Praise for

WHEN SLEEPING WOMEN WAKE

"The language is descriptive and powerful and would appeal to readers who enjoyed Min Jin Lee's *Pachinko* or Lisa See's *The Island of Sea Women*. The experiences of women during a time of war have traditionally been second place and remain unconsidered compared to those of men, but here they are brought forward center stage, and finally their untold stories can be recounted."

—*Historical Novel Society*

"Yin's debut is a riveting account of the resistance of three very different women during the Japanese invasion of Hong Kong—not only against the occupation, but against the traditions that bound them. These are women's stories beautifully intertwined with history brought to life!"

—Eve J. Chung, author of *Daughters of Shandong*

"With vivid historicity and deeply relatable characters, *When Sleeping Women Wake* is a lushly romantic and impassioned story of women's agency and resilience."

—Juhea Kim, internationally bestselling author of *Beasts of a Little Land* and *City of Night Birds*

"In this gripping tale, a close band of women is scattered by a ruthless occupation, each finding her own path through resilience, cunning, and taking high-risk chances. Through imprisonment, forced labor, torture, sickness, and starvation, the women have to use their wits and daring to survive. A riveting, fast-paced read."

—Jennifer Ryan, bestselling author of *The Chilbury Ladies' Choir* and *The Underground Library*

"In *When Sleeping Women Wake*, three women—a resourceful and literature-loving mother, a strong-willed daughter, and a devoted servant—flee Shanghai to Hong Kong, only to have their lives upended once more by the Japanese invasion during World War II. Separated by the ravages of war, each woman must navigate her own fate amid escalating danger and conflict. Compelling, beautiful, and deeply moving, *When Sleeping Women Wake* is a powerful tribute to the forgotten women and men who fought and resisted the merciless grip of the Japanese forces during a dark period of Hong Kong's history. Readers of historical fiction will be swept away by this stunning tale of love, loyalty, and survival. Emma Pei Yin is a talent to watch!"

—Weina Dai Randel, award-winning *Wall Street Journal* bestselling author of *The Master Jeweler*

"I devoured Emma Pei Yin's heart-rending, transportive, and action-packed *When Sleeping Women Wake* in a single day. Brimming with intrigue and fascinating history, this sweeping story of resistance and resilience in Japanese-occupied Hong Kong during WWII brings to life beautifully drawn characters and paints a gripping portrait of the strength of women's bonds, the hope that springs from love and chance meetings, and the grace of small acts of kindness in the most trying times."

—Ashton Lattimore, author of *All We Were Promised*

"Emma Pei Yin weaves a spellbinding tale of transformation, resilience, and the quiet power of awakening. Through evocative prose and a richly drawn sense of place, she brings to life a cast of women whose journeys are as layered as the story itself. A novel of depth and nuance, *When Sleeping Women Wake* lingers in the mind long after the final page—an exploration of strength, self-discovery, and the landscapes, both internal and external, that shape us."

—Ayesha Inoon, author of *Untethered*

"*When Sleeping Women Wake* reminds us that compassion can prevail, even against a ruthless regime that attempted to radicalize its soldiers into seeing the Chinese people as lesser than humans.

Emma's debut brought 1940s Hong Kong to life, showing me a lot about its struggles during the Japanese occupation."

—Jane Yang, author of *The Lotus Shoes*

"A heartbreaking, moving, and soaring novel. An important literary feat from an exciting new voice. Emma Pei Yin uncovers the hidden history of Hong Kong and lets us befriend the women who have the power to transform us as we witness their journeys of self-discovery and survival."

—Nguyễn Phan Quế Mai, global bestselling author of *The Mountains Sing and Dust Child*

"Epic and moving, *When Sleeping Women Wake* plunges us into Japanese-occupied Hong Kong, when World War II reached a fever pitch and it seemed as though the Imperial Army would take over the world. When the Japanese take the city, mother, daughter, and lifelong friend are torn apart, forced to endure the horror and trauma of war alone. *When Sleeping Women Wake* explores the untold histories of women's war experience under Pei Yin's steady hand and refuses to look away from the violence of war. Courage, strength, and power bleed from every page, every chapter brims with tension and turmoil as we navigate wartime Hong Kong and wonder if these women will survive, let alone find each other again. A gripping piece of historical fiction to add to your bookshelf."

—Alli Parker, bestselling author of *At The Foot of the Cherry Tree*

WHEN SLEEPING WOMEN WAKE

WHEN SLEEPING WOMEN WAKE

A Novel

EMMA PEI YIN

BALLANTINE BOOKS
NEW YORK

Ballantine Books
An imprint of Random House
A division of Penguin Random House LLC
1745 Broadway, New York, NY 10019
randomhousebooks.com
randomhousebookclub.com
penguinrandomhouse.com

2026 Ballantine Books Trade Paperback Edition

Originally published in hardcover in the United States by Ballantine Books, an imprint of Random House, a division of Penguin Random House LLC, in 2025.

ISBN 978-0-593-97558-9
Ebook ISBN 978-0-593-97557-2

Printed in Canada

2 4 6 8 9 7 5 3 1

BOOK TEAM: Production editor: Cassie Gitkin • Managing editor: Saige Francis • Production manager: Samuel Wetzler

The authorized representative in the EU for product safety and compliance is Penguin Random House Ireland, Morrison Chambers, 32 Nassau Street, Dublin D02 YH68, Ireland. https://eu-contact.penguin.ie

To my ancestors.

She wasn't a bird in a cage. A bird in a cage, when the cage is opened, can still fly away. She was a bird embroidered onto a screen—a white bird in clouds of gold stitched onto a screen of melancholy satin. The years passed; the bird's feathers darkened, mildewed, and were eaten by moths, but the bird stayed on the screen even in death.

—**Eileen Chang,** *Love in a Fallen City*

LANGUAGE NOTE

When Sleeping Women Wake takes place between 1941 and 1945, during the Japanese occupation of Hong Kong. To capture the linguistic diversity of the period, I have incorporated dialogue in Cantonese, Mandarin, and Japanese, reflecting the sociocultural nuances of the time.

Cantonese words and phrases have been romanized using the Jyutping system (e.g., *Nei5 hou2,* meaning "hello"). Mandarin follows the Pinyin romanization system, which spells words out phonetically, while Japanese words use the Hepburn system.

Although the story is set before the development of Pinyin (late 1950s) and Jyutping (early 1990s), I have chosen these systems over older ones, such as Wade-Giles, which is often criticized for inaccurately representing pronunciation.

WHEN SLEEPING WOMEN WAKE

PROLOGUE

SHANGHAI,
上海,
1906

In the depths of winter, a girl, no older than eight, trailed behind a woman on the frost-laden banks of the Huangpu River. Even the temple bells, ordinarily a grounding presence, seemed to tremble in the unforgiving cold. With each step, white streaks of mist flowed from the girl's lips, the cold biting her cheeks. She longed for the warm fire her mother used to tend with such care. In her arms, she clasped a bundle of possessions wrapped in weathered brown fabric—a pair of thin trousers, a tattered tunic, and a wooden brush she had found in a public bathhouse days before. The girl, orphaned and without kin, pressed on with determination.

The city was a tangle of commerce and life as merchants, swathed in wool and fur, darted along the streets. Vendors urged passersby to purchase sticks of candied hawthorn cakes. Their shouts were loud, and the aroma of freshly brewed *wūlong chá* that emanated from the teahouses sent a pang to the girl's stomach.

Turning a corner, she walked along a narrow footpath. The throng of the main street was replaced by imposing rows of grand houses, and the chatter of merchants dwindled into silence. She came to a halt, standing alongside the woman, who had proceeded to knock on a large red door decorated with bronze handles.

The woman nudged the girl's shoulder, prompting her to straighten her back. As the doors swung open, she was greeted by the most beautiful courtyard she had ever seen, boasting interconnected buildings, lush gardens, and plum trees dusted with snowflakes. The noble house, a *sìhéyuàn,* belonged to a distinguished scholar and his wife, a testament to his privileged position within the literati.

The girl followed the woman along a stone path until they passed the ancestral hall. Its doors stood open, tempting her to peek inside. Within, the scholar and his wife kowtowed on silk cushions. Intricate altars and gold carvings filled the space, while the heady scent of aloeswood and medicinal herbs permeated the air. Ancestor portraits hung behind the altar, their solemn gaze falling onto the couple. The wife, heavily pregnant, patted her stomach, her slender face glowing.

The woman pushed the girl forward, guiding her toward the rear of the compound to the servants' quarters. Inside one of the rooms, she goggled at ten single beds, neatly aligned. The thought of sleeping so high off the ground seemed unnatural for someone of her status. Quickly, the girl changed into her new uniform—dark-umber wool trousers and a matching long-sleeved tunic. Excitement tickled her stomach at the fine quality of the soft fabric. As she adjusted the mandarin collar, the older woman came over and began detangling her matted hair. The feeling of someone running their fingers across her scalp made her a little uneasy, but as she looked at her reflection in a small mirror, hope began to stir. Perhaps, in this new place, she could find a fresh start.

Once ready, she was escorted to the kitchens where she helped the cooks prepare Snow Fungus soup and suspend salted *huángyú* from wooden rods across the ceiling for drying—its briny odor seeping into her fingertips.

The rest of the day passed quickly, and she eventually collapsed into her bed, exhausted. Her sleep was deep but short-lived as a woman's scream jolted her awake.

Another maid had already bolted out of bed, and their eyes met in the darkness. "The baby is coming," she whispered.

In the ensuing chaos, a midwife and a nanny were immediately called upon. The girl, alongside other maids, climbed over a dozen sizable ceramic wine jars and peered over the wall into the wife's private courtyard.

Together, they watched the scholar pace. During the hour of the

Rabbit, a newborn's cries cut through the air. The scholar ran to his wife's door, robes billowing behind him.

"Have the heavens blessed me with a son?" he called out.

The nanny hurried out, her head low, eyes locked to her feet. "A daughter," she said, almost inaudibly.

The maids retreated to their quarters, murmurs of the scholar's misfortune trailing behind them, but the girl remained, leaning closer to peer within the wife's chambers, the dim candlelight casting shadows. As the scholar entered, she studied his silhouette, visible through the screen doors. He hovered over the nanny, who was cradling the baby for his inspection. She heard him muttering about the child being born in the year of the Fire Horse—a year considered too spirited and independent for a female.

When dawn broke, splashing a persimmon halo over the *sìhéyuàn,* the household bustled with whispered conversations and hushed footsteps, the announcement of the newborn daughter spreading like wildfire through the corridors.

Outside, beneath the branches of an ancient camphor tree, the head maid gathered the staff. The air carried a crispness from the lingering night chill. As the assembled servants rubbed their hands together for warmth, she asked for a volunteer to take on the role of personal maid for the newborn.

Silence greeted her inquiry, broken by the rustle of leaves overhead and the gentle cooing of spotted doves. No one wanted to take on such responsibility. Yet, amidst the hesitant glances and shuffled feet, the girl stepped forward. She had only entered the household less than one day earlier, but she would prove her worth as the newest member of the Yue family. And so, the girl became the daughter's personal maid.

As the years unfolded, the maid and the daughter grew close, sharing a bond that sisters bound by blood could only dream of. Eventually, the daughter won her father's affection with her passion for the written word. Touched by her enthusiasm, he took it upon himself to teach her. As the maid stood quietly in the corner each day, she listened to the gentle scratch of the scholar's calligraphy brushes against parchment, soothing as the patter of summer rain. Secretly, the maid pretended he was her father, too, as she had never known her own.

At the same time, the mother introduced her daughter to the *Four Books for Women,* and the maid marveled at her discipline, how each passage etched into her memory, akin to a warrior preparing for battle. The daughter learned how to sit, stand, and speak—how to ensure that every word spoken from her lips was always assured, careful, yet calculated.

In the evenings, the maid sat with the daughter, reading and writing together by the open window in her chamber, the moonlight gushing into her room.

Time marked its passage through the changing seasons, until a particular winter arrived, when destiny came in the form of a matchmaker. The daughter stood before her parents, clad in a red silk gown trimmed with golden threads that reminded the maid of the vibrant plumes of a phoenix. Bowing deeply, the maid spotted her concealing beneath her robe a precious copy of *Dream of the Red Chamber*—a parting gift from her father. The mother, teary-eyed, slid a jade bangle from her own wrist onto her daughter's. It was a symbol, she said, of their eternal bond, that despite the distance, their souls would always be intertwined, even as they parted ways in this lifetime.

Then, the maid helped the daughter ascend the horse-drawn carriage. Lifting the corner of her veil, the daughter stole one final glance at her parents. The carriage moved forward, carrying the two girls away from the comfort of home. With one hand clutching *Dream of the Red Chamber,* the daughter reached for the maid, the cool jade touching both of their wrists.

PART I

BRITISH-OCCUPIED HONG KONG, 英屬香港, 1941

CHAPTER 1

In the heart of the family library, Mingzhu turned the page of her copy of *Dream of the Red Chamber.* As the characters moved, she imagined their silk robes flowing, their whispering touch caressing her skin. A ceiling fan crafted from polished wood rotated above her, emitting a soft hum, providing relief from the torrid discomfort of July.

When the words began to blur, Mingzhu shifted her focus toward the windows. The afternoon light filtered through the glass, cascading over neatly arranged bookshelves that reached the ceiling. Having fled Shanghai and settled in Hong Kong three years earlier, Mingzhu found solace within the walls of the library. Few ventured into its depths, leaving it mainly for Mingzhu and her daughter, Qiang, as a sanctuary from the ceaseless noise of the outside world and the overwhelming presence of her husband's concubine, Cai. When guests did visit, the men retreated to the downstairs drawing room, accompanied by her husband, Wei, and the women gathered on the terrace, their conversations punctuated by glimpses of the sparkling blue expanse of the South China Sea beyond the mountains. Despite rumors of Japanese forces looming over Hong Kong, the library remained a haven where the echoes of war, which often haunted Mingzhu, felt somewhat distant.

A knock struck the door, and *Dream of the Red Chamber* slipped from her grasp. She retrieved it quickly and tucked it between plush velvet cushions on the couch. Ignoring her *qípáo*'s creased and disheveled state, she hastened to a bench near the window and reached for a threaded needle and silk handkerchief.

"Come in." Mingzhu shifted on the seat, beginning to sew.

A woman tiptoed into the room, and at the sight of her maid, Biyu, Mingzhu relaxed.

Biyu bowed and her long braid, tied neatly with a blue ribbon, slipped over her shoulder. Her tunic and matching trousers were a spotless white. "Good evening, First Madame." She stepped further into the library, her eyes skimming the room before settling on the couch. "You might want to find a better hiding place."

Mingzhu wrinkled her nose. "Too obvious, isn't it?" she conceded, rising from her seat and tossing the needle and handkerchief back onto the bench. She recovered the book from between the cushions and returned it to its rightful place on the shelf. Out the window, a spotted dove alighted on a branch of a willow tree several feet away.

Biyu began clearing a porcelain teacup and saucer from the low table. "Master Tang allows you to read. Why do you hide it?"

"Allows . . ." Mingzhu fixed her eyes on the dove. For a fleeting moment, she was transported back to her childhood, seated by a window, breathing in fresh ink and watching spotted doves land on towering camphor trees. "I wasn't hiding the book from my husband."

"Then, you must be hiding it from the second madame."

"You know how she can be." Mingzhu brushed her hands over her *qípáo*. "She doesn't think it's proper for women to read about anything but the latest fashion trends from Europe."

"But you're the primary wife. A concubine cannot dictate what you can or cannot read. It's already a compromise that you allowed her the title of second madame. Frankly—"

Her maid pressed her lips together, refraining from the tangent she had been about to start. Mingzhu gave a small laugh, noting Biyu's flushed cheeks and protective stance. At forty-one, Biyu had charcoal-black hair, tidy brows, and a gentle countenance, bearing a striking resemblance to Mingzhu. Some days, strangers even mistook them for sisters.

"You know her incessant carping does my head no good." Mingzhu sighed.

"It is nice when she speaks less," Biyu agreed thoughtfully.

Mingzhu laughed, then asked, "I assume you have come to tell me my husband is home?"

"Master Tang returned not long ago. He has requested the presence of both wives to join him in the dining hall."

"Can he not make do with Cai? What difference does one less wife make at the dining table?"

"You're the main wife. It would be—"

"Yes, I know, I know. Come on, then."

Mingzhu looked back at her bookshelves, knowing her peaceful evening had been interrupted. Why couldn't her husband have stayed in his office in the city for one more night? Perhaps two? She left the library with Biyu close behind.

A long rosewood table occupied the center of the grand dining hall. The flicker of glass sconces intensified the already hot room, painting shadows on all assembled. A knot of annoyance and concern coiled within Mingzhu's stomach as she noticed Cai comfortably seated in her own customary spot. Had Cai forgotten the tenets of family decorum, or did she believe birthing a son allowed her to flout such traditions?

Mingzhu raised a brow, and Cai let out an indignant scoff before pushing her chair back and walking off to her assigned seat at the far end of the table. "How considerate of you to finally join us," Cai said through clenched teeth.

Her words stung, yet Mingzhu remained poised. It was as if Cai had already forgotten the times Mingzhu had sat tirelessly by her side when they first arrived in Hong Kong, how Mingzhu had held her hand and provided solace during those darkest moments. She chose to ignore the provocation, redirecting her attention to Wei. "Good evening, husband," she said.

Wei merely nodded in acknowledgment, focusing on his plate of roast beef, potatoes, and sautéed vegetables. Since leaving Shanghai, he had insisted on adopting British dining customs, and the days of savoring mouthwatering braised meat and bowls of pillowy rice with chopsticks had become distant memories. Although the flavors were less thrilling, Mingzhu knew they fared better than those stranded back on the mainland, even if the sustenance lacked the familiar tastes of home. Though Mingzhu didn't love her husband, she knew that without his swift actions, transferring their finances from Shanghai to Hong Kong before the Japanese invasion, they would not be living in such comfort.

With the Peak District Reservation Ordinance of 1904 still firmly in place, many had raised their brows, pondering how a Chinese family could acquire such a grand estate on the hill. But, as Wei always said, money and connections can buy anything. It was a cruel irony that Mingzhu herself had no wealth to claim. When her parents had passed years earlier, the *sìhéyuàn* she was born and raised in was handed over to a distant male cousin—a person whom Mingzhu had never known existed, let alone met.

Over time, Mingzhu grew accustomed to the snobbish expressions of her neighbors—elegantly dressed European women who regarded her with contempt every time she ventured outside. The British had always justified the zoning law by citing the third bubonic plague pandemic. But you'd have to be a fool not to recognize it for what it truly was.

"Did you spend the morning in the ancestral hall, Wife?" Wei asked.

Mingzhu nodded at the nonsensical question. Since she had married into the Tang family, there had only ever been one day she missed performing ancestral rites, and that was the day Qiang was born.

"You lit joss sticks, too?"

Another redundant question. Mingzhu almost mirrored Biyu's eye roll, but she refrained. She replied, "I did. I lit more than usual to pay respect to those who died in the typhoon a few days ago, too."

"Good," Wei said, chewing loudly. "These are benevolent traits to have as a wife."

Cai stabbed her fork into a piece of carrot and shoved it into her mouth.

"You will follow First Madame's example, Second Wife," Wei said, taking Cai by surprise. "Even though you're a concubine, there is no harm in burning extra spirit money for my ancestors in the underworld."

Cai almost choked. "Surely your ancestors have reincarnated by now! Besides, the British don't partake in such rituals. I thought we were trying to be more like them?"

There was a hint of audacity in Cai's voice that Mingzhu found enviable. Cai wasn't entirely wrong. If Wei wanted to embrace a British lifestyle, performing ancestral rites seemed contradictory. But speaking as freely as Cai did was not a privilege Mingzhu possessed. This concubine had produced a son for the Tang family, while Mingzhu had but a daughter.

With a sturdy jawline and well-defined cheekbones, Cai projected an aura of majestic command. At least five rounds of pearls decorated her neck, and her nails were brushed with the darkest shade of red, adding a striking contrast to her powdered-white skin. She pressed her lips together, forming a subtle expression of disapproval, her authoritative presence causing unease. If Cai's circumstances had taken a different turn and she had become the primary wife in the family, she could have wielded substantial influence. To Mingzhu, the fact that Cai found herself as a concubine in this lifetime seemed a bitter jest.

Mingzhu noted the subtle flare of Wei's nostrils, a telltale sign of simmering anger. Maintaining eye contact with Cai, she subtly tilted her head, silently conveying the message of their husband's rising temper.

"Join me tomorrow, Second Madame," Mingzhu said cautiously. "Perhaps afterward, we could venture into the city and buy the shoes you have been talking about for the past few days?"

It was a strategic move, of course. Wei would have his concubine perform ancestral rites, and in return, Cai would finally obtain the shoes she had longed for since the beginning of summer. Once again, Mingzhu had skillfully defused tension and maintained harmony. How utterly exhausting.

Finally, Cai agreed, and the atmosphere lightened. But not for long.

"So," Cai began. "Is this our life now in Hong Kong? Constant rain and subpar food?"

"What's wrong with the food?" Mingzhu asked, maintaining a lightheartedness in her tone.

Mingzhu oversaw the daily menu, and she always ensured that the cooks had enough funds to purchase the freshest produce from the markets. She spared no expense in this regard, and it was in Cai's best interest not to insinuate otherwise.

"The food was better in Shanghai, that's all," Cai said. "Honestly, First Madame, there's no need to get defensive. It's not as though you cooked the food yourself. Or did you?"

"You're most welcome to take charge of the menu next week, Second Madame," Mingzhu offered, tightening her grip around the silverware.

Cai laughed. "I see what you're doing—trying to shift your duties onto me. Am I not already in charge of organizing weekend luncheons? And now you want to burden me further?"

Mingzhu stifled a scoff. It was common knowledge that Cai remained utterly idle in every aspect of her life, with her personal maid bearing the responsibility of arranging luncheons and weekend events.

"I have a son to raise, you know," Cai continued. "I'm not as fortunate as you, having only a daughter who roams freely all day and does as she pleases."

Mingzhu's eye twitched as she forced herself not to say anything. Her head began to hurt. Wei coughed, hastily picking up a copy of the *South China Morning Post* as a shield to hide behind, and Mingzhu's attention caught on the headline.

JAPANESE FORCES LAUNCH MAJOR OFFENSIVE AGAINST CHINESE DEFENDERS IN SHANGHAI

Her throat tightened. A cold sweat broke across her back as the memory of a bayonet pointed at her stomach resurfaced.

"Do you actually know where Qiang is at this moment?" Cai asked.

Mingzhu's lips thinned, the memory retreating. "Of course I know where my daughter is," she said. "What a question to ask, Second Madame."

"I heard some of the servants talking earlier," Cai said, lowering her voice to a conspiratorial whisper. "About Qiang spending time with that young gardener, Ah-Long. Don't you think you should exercise more control over your daughter?"

Cai had always been quick to criticize, but this crossed a line. Wei, useless as always in such situations, continued to hide behind the paper. Just as Mingzhu was about to speak up to defend her daughter, Biyu stepped forward, teapot in hand, and spilled hot water onto Cai's lap.

With a cry, Cai leaped from her seat, the chair legs scraping loudly against the wooden floor. She raised her hand, poised to strike Biyu, but before she could, Mingzhu slammed her hand onto the dining table, causing the silverware to clatter. Biyu quickly retreated against the wall, keeping her head low.

"Your dress is ruined, Second Madame. You should go clean up," Mingzhu said.

Cai glared between them, her face flushed with rage. She knew chastising Biyu would be akin to disrespecting Mingzhu. With no other recourse, she promptly left.

Wei continued to read the paper, never making eye contact with his wife, and Mingzhu resumed eating in silence. She pictured sitting beside her parents, sharing a meal—her mother affectionately placing the juiciest *hóngshāo ròu* pieces into her rice bowl. The more she thought of them, the fuller she became.

After dinner, Mingzhu stole a look through a jasmine bush past the cobblestone path leading to the garden. Qiang sat deep in conversation with Ah-Long at the pavilion near the pond, her smile warm and joyful. Her sharp features and full lips reminded Mingzhu that her daughter was no longer a child but a young woman, exuding confidence and charm. How had seventeen years passed so quickly yet so slowly?

She had loved Qiang from the moment she conceived her, and she had believed Wei would hold the same affection. Mingzhu thought the days of desiring sons were a thing of the past, yet her husband remained a constant reminder that some mindsets, like history, have a way of repeating themselves.

CHAPTER 2

Qiang closed her eyes, feeling the cool touch of the wrought-iron bench beneath her. As she sat beside Ah-Long, the melodies of crickets tickled her ears, and a warm breeze, carrying the scent of magnolias, gently toyed with her hair.

Quietly, Ah-Long sounded out English words from the textbook she'd lent him. For a while now, she had been teaching him English, despite the disapproval of her father's concubine. But she cared little about what Cai thought—a sentiment shared by most people in the house.

At seventeen, Qiang excelled in languages. She had won the top student award in Chinese, English, and French at McTyeire School in Shanghai four years in a row. It wasn't until she moved to Hong Kong that she began learning Japanese—a language her mother was already fluent in.

Ah-Long huffed, and Qiang opened her eyes. "What's the matter?"

"This word," he said in English, pointing to the page. "This I not know."

"Let's see." Qiang leaned closer to him. "Oh, that's easy. *Vexation.*" Ah-Long furrowed his thick brows and focused on Qiang, who pointed to her mouth. "Vex . . . a . . . tion."

"Vex . . . ah . . . shon," Ah-Long repeated, his stare still set on her lips. "Vex . . . a . . . tion."

"Yes! Well done," Qiang praised, and his cheeks flushed.

"When I can read many words like you, Young Miss?" he asked, glancing back at the book.

"You're a fast learner, so not long, I'd say. Besides, there's no hurry."

Ah-Long shook his head. "Big hurry. I learn more to get job."

"You don't like your job now?"

"I like," he said. "But I learn more to get better job, like Master Tang."

The wind picked up, and loose strands of hair tickled her brows. She looked at Ah-Long thoughtfully. In her eyes, he was already twice the man her father could ever be.

Ah-Long posed another question, interrupting her thoughts. "Vex . . . a . . . tion . . . meaning what?"

Qiang straightened. "Ah, well, it can be described as a state of increased annoyance or frustration, you know?"

"You say in sentence for me."

She pondered for a moment, then pulled up the sleeve of her satin blouse and pointed to a pink dot on her elbow. "The vexation caused by mosquitoes can ruin a lovely evening in the garden."

"I see. This good sentence!" He smiled. "You is right, Young Miss. Tonight very lovely in garden."

Qiang pouted. "Ah-Long, how often must I tell you not to call me that? It makes me feel old."

"But I say *Young Miss,* not *Old Miss,*" he said, and she laughed. "House rules, I must say *Young Miss*. I not say your real name."

"But I call you by your name," Qiang countered. "It's only fair for you to address me by name, too. It would make us more equal."

"We not equal, Young Miss. You are you, and I am me."

The words stung. His eyes held a deep, piercing gaze. His skin bore the gentle touch of the sun, freckles dotting his cheeks, and his nose was wide, lacking the defined contours of her father's or any other man's she had seen before.

"You look me funny. What you think?" Ah-Long said. Qiang didn't answer. Revealing that she was studying his features seemed inappropriate. A beat of silence passed, and Ah-Long pointed to her sleeve. "Pull down before more bite."

"Oh, right," she said, tugging at her sleeve. "Anyway, it's your turn now. Use the word *vexation* in a sentence."

Ah-Long tapped his fingers on the book, deep in thought. After a minute or so, he closed the book with a smile. "I have good one," he said. "Second Madame vexation the first madame!"

Qiang burst into laughter, and Ah-Long chimed in, and for a moment, the world around them faded into the background.

"I'm sorry to interrupt all the fun."

Startled, Qiang and Ah-Long stood, and the book fell to the ground with a soft thud. Her mother was making her way toward them, smiling.

"Good evening, First Madame." He bowed.

"Good evening, Ah-Long," she replied, her focus shifting to the fallen book—a hint of amusement in her eyes.

He picked up the book and bowed again. "I'll leave. Good night, First Madame. Good night, Young Miss."

Qiang watched Ah-Long disappear back into the house.

"You don't have to worry about him, you know," her mother teased.

"Worry?" Qiang laughed nervously. "I'm not worried, Mama."

"If you say so." Mingzhu clicked her tongue and took Qiang's hand, leading her to sit back on the bench. "My dear, there have been some more reports on recent Japanese movements. It's in all the newspapers. You remember what I said about talking to the Japanese, don't you?"

"Of course," Qiang confirmed. "I remember everything you teach me. You look concerned, Mama."

"I just wanted to make sure you don't forget, that's all."

"I know to avoid the Japanese at all costs. That should I ever find myself in their presence, to find a way out immediately. To never speak to them, befriend them, trust them, or be alone with them. I was in Shanghai too, Mama. The things we saw there—"

"Don't think about it," Mingzhu interjected. "There's no need to bring up painful memories. I'm just glad you remember what I said."

"But . . . do you honestly believe them all to be bad, Mama?"

"Oh, Qiang." Her mother sighed. "When a majority of a particular nation has demonstrated an incapacity for humanity, it becomes difficult to believe otherwise." She paused, her expression conveying a touch of contemplation. "Think of it like the moon. Even on the darkest of nights, there's always going to be a glimmer of light—of hope. So, no, I do not believe that all Japanese are shrouded in darkness.

But in the current circumstances, being alert is the best course of action."

"I understand," Qiang said.

Deep down, she wanted to believe that there was more good than bad in the world. If the Japanese were all monsters, then what kind of world would this be?

CHAPTER 3

Wei slept deeply under their silk blankets, his snores loud. Morning light pierced through the blinds. In the reflection from the vanity mirror, Mingzhu noticed the subtle changes in him—his once-thick hair now thinning and streaked with silver strands, his deep frown lines softened in sleep. Reaching for her lipstick, housed in a sleek gold-toned bullet, she smoothed it across her lips. Its cerise hue, reminiscent of a budding rose's delicate blush, suddenly took her back to the morning of her wedding day.

The journey to Wei's home had been long. She'd held on to Biyu's hand inside the carriage, unsure if she wanted to live or die. The edges of *Dream of the Red Chamber* pressed against her thigh, a reminder of the parents she had left behind.

Her pearl-and-emerald crown had shimmered like constellations in the night sky, straining her neck. The veil, matching the red of her lips, concealed her face, masking her uncertainty and fear.

"If I'd been born a son, I wouldn't have to leave my parents," she had said.

Biyu's hold on her hand strengthened. "Son or daughter, it doesn't matter in the end. The parents ordain marriage. It has been this way for centuries. Even if you were a son, you'd still have no say in who you married."

Mingzhu pressed her lips together. "If I ever have a daughter, I'd let her marry whoever she wants."

Biyu chuckled. "You swear?"

"On my life."

When they finally arrived at Wei's house, Mingzhu was ushered out of the carriage by the matchmaker. As she stepped across the threshold, her heart hammered in her chest like a frantic bird trapped in a cage. The air was heavy with the scent of sandalwood and the mustiness of old furniture. The whispered conversations of unseen guests brushed against her ears and her breath came in shallow gasps as she moved forward, her steps slow and uncertain.

She finally came to a standstill, to perform the customary three bows in front of the Double Happiness altar. Trembling, she offered the first bow to Wei's ancestors, acknowledging a lineage that held no power to bring her happiness. Her movements were stiff and awkward, and she could feel the eyes of the guests upon her like a weight pressing down upon her shoulders. The second bow, suffused with a deep sense of resignation, was directed to Heaven and Earth. Then, the third and final bow was to Wei's deceased parents, represented by two large wooden tablets on empty chairs. Mingzhu bowed three times, not to symbols of love and devotion, but to the ghosts of tradition and the hollowness of an unfulfilled heart. Feeling dizzy, she rose to her feet, fighting back the urge to run away.

Following the ceremony, Biyu assisted Mingzhu to a secluded bridal chamber, where she sat like an ornament on the edge of the bed, awaiting Wei's arrival. Time passed with agonizing slowness until, at last, her new husband stumbled into the room, his breath thick with the scent of *báijiǔ* and his movements heavy. In a display of callousness, he tore away her veil, and her golden headpiece slipped from her head, shattering into fragments on the floor.

That night, Mingzhu became a wife.

A light touch on her shoulder snapped her back to the present. Biyu stood behind her. "He's here, Madame," she said quietly, so as not to wake Wei, who was still snoring.

"Who?"

"Mr. Beaumont, Qiang's new tutor."

Mingzhu stood, quickly slipping her feet into brocade heels before leaving the room. Before entering the library, she checked her reflection in a mirror on the hallway wall. She appreciated the meticulous work executed by Biyu, who had pinned her hair into a neat bun and combed strands into waves across her forehead. Her green silk *qípáo* boasted hand-stitched embroidery with golden threads that caught the sunlight streaming through the windows. For a moment, she worried about how the hem of her dress flared out, revealing a flash of her ankles, but it was too late to change.

Standing by the library window was a tall, lean man, dressed impeccably in a pewter-gray suit, crisp white shirt, and navy tie. His brown hair was neatly combed, and his cut jawline and sharp features were softened by a pair of wire-rimmed spectacles perched on his nose. But what intrigued Mingzhu most was that he was reading her copy of *Dream of the Red Chamber.*

"You read Chinese?" Mingzhu asked, walking further into the library.

Startled, he looked up and replied, "Not very well, I'm afraid. I know some characters here and there. I have the English edition of this novel."

"I see," Mingzhu responded, her interest deepening. She had never known a *báirén*—a white person—to have an affinity for Chinese classics. It was an opportunity to test him. "Then I suppose you wouldn't mind quoting a passage for me?"

He seemed amused by her request. Closing the book, he locked his meadow-green eyes with hers. "Of course not, but let's make it more interesting, shall we?"

"How?"

"Let's see . . ." he said, tapping on the book. "Ah! How about I quote the first part of my favorite passage of this novel, but you finish it?"

Mingzhu nodded in acceptance, inclining her head just low enough to conceal the fleeting excitement. This was hardly a challenge.

He cleared his throat. "Upon oneself are mainly brought regrets in spring and autumn gloom . . ."

Mingzhu smiled. "A face, flowerlike may be and moonlike too, but beauty all for whom?" she finished.

"I'm impressed." He returned her smile.

"Likewise."

"I'm Henry Beaumont," he said, returning the book to its place on the shelf before approaching her, strides long and confident, hand extended.

Biyu let out a small gasp at the breach of protocol, and Mingzhu instinctively stepped back, declining the handshake. Instead, she offered a slight tilt of her head.

"Nice to meet you, Mr. Beaumont. I'm Ming—" She halted, realizing her lapse in decorum. What was she thinking? Why had she almost introduced herself with her first name?

Henry withdrew his hand at her hesitation. "Madame Tang, I presume? Qiang's mother?"

"Yes, that's right."

"It's a pleasure to meet you," he replied. "I recognize your voice from our telephone conversation last week. I understand that our societies may have different customs regarding names, but please call me Henry. I'm not one for formalities."

Mingzhu's cheeks warmed, and no suitable response came to mind.

"But . . . I suppose a bit of formality here and there can't be too bad," Henry concluded.

He had just turned twenty-six, which Mingzhu had asked him about during his telephone interview. She couldn't stop looking at him. How could a man seven years her junior intrigue her so much?

Biyu stepped between them, inviting Henry to sit on the armchair in the center of the room. With a gentle nudge, she signaled for Mingzhu to sit opposite him.

"I'll prepare some tea and snacks," Biyu announced before leaving the room.

They sat across from each other as the clock on the wall ticked, both briefly scanning the room until their eyes met again. To her relief, he broke the silence.

"I have always been interested in Chinese literature. Have you read the four classics?" Henry asked.

"Of course," Mingzhu said stoutly. As an afterthought, she added, "Though, I didn't enjoy them all equally."

"How interesting. Which impressed you the least?"

Leaning forward, Mingzhu propped her chin on her palm. "I took issue with *Romance of the Three Kingdoms*," she began, her voice filled with passion. "The way Luo Guanzhong portrayed women was abysmal. You'd think a novelist of his skill could have shown more depth."

Henry's eyes softened, and his face flushed ever so faintly. "You're a passionate reader. In what way could Luo have done better?" he asked.

Noting the gentle admiration in his gaze, Mingzhu folded her hands in her lap and leaned back with a composed smile. "Well, first, other than Lady Sun, Guanzhong scarcely wrote about women and their strength at all."

"Lady Sun?"

Mingzhu raised an eyebrow. "*You* have not read the four classics, I see."

"I have not," he admitted. "But I will."

"You must," she enthused. "Lady Sun, otherwise known as Sun Ren, is described as a fiery, heroic woman skilled in martial arts." Henry leaned forward, mirroring the same attentive posture that Qiang used to adopt when she listened to comparable stories. "She is the youngest sister of the ruler of Wu and is married off to Liu Bei, a warlord who later establishes the Shu Kingdom." Mingzhu grew animated as she continued to tell the story. "She's strong and is fiercely loyal to those she loves. A woman with such strength should not be overlooked."

"The saying is true, then." Henry cupped his hands together and looked intently at Mingzhu. "Behind every great man is an even greater woman."

Mingzhu gaped at him, then snapped her mouth closed as Biyu returned, carrying a tray of English tea and almond biscuits. Instinctively, she tapped the cool jade bracelet on her wrist, finding solace in its touch against her skin. She caught Henry stealing a glance in her direction and maintained her focus on the vibrant green of her bracelet, which mirrored the color of his eyes.

"Perhaps I may tidy your poetry collection for you this afternoon, Madame?" Biyu suggested.

"That would be most welcome, Biyu," she replied. "So, Mr. Beaumont, have you delved into the world of Chinese poetry? Beyond the ones featured in *Dream of the Red Chamber*."

Henry picked up a biscuit and took a bite, his response quick. "Not enough, I'm afraid. Teaching has taken up much of my time. But when I used to work as a journalist in Japan—"

"You have lived in Japan?" Mingzhu asked.

"Yes. Only for a year."

"A short time," she said, bringing a teacup to her lips.

"With the current political climate, there was only so much I could write as a journalist. Besides, teaching pays far better." Henry smiled.

"I see," she said. "Well, if you have time to spare in the coming days, I'd happily offer my recommendations on some poetry."

"I would like that very much. Who is your favorite poet?" he asked, sparking another conversation.

The next hour slipped away unnoticed as they immersed themselves in the world of literature and poetry. Henry's insights on education and his effortless charm captivated Mingzhu; each word he spoke stirred something deep within her. Looking at the clock, she realized how time had escaped her. When he excused himself to begin his lesson with Qiang, loneliness washed over her—a sensation she had never before encountered amidst the library's serene confines.

Later, in the ancestral hall with mala beads in hand, Mingzhu went about the ritual of ancestor worship. But with every kowtow, her mind was not on the age-old words, or on the scrolls painted with the solemn faces of her husband's ancestors. Rather, her thoughts were firmly placed on Henry Beaumont.

CHAPTER 4

Through the open windows of the study, willow branches swayed against the soft melody of Cai's gramophone. The music was distant but clear, forcing Qiang to pay closer attention when Henry spoke. Her father had had builders refurbish the study, but his patience waned over the weeks as workers came and went. He eventually leased an office in Kowloon and worked away from home, which meant that Qiang could now call the study hers. The freshly painted maroon walls gave off a chemical tang which stung her nose, but she didn't care.

The grandfather clock chimed, marking the end of her lesson. Henry closed his copy of *The Elements of Style* and clapped his hands together. "I think we did quite well for the first lesson, Qiang. Do you have any questions?"

She smiled and shook her head, content with her mother's choice of such a good tutor.

A rustle sounded near the study door as her mother strolled past with Cai. Qiang glanced at the grandfather clock again. It was lunchtime, and she had promised her mother she'd stay home today instead of going to the city to meet her friend Camille.

"Your mother must have many friends visit," Henry mused.

"Friends?" Qiang shot him a quizzical stare. "*That* woman is my baba's concubine."

"Ah, my mistake. I forgot about that," Henry said.

Qiang clutched her books to her chest. "Actually, I do have a question, Teacher. May I?"

"Of course, Qiang," he replied, busying himself with gathering his books. "And please, call me Henry."

"Henry." Qiang nodded. "Do you think a friend of mine could sit in on our lessons starting tomorrow?"

"A friend?"

"He's learning English," she explained. "I've been teaching him, but he's ready for more, and it would mean the world to me if he were allowed to sit in and listen."

Henry contemplated her request. "I see no issue with having someone join us. Another person brings different opinions and views that we can all share. If your mother approves it, then I have no objections."

"Mama won't have any concerns. Ah-Long and I will greet you tomorrow. Good day, Henry!"

Excitement bubbled in Qiang, and she skipped out of the study, quickening her pace through the kitchen and bursting into the garden, where Ah-Long was watering the hibiscus plants. Mindful of the other staff, she tapped him on the shoulder and whispered the good news before retreating into the house for lunch.

Strolling into the dining hall, she kissed her mother on the cheek and greeted Biyu warmly before taking a seat.

"Your manners have escaped you, Young Miss," Cai scorned.

Her mother gave Qiang a telling pinch under the table. Reluctantly, Qiang smiled at Cai. "I apologize. Good afternoon," she said.

"Good afternoon . . ." Cai pushed.

"Good afternoon, Second Madame," Qiang replied, her smile tinged with displeasure.

A couple of kitchen maids delivered an English-style lunch of prawn cocktail, roast chicken with vegetables, and a side of Waldorf salad. Qiang's mouth began to water, and she quickly tucked into the prawns, then paused, noticing her mother push her plate aside, face pinched. Qiang couldn't remember the last time she saw her mother eat lunch. Back in Shanghai, she never skipped a meal.

Between bites, Qiang mentioned the topic of Ah-Long joining her lessons with Henry. Her mother agreed without hesitation, even saying it was a promising idea.

"Don't you think you're overstepping your bounds, Qiang?" Cai asked.

"I hardly know what you mean, Second Madame," Qiang replied, never once looking away from her food.

"A young lady of your social standing should know better than to mix with servants."

"Ah-Long is just as deserving of an education as anyone else. It's a shame you can't see that," Qiang retorted.

From the corner of her eye, Qiang saw her mother and Biyu exchange a knowing glance, but they remained quiet. Cai mocked, "Don't be foolish, Qiang. Ah-Long is a servant of this house, a gardener at that. What use could he have for education? It was already a stretch for your baba to grant *you* one."

Her condescending tone was like a punch to the gut. Qiang glared across the dining table at Cai. "Even those who serve are not devoid of aspirations and dreams, no matter how humble their station in life may be."

"What would your baba think of your behavior toward the servant boy? He wouldn't be pleased to see his daughter associating with such people."

"My baba doesn't need to know about everything I do. And even if he did, I wouldn't let his opinions dictate my actions, let alone yours."

"Why, you little—" Cai slammed her palm on the table and turned to Mingzhu. "I can't believe you let her speak to me like that. What sort of mother are you that you cannot control your own flesh and blood!"

"Second Madame," her mother said smoothly. "Every woman has her unique approach to motherhood. I have no desire to diminish your influence on Jun's upbringing, just as I expect you to respect my role in raising Qiang."

Cai's mouth dropped, but before she could respond, the bone-chilling wail of air raid sirens filled the house, causing Qiang and her mother to freeze in terror. Biyu's eyes bulged, and Cai released a piercing shriek, collapsing from her chair and hurrying for refuge under the table.

The siren echoed again, and Qiang could hardly breathe. She clamped her eyes shut and her thoughts spiraled back to Shanghai. She was running barefoot across the boardwalk of the Bund, bombs detonating around her as she fled with her mother, Biyu, and Cai close behind. The horrifying explosions muffled their frenzied steps. They sprinted down the boardwalk, splinters puncturing Qiang's already wounded feet, toward the boats, where the screams of children and desperate cries of women filled the air.

When they reached the dock, Qiang watched her mother speak to a Japanese soldier, his bayonet pointed at her stomach. Her mother's voice was taut with fear, but steady, as she presented him a set of papers. She pleaded with him, claiming they weren't locals but visitors from Hong Kong with British ties.

Another bomb dropped, shaking the wooden planks beneath them. Miraculously, the soldier yielded. Qiang had gripped her mother's hand and followed her onto the boat.

"Qiang? Qiang, can you hear me?" Her mother's voice pulled her back to the present.

Qiang opened her eyes. Two maids ran into the dining hall and scrambled to join Cai under the table. They huddled together, rank forgotten, clasping each other.

The siren wailed once more, and another knot burned in Qiang's stomach. Her mother cupped her cheeks.

"Stay calm, Qiang," she said. "Everything is fine. Just stay calm. Find something to distract yourself."

Qiang nodded dutifully, digging her fingers into the flesh of her palms, and forced herself to concentrate on the dinnerware in the center of the table. She began counting the petals on each painted flower of the prawn cocktail glass, one by one.

One.

Two.

Three.

"My Jun!" Cai wailed. "Somebody, get my Jun!"

Her mother's jaw stiffened, and she turned to Biyu. "Jun is in the nursery with the nanny. Go and bring him to the second madame."

"Yes, First Madame." Trembling, Biyu hurried away.

"Qiang," her mother said. "It's a drill. It must be. And please, stop clawing at your hands."

"A drill?" Cai screeched, her tone as piercing as the siren's shriek.

"How can you know? We haven't had a drill in weeks! What if the Japanese have finally penetrated Hong Kong? We're doomed. Oh, we're doomed!"

The words hit Qiang hard, the panic rising into her throat. Was Cai right?

Qiang watched as her mother crouched next to Cai and patted her back. "This must be a drill."

"We said the same for Shanghai and look at how that ended." Cai pushed Mingzhu away. "Or have you already forgotten the number of dead bodies we climbed over to get here?"

"*Zhùkǒu*!" Mingzhu commanded. "Pull yourself together, Second Madame."

At that moment, Qiang's father walked into the dining hall, scanning the room. "Where is my son?" he shouted.

"Biyu has gone to fetch him," Mingzhu answered, rising to her feet.

"You should have gone yourself." Wei shot an accusing finger at Mingzhu.

"Jun is not my responsibility," Mingzhu said bluntly.

"You're responsible for every woman and child in this household. That is your only role!"

Mingzhu's lips thinned.

Qiang got up and stood between her parents. "Mama was busy trying to soothe Second Madame—"

"Tang Qiang, hold your tongue," her father snapped. "Your opinions in this matter are neither required nor desired. What if the Japanese did come? What then? Jun's safety is paramount. He must be protected at all costs!"

Qiang's cheeks burned with shame and fury at her father's blatant favoritism. A multitude of words simmered within her, but they remained clogged in her throat.

Her mother pulled Qiang closer to her side, shouting over the siren at Wei, "Why such concern, dear husband? The British are stronger than anyone else. The Japanese would be crazy to attack the colony. Isn't that what you always tell us?"

Wei narrowed his eyes.

"Surely, we are beyond the reach of the Japanese here," Mingzhu persisted, undeterred, "and Jun should be secure within any corner of this house."

Qiang pulled at her mother's hand, silently urging her to give up. She watched her father's eyes grow redder and his forehead veins bulge. Thankfully, Biyu's entrance with Jun broke the growing tension.

"My precious Jun!" Cai rushed to hold her son, resting her cheek against the little boy's forehead and whispering soothing words to calm him. The siren stopped, leaving only Jun's wailing to puncture the silence.

That evening, the family discovered that it had indeed been just a drill. After the siren's wail had ceased, Qiang sought the sanctuary of her room for the rest of the day, staying there until Ah-Long showed up with a plate of osmanthus jelly cakes. She invited him to accompany her to the library, where they found her mother writing by the window. Upon hearing them enter, she hastily stowed the paper into *Dream of the Red Chamber* and returned it to the bookshelf. She bid them goodnight and cautioned Qiang not to be discovered by the others.

Ah-Long and Qiang lit a small candle in the corner of the room and sat on the floor with the cakes between them. He asked Qiang about Shanghai, and she recounted her experiences. First of their escape, then of her childhood. He listened attentively as she described the thriving streets, the pungent yet alluring fragrance of the street food stalls, and the colors of the city she had once called home.

"And what about you?" Qiang asked self-consciously. "Tell me something about your childhood. In English, too. It's good practice."

Ah-Long scratched his chin and began to speak, his hands forming dancing shadows on the walls.

"I was born in fishing village in Jīnshān. Everybody know everybody there. There is big lake and in summer, there is many lotus flower. I have big family. We not have much, you see. But we happy. My father? He was how you say . . . *yúfū*. I learn from him."

"A fisherman," Qiang said.

"Yes. *Yúfū*. Fish-ar-mun."

"Fish-*er*-man." Qiang pointed to her lips.

"Fish-er-man," Ah-Long repeated, and she nodded. "Every day, I wake with my father, the fish-er-man. We fix the net to catch fish. Many fish on good day. The smell of the sea is inside my head. We work very hard." He looked at his hands. "Life not easy but we happy. Happy like you and First Madame."

Qiang smiled. Her mother meant the world to her. She was glad he had noticed.

Ah-Long lapsed into quietness, lost in his memories. "I not talk of past too much," he finally admitted, his voice barely above a whisper. "My life now is good. I like here. I like you."

Qiang held back a laugh. Surely, he didn't mean it *that* way. His English was still not proficient enough. Yawning, she replied, "I like you too, Ah-Long."

•

Later, Qiang stirred awake on the library couch. Ah-Long had laid a shawl over her, and the candle had been snuffed out. Heavy curtains hung over the windows, and she could barely discern the outlines of the furniture. She snuggled deeper into the shawl, appreciating the tranquility of this secluded space. It was no wonder her mother favored it so much. It was almost enough to make her forget about the echoes of sirens still ringing in her mind, like wind chimes jangling in the presence of lonely ghosts.

CHAPTER 5

As summer turned to autumn, the air raid drills became more frequent, and although Wei remained dismissive of any threat of Japanese invasion, secretly Mingzhu had doubts. But that seemed distant in the tea parlor where she now sat, marveling at the Parisian décor—chandeliers, plush suede chairs, and floral motifs. Around her, gracefully dressed women chatted, enjoying tea and pastries. The company, however, did little to inspire her admiration. There were five wives present today, herself included. Mingzhu had coined nicknames for them—London Wife, California Wife, Mississippi Wife—as she had never invested much effort into getting to know them better. Francine was the sole other Chinese woman in the group and the only one who had shown genuine interest in her.

Mingzhu assumed a posture of quiet observation as the women discussed the latest scandalous gossip. Allegedly, an absent wife was having an affair with her tailor, provoking a flurry of whispers. London Wife boasted of her daughter's early admission into Château Mont-Choisi, while Mississippi Wife recounted how she'd threatened her husband with divorce if he persisted in his dalliances with an American singer from a gentlemen's club in Kowloon. The conversation, though mind-numbingly superficial, demanded Mingzhu's participation. So, she played her part, punctuating their dialogue with nods, intermittent laughter, and the occasional exclamation. *A divorce? How shocking!*

As Mingzhu raised her teacup for another sip, her reflection in a nearby mirror caught her attention. Her simple yet tasteful *qípáo,* with its high collar and subtle embroidery, stood in stark contrast to the extravagant attire of her companions. They wore short-sleeved V-neck dresses in expensive fabrics—deeply colored navy, maroon, and floral prints—each finished with pearls and lace. Their skirts flared modestly below the knee and their waists were cinched with belts. One wife even had an array of brooches pinned to her chest, as if she hadn't quite been able to decide which to wear that morning. Mingzhu had to remind herself that her presence was out of obligation to her husband, not to compete with these women for attention.

California Wife leaned forward. "My dear Albie is hosting a birthday celebration for me next weekend. Invitations were dispatched to your respective residences early this morning."

London Wife clasped her hands together, her brooches knocking against one another. "Oh, how delightful!"

"Where shall this splendid affair take place?" Mississippi Wife asked.

With an air of nonchalance, California Wife replied, "Nowhere over-the-top, just a gathering at the Hong Kong Club."

Mingzhu and Francine exchanged a knowing glance. London Wife's shoulders slumped, and she turned to them. "Oh, what an unfortunate predicament for both of you."

California Wife brought her hand to her mouth. "Oh my! I completely forgot about that."

Francine remained silent, but Mingzhu raised her chin and smiled reassuringly. "There's no need to apologize," she said. "You need not bear the burden of the policy that forbids Chinese civilians from setting foot inside the club."

California Wife avoided eye contact. "I apologize, Madame Tang. I should have been more considerate when my husband suggested the venue. But in fairness, women, in general, aren't usually permitted. It's only because my sweet Albie made a substantial donation to the club recently—"

"Truly, there's no need to explain yourself," Mingzhu interrupted. "I will arrange for a birthday gift to be sent to your residence before the event."

"I'll do the same," Francine said softly before adding, "Chances are, I wouldn't have been able to attend anyway."

Mississippi Wife shook her head and sighed. "It's truly pitiful how Chinese civilians are treated at times . . ."

A discussion unfolded between the wives about the restrictions placed upon Chinese civilians in Hong Kong. Mingzhu pretended to listen, but she understood that all this talk was merely a façade. What, after all, would these women ever do to effect change and reduce discrimination against the Chinese? The answer was painfully clear.

Nothing.

They would do nothing.

Eventually, the conversation stilled, and the women commenced their drawn-out routine of farewells, accompanied by perfunctory hugs and air kisses.

"Will you join me for a stroll through the park?" Francine asked, pulling Mingzhu aside.

Mingzhu checked her watch. Should she return home now, she would be required to share a meal with Cai, and there was nothing she desired less.

"A stroll would be nice," she replied.

As they bid farewell to the remaining wives, they stepped out into the warm sunlight, and a refreshing breeze brushed against her face, carrying the intoxicating fragrance of nearby jasmine bushes. They walked side by side, relishing the comfortable silence.

Francine was the first to break it. "Can you believe the audacity of those women? They speak of the mistreatment of our people as if they forget they are the occupiers! Sometimes, I just want to grab them by the shoulders and give them a good shake."

Mingzhu laughed. "That would be quite the sight."

"It truly would, wouldn't it?" Francine said. With a sigh, she added, "But, really, do you ever think of what a free Hong Kong would look like?"

Mingzhu didn't know how to respond. Hong Kong or not, she would still be the first wife of the Tang family. The word "freedom" was itself an echo of an idea she would never be able to catch.

As they continued their walk, Mingzhu found herself involuntarily drawn to Francine. Her chestnut-brown hair was neatly twisted into a bun and secured with a golden hairpin. The warmth of her brown eyes contrasted beautifully with her pastel pink *qípáo* adorned with exquisite floral embroidery.

"What's that?" Francine pointed to the leather purse swinging from Mingzhu's arm, where the spine of a book was just visible.

"It's a book I'm reading. *Midnight* by—"

"Mao Dun!" Francine exclaimed. "I've read it. What a thought-provoking novel. Have you finished it?"

Mingzhu shook her head.

"But surely you have formed an opinion on it?" Francine pressed. "What do you make of Mao Dun as a writer? I find him to be a remarkable realist."

"From what I have read and know, I somewhat agree," Mingzhu admitted, intrigued. She had never imagined Francine to be an avid reader and felt delighted to discover this new aspect of her personality.

Crossing a small road, they arrived at the park, welcomed by the fragrance of flowers and the melodious song of orioles through the trees, whose yellowing leaves were falling gently. They continued discussing literature and art as they strolled past a pond, where a group of ducks floated lazily on the serene water. Francine sighed. "I envy them. Look how the ducklings follow the mother around. Just the other day, my son wrote to tell me he has decided to continue his studies at Oxford and won't be returning to Hong Kong. Can you believe that?"

"You miss him," Mingzhu said empathetically.

"More than words can express," Francine confessed. "I had Samuel when I was just fifteen. He's more like a friend than a son. When he left for his studies, a part of my soul was torn away. Now, I'm left alone at home. My husband is hardly ever around. Sometimes, I secretly wish for him to have an affair. That way, he can bring home another woman for me to talk with!"

Mingzhu gave an uncomfortable laugh. "You don't mean that."

"I do!" Francine chimed. "At least you have a sister-wife. I'm sure she's good company."

"If you say so."

"I have a proposal." Francine eyed Mingzhu. "How about we become friends? *Real* friends. We can see each other more frequently, not only during the wives' gatherings. I don't think I'm the only one who needs a companion."

Mingzhu mulled over Francine's words. She had never considered forming a close friendship with any of the other wives.

"Well?" Francine asked, looking like a puppy awaiting a pat.

After a moment's pause, Mingzhu accepted the proposition. "Friends," she agreed, and a warmth bloomed in her chest.

On her way home, settled in the back seat, a shiver ran down Mingzhu's spine as the coolness of the car's upholstery seeped through her *qípáo*. The weather in Hong Kong was unpredictable. Every day, all four seasons presented themselves. Despite autumn's dropping temperatures, today's humidity had left a thin sheen of sweat on her skin.

She stared out of the window onto the lively streets of Wan Chai District. Shop fronts compressed tightly together, vying for space, each sign in colorful Chinese characters, beckoning people in. She rolled down the window and was hit by a pungent amalgamation of street food and burning incense. Beads of perspiration trickled down the brows of diligent men pulling rickshaws, and when they sped past the car, Mingzhu pinched her nose at the stench of their body odor.

A white man dressed like Henry and seated in a rickshaw caught her interest. As the rickshaw sped by, she realized it wasn't him.

Her connection with Henry had grown since their first encounter three months earlier. She had been studiously selecting poetry collections and presenting them to him with great thought and care, and their interactions had evolved into an artful dance of intellectual engagement—a captivating pas de deux centered around literature and poetry.

With Wei's approval, Henry had become a regular visitor to their home, giving Qiang's lessons four times a week and gaining free access to the family library. At first, Mingzhu had had reservations about sharing her precious space, but her concerns had proved unfounded. Henry's visits were restricted to the morning hours, coinciding with her engagement in ancestral rituals elsewhere within the house. Their discussions unfolded discreetly in secluded corners and hushed moments in hallways, through tender notes pressed and folded into the weathered pages of *Dream of the Red Chamber.*

Mingzhu had initiated it. One morning, Wei had ordered her to accompany him to a charity brunch in the city. Knowing she wouldn't see Henry that day, she wrote a note and concealed it within *Dreams of the Red Chamber,* then entrusted Biyu with informing Henry of its location. From then on, their correspondence followed the same clandestine method. The words she had penned that day would not be forgotten, for they mirrored her thoughts.

Perhaps tomorrow, when I am not bound by duty,
our paths may cross again.

Soon, their notes evolved into letters. Henry's words crafted fanciful tales of his youthful travels through Asia, vividly illustrating distant lands and cultures. Each letter offered a gateway into his past, filled with anecdotes from his hometown of Kent, England, describing quaint houses, winding roads, verdant trees, and wildlife, and she found herself transported by the beauty of his recollections. Reading his letters felt like journeying across the vast ocean, experiencing the world through his perspective.

She reciprocated with her own stories of Shanghai, narratives she had never shared with anyone before, infusing her writing with her feelings. She found comfort in his words—a profound connection that surpassed the physical realm—and she couldn't help but wonder if he might harbor similar sentiments. As much as she relished their exchanges, they were accompanied by a nagging guilt that unsettled her stomach.

The car began moving again, and a small sign in a bookstore, tucked between a bakery and a pharmacy, caught her attention.

"Stop the car," Mingzhu said, and pointed out of the window. "Let me out here." The driver steered the car to the roadside, and she instructed him to return to the house. She would make her own way back.

A bell chimed overhead as she entered a dim yet attractive interior. Bookshelves stretched from the floor to the lofty ceiling, and she traced the textured spines, navigating a few towering stacks of books piled on the floor. An older man scuffled over, his figure draped in a dark blue *changshān* fastened with frog buttons. His white hair, arranged into a queue, hung over his shoulder. "Welcome, welcome. Everything is marked for a low price. All books must go."

"You're closing down?" she asked.

The man rubbed his weary face. "Of course. There's talk of an occupation. I'm not the only business closing."

"Occupation . . ." Mingzhu repeated.

She didn't share Wei's confidence in the power of the British. If the Japanese were to invade Hong Kong just as they had Shanghai, how long would it be before the British decided to abandon them to their fate?

"*Ai-yah.* You're a woman. What do you know of politics?" the man said. "You just buy books for husband and son, okay? Buy many."

Mingzhu met his critical stare with a spark of defiance. "I may not know much about politics, but I would wager I know more about books than you."

"Is that so?"

"Take this, for example." Mingzhu plucked a small book from the shelf and waved it between them. "This should be in the poetry section, not short stories."

The man laughed. "You have a sharp tongue," he conceded.

"So, do you believe in the talk? You think the Japanese will attempt an attack on us here?"

"Without a doubt," he said. "The Japanese are among us now. Everything may look normal out there"—he gestured toward the shop window, providing a glimpse of the busy street beyond—"but do not be fooled. Death lingers. It's coming for us."

Mingzhu fell silent. No matter how much she reassured her daughter and the others that the air raid drills were merely an exercise, even as they became more frequent, she had a lasting worry that the Japanese would come.

"Anyway, enough talk of war. Look around!" the man declared, motioning to the shelves and walking away. "You never know when you'll be in a bookshop again. Enjoy it while it lasts."

Feeling uneasy, she browsed listlessly for a few more minutes before deciding to leave, but barely had she touched the knob when the door swung open, the bell tinkling overhead, and her eyes met a gaze reminiscent of the emerald depths of a forest.

"Mr. Beaumont," she said, startled. He wore a white linen shirt, cream trousers, and a pair of brown loafers, and his wavy brown hair was mussed instead of his usual combed style—much more casual than when he attended Qiang for lessons at the house.

Suddenly, her concerns seemed insignificant. Looking at Henry was like inhaling fresh air.

He stepped into the shop, the door closing behind him. "We've known each other for three months, Madame Tang. Surely you can call me Henry by now?"

"Yes, well . . ." Mingzhu said.

"It's no trouble," Henry said, reassuring her. "I will patiently await the day you deem us close enough acquaintances to call each other by our given names."

The corner of her mouth curved into a smile. "I admire your patience, Mr. Beaumont."

"Say." Henry shuffled his feet. "Have you had lunch?"

"Lunch?" she said.

The bookstore owner observed them, his brows raised.

"Yes, lunch," Henry replied with a teasing tone. "It's the meal between breakfast and supper."

"Yes, and no, I haven't had lunch yet," she said, suppressing a laugh.

"Would you consider joining me?"

Her stomach flipped, and not just from sudden hunger at the mention of food. It wouldn't be proper for them to share a meal out in public. What would Wei or Cai say if they ever found out? Her head started to ache.

"Didn't you want to browse? I don't want to interrupt you."

"Not at all. I realized I'm quite starved." His eyes flicked away from hers, and he cleared his throat. "There's a great *caa4 caan1 teng1* nearby. They serve delicious beef brisket noodles."

"Beef brisket?" Mingzhu bit her lip.

Henry smiled. "Come on, I'll show you the way."

. . .

The *caa4 caan1 teng1* was a modest restaurant with simple wooden tables, chairs, and a counter. In one corner, a chef busily prepared food with great intensity and fervor, bits of meat flying every time his cleaver hit the chopping board. When Henry asked her what she'd like to eat, she left the choice to him, as she did with Wei. He ordered two bowls of steaming hot noodles, and when they arrived, Henry held a pair of chopsticks, tapping them against hers as if they were wineglasses.

"Cheers!" he declared.

Her laughter was so vigorous that nearby patrons turned their heads. She pressed her lips together and cast Henry a playful grin, surprised at how comfortable she was around him.

She savored each bite, her taste buds leaping. The broth was rich and savory, the noodles tender, and the brisket melted in her mouth almost instantly. She couldn't recall the last time she had eaten something so delicious.

"So," Henry began. "What do you think?"

"It tastes like home."

He shifted in his seat. "Ah. Right. You must eat this all the time at the house."

"No," Mingzhu said, her eyes beginning to water. "It tastes like my first home in Shanghai, where I was born and raised."

"I'm glad you like it," he replied.

Suddenly, a cluster of children, no older than twelve, trooped into the tea restaurant with stacks of rolled paper beneath their arms, yelling something indecipherable. One child slammed a leaflet onto the table between Mingzhu's and Henry's bowls. The colorful image depicted a Japanese soldier holding a European woman against her will, and the bold black headline screamed:

**PREVENT THIS TERROR FROM
REACHING YOUR DOORSTEP.
INVEST 10% IN WAR BONDS TODAY!**

Mingzhu couldn't swallow her brisket. Henry grabbed the leaflet, crunched it into a ball, and shoved it into his jacket pocket.

The chef raised the cleaver and screamed at the children to get out, causing most diners to jump in their seats. "Before I chop your hands off!" he added.

Once the children left, Henry asked, "Are you all right?"

Mingzhu nodded, her appetite gone.

"There's been more activity going on these past days," he said. "Has your family prepared an evacuation plan? You know, in case—"

"My husband stands firm in his belief that the British will not let danger into the colony."

"But you wrote in your latest letter to me that you don't share the same belief as him. Is that still the case?"

The fumes seeping from the cars and trams outside made her lightheaded. "Perhaps we should talk of something else," she said.

"Of course," Henry said. "I'm sorry. I didn't mean to cause you any discomfort. It's probably best not to give it too much thought."

Mingzhu gave a weak smile. How could she not think of everything that was happening? The whispers, rumblings, and rumors of a potential war breaking out in Hong Kong were impossible to ignore. This was precisely what had happened in Shanghai right before the occupation. How could she not give it too much thought?

When they eventually exited, the late afternoon sun began to dip lower in the sky, casting long shadows on the buildings around them. Henry glanced at his watch.

"I should be going," he said. "I'm giving a lecture at the university tonight."

"Of course," Mingzhu replied. "Thank you for lunch and for showing me this place."

"The pleasure was all mine," Henry said, his gaze lingering on her. "Perhaps we can do it again another time."

"*Haang4 hoi4*! *Haang4 hoi4*!" A vendor who had lost control of his cart barreled toward them, its wheels clattering loudly over the uneven pavement. Before Mingzhu could react, Henry grabbed her and pulled her out of harm's way, her body pressing flush against his as he encircled her waist in a tight embrace. A gasp escaped her lips. At that moment, she became acutely aware of his broad chest pressed warmly against hers.

"Are you all right?" he asked, his voice close to her ear.

"Yes, thank you." Her hair fell over her eyes as she peered up at him. The intensity of his gaze upon hers sent her heart racing, and she wondered whether he could feel it. She quickly pulled away, and it was evident from his expression of loss that he didn't want to let go.

"Thank you," she said, steadying herself.

"I should be going," Henry murmured.

Mingzhu couldn't speak. The moment was charged, almost electric, as if something were happening between them that neither of them could control. "Yes, right. Thank you again for the lunch," she finally managed to say.

"Will you be home tomorrow morning?"

"Yes," she replied, brushing her hair behind her ears.

"I shall come an hour before Qiang's lesson." Henry leaned in closer. "Perhaps there may be a book worth reading in the library?"

"There's always a book worth reading," Mingzhu said, smiling.

"Well, then, perhaps you will recommend one to me? If you have time, that is."

"I have time," she replied almost too quickly.

Henry grinned. "Until tomorrow, then."

Mingzhu watched as Henry faded into the crowd. Her mind was hazy, and she was reminded of Jia Baoyu and Lin Daiyu from *Dream of the Red Chamber,* who defied societal expectations and fell in love. Could it be that she was experiencing the same thing, this spark Henry ignited within her? Such a thought both thrilled and terrified her. She had married for duty, and now the idea of falling in love seemed both exhilarating and dangerous.

Too dangerous.

CHAPTER 6

As the weeks passed, and drills became a routine part of life, the looming threat of a possible invasion remained constant in Hong Kong. Qiang was overjoyed to learn that her father had planned a night away at the Kowloon Hotel for the family. They were to attend a fundraising gala for the RAF bomber fund, and her father eagerly penned a generous check as their donation.

Qiang had chosen to wear a knee-length satin dress, the deep-navy fabric finished with delicate silver embroidery that caught the light. Its modest neckline and short sleeves befitted such an occasion, and the matching pearl necklace she'd borrowed from her mother added a touch of sophistication, making her feel older than seventeen. Her hair was fashioned into a loose bun, courtesy of Biyu, and held in place with a silver pin that complemented her attire.

Entering the dance hall alongside her mother, Qiang felt giddy as the pulsating music from a band reverberated through the air, infusing the room with irresistible energy. The spotlight shifted to the stage, where a young *shídàiqǔ* singer approached the microphone. Her embroidered red-and-gold silk *qípáo* shimmered under the spotlight, and with the first notes, she enclosed the room in a unique blend of Chinese folk music and American jazz. Qiang noticed a naval officer swaying to the beat with a partner, the smoke from his cigarette swirling mystically over the dance floor.

"Look, Mama, it's Henry," Qiang exclaimed, pointing toward the bar.

Her tutor had dressed for the occasion, sporting a blue suit, a crisp white shirt, and a silk tie, his hair slicked back with a trace of pomade. He moved deftly through the crowd, drawing attention with his confident stride.

Her mother fiddled with her jade bracelet, and Qiang wondered what had gotten her so nervous.

"Wei," Henry greeted him warmly, extending his hand for a firm shake. "What a delightful surprise to see you and the family gathered here."

"Henry," her father replied, his voice filled with genuine pleasure. He scanned the room briefly to ensure their encounter didn't go unnoticed. "Wonderful to see you."

Cai pushed her way past Qiang and her mother, sidling up next to Wei. She extended her hand to Henry, who raised an eyebrow ever so slightly and instead nodded politely. "Good evening, mistress."

Qiang chuckled at Henry's word choice, but her mother quickly nudged her with a silencing look. Cai's face, already heavily rouged, flushed a deeper shade of red.

"I'm sorry to interrupt," said a woman with brown eyes and snowlike skin. Looking at Henry, she took him by the arm and turned to lead him to the dance floor. "You owe me one," she said playfully.

"Excuse me," Henry said as she pulled him away.

"What a fine-looking woman," Wei said. "She'd be lucky to end up with a man like Henry."

Her mother lowered her voice so that only Qiang could hear. "A woman's luck isn't determined by the man she marries."

Qiang gave her hand a reassuring squeeze.

Her father led them to a round table and invited other associates to join them. Over cigars and wine, conversations about the occupation back on the mainland saturated the air.

Qiang rolled her eyes as Cai eagerly showed off her latest jewels to the other wives. Meanwhile, her mother seemed to be in another world entirely, her gaze locked on the dance floor where Henry was dancing effortlessly with the woman from before.

Cai gave a little cough and leaned toward Mingzhu. "That lady dancing with your daughter's tutor is a taxi dancer."

Qiang watched as her mother brought her wineglass to her lips, ignoring her father's concubine.

Not taking the hint, Cai continued, "Don't you think you ought to warn him?"

"Warn him?" Qiang asked. "Of what?"

"Oh, Qiang," Cai said. "It seems you don't know *everything*. Taxi dancers have been known to be spies planted by the Japanese!"

"Is that true?" she asked her mother, who responded with a nonchalant shrug.

"I wouldn't know, Qiang," she said, tracing the rim of her wineglass. "He's his own person. It's his choice who he dances with."

A pair of hands covered Qiang's eyes, startling her. "Guess who?"

As she breathed in notes of bergamot and jasmine, a smile spread across her face. She would recognize that voice and scent anywhere. "Camille!" she exclaimed and pulled her into a warm hug. "What are you doing here? I thought you were in Macao with your parents."

A twinkle of rebellion danced in Camille's eyes. "I may or may not have feigned illness to escape the trip."

"You rebel!" Qiang laughed. "Did you come alone?"

"Of course not. I came with friends from school." She gestured toward the main doors of the hall, where a group of young men and women waved back. "We're going to the park for a spot of adventure. Come with us."

Qiang tapped her mother on the shoulder, informing her she was stepping outside with Camille to catch some fresh air. Her mother nodded, but her sights remained on the dance floor.

The clamor of the hotel gradually yielded to the brisk autumn winds that feathered through the trees, brushing against Qiang's cheeks. As they skipped through the moonlit streets, the city took on a different charm, revealing hidden corners and stories waiting to be discovered. Qiang's ears pricked at the occasional hum of sleek cars, their headlights slicing through the dark alleys like shards of silver, highlighting the art deco façades of the buildings.

Why did Cai complain so much about Hong Kong, constantly comparing it to Shanghai? Hong Kong was just as beautiful and enchanting, with its unique allure. But, then again, what didn't Cai complain about?

Camille's friends from school chattered ahead of them, the young men passing around a flask. "You know, they're a fun bunch, but I wouldn't rely on them for anything serious," Camille whispered. "Except Edward. I rather like him."

"Don't be so loud!" Qiang giggled, plopping onto the grass with the others.

"How about a game of truth or dare?" Edward proposed, sparking excitement among the group. Camille, always up for a challenge, took the flask from one of the other men and spun it on the grass. When it landed on her, she smirked, a mischievous glint in her eyes.

"I choose Edward," she said. "Truth or dare?"

He sat up, a grin spreading across his face. "Dare, of course."

Camille surveyed him. Leaning closer, she said, "I dare you to kiss me right here, in front of everyone."

Qiang gasped, along with some others. How could she be so bold?

The men jumped in excitement, cheering Edward on. He wasted no time, leaning in and pressing a quick, enthusiastic kiss on Camille's lips. Qiang flushed, torn between watching and turning away.

As he pulled away, Camille whispered to Qiang, "I'm going to marry him one day. He just doesn't know it yet."

The game continued, each person taking turns. Camille dared another girl to put her shoes on the wrong feet and then run around a nearby bush, and cheering and howls of laughter filled the air.

After a while, a faint sound caught Qiang's attention, coming from behind a walled building at the edge of the park. It was a child crying, and soon, the group noticed.

"Qiang," Edward challenged. "I dare you to climb over the wall and see if it's a ghost!"

"Very well." Qiang rose from the grass, the chill raising goosebumps on her skin.

"That's a police station, Edward," Camille interjected.

"So?" he replied. "What are they going to do, arrest a young lady from an elite family? Go ahead and do it."

Qiang ignored Camille and approached the wall. The coldness of the brick against her palms sent a shiver down her spine, but the sense of adventure propelled her forward. Besides, she wasn't afraid of ghosts.

Her heart raced as she scaled the wall. The heels of her shoes proved burdensome, so she kicked them off. Camille ran over, picked them up, and said she'd wait for her there.

The cries grew louder, guiding her barefooted steps, and she found herself in a small courtyard. Beneath a banyan tree stood a little girl, her tear-streaked face turned upward to a man perched in its branches. What was he doing up there?

The little girl's eyes widened when she saw Qiang.

"Are you all right?" Qiang asked.

The man peered down, but it was too dark to see his features. "Her kite got caught in the branches," he explained, his voice calm and gentle.

"I see." Qiang knelt beside the girl and offered a reassuring smile. "Don't worry, your father will get the kite down soon."

"He's not my baba! My baba is inside there," the little girl sobbed, pointing a finger back at the station. "My kite, I want my kite!"

The kite was entangled in a narrow crevice between two branches. There was no chance the man's arm would fit through.

"Excuse me?" Qiang raised her voice. "Perhaps I should try?"

"You want to climb this tree?" he asked.

"Well, I don't *want* to climb the tree," she said. "But I believe I can reach that spot more easily than you can."

Carefully, he descended the tree, his movements sharp and controlled. Once his feet touched the ground, he stepped back and dusted bits of bark from his hands. He wore a button-up shirt and black trousers, accompanied by a black belt. His hair, thick and dark, fell across his forehead in a way that was both charming and deliberate. Qiang couldn't help but notice his lithe, muscled frame and the deeply intense gaze that he was directing at her from under thick brows. For a moment, Qiang found it challenging to look away.

"Go on, then." A glimmer of amusement shone in his eyes.

"Right, yes, of course," Qiang replied quickly.

She began her ascent, the rough bark biting into her palms and feet as she used the sturdy branches like a ladder. She could sense the man watching her intently.

"Say, miss," he called out, his voice tinged with curiosity. "Where are your shoes?"

"Oh, they're around," Qiang said. "Please don't talk to me. I'm trying to concentrate."

The man kept quiet, and even the little girl stopped sobbing momentarily. As Qiang reached the spot where the kite was ensnared, she steadied herself, balancing on the branches, and stretched toward the trapped kite and untangled it with precision and care.

The little girl's voice soared with joy. "My kite! My kite!"

Lowering the kite to the ground, Qiang descended the tree. The man approached her, his smile wide.

"Impressive," he commended, extending a hand to help her with the last step. Qiang politely declined and instead jumped to the ground.

The little girl snatched her kite and dashed toward the entrance of the police station. She waved goodbye before disappearing inside, leaving Qiang alone with the man.

"Thank you for your help," he said, his smile warm and genuine. Splatters of gold paint on his hands flashed in the moonlight. "I'm Hiroshi Nakamura."

"You're Japanese," Qiang blurted. Her mother's teachings were loud and clear.

Never speak to the Japanese.
Never befriend the Japanese.
Never trust the Japanese.
Most of all, never be alone with the Japanese.

"I am," Hiroshi replied. "You seem troubled. Are you hurt?"

"No, I'm fine." Qiang squared her shoulders, attempting to maintain an impression of composure.

Hiroshi stepped back, offering her space. "You're distressed because I'm Japanese," he stated.

Was she that obvious? Before she could respond, a hissing sound came from over the wall.

Hiroshi gestured toward the sound with a thumb. "Is that a friend of yours?"

She gave a partial nod. “I climbed the wall as part of a dare. I had no intention of disturbing the station.”

“A woman who jumps over walls, climbs trees, and embraces dares,” he said playfully. “You’re quite bold.”

“What are you doing in Hong Kong?” she asked, immediately regretting it as he studied her.

“I’m here for work,” he answered. “I’m sorry, did I miss the part where the Japanese weren’t allowed to work in the colony?”

“What type of work?” Qiang blurted, then bit her tongue. Why couldn’t she control herself?

“We have an interrogation room inside if you’d like to continue this line of questioning there,” Hiroshi said, amusement flickering in his eyes.

She gave an awkward laugh. “I wasn’t interrogating you.”

“Well, it certainly felt that way, miss,” he said. “Say, may I know your name?”

“You may not.”

“Qiang? Qiang!” Camille called, and heat rushed to her cheeks at her friend’s awful timing.

“Qiang, is it?” Hiroshi asked, his voice carrying a note of understanding. “I work for the Imperial Army. I assure you that my intentions here are good.”

“I see . . .” Qiang started fidgeting with the pearl necklace around her neck.

“I don’t think I’d be standing here so freely if I were a threat. Wouldn’t you agree?”

“Why do you have gold paint on your hands?” she asked, diverting the conversation elsewhere.

“Do you know much of Japanese art?” he asked.

“Are you going to tell me you’re an artist as well as a soldier?” Qiang asked, somehow more confident.

Hiroshi laughed. “Painting is more of a hobby. There’s a Japanese art form known as *kintsugi*. You have not heard of this?”

“I think we can establish I know little of Japanese art,” Qiang quipped.

When Hiroshi smiled this time, the dimples on either side of his mouth deepened. She couldn’t help but mirror his expression.

"*Kintsugi* is an old art form. To put it simply, it's fixing broken pottery."

She frowned. Was he putting it simply because she was a woman, and he thought she couldn't comprehend the intricacies of the ancient art form?

"Explain it to me properly. What is the gold paint on your hands for?"

Hiroshi stepped forward, holding out his hands for Qiang to see. She peered closely at the gold flecks splattered across his skin.

"I repair broken vases with lacquer mixed with powdered gold. When there is no gold, I use silver. Any metal works."

"What's the point?" she asked, raising a brow. "Would it not be better to buy a new vase?"

"Perhaps," he said. "But is it not better to try to mend things, to restore them to functionality? Do you generally throw things out of your life so easily?"

"Well, I suppose it depends on what it is."

"A broken vase," Hiroshi challenged.

"I'd throw it out."

"A broken chair."

"I'd throw that out, too."

"What about a broken heart?"

Qiang hesitated. Hiroshi's brows grew closer together as he waited for her to answer.

"I have never had a broken heart," Qiang admitted.

"Ah." Hiroshi relaxed his shoulders. "Then, you're lucky."

"That is not to say I haven't seen things broken, Mr. Nakamura—"

"Please, call me Hiroshi."

"As I said, Mr. Nakamura, I have seen many broken things."

"I believe you."

"And so you should. I may not care so much for a broken vase or a broken chair. But I do care for the broken families, homes, and land your Imperial Army has so ruthlessly stripped from my people. So, tell me, Mr. Nakamura, are those things that lacquer mixed with gold can fix?"

Hiroshi blinked, as if taken aback by her sudden outburst. Even she didn't know quite where to look after her heated words. What had gotten into her? Where did such boldness to speak to a Japanese stranger like this come from?

Camille called out again, but Qiang ignored her.

"The Imperial Army have their beliefs," Hiroshi said. "I have mine."

"And what exactly are your beliefs, Mr. Nakamura?"

"You wouldn't believe me if I told you."

Qiang raised her eyebrows in silent invitation.

"All right." Hiroshi exhaled. "I believe in peace. I believe in a world where there is no war, no famine, no hate. Just peace. Is that something you believe in, too?"

Qiang absorbed his response for a moment. She couldn't quite fathom why she felt such a strong pull toward him. Was it how his eyes seemed familiar, as if she and he had crossed paths in another time? Or perhaps it was his remarkable calmness, a quality she had not encountered when conversing with Japanese men before. Whatever this feeling was, she was sure of one thing: she didn't want to part ways just yet.

"I believe in many things," Qiang finally replied. "But until your fellow countrymen stop what they're doing, peace is not a luxury I can afford to believe in."

Hiroshi tucked his hands into his trouser pockets. "You should go." He tilted his head toward the wall. "I have work to do."

Without saying another word, Qiang climbed over the wall.

"Who were you talking to?" Camille asked, concerned. "Did you get in trouble?"

"I don't think so," Qiang reassured her, slipping her feet back into her shoes.

Toward the end of the evening, Qiang found herself wedged between her mother and Cai in the back seat as the car glided through the night, an uncomfortable silence in the air. She couldn't help but notice her father's tense expression as he sat opposite them. Only the hum of the motor dared to disturb the stillness.

"My love, why are you looking at me like that?" Cai asked.

A faint quiver ran across his nose—a telling sign of the anger that was to come. "You have humiliated this family with your disgraceful behavior. How could you allow a stranger to touch you so intimately?"

"It was just a dance, my love."

Qiang couldn't look away from the unfolding scene, and her mother closed her eyes and began massaging her temple. Qiang knew that this could have been avoided if Cai had simply heeded her advice and remained home to care for Jun, who had fallen ill with a fever.

"Just a dance? Don't think I didn't see, and don't think my associates didn't see either! You demeaned yourself. Did you not think of my *miànzi*?"

"Oh, my dear," Cai replied. "First Madame spent most of the evening sitting with your daughter's tutor at the bar. Does that not make you lose face?"

Her mother snapped her eyes open.

"First Madame engaged in a proper conversation with a respected English tutor, a trusted family friend," her father said, his voice laced with disdain. "You, however, were entwined with that officer, moving in the most nauseating manner."

"Trusted family friend?" Cai shrilled. "Mr. Beaumont has only been a tutor in our house for less than a year. I, on the other hand, have been your wife for many!"

"You're a concubine, woman!" Qiang's father shouted, shutting her up.

When the silence proved too stressful, Qiang was thankful her mother interjected with a calm yet firm voice. "Husband, I assure you that the dance meant nothing on Second Madame's part. The officer she danced with was Mr. Ian Whittaker, the husband of one of my friends from the Wives Club. You know the British have a more open-minded perspective and consider dancing as nothing more than a simple social interaction."

"Is that so?" Wei asked, sounding childish even to Qiang.

"Of course," her mother continued. "The fact you *allowed* Second Sister to dance with him only showed your generosity and social standing among the British people. They must think you're highly educated."

Qiang dropped her jaw slightly, impressed by her mother's quick wit.

He took a beat to digest her words, then exhaled heavily and turned his attention to the passing city lights outside the window, their fleeting shadows producing an ephemeral dance upon his face.

Qiang looked at her feet, the mud from the park smeared on her shoes. She quickly tucked them as far back against the seat as possible. For the rest of the journey home, she could not shake the image of the Japanese man, Hiroshi Nakamura, and his golden-flecked hands.

CHAPTER 7

Mingzhu couldn't spend time alone with Henry until a few weeks later, when she was able to sneak out to meet him again for lunch. Afterward, they stepped out onto the lively streets of Wan Chai, her stomach and heart full. Newly installed neon signs and swaying paper lanterns overhead competed for Mingzhu's attention, generating a series of colors across the bustling shop fronts.

Rickshaws and trams rumbled past, their bells chiming loudly, while street vendors filled the sidewalks with their enticing offerings. The last traces of autumn painted themselves across the city. Fallen leaves scattered the roads, forming tiny rustling mounds, and a chilly afternoon breeze brushed against her face.

As they passed a quaint storefront with a glistening glass window, Mingzhu stole a glance at her reflection beside Henry. Her beige cotton *qípáo* and cardigan, both decorated with a simple floral design, paired well with his sharply pressed trousers and his tailored white shirt with rolled sleeves. With one hand, he clung to a linen jacket, the hairs on his forearm golden in the sunlight. Wei didn't have much body hair, and she wondered what it would feel like to run her fingers along such fine strands.

A group of men chatted animatedly in Japanese near a telephone booth, drinking from takeaway cups. One man, deeply absorbed in the discussion, slammed his arm into Mingzhu, and she let out a startled cry as scalding liquid cascaded down the front of her *qípáo,* staining the once-pristine garment and burning one of her exposed hands.

Henry stepped forward. "Move aside," he said to the man.

The man turned toward his companions, their previously boisterous conversation diminishing to hushed murmurs.

Guiding Mingzhu away from the group, Henry spoke in a low tone, concern evident in his voice. "They are speaking Japanese," he warned. "It would be best to avoid further interaction with them."

"You're right. Let's go."

"Wait. You're injured." Henry took her hands into his and blew on her skin.

"I will be fine." Mingzhu blushed, withdrawing from his grasp.

Henry wrapped his jacket around her waist, shielding the stained dress from prying eyes. As he knotted the sleeves, a faint scent of his earthy cologne encircled her, eliciting a deeper flush to her already warm face.

"I'm so sorry, Henry," she said, her voice filled with regret. "I never intended to cause any trouble."

"Trouble? You haven't caused any trouble." A smile graced his lips. "Wait . . . what did you just call me?"

Mingzhu gasped and covered her mouth, and his laughter filled the air, infectious in its joy. At that moment, it had felt so natural to address him by his given name.

Henry returned to her burns. "Your hands do not look in good shape. I have medicine at home, just two blocks from here. Will you accompany me? If not, I can arrange for a driver to take you home."

Considering the state of her *qípáo* and stinging hands, Mingzhu weighed the consequences of returning home in such a condition. How would Wei react if he saw her like this? And worse, what would Cai say?

"Do you have a telephone?" she asked, and he nodded. "In that case, I will accompany you. I can call my dressmaker to deliver a fresh outfit for me before I return home."

They proceeded down two blocks, gradually leaving behind the commotion of the busy city, until they approached a shabby cement stairway, the peeling paint revealing the worn concrete underneath. Henry gestured for her to follow, and together, they ascended the stairs, their footsteps echoing.

At the landing, a row of pale grayish-blue front doors, each secured behind black metal gates, greeted Mingzhu. The air carried a musty scent, intertwined with the distant aroma of spices wafting from nearby kitchens.

Inside the apartment, Henry strode across the room, hopping around piles of clothes and books on the floor. He pulled the wooden shutters open, letting rays of afternoon light pour in. There were two rooms—the bathroom and what appeared to be the "everything else" room, with a medium-size bed in the middle, covered with thin white netting to keep the mosquitoes at bay. A small study desk with a steel lamp atop it rested near the window.

"Here, take a seat by the desk. I'll be back in a moment."

Mingzhu sat down and waited until he returned with a small medicine kit. She positioned her hand on the table while he tenderly applied the cream to her burned skin. She glimpsed a family of four in the apartment across the way, gathered around a circular table with huge smiles on their faces. With determined persistence, the mother fed spoonfuls of rice to the youngest child while the father entertained the other in a game of fighting chopsticks. The scene was so different from the dining hall back at the Tang residence. Mingzhu thought hard but couldn't remember the last time she sat around a dining table with Wei and Qiang when they all laughed and smiled.

Henry offered a comforting squeeze of her hand. Mingzhu's stomach tensed as they locked eyes. He quickly directed his attention toward the family across the street.

"They look happy," he said.

Mingzhu swallowed hard, trying to hide the fact her eyes had begun to water. "Sorry," she whispered. "Seeing such a sight makes me . . . makes me . . ."

"Upset," Henry said, tightening his grip on hers, and Mingzhu nodded. "And rightfully so. You are in a tough predicament. I'm sorry."

"I sometimes wonder if perhaps I would be happier married to someone else."

"That's understandable," Henry replied. "You didn't have a choice in your marriage. It must've been difficult."

"It wasn't, at first." Her shoulders relaxed, and she could feel the anxiety that had been brewing in her stomach begin to settle. "When I married my husband, I was confident in what my role was."

"Your role?"

"Yes," Mingzhu answered. "My role as a wife. I knew what I had to do, what I had to say, and how I was to perform my duties."

"Perform your duties . . ."

Mingzhu laughed. "You sound like a parrot."

"I'm sorry," Henry said, laughing with her. "I'm just taking in every word you have to say. That's all. May I ask you a question?"

"Of course."

"If you could turn back time and you had a choice in the matter, would you still have married your husband? Or do you think you would have held out and waited for love?"

"Love . . ." she said.

"Who's the parrot now, Mingzhu?" Henry smiled.

Her name on his lips sent an electric wave through her chest, low into her body. She allowed him to hold her hand a little longer, their touch becoming a channel for unspoken desire. The world around her gradually receded into the background, overshadowed by the way his jade green eyes burned into hers.

The tension between them was shattered by a knock on the door. Henry reluctantly relinquished her hand and approached the entrance. A delivery man stood on the other side, holding a package.

"Delivery for a Madame Tang," he announced, extending the box toward Henry.

Realizing that it must be the dress she had ordered upon arriving at Henry's, Mingzhu stepped forward, her heart still fluttering. "Thank you," she murmured.

With a quick nod, the delivery man departed, leaving Mingzhu and Henry alone again. Knowing the need for discretion, Mingzhu excused herself. "I should change and go."

"Right, yes. Of course," Henry said, gesturing toward the bathroom.

Moments later, Mingzhu walked out of the bathroom to see Henry standing near the bed, his eyes tracing the contours of her new outfit.

"I must be going now," she murmured, trying to keep her tone steady. But there was a subtle longing beneath her words, a reluctance to leave.

"Please." Henry gestured to the front door, his expression tinged with regret. When she approached the door, he said, "Mingzhu?"

"Yes?" She turned back to him, her heart racing.

"I apologize for the inappropriate act of holding your hand. I didn't mean to put you in such a compromised position. Will you forgive me?"

Mingzhu pressed her lips together. "You're sorry?"

"Perhaps *sorry* isn't quite the right word," Henry replied, taking a step closer to her.

"Regretful, then?"

"No, not regretful." He took another small step toward her.

"I didn't regret it," she admitted softly.

"Nor did I. But it was inappropriate," Henry acknowledged.

"Regretfully inappropriate," Mingzhu echoed, feeling a rush of warmth as he drew nearer.

"It won't happen again," Henry vowed, inches away from her now.

"It can't."

"It can't," he repeated.

Their proximity sparked an undeniable tension between them. Henry leaned in, then hesitated, pulling back slightly. Before he could fully retract, Mingzhu rose to her tiptoes and pressed her lips against his.

She gasped, taken aback by her boldness. The tiny hairs on the nape of her neck stood on end as though she had been brushed by a jolt of electricity.

Henry's cheeks flushed pink, and he grinned widely. "I wasn't expecting that."

Mingzhu couldn't help but smile, though she tried to hide it behind her hand. "But you had hoped for it, hadn't you?" she teased, her eyes locking with his in a playful challenge. "I really should go," she added, a sense of urgency creeping into her voice.

"Right, yes," Henry agreed, his smile unwavering. "Of course."

As Mingzhu went to leave, a flicker of hesitation held her back. She threw Henry another glance. When she found the same longing reflected in his eyes, she rushed back to him without another word and grasped the collar of his shirt and kissed him again, this time with a slow and deliberate intensity. He wrapped his arms around her, drawing her even closer. Aching desire lit her from the inside out, setting her nerve endings aflame. Nothing else mattered. For a dizzying moment, she imagined letting it carry her away to his bed in the center of the room. She breathed him in, pressing closer to him, and he groaned. It would be so easy.

But she couldn't. She was married. The thought was like jumping into a cold river.

Still, it took all her strength to eventually pull back and walk out the door.

On the journey back to the house, Mingzhu couldn't shake off the thought of what her life would be like if she were married to Henry instead. *Stop it,* she told herself, trying to get a grasp of reality.

Settled in the games room that night, Mingzhu joined her husband, Cai, and Qiang in a game of *májiàng*. The ivory tiles clacked rhythmically, filling the air with their distinctive sound as each player executed strategic moves. She was disturbed at how no one looked at her differently, though she felt changed.

"There are more riots, you know," Cai said.

Mingzhu rearranged her tiles, hiding the sudden tremble of her hand. "Yes. I have heard this news."

"There are whispers that Japan will invade," Cai continued. "We should consider moving to a safer place. How about America? Hawaii, for instance, seems peaceful, according to my cousin."

Wei's knuckles whitened around a tile. "I've said it before, and I'll repeat it: the British will protect us. Stop this nonsense and focus on the game."

Taking advantage of the fact that no one was paying attention, Mingzhu laid down her winning tile, declaring her victory with a confident *"Hú!"*

Wei grumbled in defeat. Mingzhu's triumph was short-lived, though, as he pinched her thigh beneath the table. Discomfort prickled across her skin, and she pushed his hand away, her face stoic as she resumed shuffling her tiles. Undeterred, Wei persisted, his touch audacious and familiar.

"My friend Francine has offered us a place to stay in case of trouble," Mingzhu said impulsively, hoping it would divert his attention. The two women had grown close, bonding over shared secrets and laughter while arranging their own outings without the company of the other wives. Last week, Francine had told her that she'd be leaving for her father's residence for a while, to be safe. Having just arrived, Francine had sent a letter to Mingzhu and her family, inviting them to stay in Sai Kung if there was a Japanese invasion. Mingzhu had intended to keep this invitation to herself, ensuring that only she, Qiang, and Biyu would have a secure haven should war erupt. She cared little for Wei and Cai's safety; the only reason she would consider bringing Cai along would be because of Jun. Hiding out with her husband and his mistress seemed as dreadful as a potential war.

Wei pulled his hand from her. "Enough! What rubbish are you women spouting? I'm sick and tired of repeating myself. The British have a strong foothold here in Hong Kong. They are only making this land more prosperous. Japan might have taken over Shanghai, but there's no chance they'll take Hong Kong, too. Now, for heaven's sake, focus on the game!"

Mingzhu was glad for his anger, for he had stopped trying to touch her beneath the table. But in the absence of his touch came an even more frightening thought. What if Japan did occupy Hong Kong?

As the night dragged on, fatigue settled upon the group. Once everyone had departed, Mingzhu began putting away the tiles.

Wei moved in closer, his hands encircling her waist. She could feel the warmth of his breath against her ear.

"I am not feeling well," she said. "Perhaps you could seek out the second madame tonight?"

He firmed his grip around her. "It is you I want, First Wife."

Mingzhu pushed herself from him and continued to tidy up. "Please, husband," she uttered. "I truly am quite exhausted. I have a terrible headache . . ."

Wei seized her hand and shook the tiles from her grasp. Each one that smacked the table sent a jolt of annoyance through her entire body.

"You would refuse me?" He twisted her hand back.

Mingzhu couldn't find the words to get out of such a predicament. She conceded and closed her eyes, allowing the engagement to unfold. Even as Wei's hands explored her body and his lips left a trail of forced kisses along her neck, her thoughts drifted elsewhere—to Henry.

With each touch, each whispered word, she surrendered further to the illusion of Henry's presence. He became her refuge from the rough touch of her husband. She allowed herself to entertain the fantasy and believe in a world where Henry's hands were on her body, tearing away at her *qípáo*. It was Henry's lips parting hers. The falsehood was bittersweet, but she clung to it for dear life. Soon, she began kissing Wei back passionately.

He groaned into her ear. "Now, that's more like it."

Mingzhu flinched and pushed her lips back onto his. The more she kissed him, the less he spoke. The less he spoke, the more she could imagine Henry. She fought the urge to call out his name, to give voice to her true desires. Instead, she kept her eyes closed and pushed herself closer to him.

The next morning, as a chilly draft slipped through the window and brushed across the bedroom, Mingzhu lay wide awake. Beside her, Wei's steady breathing indicated his deep slumber. Her mind was conflicted from the events that had occurred the night before. She crept out of the bed, careful not to wake her husband, and moved to the window, her bare feet padding on the cool marble floor. The outside world was just beginning to stir, and the touch of the early morning light revealed a familiar figure approaching the house.

Henry.

Excitement coursed through her body, quickening her heartbeat. His early arrival presented an opportunity to see him and engage in conversation. Without hesitation, she made her way to the closet, her movements filled with anticipation. Selecting a simple yet elegant silk robe, she slipped it on, then combed her fingers through her hair, arranging it in a loose bun that accentuated her features. A final glance in the mirror assured her that she appeared presentable, even if she wore clothing only her husband should ever see her in. Then, with one lingering look back at Wei, she set off.

A stillness hung in the air as she hurried through the tranquil corridors of the house. The servants had yet to wake and begin their daily routines. Only the doorman would be up at this time.

Reaching the library, she pushed open the door. Henry was already seated and flicking through one of her classics. When their eyes met, he stood and greeted her.

"You have come early today," Mingzhu said.

Henry smiled. "I'm halfway through *Romance of the Three Kingdoms*. I must admit, it's not a light read. Would you sit with me and explain the parts I don't quite understand?"

Returning his smile, she closed the door behind her. There was nothing she wanted to do more.

CHAPTER 8

A little past noon, Qiang made her way home from Luk Yu Teahouse, and she shivered from the chill winds. Graying November clouds lingered from the morning rain. She wiped her tears, still reeling from saying goodbye to Camille, who had told her she was moving to Macao with her parents.

"It's only a matter of time before Japan invades Hong Kong," Camille had said over tea that morning. "My parents have family in Macao. It's the safest place for us to go."

"My baba is adamant that the British will protect us. He says we have nothing to worry about."

The waitress, who had clearly eavesdropped, gave a small scoff. Facing Camille with her entire back turned to Qiang, she inquired, "Can I get you anything else, miss?"

Qiang had grown accustomed to this differential treatment whenever she was out with Camille, who was half Chinese, half white, and had inherited her father's lighter complexion and distinctive features. Dismissing the waitress, Camille continued, "Oh, Qiang, the reality is different. The British have their own interests to protect, and when it comes to war, it's every man for himself."

"The British have protected us well so far, have they not?" Qiang asked, knowing full well she sounded like her father.

"They have?" Camille said. "You're forgetting they're occupiers, too. Listen, Qiang, you should talk with your mama. She is realistic and always supports you. You must tell her to consider leaving Hong Kong."

On her walk home, Qiang didn't know what to do. What would her mother say if she were to make such a suggestion? Leaving Shanghai had been no easy feat. Where would they go from here, from this new life they'd built since arriving in Hong Kong?

But Qiang had seen what the Japanese were capable of. One memory clung to her like a bad dream—a mother cradling her newborn on the street. Japanese soldiers had stabbed the baby dozens of times and blood from its lifeless body had seeped into the mother's tunic. The mother cried for help, wailing at the top of her lungs. People heard her. People stopped to look. But no one helped her, not even Qiang.

Upon her return home, Qiang entered through the double doors, making her way into the vast entryway of the residence. The household staff—maids, chefs, and gardeners—had congregated, their low conversations and urgent movements centered around the library door on the upper floor.

A maid hurried to Qiang, bowing.

"What is happening?" Qiang inquired, handing her purse and coat to the maid. "Where's my mama?"

The maid merely shook her head, glancing briefly up toward the library before retreating.

Ah-Long was at the foot of the staircase, his face contorted in distress. Noticing Qiang's arrival, he approached her. "The first madame . . ."

Dread pinched Qiang's stomach. She pushed past Ah-Long, ascending the stairs until she was outside the library, standing beside Biyu.

"Your baba refuses to come out," Biyu sobbed, as she pounded on the door.

From within, her father boomed, "You wicked woman! What kind of wife are you?"

"What has happened?" Qiang asked, desperate. "Why is this door locked?"

Shaking, Biyu began fiddling with a butterfly pendant that hung around her neck. "Jun has fallen ill with another fever. Your baba is blaming your mama."

"What?" Qiang spat, glancing around. "Where is Cai? Why isn't *she* the one facing the consequences?"

"You know that's not how things work around here, Qiang," Biyu said.

"Baba!" Qiang struck her palms against the door. "Baba, open the door!"

"Stay out of this, Tang Qiang," he spat back.

Qiang pried Biyu's hands away from her necklace. "Is there a key to open the door?"

Biyu shook her head, lost for words.

"Think harder, Biyu! There must be a key somewhere."

Her father shouted, "Repeat the rules of being a first wife! Repeat them to me!"

"Respect and loyalty," her mother began, her voice low but resilient. "The first wife must demonstrate the utmost respect and loyalty to her husband and his family."

Ah-Long appeared behind Qiang with a tool she'd seen him use in the garden. "Use this mattock. It'll work."

Grabbing the mattock, Qiang struck the doorknob, hitting it repeatedly until her fingers numbed. All the while, her mother's voice flowed through the door.

"Managing the household is crucial," she recited, her voice tired. "The first wife is responsible for overseeing the efficient running of the household—this includes supervising the help, managing household expenses, organizing meals, and maintaining cleanliness."

Finally, the doorknob gave way, clattering onto the floor. Qiang pushed the door open, and her heart sank. Her mother was kneeling in front of her father, who sat in the armchair with a tightly rolled leather belt in his hand.

"Get out!" he shouted.

Sweat trickled down her mother's face, pooling at the base of her neck. Her arms bore red welts, and her hair had come undone, flowing down the back of her *qípáo*.

"Mama!" Qiang rushed over, wrapping her arms around her mother. Despite her sweat, she didn't cry, and she didn't shake. She was as steady as a rock.

Her father stood, the leather belt swinging in his hand. He towered over them, his face scrunched in anger.

"Did you not hear me, Tang Qiang? I said get out!" He slapped the belt down, and it swiped against Qiang's cardigan. Her nostrils flared at almost being hit.

Her mother's body was tense, her back rigid against Qiang's chest, but her voice was calm and steady when she spoke. "It's all right, Qiang," she soothed, patting her hand. "Go. I will handle this."

"I will not leave you, Mama."

"You wicked woman," her father continued. "You were to call the doctor first thing this morning! But, no, what did I hear? You went to the damn city! What could be more important than Jun?"

"I did call the doctor," she defended. "I told the second madame he would be coming. I arranged it as requested. I made sure everything was organized before I left."

"You should've stayed at the house and cared for my son. It's your sole purpose and duty as the first wife. You're a failure of a wife. You have failed me. You have failed the entire Tang family!"

"I am more than just a wife!" Mingzhu shrieked.

Qiang jumped at her mother's words. She had never seen her in such a state of rage before.

Wei lifted his arm, ready to strike again, but Qiang positioned herself before her mother. The leather belt cracked against Qiang's arm, slicing through her skin, and searing hot pain shot through her body.

Her mother rushed to cover her. "Enough!" she cried.

Wei dropped the belt to the floor, his shoulders falling, and he frowned at Qiang. "Get your mama to the ancestral hall at once," he said. "She will kneel there until I say so. She will not eat. She will not drink. She will only pray. If anyone dares comfort her during this time, I will kill them with my bare hands." He towered over her mother with utter contempt. "Remember this day, First Wife. If my son falls sick again, you will owe me your life."

After he exited the room, Biyu rushed into the library, brushing past Qiang to assist her mother to the sofa. Biyu set about retying her hair, and Qiang grabbed a shawl from the armchair, draped it around her mother's shoulders, and wiped the sweat from her neck and cheeks with a handkerchief.

Meanwhile, her mother sat unresponsive, staring across the library at a small table beside the window. Her copy of *Dream of the Red Chamber* was situated neatly atop it.

"Qiang," she said finally. "Will you promise me something?"

"Anything, Mama."

Her mother peeled her gaze from the small table and locked eyes with Qiang. "In this life, let no man treat you the way your baba treats me. Promise me, Qiang."

Qiang's eyes stung. "I promise, Mama."

CHAPTER 9

As Hong Kong folded into winter, bringing colder nights and paler skies, ominous whispers of a possible invasion persisted. Staunch in his trust in the British, Wei threw an extravagant party for Jun's second birthday. Mingzhu was tasked with meticulously crafting handwritten invitations to British expatriates and wealthy Chinese families across the city. A month had passed since the Jun incident, and as punishment, Wei still forbade Mingzhu from attending any social events—although whether it was truly a punishment was debatable. As guests began arriving, Mingzhu remained confined inside the ancestral hall. While she disliked kneeling for hours on end, it was also a relief not to have to socialize with her husband's acquaintances. At least the dead didn't engage her in fruitless conversation.

Mingzhu's ears perked up as she caught the sound of a familiar voice amidst the raucous laughter and chatter echoing from outside the ancestral hall. She had been surrounded by staff the past month and had hardly been able to speak with Henry, though they had managed to exchange a few letters.

"Is she in there?" Henry asked urgently.

"Yes, Mr. Beaumont," Biyu answered.

"I must speak with her at once."

"First Madame is not permitted to speak with the guests, Mr. Beaumont. Master Tang has made it clear that—"

Henry cut her off. "It's imperative I speak with her now, Biyu. If you care for your Madame, you will allow me inside. There is no time."

Mingzhu pushed herself from the floor and began straightening her *qípáo*. When the doors opened and Henry stepped into the sacred space of the hall, she refrained from rushing over to him.

"Henry," Mingzhu said, noting his concerned expression. "You shouldn't be in here."

"It's the Japanese!" Henry exclaimed. "They—"

The air raid sirens began to blare, cutting off his words. Mingzhu rushed out to the hallway, catching sight of panic stirring among some of the guests. Within the chaos, some continued their conversations, feigning indifference as they downed their wine, while others made hasty exits, eager to seek shelter in their awaiting vehicles.

"Quick, get back inside." Henry pulled Mingzhu into the ancestral hall with Biyu following closely behind. He closed and locked the heavy wooden door with a single, decisive motion, creating a barrier between them and the frenzy unraveling outside. The sound of the sirens was muffled; the relentless shrillness, which seemed to be persisting longer than usual, was replaced by a distant, muted drone.

"This isn't another drill?" Biyu interjected, placing her hands over her ears.

Henry shook his head, his focus never leaving Mingzhu. "Listen to me, Mingzhu. They're really here this time. But I have a plan. No matter what happens next, I need you to follow my lead. Do you trust me?"

Mingzhu looked at him wordlessly, dread closing her throat. Outside, she heard the roar of trucks, and then screams.

The invasion was really happening.

"Answer me, Mingzhu," he said. He was clearly panicked, and his voice, urgent and demanding, pierced through her shock.

"Qiang . . ." Mingzhu stammered, leaping toward the door only for Henry to pull her back. "I need to get to Qiang!"

"Mingzhu, stop!" Henry grabbed her shoulders, his eyes meeting hers. "I have a plan. Again, do you trust me?"

Mingzhu clutched her mala beads, seeking strength and guidance from their smooth texture against her skin. "Yes. I trust you," she finally said.

"Good. Stand behind me." His voice was clear and resolute. "Follow my lead and speak only when necessary."

"Wait!" Mingzhu pointed at a large chest between the wall and the ancestral shrine. "I think you can fit in there, Biyu."

"Absolutely not, First Madame! You hide. You're more important."

"Biyu, listen to me," Mingzhu implored. "You have devoted your entire life to me, from the moment I took my first breath until now. I am asking you—no, I am begging you, for once, let me protect you."

The thuds intensified, and Henry said, "Hurry! Biyu, you must hide. I am only able to help your madame."

Mingzhu pushed Biyu forward, guiding her into the wooden chest, then quickly stuffed several prayer cushions on top of her before slamming the chest shut and returning to Henry's side.

One desperate thought repeated over and over: *Please stay safe, Qiang.*

CHAPTER 10

One moment, Qiang stood by her father, welcoming the arriving guests; the next, the sirens blared, and a jarring rumble tore through the air as a convoy of trucks surrounded the entrance, their engines roaring before coming to a halt. She froze in place, overwhelmed by the sudden chaos that engulfed the household.

Her father turned to her, his voice low. "Protect your brother, Qiang. Find him and get him to safety."

The truck doors swung open, and from within emerged a horde of Japanese soldiers, their boots landing on the ground with a resounding thud. Clad in dark-khaki uniforms, they exuded an aura of menace that made terror grip her throat.

"Go!" He pushed Qiang further into the house. "Protect my son!"

The soldiers moved with unsettling synchronicity, their movements precise and purposeful, forming an impenetrable, inescapable wall of authority. Qiang pushed her way through a sea of people. Most of the guests had begun walking closer to the door to understand better what was happening. Why was Qiang the only one running the other way? Did these people not know what the Japanese were capable of? Were they not scared?

A Japanese officer shouted in broken English, "Men one side, women other side! All of you! Raise your hands!"

The house trembled with fear and disbelief as terror-stricken eyes darted in every direction, desperately seeking understanding amidst the unfolding chaos. Hurried footsteps scattered across the marble floor, accompanied by whimpering voices.

Qiang found herself stuck, encircled by a group of women. She knew she had to get out of there. Where was Mama? Where was Biyu? Ah-Long?

"Are we going to die?" a short woman beside Qiang sobbed, her fingers tugging at her sleeve.

"Shh." Qiang brought a finger to her lips.

"Women, here!" an officer barked, waving his pistol toward them. The short woman gripped Qiang tighter.

Looking to the main door, she watched as a soldier dragged her father onto the graveled path outside. When he refused to kneel, the soldier punched him in the face, and he dropped to the ground, his knees digging into the gravel as he spat out chunks of blood. Tears blurred Qiang's vision, and she slapped her hand over her mouth to keep from screaming.

The Japanese herded the Chinese men toward the waiting trucks outside. The Western guests who had gathered for Jun's birthday were organized into a queue and subjected to questioning, and their information was recorded with painstaking attention to detail.

"We have rights, you know!" Mr. Lupton, her father's business associate, bellowed. "How dare you detain us like this!"

In response, the officer drew his pistol, the cold metal glinting under the sun that had begun to set. Before anyone could react, a deafening gunshot shattered the air, the bullet piercing the space between Mr. Lupton's eyes. In an instant, he collapsed to the ground, lifeless.

Horrified screams broke out in the crowd, and a man nearby vomited onto the ground. He was captured and pushed onto one of the waiting trucks. The short woman's grasp weakened, and her eyes rolled back as she lost consciousness. Instinctively, Qiang lowered the woman to the floor, cradling the back of her head to prevent it from hitting the hard marble surface.

"Does anyone have any other questions?" The officer waved his pistol before the remaining men, who all shook their heads and looked down. Then, under rigorous scrutiny, the Western men all surrendered their names, addresses, workplaces, and social standing. Some were released, while others were steered into the waiting trucks.

It was Shanghai all over again.

"Do you think they're selecting based on occupation?" another woman asked, but no one dared answer her. No one dared to speak.

Qiang crouched watchfully beside the unconscious woman as the Japanese continued their methodical roundup, corralling men onto the trucks with chilling efficiency. With each passing moment, any hope for escape seemed to slip further away.

Pressing her back further into the comforting shadows beneath the staircase, Qiang began praying for a miracle. Her mother's voice muffled her father's earlier command of finding Jun and getting him to safety.

Should the Japanese invade or make it to our doors, hide.
Hide and survive. Never let them take you.

The floor shook beneath her as fighter planes tore through the sky overhead with a deafening roar. A distant explosion thundered through the house, violently rattling the walls. She propelled herself forward, crawling down the hallway toward the kitchen. The cold marble floor was hard against her knees and palms.

In the kitchen, the cooks and several maids huddled in the corner. Ah-Long was in front of them with his arms held out, protecting them. When he saw Qiang, he ran toward her.

"Th-they're here," Qiang stammered.

Ah-Long whipped his head back to the others. "Go. Everyone, go now. Take the road at the back of the house and go downhill. Go!"

The maids and cooks gathered, pushing and shuffling out through the back door.

"Come with me," Ah-Long said, holding Qiang's hand.

"I need to find Mama. I can't leave her in the house."

"Too dangerous, Young Miss," Ah-Long warned. "Come. Trust me."

"But Mama . . ."

Loud footsteps thumped down the hall toward the kitchen.

"Hurry!" Ah-Long pulled her outside and they raced toward the back end of the yard until they came to a small wooden shed. He ushered her inside and removed the wooden planks from the floor, unveiling a hiding place. The sound of approaching boots grew louder. In a hushed tone, he directed Qiang's attention to the hole in the ground. "Inside here. Hide now," he said.

"Hide with me," she urged.

"No. You hide. I have to put the wood back."

"No, no, no. Hide with me, Ah-Long. Please."

Ah-Long tenderly brushed aside a stray lock of her hair. It was the first time he had touched Qiang in such a way, and despite the horror unfolding outside, she was briefly comforted.

"I will come back. I promise."

Qiang began to cry. "Please . . . Ah-Long . . ."

"I never lie to you, Young Miss." Ah-Long looked intently at Qiang. "I will come back. I will find First Madame."

Japanese voices could be heard outside and with a reassuring nod, Ah-Long rose to his feet, his movements deliberate as he guided Qiang to lie down and wedged the wooden planks back into place.

Time passed agonizingly slowly as she hid in the suffocating darkness. The air grew stagnant and oppressive, thick with the scent of cold, damp wood. The staleness of it all seemed to press down on her lungs, making it difficult to draw even the shallowest breath. With each inhale, she struggled, haunted by the memory of her father's intense concern for Jun. As she fought to draw air into her lungs, she clenched her fists, feeling anger coursing through her. She resented her father for bestowing so much love on Jun that it seemed he had forgotten about her existence entirely. How, at that moment, with almost no air to breathe, she wanted to wrap her hands around her father's neck and squeeze out all the hatred she had fostered over the years. The tears that poured from the corners of her eyes began soaking into the mud beneath her.

Suddenly, the shed doors were thrown violently open, and heavy footsteps caused the wooden floor to creak in protest above her. She remained motionless. Flecks of dirt fell on her face through the narrow cracks, and she held her breath, desperate to stifle any noise that might betray her presence. Muffled screams echoed from above, the desperate pleas of a woman met with the forceful intrusion of a Japanese soldier.

"Get off me!" she hissed. It was Li Mei, one of the kitchen maids. Qiang's heart battered against her ribs. She had to help her. She began pushing against the wooden planks above her, but they wouldn't budge. Li Mei's weight pressed down on them, preventing Qiang from breaking free. She heard the sound of a belt being unbuckled, and Li Mei's whimpering filled the air.

Tears continued streaming down Qiang's cheeks, their salty trails merging with the dirt that clung to her face and dripping into her ears. The Japanese soldier erupted in laughter. "Stop moving!" he ordered.

Through the crack in the wood, Qiang saw Li Mei pushing herself up from the floor, grasping a garden weeder in a trembling hand. Her disheveled hair clung to her sweat-soaked face. The soldier took a step forward as Li Mei drove the weeder into her own neck. Qiang squeezed her eyes shut and bit her tongue. Li Mei's body collapsed to the ground, her blood seeping through the cracks in the wood, splattering Qiang's face with its warmth.

"*Subeta!*" the soldier hissed. He proceeded to kick Li Mei before storming off in fury.

The silence that followed threw Qiang into a forceful breakdown as she choked back a scream. Through the gap, Qiang saw Li Mei's eyes wide open, lacking any trace of life.

CHAPTER 11

With an explosive crash, the ancestral hall door finally splintered open under the relentless assault of the invading soldiers. Mingzhu stood tall with her head high. She had faced Japanese soldiers before. She was terrified, but she would not show it.

One figure stood out among the three soldiers, his attire subtly distinct. Henry's gaze locked with his, silently conveying a shared understanding. Mingzhu's grip on the mala beads tightened further.

"Captain Sato," Henry said, breaking the silence.

The Japanese captain responded with a smile, curiosity dancing in his eyes. "Mr. Beaumont. What a surprise to see you here."

"I was attending a birthday celebration," Henry said.

Sato paced, exuding a sense of calculation. His sight fell on Mingzhu, and he scrutinized her with interest. "Acquaintance of yours, Mr. Beaumont?"

"She is my assistant, Captain," Henry lied.

"An assistant," Sato mused, clearly eyeing Mingzhu's attire. "Do you have papers?"

"Yes, Captain. Her contract was issued a couple of days ago."

Sato crossed his arms behind his back. "How conveniently timed."

Questions spun in Mingzhu's head but she remained quiet, listening to their conversation. The other two soldiers kept their guns pointed toward her. How did Henry know this Japanese captain? What else was he hiding?

Sato approached Mingzhu. The overpowering scent of mint aftershave made her nauseous. He closed the distance until their noses were nearly touching, a deliberate attempt to unsettle her. She dropped her gaze.

"Do you speak English?" Sato asked.

Mingzhu nodded, her voice steady. "Fluently."

"*Nǐ shuō zhōngwén ma*?" he inquired, asking if she could speak Chinese.

"*Huì*," she replied. Yes.

Sato laughed, stepping back, and wagged a finger at her as if she had uttered a great joke. He turned to Henry, a broad smile on his face, before shifting his attention back to Mingzhu. "*Watashi no mitame wa suki desu ka*?" he asked in Japanese.

Mingzhu studied him intently, from the top of his hat to the tips of his leather boots, before responding in English. "The way you look is of no concern to me."

Sato produced a knowing smile. "Show me her contract, Mr. Beaumont."

Henry nodded, his actions quick and decisive as he retrieved the documents from his jacket. "Here is the contract. And these are the signed agreements between Tang Mingzhu and me, pledging our allegiance to the Japanese Empire. We are willing to offer our language services to your cause."

Mingzhu shot Henry a look of disbelief. Her mind raced and ice crept into her heart as Sato scrutinized the forged documents, his thick brows furrowing with concentration.

"Do you often carry such papers in your pocket?" Sato's voice cut through the tension.

Henry hesitated only for a second before seemingly improvising. "There wasn't a chance to give them to her until today," he said.

As Sato's attention shifted back to Mingzhu, she kept her gaze lowered, doing everything she could to avoid looking at him.

"Very well," Sato finally conceded, holding out two badges. "Pin these to your chest and meet the convoy out front—" He dropped his hand as another soldier entered the room. "Yes?"

The man bowed his head briefly. "We've breached the borders, Captain," he said.

Sato turned his back to Mingzhu and Henry so they were out of earshot and resumed the discussion with the soldier in a hushed voice.

Mingzhu turned imperceptibly toward Henry.

"How could you do this?" she muttered, hurt and anger imbuing her voice.

"Mingzhu, please try to understand," he pleaded. "I had no choice."

"No choice? You created this contract without even asking me," she hissed. "Did you not consider what I might have wanted under these circumstances? What about Qiang? You didn't consider her for even a second! Besides, I would never willingly work for the Japanese."

Henry reached out to her, but she moved her hand away. "Mingzhu, I am truly sorry. I intended to discuss this with you today to allow you to decide. The contract was just one option among many. But . . ." His eyes flitted to the soldiers. "I had no choice. It was the only way I could think of to protect you."

"Protect me?" Mingzhu's voice trembled as she struggled to maintain composure. "When have I *ever* asked for your protection?"

"You haven't," Henry answered, gently clasping her hand. "But I had to do something, you're on my mind constantly. And you must understand how I feel about you. I had to try."

Mingzhu felt immobilized, unable to withdraw her hand from his reassuring grip. Despite her anger, she found herself reluctant to let go. "You even forged my signature." A hot flush of shock and anger crept up her neck.

"I traced it from your letters."

"Unbelievable—"

"No talking!" one of the soldiers shouted.

Sato turned back to face them, and the others followed. Mingzhu pulled her hand from Henry's.

Sato started to speak, but Mingzhu paid no attention. Instead, her eyes darted to a flicker of movement by the door. Another face appeared, only half visible. It was no soldier. It was Ah-Long. Mingzhu tried to keep her breathing steady.

He mouthed, *Qiang. Safe.*

Then, he was gone.

Tears of relief and fear burned her eyes. She desperately needed his words to be true.

"Join the convoy outside," she heard Sato say as Henry took the two badges from Sato's hand.

"Captain?" Another soldier nodded pointedly. "Your presence is required in the main hall."

"Let's go," Sato said, following his soldiers out of the room, leaving Mingzhu and Henry alone amidst the lingering tension.

The chest was flung open, and Biyu pushed her way out. "Madame?"

"Biyu." Wiping her tears, Mingzhu pulled her in close. "We don't have long."

"Madame, are you all right? Did they hurt you?"

"I'm fine, Biyu. They didn't hurt me."

"What will happen to us now?"

Mingzhu composed herself. She held onto Biyu's hands tightly. "Biyu, I must go with Henry."

Biyu shook her head in protest. "What about Qiang? What about me? You can't go with the Japanese."

Mingzhu's eyes watered. "I have no choice. You heard what they said."

"Madame . . ." Biyu wept. "This is insanity. Come with me. Mr. Beaumont can come with us, too. Those officers out there, they're not human! Remember Shanghai?"

Mingzhu remained resolute, comforting Biyu with a gentle touch. "There, there," she said, maintaining her composure. "It's going to be all right. My language skills and Henry's will be a safety net for us. At least for now. But, Biyu, I need you to promise me something."

Biyu sobbed. "Anything."

Mingzhu's eyes stung, but she refused to shed another tear. "You must find Qiang and get her away. Do you remember the address Francine gave me?"

Biyu nodded, sobs racking her body, and Mingzhu could see she was on the verge of being overcome with grief. But Mingzhu tightened her grip on her friend, and the two women looked at each other, drawing on each other's strength. For a moment, they were just two girls again.

Mingzhu could see Biyu's resolve hardening and her tears slowing. "It's in the library."

"Find Ah-Long. He knows where Qiang is and he can get you to Francine's. Promise me, Biyu, promise me you will do this."

"I promise."

Mingzhu's voice wavered. "You're my family, Biyu. The sister of my soul. You always will be."

"I will protect your daughter with my life," Biyu vowed.

With a final embrace, the two women released each other. Biyu took one last look at Mingzhu before running from the hall.

"We should go," Henry said.

"Wait." Mingzhu turned to the ancestral altar. She bowed three times, silently affirming to herself that she would never kowtow to her husband's ancestors again—no matter what happened next.

CHAPTER 12

Shivering, Qiang tried unsuccessfully to push up the wooden planks. Time had lost all meaning in the darkness. Trapped between the fear of what lay beyond and the torment of her thoughts, she couldn't help but wonder: *Is this how I die?*

Footsteps entered the shed, and a loud rustling followed. Li Mei's body was being dragged away. Soon, the planks were lifted. Qiang's hand shot up, shielding her from the intense light that flooded in. Peering through her fingers, she saw Ah-Long and Biyu.

"You came back," she choked.

Ah-Long pulled Qiang up onto the shed floor. Biyu set the oil lamp beside them and rushed forward, holding Qiang tightly and rocking her back and forth.

"I made a promise to you, Young Miss," Ah-Long said. "I promised I would come back."

Biyu pulled away. "We should get you cleaned up."

"Where's Mama?" Qiang asked.

Biyu turned away, and a hollowness filled Qiang. Had something terrible happened?

"The first madame is alive," Ah-Long said quickly. "Biyu will tell you everything, but first, we must get inside. Come."

Qiang's legs shook as the trio huddled together and slowly walked out of the shed into the evening light. On the grass, Li Mei's body lay motionless. Ah-Long gestured to the house. "Come. Keep walking."

Returning to the house through the kitchen door, Biyu led Qiang to a table next to the pantry and fetched a basin of water and a clean cloth. As she cleaned Qiang's face, tenderly wiping away the dried blood, Ah-Long paced deeply in thought.

"Tell me what happened with Mama," Qiang said.

Biyu splashed the bloodied cloth back into the basin and told Qiang what had transpired, and her heart filled both with relief that her mother was alive and dread at the uncertainty of her fate.

"Do you know where they are taking Mama, or Henry?" she asked, but Biyu shook her head. "What about that Japanese captain? What was his name?"

Biyu fell silent, clearly trying to remember. But when Qiang saw the pain in Biyu's eyes, she decided to stop asking so many questions.

"We must leave," Ah-Long said, his voice steady but urgent. "They have gone for now but will likely return. We must get someplace safe."

Together, they entered the main hallway of the house. Lifeless bodies littered the ground, their eyes staring blankly into the void, and empty bullet casings were strewn across the marble floor like scattered stars. The air was heavy with the scent of death.

Qiang scanned the bodies and didn't spot her father. "They've taken Baba," she said.

"Better they took him than for us to find him here among the dead," Biyu said, urging her to continue walking. "Come on."

Ah-Long was already at the top of the stairs and whistled down to them. Biyu and Qiang quickly ascended and followed him into the library, which was both serene and haunting. The curtains hadn't been drawn shut yet, and the moonlight lit the dust floating around the shelves.

"Your mama's friend Francine has a home in Tseng Lan Shu in Sai Kung. We must go there and seek her help." Biyu hurried to the wall, pulled out Mingzhu's copy of *Dream of the Red Chamber,* and began flipping through the pages until a small piece of paper pirouetted to the floor. Biyu picked up the note and brought it over to Qiang, who read the address scrawled across it.

Ah-Long peered over her shoulder. "We should leave now, while it's dark."

"Do you know the way to Tseng Lan Shu from here by foot?" Qiang asked.

Ah-Long knitted his brows. "Yes, Young Miss. There aren't many places in Hong Kong that I haven't explored. But this won't be an easy walk. The mountains are dangerous. If we go now, we should get there by morning."

"Can we not call for a taxi?" Biyu asked. "I saw some kitchen maids leaving in one just before."

Ah-Long shook his head. "It's too dangerous."

"Then we must walk," Biyu said. She pushed Mingzhu's book into Qiang's grasp. "We should change your appearance, too."

"Just like we did in Shanghai?"

"Yes, just like then, Young Miss." Biyu eyeballed Qiang's pearl earrings and necklace. "Let's get you into a set of my clothes. I'll sew your jewelry into the lining. It'll only take a few minutes. Wait here. I'll come back with fresh clothes."

Left alone with Ah-Long, Qiang joined him by the window. Fires danced in the darkness, illuminating the shattered buildings and streets in the distance. The rumble of explosions and sporadic gunfire blasted through the air, and smoke billowed into the sky, obscuring the stars.

"This is really happening," Qiang said.

"Is this what happened in Shanghai?" Ah-Long asked.

"Yes," she muttered.

They remained silent, a shared understanding passing between them, until Biyu returned with fresh clothes and *mántou* wrapped in cloth. "You haven't eaten anything today, Young Miss. Take this."

The last thing Qiang wanted was to eat. She shook her head and watched Biyu shove the *mántou* into the deep pocket of her tunic. Qiang accepted the garments and changed into them, then as she was braiding her hair into a long plait, she caught Ah-Long's gaze in the reflection of the window. He let out a cough and quickly looked away. With Qiang changed, Biyu quickly sewed the jewelry into her tunic.

They moved cautiously through the ravaged hallways of the house, careful to avoid stepping on shattered glass littering the floor. As they passed the study, Qiang stopped at the sight of Cai. Her father's concubine lay still—her silk *qípáo* ruffled to her waist. Terror had replaced Cai's once-audacious expression, and in her arms, Jun lay spiritless.

Bile rose in Qiang's throat. For years, she had resented Cai and her half brother. For years, she had wanted them gone. But not like this. No one deserved this.

Biyu quickly pulled Cai's *qípáo* back over her thighs. She yanked an oversized coat hanging near the door and covered Cai and Jun beneath it before turning to Qiang and Ah-Long. "Come, let's go."

The night deepened as the three of them descended Victoria Peak into Mount Cameron. The December winds slapped Qiang's face with every step, but she pressed on. As they rounded a bend in the narrow trail, thick branches of white oak trees began to rustle.

Biyu jumped at the sound and tugged on Qiang's arm. "What was that? A tiger?"

Ah-Long snatched up a rock and threw it between the branches ahead. "No, it's nothing."

Reassured, Biyu loosened her grip on Qiang's arm, and they continued along the trail.

Hours passed until they reached the base of Mount Cameron, and Qiang's lungs were beginning to feel heavy. The flora covering the foothill offered a brief respite. Towering trees swayed as the night sky began giving way to the dawn light. The air around them bore the heady fragrance of dewy earth, mingled with the distant saltiness of the sea. All the while, distant explosions continued.

Ah-Long gestured to a massive fallen tree trunk. "Sit. Rest," he urged.

Qiang settled down, and her feet pulsated with pain. Biyu pulled out the *mántou* from her tunic and tore it apart three ways, handing one piece to Qiang and one to Ah-Long. Qiang still wasn't hungry, though. Her stomach was full of angst and fear. How could she possibly fit anything else in there? She returned her piece to Biyu, who shoved it back into her coat pocket.

"Save for later, then," Biyu said.

Qiang stretched to better view a small cluster of Eurasian tree sparrows perched on a branch. From between the dense leaves, the faint clicking of crickets brought back memories of a time she could never revisit. The moments she had spent in the garden, sitting next to Ah-Long and teaching him English, felt like they belonged to a different lifetime.

After a brief rest, Ah-Long began guiding them across two smaller hills. This time, they were more cautious, steering clear of main roads. The last thing they wanted was to encounter any Japanese soldiers. Finally, after several more hours and detours, they reached Tai Koo dock. They had been alone for so long, just the three of them, that the scene that unfolded before them almost brought Qiang to her knees.

The docks were swarming with people, a chaotic mêlée stretching in all directions as men, women, and children fought desperately for a place on any available vessel to escape the island. Dozens of boats and sampans of varying sizes bobbed on the water, each one dangerously overcrowded. People were being forced overboard, and families were torn apart, with no other choice but to separate in the madness. As another bomb struck nearby, the ground shook, sending even more victims into the sea. Some swam, while others tried but could not.

"How are we going to cross to Sai Kung?" Biyu asked.

"I do not know," Ah-Long admitted.

Qiang watched the scene. She wanted to run to the dock and help people onto the boats, but she knew this was impossible. She was incapable of bringing any order to such chaos. Her chest began to hurt, and she stumbled back a couple of steps into a pile of bamboo. Suddenly, she knew exactly what to do.

"Look," she called out to Biyu and Ah-Long. "I have an idea."

"What is it, Young Miss?" Ah-Long asked.

"We can tie these bamboo rods together to create a small raft. That should be able to carry us across."

"You're right," Biyu agreed, nodding. "But what will we use to secure them?"

Ah-Long scanned the area. "There is a curtain shop over there. You two stay. I'll find something for us to use."

While Ah-Long ventured across the street, Qiang and Biyu gathered bamboo rods and laid them together in neat rows. By the time Ah-Long returned, they had assembled a sizeable float. Ah-Long had procured fabric and a pair of scissors from the shop, and he cut off strips while the two women wove the fabric around the rods to bind them together, tightening them with as much strength as they could muster.

As fighter planes streaked across the sky above, Qiang helped lift the float and they rushed toward the water. Others nearby had observed their actions and followed suit. But there was only so much bamboo to be shared. Fate would determine who would be lucky enough to get there first.

In the water, Qiang worked hard alongside Ah-Long and Biyu, frantically paddling the float to move it as quickly as possible. As they ventured into the sea, Qiang saw her reflection staring back at her from the water and thought back to their journey out of Shanghai. It was like no time had passed at all since she had been seated in the small trading boat between her mother, Biyu, and a newly pregnant Cai. Several other passengers had been on board, but only one elderly man had sought refuge below deck, where the women were situated beneath an array of oil lamps hung from a thick rope.

"We could've taken the train instead of this repulsive thing," Cai had grumbled, sweat forming on her brow.

"You're the reason we're in this predicament," Qiang countered. "You're the one who nearly got Mama shot!" Her mother took Qiang by the hand to calm her nerves. Usually, that would have worked, but Qiang had had enough of Cai's unabating complaints. "If you hadn't taken so long to gather your belongings, we could have left yesterday!"

Cai's jaw whitened. "Do you know the worth of my belongings? How could I possibly leave such luxury behind?"

"And where are those things now?" Qiang snarled. "Half of your bags were taken by looters!"

"Well, if your baba hadn't left for Hong Kong without us, perhaps we would've had more help!"

"Enough," her mother snapped. "Both of you."

Suddenly, Cai pressed her hands against her stomach. "*Argh,* something isn't right."

"What's the matter? What are you feeling?" Her mother moved closer to Cai.

"My stomach . . . it's . . ." Cai collapsed onto her side and let out a scream of agony.

Biyu pulled Cai toward her, allowing her head to rest against her chest. "Take a deep breath, Second Madame," she advised.

"I can't!" Cai cried. "It hurts! Someone, do something!"

The elderly man, who had watched the scene unfold, backed away, repulsed. "What's happening to her?" he shouted. "Her face is as pale as a ghost! Is she dying?"

"Lower your voice!" Biyu hissed at him. Turning to Cai, she continued, "Breathe . . . just breathe . . ."

Her mother clasped Cai's hand. "Listen to Biyu, just breathe. I promise we'll be in Hong Kong soon. We'll get you to the doctor immediately. Qiang, soak a handkerchief with fresh water from that bucket over there and put it on Second Madame's forehead."

Qiang, slightly reluctant, did as she was told. As she wiped the sweat from Cai's neck and arms, a warm, sticky substance met with her knees, and she looked down to see blood pooling out from between Cai's legs, soaking her dress. She shot a quick, concerned look at her mother. "Mama . . ."

"Heavens," her mother murmured.

"She's bleeding!" the man shouted hysterically. "What bad luck is this? Throw her off the boat!"

"Blood?" Cai cried, her distress escalating. "Did he say blood? Why am I bleeding? What's happening to my baby? Answer me! Why aren't you answering me?"

On the bamboo raft, seawater splashed into Qiang's eyes, pulling her back to Ah-Long and Biyu. People had begun hurling their children off the dock into the water and jumping in after them. Qiang thought of Cai and the baby she had lost on the boat, and of Jun, the child she had afterward and had treated like gold. How could this be happening all over again?

"Young Miss," Biyu said, touching Qiang's cheek.

"I'm fine," Qiang said, wiping away the sweat from her face and neck. She moved in tandem with Ah-Long, propelling the float away from the dock. Gradually, her mind grew blank, the voices around her becoming dim, and she had no recollection of how she got from Tai Koo dock to Kun Tung shores. Once on dry land, it wasn't long before they were at the top of a small hill. On one side was a large river, and on the other, Tseng Lan Shu.

The ebony sky was shot through with a delicate palette of pastel tones, and the first timid rays of sunlight pierced through the dense canopy of trees like golden spears. Surrounded by ancestral shrines, the hill's peak offered a vantage point to what lay below.

Ah-Long shielded his eyes from the sun and squinted. "We are here."

Qiang stepped closer toward the edge, her eyes fixed on the sight before her. Nestled amidst the rolling hills was a small village—a sanctuary of stone houses and square courtyards. At that moment, she should have felt relieved, but the only sensation was the gaping void left behind by her mother's absence.

Mama, Qiang thought, tears rising. *Will I ever see you again?*

PART II

JAPANESE-OCCUPIED HONG KONG,
香港占領地,
1942

CHAPTER 13

Biyu couldn't sleep. She lay between Qiang and Francine on thin piles of cotton sheets with rolled-up clothes for pillows. Staring at the roof made of overlapping curved tiles, held up by thick wooden rafters, she could scarcely believe that they had made it to Francine's village house alive only several days earlier. A radio in the corner crackled intermittently, and distant voices droned through as if underwater.

The house belonged to Francine's father, Mr. Gok, who occupied a bedroom toward the back. Small yet spacious, the house had minimal furniture—a dining table, three chairs around a small desk with a radio that Mr. Gok kept on throughout the day, and a tall altar where he displayed his family's ancestral tablets, along with three oranges in a bowl as a humble offering. Each morning, he lit incense sticks, their fragrant tendrils curling through the air as he silently paid tribute to his deceased wife. In those moments, Biyu thought of Mingzhu back at the house in the ancestral hall, kneeling on a silk cushion, bowing, and praying with devotion.

Francine had forbidden Biyu from cleaning or cooking, insisting she take charge of everything. Instead of putting her at ease, it made Biyu uncomfortable, and she grappled with a sense of inadequacy. Observing a married woman of such esteemed social stature cook and serve meals felt out of place, and it took Biyu a while to adjust. Sharing the dining table with Qiang and Francine was a breach of propriety. Ah-Long, though, had no reservations, as he sat comfortably beside them, selecting the meatiest chicken pieces and placing them into Qiang's rice bowl as though life had always been like this.

Outside, Ah-Long remained vigilant beneath the lychee tree in the courtyard, listening for any signs of danger. Inside, the house had no heating, and Biyu shivered. Since the battle for Hong Kong began, electricity and water supplies had been shut off. Luckily, Mr. Gok had instructed Francine to fill the bathtub with water five days earlier. It was from that bathtub that he, alongside the women, drank and cooked. Biyu longed to wash her hair and feel the water soaking her scalp, but no one knew when the water would return. Until then, there was nothing she could do.

Rubbing her butterfly pendant, Biyu pictured the day she first entered the Yue household in Shanghai many years ago. She remembered the courtyard of the *sìhéyuàn,* the snow dusting the ground, and the cries of a newborn. It felt like only yesterday when she had stepped forward to become the faithful maid to Mingzhu, a baby at the time. Biyu had been just a child herself. But from the moment she laid eyes on Mingzhu, gently cooing and sucking her thumb, she wanted nothing more than to love and protect her to the best of her ability.

And now, who knew if she'd ever see Mingzhu again.

Qiang stirred, shaking and mumbling in her sleep. Biyu reached out and caressed her hair. Since their arrival in Tseng Lan Shu, not a single night had passed where Qiang didn't wake in tears. Biyu held her promise to Mingzhu close to her heart. Now that they were at Francine's, she would do everything within her power to protect Qiang.

Most nights, the distant explosion of bombs punctuated the darkness. Biyu could only offer prayers, hoping the voice crackling through the radio was right and the British Allied forces would prove strong enough to repel the Japanese. Yet, she couldn't rid herself of the overwhelming sense of futility. What was the point of fighting against such brutality now? Evidently, the Japanese had already infiltrated the colony, like a seed planted in the heart of Hong Kong months ago that was now sprouting, wreaking havoc throughout the city.

"Is that you, Biyu?" Francine croaked. "You cannot sleep?"

Biyu lit the oil lamp, and Francine stretched and sat up. "Qiang was crying in her sleep again," Biyu explained, her hand returning to Qiang's hair. She didn't mention that she herself had been wide awake.

"Mingzhu would be pleased knowing how much you care for her daughter." Francine reached over to the radio and clicked it off. "God, I hate this awful thing. It only ever conveys bad news."

"Why did you offer my first madame a place to stay?" Biyu asked. "You hadn't known her for long."

Francine shrugged airily, a touch of melancholy lingering in her expression. "From what Mingzhu told me, it didn't seem her husband believed the war would ever come. But I could see it in her eyes; she knew. So, I wanted her to know there was somewhere she could escape to if she needed. We must look out for our own."

"I'm not sure Sai Kung is as safe as you expected." Biyu pressed her lips together. "The battle is happening all over the territories. Sometimes I wonder if we would've been better off hiding back at the Peak."

"As if it would be safe there," Francine said. "The rich and the educated were the first they came for. You saw it for yourself. My husband is in London. As far as I know, he's safe, but I haven't heard from him since the battle started."

"Why didn't you go to London with him?"

"I had intended to." Francine sighed. "He went ahead on business, and I was to follow. My son, Samuel, is studying there. We had planned to spend the New Year together."

"But then the monsters came." Biyu clenched her jaw.

"The monsters came," Francine repeated. She placed a gentle hand on Biyu's knee. "But I'm glad I'm here, Biyu. At least I can be with my father."

"Your father hardly speaks to you or acknowledges your presence," Biyu blurted. "I'm sorry, that was rude. I must be tired. I don't know what came over me."

Francine chuckled. "You don't have to apologize. You're right. My father still hasn't forgiven me for marrying my husband."

"Why?" Biyu asked. She didn't understand why a father of lower standing such as Mr. Gok would be displeased with gaining such a son-in-law.

"When I was fifteen, my husband and his father, a businessman, came to our village," Francine said. "They offered to buy the land, and everyone in Tseng Lan Shu accepted except my father. He's never cared much for money. His whole life has been bound up in this land, working in these fields day in and day out. It's all he knows—all he's ever lived for. Without it, I daresay, he'd be utterly lost."

"How did you end up marrying, then?" Biyu asked.

"My husband visited the village frequently, helped in the fields. Unlike the arrogant sons of other wealthy families who had tried to buy the land before, he was kind, hardworking, and most important, he made me laugh."

Biyu listened with keen interest. She thought of the first madame and Master Tang. Never had she seen them laugh together. It struck her then that no one had ever made her laugh in such a way before either. The closest she had come to such joy was her sisterhood with Mingzhu, whose laughter always felt like a rare gift.

Francine continued, "But love doesn't always endure, does it? I'm not sure when we began to drift apart, but we did. In any case, it hardly matters now. There's a war going on, and I need to focus on my father's safety. I don't know how much longer the British can hold back the Japanese."

"Hong Kong is a British colony," Biyu said. "Surely they will fight hard for it, no?"

Francine raised a brow. "I think you'll find that the British like to fight their way *into* places. Whether they care enough to fight *for* Hong Kong's people . . . that is debatable."

"So you think Japan will win?"

"Oh, Biyu. I don't know anymore. I don't know what I think. These are all tired thoughts pouring from my lips. I hardly make sense."

"I understand," Biyu replied. "I'm scared of Japan occupying Hong Kong, though. I'm scared of what they will do."

Francine lay back down and stared at the ceiling. "I'm scared too, but where the British may fail, there may be hope in the resistance."

"The resistance?"

Francine cast a knowing look at Biyu. "My father was telling Ah-Long all about them. They are a group called the East River Column. He said they've grown in numbers since partnering with Huiyang Bao'an People's Anti-Japanese Guerrillas. Most of them are Hakka, too. They've set up their headquarters just an hour north of here."

"Hakka?" Biyu repeated. "They're known to be strong. You think this resistance will fight the Japanese?"

Francine turned back to the ceiling. "That's what people say, yes."

Biyu and Francine spoke until dawn, interrupted only by a rooster's shrill cry that woke the village. In the morning, Francine asked Biyu to help her prepare breakfast. And just like that, her spirits lifted ever so slightly as she arranged the firewood beneath the gray brick stove.

CHAPTER 14

A sudden blow to her head upon boarding Sato's truck seventeen days earlier had left Mingzhu unconscious. When she finally came to, she found herself in a room she had never seen before. She had spotted children's bags and notebooks kicked to the far corner and concluded that this place must've been a school once. The room's design seemed purposefully devoid of comfort, and the chill in the air seeped into her bones, disorientating her further. The only dim light came from two small windows, its panes obscured by a thin layer of black paint barricading her from the outside world. A wooden bucket stood in one corner with a persistent leak staining the concrete ground beneath it.

For the past seventeen days, she had been sharing her room with one other person. First, with a woman who had reminded her of Cai. Perhaps it was the curve of her lips when she once met Mingzhu's eyes and offered a somber smile; yet she had been sickly pale, her complexion drained of the vitality her sister-wife always radiated. No matter their differences, Mingzhu hoped both Cai and Jun were safe. When the first woman was taken by soldiers, a much older woman was thrown into the room. The other woman never returned.

Each passing moment was tainted by the relentless fear that she was next.

"Why do you bother?" the older woman spat one day as Mingzhu crouched and scraped the heel of her shoe against the concrete wall, marking her eighteenth day in the room with a thick line. "What does it matter how long we are here?"

"I suppose it doesn't," Mingzhu said, her hands shaking from the cold.

Since her arrival, Mingzhu had fallen into a monotonous routine that revolved around sleepless nights, the meager rations brought to her by her captors, and finding solace in prayers dedicated to Qiang and Biyu. She lamented the loss of her mala beads and jade bangle, not knowing which soldier had stripped her of them.

There had been no word from Henry. The last time she saw him, they had walked toward the same truck. The only indication of his well-being had come several nights before when she heard the guards speaking of a band of British journalists who had been taken to work for the Imperial Army. Mingzhu didn't understand why she was not among them. They had seen Henry's documents. Sato had accepted their story. So, what had happened?

Running her finger across the wall where she had tallied up her eighteenth day, a memory came to her of the last time they had been in the library together.

Mingzhu had been engrossed in her books, her finger tracing idle circles on the spines, when Henry had strolled into the library.

"I couldn't help noticing you do that quite a lot," Henry said.

She met his gaze. "Is that to say you notice *me* quite a lot, then, Mr. Beaumont?"

Henry gave a coy smile. "What are you planning to read today?" he asked.

Mingzhu sighed and continued tapping her finger along the shelf until she found *Romance of the Three Kingdoms*. With a mischievous gleam, she held it up for him to see.

"Our favorite," Henry remarked. "You know"—he glanced back to the door, ensuring privacy before continuing—"Mingzhu, since the first day we met, I have been meaning to ask you something."

"You're full of questions, aren't you?" she teased, clutching the book to her chest as she moved to stand by the window. "Go on, then. Ask away."

Henry approached until he was a mere breath away. The afternoon sunlight beaming through the window only flushed their cheeks further.

"I've been wanting to ask you about one of the characters in this novel," he said, reaching for the book's cover. When his hand brushed against hers, he allowed his touch to linger, as if savoring the connection for a moment longer.

"Oh?" she murmured, feeling the hairs on the back of her neck stand to attention. *Please don't let go,* she wished.

"You once told me of Lady Sun's strength—her fierce loyalty to those she loved. You said that a woman like her should not be overlooked."

"I did say that, yes," Mingzhu agreed.

Henry pulled his hand away, but not before stroking her fingers. "Well, I've always wanted to ask: would you say you're like Lady Sun, or are you a woman who lacks agency?"

Mingzhu swallowed hard, taken aback by the directness of the question. No one had ever asked her such a thing before. She looked into Henry's green eyes, knowing precisely the implications his question held. He wanted to see if she was brave enough to follow through on their mutual feelings, and if she would, like Lady Sun, fight for what she desired. But, in the library, within the cage of the Tang residence, Mingzhu realized she was not only restricted in what she could openly say, but also that she had never allowed herself to consider exactly what kind of woman she was, or could be.

The distant rattling of keys resounded through the corridors, extinguishing the memory. The older woman instinctively retreated to her pallet, her body tense with fear. Mingzhu hastily shoved her shoe back on and positioned herself to face the barren wall. She fixated on the eighteenth line she had etched. As the sound of heavy boots drew closer, a knot of apprehension formed within her chest. The door creaked open and a Japanese soldier entered with a shout of, "Hands on your head!"

Mingzhu interlaced her fingers tightly, resting her palms on her head. The light in the room created shadows on the walls, and she could tell from the way the soldier rolled his neck from side to side that his interests did not lie with her. Her shoulders relaxed ever so slightly.

The soldier seized the other woman from her pallet, gripping her mercilessly by the hair. Mingzhu's eyes widened as she witnessed the struggle within the half-light of the room. The woman flailed, desperate and defiant, striking the soldier in a futile attempt to break free from his grip.

"Get off me!" she hissed.

Get off her, Mingzhu begged silently.

The officer didn't speak. With a chilling swiftness, he raised his gun high above his head before slamming it down upon the woman's skull. Time slowed as Mingzhu watched the woman buckle to the ground, the soldier dragging her away like discarded refuse.

When the door slammed shut, and she was left alone, Mingzhu fell forward, her forehead hitting the cold concrete of the wall. She cried until her eyes were so heavy that she fell into another nightmare.

A new person was brought into the room a day later. She was much younger than the woman before. Thirteen, fifteen, at most. Mingzhu offered the girl a smile, but it was not returned. She wore a school uniform Mingzhu didn't recognize, and the school badge stitched to the shirt pocket was stained with dried blood.

"What is your name?" Mingzhu asked.

The girl scowled and turned to face the wall. A sharp pain sliced through Mingzhu's stomach as she thought of Qiang. Where was she now? Was she with Biyu? Had they managed to escape and get to Francine? Mingzhu kneeled on the pallet and began to pray, calling upon her parents and all the ancestors of her natal clan.

The days that followed were unnerving. Bombs blasted endlessly, getting closer and closer each day. Outside, glass shattered, and the smell of burning wood seeped into the room, making Mingzhu think of Wei. She pictured him sitting at the dining table back at the house, chewing on a piece of meat, and declaring his admiration for the British.

"Stupid fool," she muttered as she began scraping the heel of her shoe into the wall to mark another day.

Keys turned in the door. She immediately slipped her shoe back on and kept her eyes on the wall. The young girl began crying, calling out to her mother. *Ma, Ma, Ma.* Mingzhu bit her tongue. It was all she could do not to run to the girl and wrap her in her arms. The door opened, and two soldiers entered.

"Hands on your head!"

Mingzhu did as she was told.

"Stand up," one of the soldiers ordered. "Both of you."

Mingzhu stood, her ankles weak and her balance shaky.

"Turn around."

Again, Mingzhu did as she was told. She kept her hands on her head and looked at the girl. She offered her a smile. This time, the girl smiled back, her lips trembling. The shorter soldier walked over to the girl and tied her wrists before gripping her by the neck and yanking her out.

"Stop!" Mingzhu cried. "Where are you taking her?"

"Shut up!" The taller soldier lunged at Mingzhu. She fought back, punching him in the chest with her fists until he pulled out his pistol and dug it into her stomach. "Why are Chinese women always so disobedient?" he growled. He pushed Mingzhu off him, raised the gun to her head, and called out. Another soldier, almost the same age as the young girl, came running in.

"Tie this one up. She's been summoned."

"Hai!" The young soldier wrapped rope around Mingzhu's wrists, his face blank. The corner of her eye twitched as she tried to comprehend how someone so young could partake in something so cruel.

Once the rope was tight, the young soldier stood behind Mingzhu and pushed her forward as they followed the taller soldier. Mingzhu scoped her surroundings. If there was a chance for an escape, she wouldn't hesitate to take it. She walked with difficulty as the heels of her shoes had been shaved down to unevenness. But as they reached the top of a small stairwell and stepped onto the massive campground, Mingzhu knew her chances were slim.

All around her, large military tents had been set up. When she risked a glance back, it confirmed her previous thoughts: the building she had walked out of was indeed a school—a small one at that. She squinted as sunlight shone through a gap between the hills. A family of fork-tailed sunbirds nested in a tree nearby, and a small smile appeared on Mingzhu's face. At least she was still in Hong Kong.

A roar of laughter came from one side of the camp. The young girl Mingzhu shared a room with was being dragged toward a small chapel, where a line of soldiers stood outside, cheering and reaching out to pinch her flesh. The fear in her eyes was indescribable as she disappeared inside.

"Where are they taking her?" Mingzhu questioned.

"Keep walking." The young soldier shoved her forward.

Mingzhu thought she might be sick. If she did find a way to escape, would she be able to get to the girl and save her, too? Smoke ballooned from a large fire at the other end of the camp, and the smell of roast meat made her stomach turn.

She watched as men and women, both adults and children, lined up in front of a dense forest. Soldiers hauled them into the depths of the trees, and gunshots followed soon after.

A man, kneeling on the ground, begged the soldiers for mercy. "Please, please spare me!" he beseeched.

The soldier snorted, his breath fogging the cold air. "The British have retreated. Even they have forsaken you!"

Mingzhu stumbled. The British had retreated? It couldn't be. It had to be lies. It had scarcely been three weeks. Was that all Hong Kong was worth in the end? Less than twenty-one days of fighting? She didn't have time to think as her escorts pushed her inside a sprawling tent where two soldiers stood guard. Without a word, her escorts severed her bindings and departed.

"You're here," a voice called out, instantly recognizable. Mingzhu stepped around a wooden screen to where Sato sat behind a large desk, the ember of his cigarette forming a ghostly haze in the dimly lit space. His eyes flickered toward the chair opposite him, indicating her place.

Suppressing the discomfort caused by her worn-out heels, she cautiously took her seat. The tent was big but crowded. Large trunks sprawled everywhere, and one lay open, revealing a cache of weapons within. A small bed was tucked in one corner, while numerous *kakejiku* splashed with calligraphy and scenic paintings were suspended from a horizontal bar that hung from the tent's apex.

"You're not so easy on the eyes today. Not eating well?" Sato asked, appraising her once again.

The urge to lunge across the table and confront him swelled within her. How dare he mock her? But she remained silent, her stare fixed upon him, unyielding.

Sato drew leisurely on his cigarette, exhaling smoke in thick rings. "Men!" he bellowed, prompting a soldier to rush into the tent, saluting his superior. "Fetch a plate of food."

"Hai!"

The soldier marched out and returned with a plate filled with chopped pork.

Saliva pooled in Mingzhu's mouth, a reminder of her forgotten hunger. Until that day, she had been given only rice, water, and a handful of vegetables. She clenched her fists and looked away, not wanting to show any sign of weakness.

"Eat," Sato insisted, pushing the plate closer to her. He crushed the cigarette into his desk, dismissing the soldier who had fulfilled his order.

Mingzhu shook her head.

"Eat," he repeated, rising abruptly, his fists crashing onto the table. He whipped out his pistol and pointed it at her.

Startled, Mingzhu recoiled and stared at him. His thick brows were furrowed, but her resolve was steady. "Why?" she asked without considering the consequences of her words.

"Men!" Sato shouted again, calling two soldiers into the tent.

Mingzhu dug her nails deeper into her palms, drawing blood as she braced herself for what would come next.

"Remove the screen and open the tent," Sato commanded.

The soldiers lifted the screen, sliding it across the ground with precision and revealing the tent's entrance. They parted the heavy fabric and exposed an almost unobstructed view of the campsite beyond.

"Do you see those two lines?" Sato closed one eye, pointing toward the campsite with his pistol as if marking prey. When Mingzhu offered no immediate response, he bellowed, "I asked you a question!"

Beads of sweat trickled down Mingzhu's back. "Yes," she forced out, fixing her attention on the line of soldiers stationed outside the chapel. She knew what transpired within its walls, what was being done to that young girl, but a part of her resisted accepting the truth.

"Unlike everyone else here," Sato said, a threatening edge to his voice, "you're going to get a choice."

Mingzhu's head pounded.

"There are three paths I will offer you," he said, sitting back down. Pointing his gun first toward the line outside the chapel, he continued, "The first will take you into that chapel. You'll live, of course, but for how long? I cannot say."

The wind grazed the tender skin beneath Mingzhu's bloodied nails, sending a shiver down her spine. Sato redirected his gun in the opposite direction, where two soldiers were dragging an elderly Chinese man away. "The second doesn't seem so bad compared to the first."

She surveyed the heavily guarded campsite. There was no escape. But her desire to survive burned fiercely within her. "You mentioned three," she interjected, her voice steady despite her desperation.

With a resounding thud, Sato collapsed into his seat, his once-threatening demeanor replaced with an unsettling gleam of satisfaction. "The third is quite simple. You eat," he commanded. "And then, we discuss your appointed position."

Her eyes narrowed. "My position . . . alongside Mr. Beaumont?"

Sato waited, and Mingzhu picked up a piece of chopped pork and popped it into her mouth. Its smokiness, mixed with fat, coated her tongue, and she devoured the meal ravenously.

He lowered his gun. "The position Mr. Beaumont spoke of is no longer available. I have something else for you."

"No longer available?" she asked, the meat's saltiness stinging her dry lips.

"Forgery is no small offense," Sato said. "You should both be dead."

Mingzhu held her breath.

"But we need translators," Sato continued. "Your friend Mr. Beaumont will do well in serving us."

Mingzhu stilled at the confirmation that Henry was alive. "Where is he?"

"That is none of your concern. Now, let's talk about you."

"What of me?"

"I've done my research on you, Tang Mingzhu. You're a descendant of one of the last most elite families from the Qing dynasty in Shanghai. It's lucky your parents died early and never saw the war."

Mingzhu vividly recalled the day she received news of her parents' demise in the second wave of the Great Manchurian plague. She had pleaded with Wei for permission to return and provide them with a proper burial, but he had remained resolute in his refusal. She learned her parents had received a humble funeral through accounts from old servants, and their tablets were enshrined in the ancestral hall of the *sìhéyuàn.* While her distant cousin inherited everything, she at least found comfort in knowing that her parents had been laid to rest with dignity, spared from being abandoned without a rightful place of burial.

"You know," Sato continued, "we didn't think much of the educated back in Shanghai. But we've learned our lesson and we will do things differently this time."

Mingzhu pushed the plate away. "I don't know what you're implying," she said.

"It means that good fortunes are upon you today, Mingzhu. Today, I will make you my personal secretary."

Mingzhu's glare intensified. "Your personal secretary?"

Sato leaned forward from the depths of his seat, his voice menacing. "Starting today." His words were pregnant with possessiveness. "You will work for me. And anyone who works for me belongs to me. You understand?"

In that pivotal moment, sitting opposite Sato, her eyes level with his, Mingzhu grasped the gravity of her choice—or lack thereof. If she took the chance to navigate the treacherous waters of Sato's world, she might retain a flicker of hope of being reunited with her loved ones. Besides, if Sato wanted her dead, she would already be gone.

Henry's question rang loudly in her ears. *Would you say you're like Lady Sun, or are you a woman who lacks agency?* At that moment, she knew the answer.

Clenching her fists, she said, "I will work for you."

Sato's laughter boomed through the tent. Yet, beneath it, an undercurrent of unease tinged his expression. Had he noticed the slight defiance in her tone?

"I will work for you," Mingzhu repeated, raising her chin. "But let it be known that I belong to *no* man."

Sato arched an eyebrow, his response limited to a wordless gesture. Mingzhu recalled how effortlessly Sato had spoken various languages back at the house, his fluency surpassing hers. So, why did he need her assistance at all? What could she provide for him? But now was not the time for overthinking. She had to focus on finding a way back to Qiang and Biyu; this opportunity was her only chance.

CHAPTER 15

Trudging through blankets of blackened snow alongside Biyu and Francine, Qiang was burdened by exhaustion from a grueling twenty-six hours of work without rest. The approaching spring did little to alleviate the icy gusts of the early evening, which seeped into her aching bones, a reminder of the Japanese occupation that continued to hold Hong Kong in its grip. She thought of her mother. Three months had passed since she had last seen her. Was she still alive? Where had the Japanese taken her? At least Qiang had Biyu, but who did her mother have?

"Watch out!" Biyu warned.

Two soldiers marched toward them, their imposing strides threatening. Qiang quickly stepped to the side with Biyu and Francine, lowering her head into the required position of the *keirei*. Her face burned thinking of how Biyu and the others used to bow to her. She vowed never to let anyone do that again.

The soldiers passed without sparing the women a second glance, and Qiang released the pent-up breath she had been holding, the condensation swirling into the air around her. She tried to regain composure, preparing to resume the walk.

"Stop!" one of the soldiers shouted from behind them.

Qiang froze. The soldiers made their way back to her. Knowing what was expected, she rummaged in the depths of her tunic pocket in a desperate search. Trembling fingers retrieved a small card, and she handed it over. The other soldier repeated the process with Biyu and Francine.

"Name," the officer demanded, his voice dripping with authority. When she mumbled her response, he barked, "Speak up."

"Tang Qiang."

"Age?"

She paused. "Seventeen."

"Occupation?"

"Factory worker."

"Which facility?"

"The textiles production factory over at Middle Hill."

The officer returned the card to Qiang. "You may go."

Gripping the hands of Biyu and Francine, Qiang hastened from the soldiers, but as they veered down a narrow path into Tseng Lan Shu, her hopes for respite shattered. As they neared Francine's house, her stomach coiled at the sight of soldiers tossing lifeless bodies into a ditch one after another. Qiang's breath hitched in her throat.

"My father!" Francine ran toward the house.

"Get inside." Biyu pulled Qiang behind her. "Keep your head down."

Inside, the chairs lay toppled on the floor. Francine barged into Mr. Gok's room. When she came back out, she shook her head and began to cry.

"He will still be at the farm," Biyu offered.

Francine slapped a hand against the wall for support. "He's so old," she said, her voice trembling. "They reduced his rations last week as punishment for working too slow. What will they do to him if he doesn't meet his quota again?"

"He'll be fine," Qiang interjected, trying to reassure her. "He's not usually home until late evening. Let's wait."

"But what if he's . . ." Francine gestured toward the atrocity unfolding outside.

"He wasn't here," Biyu said firmly.

"Are you sure?" Francine asked, her voice heavy with worry. "There were so many—"

"Trust me," Biyu said. "I saw every face. None of them belonged to Mr. Gok."

Qiang picked up the chairs and put them back to their original positions while Biyu guided Francine to a seat, patting her on the back. The radio Mr. Gok had played every day had been taken.

"My father is going to be beside himself," Francine said, staring at the now-empty spot on the desk.

Qiang turned back to Biyu, who stared glumly out beyond the courtyard. Even though the walls were high enough to shield them from the sight of the bodies, they offered no protection from the sounds that echoed through the air, every loud thump of a body tossed onto another. Qiang sat down quickly next to Francine, her shaky knees unable to support her any longer.

"They did this to the residents down at Ngau Tau Gok last month," Biyu said. "A man from the factory lives there. He said an entire row of houses were burned to the ground. And all because one family refused to demolish their ancestral altar!"

Qiang turned to the corner of the room, where Mr. Gok's family altar had once stood. A band of sorrow tightened across her chest as she recalled the day Japanese soldiers had charged into the house and torn it down. She squeezed Francine's shoulder, silently conveying the shared significance of their memories. In that corner of the room, she had witnessed the heart-wrenching scene unfold before her—Mr. Gok had crumbled to his knees, his voice hollow with anguish as he called out to his dead wife.

The image of Mr. Gok's face, etched with grief, haunted Qiang. The raw intensity of his pain as a soldier had grabbed the wooden tablet and cracked it in half was too much for anyone to bear. As if losing the one you loved wasn't hard enough, Mr. Gok had had to lose his wife a second time.

"Come, Qiang," Biyu said. "Let us prepare a meal so the men have something to eat when they return."

When Mr. Gok finally returned, shortly after Ah-Long, Francine squeezed him so tightly that he groaned and shooed her away. Together, they sat cross-legged on the floor and began to eat.

The meal was simple: steamed tofu and a handful of snake beans. On a small plate were two boiled eggs Ah-Long had brought home from the farm. Mr. Gok stabbed his chopsticks into one of the eggs and swallowed it whole. Francine cringed at her father's actions. Qiang watched on, knowing her father would have done the same thing.

Ah-Long cut the second egg into four-quarters. "Eat," he said to the women. Gratefully, Qiang popped a piece of egg into her mouth, savoring its creamy texture and saltiness.

Since the occupation had taken hold, most inhabitants of Hong Kong had been issued a ration card, an identity tag, and employment. Francine had lied when the officers came knocking at their door, claiming that Qiang, Biyu, and Ah-Long were distant relatives visiting from rural China with no means of returning to the mainland. The officers, eager to fulfill their quotas, gladly dispatched them to a factory job. It wasn't as though they had any real say in the matter. The rule was clear: toil for the Imperial Army and, in exchange, receive food rations, or get nothing and starve.

Despite the scarcity of meat, they managed to ward off hunger, thanks to the vegetable garden Ah-Long and Qiang had constructed together. Just before the news had confirmed the British concession and the subsequent Japanese occupation of Hong Kong, Qiang had given Ah-Long her pearl earrings and necklace. He took them to a nearby town and pawned them for seeds. Upon returning, he and Qiang worked tirelessly to plant bok choy, radishes, and snake beans around the lychee tree in the courtyard.

Ah-Long taught Qiang to feel the soil and sense its texture and moisture levels with her hands. She discovered the magic of sifting soil through her fingers, separating clumps and stones to create a soft bed for the seeds. Since the water had come back on, gardening had become a ritual. She held the can, feeling the pull of the water as it sloshed within, and poured it over the soil. Ah-Long watched, ensuring the cascading droplets soaked through. Qiang couldn't help but smile at the situation and how their roles had changed. She was now the student, and he was the teacher.

Weeks passed until one day, at the start of spring, Qiang witnessed the first green shoots emerge. As the vegetables grew, her involvement deepened. She learned to differentiate between the plants' needs, discerning when they thirsted for water or craved the touch of sunlight. Her hands became attuned to their silent language, capable of deciphering their subtle cues. With everything happening around her, she relished the sensation of earth between her fingertips, grounding her—anchoring her to the present moment.

. . .

One night, as the season coninued to warm, Qiang couldn't sleep. She got up, careful not to wake the others, and made her way toward the courtyard where Ah-Long was crouched, planting new seeds beneath the moon's glow. Mr. Gok sat on a wooden stool, sniffling from the evening breeze as he watched.

"People say the resistance has grown in numbers. They're in Tai Po and Sha Tin now, too," Ah-Long said.

Qiang tiptoed back inside the house and hid behind the door. She peered through a small crack.

Mr. Gok was nodding. "I saw the children secretly handing leaflets to all the men in the village. They're recruiting."

"Yes, I saw."

"So, what do you think?" Mr. Gok asked, leaning forward to inspect Ah-Long patting down the soil.

"I'm not thinking much," Ah-Long said.

"Oh?" Mr. Gok sounded surprised. "For weeks, you ask me about the resistance. You want me to tell you anything I hear about Sai Kung, but now, you say you're not thinking much?"

Ah-Long gave a little laugh. "Now, my focus is on the garden. Mr. Gok, you should go to sleep. It's late and Miss Francine gets very upset when you do not rest enough."

"Francine?" Mr. Gok scratched his head.

Ah-Long gave a concerned expression. Qiang was equally worried. For days now, Mr. Gok had consistently forgotten who Francine was.

"Ah! Francine." Mr. Gok grunted. "That daughter of mine is never happy these days. Nothing to do with my sleep. But you have made your point. I'll see you in the morning."

"Goodnight, Mr. Gok."

Qiang quickly pulled away from the door and squeezed herself as far behind it as possible so that Mr. Gok would not see her. When he finally entered his room and clicked the door shut, Ah-Long approached and gave a subtle cough.

"You stop hiding now, Young Miss," Ah-Long said in English.

Qiang flushed, and she walked around the corner.

"You listen to me and Mr. Gok?"

"I didn't hear much," she lied. "What are you planting?"

"You want to help me?" Ah-Long asked, handing her a tool.

Qiang took the weeder and immediately dropped it, its metal thudding to the ground. She was back at the Peak, stuck beneath wooden planks, unable to breathe. The memory of Li Mei's body smashing into the floorboards above her made her lose her balance, and she quickly crouched to the ground.

Ah-Long went to offer her a hand but then looked at the weeder, immediately picked it up, and threw it aside, out of view. He squatted beside her. "Sorry, I forget. Here, we use hands instead. I show you. Watch."

Grateful, Qiang breathed slowly and watched as he began digging into the soil. "These don't look like vegetable seeds," she finally said.

"You clever, Young Miss," Ah-Long said. "This something else."

"What are they?"

"When grow, you will see."

Qiang crouched beside Ah-Long for the next hour and helped him plant the seeds. When they finished, Ah-Long instructed her on how often to water the soil, then told her to head back in to get some sleep.

"You should sleep, too," Qiang said.

"Soon."

Qiang rose, feeling a tingling numbness in her thighs. Stepping over the threshold into the house, she glanced back and saw Ah-Long's solemn gaze. "Why are you looking at me like that?" she asked, cocking her head.

"Look how, Young Miss?" he asked, scratching his ear.

Frowning, she said, "I'll see you tomorrow."

"Goodnight, Young Miss," he replied, returning his attention to the flower bed.

Back in bed, Qiang couldn't sleep. The tips of her ears twitched, trying to catch any sound from the courtyard. Something wasn't right. She pushed herself up, hurried back outside, and made her way to the side of the house where Ah-Long lay on a pallet against the wall beneath the stars. His eyes were closed, and his chest rose and fell peacefully. She dropped her shoulders and let out a small sigh. She was overthinking.

. . .

The following morning, Qiang woke to Biyu shaking her aggressively. "Young Miss, wake up!" she exclaimed, waving a piece of paper. "Ah-Long has gone."

Rubbing the sleep from her eyes, Qiang pushed herself up. Across the room, Francine stood near the kitchen door, a look of concern etched on her face. Qiang took the letter from Biyu's trembling grasp. There, in messy Chinese characters, was Ah-Long's handwriting.

> Young Miss,
>
> I'm sorry, but I must go.
>
> For three months, I have followed the Japanese and their every demand. They say bow, I bow. They say work, I work. They tell me not to honor my ancestors, I obey. But they have taken too much now.
>
> I could not tell you in person because you would tell me to stay. And you know I find it difficult to go against your word.
>
> Hong Kong is dying, and I must do what I can to save it. I have planted flowers in the garden for you. Whenever you look at them, I hope you will think of me.

Qiang's vision blurred at the final line of the letter:

> I will see you again one day. I will never fail you.
> Ah-Long

Biyu pressed the sleeve of her tunic to Qiang's cheeks. "Save your tears, Young Miss," she said. "Ah-Long is strong. He will not suffer."

Francine approached with a sympathetic expression. "Biyu is right, Qiang. Ah-Long is a capable young man. He—"

Qiang crumpled the letter in her palm and flung it onto the floor. Biyu and Francine jumped in shock. Then, pushing herself up, she stomped to Mr. Gok's bedroom door and gave it three sharp knocks.

"Who is it?" Mr. Gok groaned.

"It's me, Mr. Gok. It's Qiang."

Silence.

"Young Miss, what are you doing?" Biyu asked.

Qiang ignored Biyu. If she spoke to her, she'd only cry and never stop. Entering Mr. Gok's room without permission, she slammed the door behind her. Mr. Gok was sitting on the edge of his bed, staring at a black-and-white photograph. A woman in a loose-fitting tunic paired with trousers stared back at him with a smile.

"*Ai-ya!*" He scowled. "Such bad manners! What do you want?"

"Where is the resistance?" Qiang asked, looking away from the photograph.

Mr. Gok's hands shook as he tucked the picture into his trouser pocket. "What resistance?" he asked, evading her eyes.

"The one Ah-Long left to join." Qiang crossed her arms. "I heard you two talking last night. You know where he's gone. So, tell me."

Mr. Gok let out a shaky laugh. "Why? Will you go and join them and fight?"

His words hit a nerve, but she refrained from letting her annoyance show. Dropping her arms to her sides, she clenched her fists and said nothing.

"Didn't think so," Mr. Gok belittled. "You're just a girl. What do you know about fighting? Get out of my room."

The next day, Qiang spent her fourteen-hour shift at the factory questioning why a woman couldn't fight in a war. She was just as strong as Ah-Long, as unrelenting as Mr. Gok, and as motivated to succeed as her father. So, who was to say she couldn't fight?

CHAPTER 16

Lost in sadness, Mingzhu barely noticed the shift from spring to summer. Sheets of hot rain splattered against the window and fogged the edges, obscuring her view of Victoria Harbor. The dock, once teeming with ferries and cargo ships, had undergone a grim transformation. About a dozen cranes, once constantly in motion within the colony, now stood still under Japanese occupation. Nearby, a pile of rickshaws, their wheels caked in mud, lay discarded. She couldn't help but think of Henry. Was he still alive? Was he still in Hong Kong? If she could turn back time and find a way back to the house before Sato had separated them, she would at least have looked into his eyes a moment longer—to memorize their warmth, the way they always seemed to reassure her. She would have held on to that look, that memory, for as long as she could.

Reality pulling her back, she shifted her attention from the window to something else that had changed. Sato's office was now set up in one of the suites at the Peninsula Hotel. She remembered the place well; it was where Wei had attended numerous events, with her by his side, fulfilling her duty as an obedient wife. Now, with the Japanese in control, transforming the grand hotel into their headquarters, those days felt like a lifetime ago.

She caught sight of her reflection in the glass cabinet nearby. Clad in the uniform of her captors, she scarcely recognized herself. The severe lines of her primly buttoned khaki jacket emphasized the precision and discipline demanded by her role as Sato's secretary. For eight months, her days had been filled with administrative tasks, ensuring the smooth flow of information and correspondence between the different makeshift offices. The single golden stripe on her collar denoted her position, which afforded her protection from other soldiers. But it also marked her as a prisoner. Sato treated Mingzhu the same way he had when they first met. He continued to talk down to her and mock her actions. He granted her accommodation in one of the unoccupied hotel rooms and allowed her two meals a day, which was more than other secretaries received. She was permitted to leave the hotel only to run errands in his name, during which she was granted a pass and a soldier as escort.

Only once had she attempted to escape. She had been waiting for an opening since arriving at the hotel with Sato. During those earlier days, she noted any unmarked exit, regular guard schedules, any naïve and unsophisticated soldiers. All were few and far between. Still, she had decided to take her chance during the revelry of the occupation declaration. Amid the drunken soldiers, she saw an opportunity. She waited until the early morning hours, silently navigating the hotel's hallways, strewn with sleeping men, and slipped through the kitchens and into the gardens before soldiers on patrol caught her. If it hadn't been for that single golden stripe on her uniform, they would have executed her on the spot. Instead, they dragged her to Sato, who was already awake in his office and reading the paper.

When Mingzhu didn't answer Sato's inquiry about her attempt to flee, he had asked, "You think your daughter is out there, don't you?"

Mingzhu froze and remained silent, remembering how Sato had done his research on her. Did he know where Qiang was?

"Work well for me, and you might see her again one day," Sato had stated. "Try to escape once more, and you never will."

And so, Mingzhu stayed. She submitted to her new life. In addition to organizing Sato's schedule and maintaining his records, she acted as interpreter in meetings between him and several Chinese officials. Why Sato refused to speak Chinese himself remained a mystery to Mingzhu. The meetings were usually brief, and often involved Sato coercing Chinese business owners into signing over their finances and land leases to the Imperial Army.

During these meetings, Mingzhu grew to resent herself. Whenever she encountered another Chinese person, she saw in their expression the disdain they felt toward her for working for the Japanese. Mingzhu harbored a quiet restlessness. While she performed her duties competently, she burned with rage at her contribution to her people's struggle. But what could she do? During those times, Mingzhu thought of Qiang. She longed for the day when they would be reunited—when she could wrap her arms around her daughter and comfort her. Biyu was often on her mind, too. Whenever she saw someone of similar height and build, she'd check to see if it was her. And every time it wasn't, longing stabbed her chest.

The suite door swung open, and Sato strode in with two younger soldiers following behind. Their boots squeaked against the marble floor, leaving wet trails in their wake.

"I told you not to kill him!" Sato shouted. He covered his mouth with a hand and began coughing forcefully.

Mingzhu bowed, extending her hands to receive Sato's sword. Cold steel pressed against her palm. Her fingers traced the carved patterns on the blade, capable of altering destinies with a single stroke. As always, she imagined wielding it against Sato and his men as she placed it on a wooden rack behind his desk.

"I didn't kill him, Captain," one of the soldiers protested. "The man hadn't eaten in days."

"Damn it, I told you not to starve the prisoners," Sato growled. She wondered who this prisoner was to have stirred such emotions in him.

Sato settled into his seat, his face flushed red. Mingzhu observed him suppressing another coughing fit. He had been struggling with a persistent, hacking cough for nearly a week. In an effort to help, Mingzhu had several times prepared medicinal soup with the assistance of Fung, the army chef. While Sato's illness brought Mingzhu a certain satisfaction, she knew his well-being was tied to her own. His demise would leave her vulnerable. For Mingzhu to live, Sato had to as well.

One of the soldiers lowered his gaze toward Sato. "Are you sick, Captain? Your office stinks of medicine."

"Of course not," Sato grunted.

Being sick had its repercussions. Many times, when a captain or commander had fallen ill, they were promptly removed from their station and replaced. Mingzhu depended on Sato, and she couldn't afford for him to be questioned like this.

She stepped forward, almost standing between Sato and the curious soldier. "I'm sorry," she began. "The smell is coming from me. I had a slight temperature this morning—"

The soldier waved his hand to stop her from talking and turned back to Sato, bowing and apologizing for his line of questioning. Sato gave Mingzhu a subtle nod.

Someone knocked on the door, and a young lieutenant walked in and approached Sato's desk. His hair was thick and neatly combed back. To her surprise, he offered her a polite smile, the dimples on his face deepening. She guessed that he must be only slightly older than Qiang, his youth evident in the radiance of his tanned skin and lively gaze.

The two soldiers straightened their backs. "Lieutenant Nakamura."

"Soldiers," the lieutenant said. He turned to Sato and bowed. "Captain."

"Hiroshi."

"I have an updated list of names of the internees in Stanley Camp. More women have been arriving these past few days."

Mingzhu glanced at the document. More women at the camp? What if Qiang and Biyu were among them? She shook herself from such thoughts. It was well-known that local Chinese civilians had been left to roam the city, hungry and dying. The people who ended up at the camps were most often *báirén* and the Eurasians.

"Ah, yes." Sato glanced at the soldiers. "You may leave us." Once they had left the room, Sato gestured to the seat before him. "Sit, Hiroshi. Mingzhu, you may leave, too."

She nodded and slipped out of the room, but an odd feeling tugged at her, and she pressed her ear against the door. Sato's and Hiroshi's voices were low, but she made out their words without too much difficulty.

"I'm afraid I come bearing bad news," Hiroshi said. "I have been reassigned by General Tanaka."

"Tanaka?" Sato repeated. "Since when does a general oversee the assignments of a mere lieutenant?"

"That is why I came today," Hiroshi said. "Tanaka turned up at

Stanley and requested my transfer personally. He's also requested that all documents that have passed between you and me be sent to his office for review."

Two soldiers walked by, and Mingzhu straightened her back, swiping a finger between her collar and her neck to cool herself from the stuffy hallway. When she was alone again, she subtly leaned back to listen.

"You think he is on to us?" Sato questioned.

"I'm not certain," Hiroshi replied. "But, like you said, what care does a general have in a lieutenant's station? I think we should be careful."

"You're right," Sato said. "Where is he sending you?"

"Middle Hill. To a factory where our military uniforms are produced."

"That's out in Sai Kung."

"Yes, Captain."

They fell quiet again. Mingzhu pictured Sato sitting there with his thick brows knotted in concentration. She pressed her ear harder against the door.

"Well," Sato finally said. "Lucky for us, our communication has never been through the written word. Tanaka will soon know there's nothing to gain from our documents."

"Exactly," Hiroshi said. "Tanaka is playing it safe, trying to keep an eye on everything. That is all."

"Then there is nothing much more for us to discuss," Sato said.

"I am still with you, Captain," Hiroshi said eagerly. "I have made new connections with the ERC. I can continue our work if you let me."

"Absolutely not," Sato spat. "Too dangerous."

Mingzhu bit the inside of her cheek. Did she mishear? Did he really say ERC? She had been privy to the murmurs and hushed discussions among the Japanese for the past few months, detailing the hardships they had endured at the hands of the rebel group.

"Then, what should I do?" Hiroshi asked.

"You will do as Tanaka has ordered. I know where to find you should anything change. If you must do something, stay alert. Sai Kung is a large territory with many connections to the ERC. Monitoring our troop movements might not be a bad idea. Every district has a blind spot. Finding them may prove useful to us one day."

"Yes, Captain, I understand," Hiroshi answered. "But what about your secretary?"

Mingzhu's heart pounded.

"What about her?" Sato asked.

"Does she know?"

"No."

"Did you not bring her here to aid us?"

Silence fell. Mingzhu pushed herself off the door and adjusted her jacket as another uniformed woman approached. Once she had disappeared out of view, Mingzhu pressed her ear to the door again, but nearing footsteps made her jump back. The door swung open, and Hiroshi stepped out and offered Mingzhu a brief nod before leaving. She watched him stroll down the hallway until he turned the corner, anxiety squeezing her stomach. What did Sato want with her?

That night, Mingzhu lay awake staring out of the window, entranced by the moon's hazy glow as it peeked through the clouds in the rainy night sky. The evening heat was intense, and she was sweating under the heavy blanket, seeking security in its weight. The conversation between Sato and Hiroshi, which had occurred several hours earlier, played on an endless loop in her mind. As she attempted to decipher the hidden implications within their words, her head throbbed. How she wished life would return to how it used to be, when her only headaches had stemmed from Cai. What exactly were Sato and Hiroshi trying to hide? Why had Sato spared her life when he had the chance? But most of all, she needed to know whether Qiang and Biyu's names were on the list of Stanley Camp internees that Hiroshi had delivered.

Restless, Mingzhu threw the blanket off herself and changed back into her uniform. Cracking open the door, she peered into the low-lit hallway to find it empty and stepped outside cautiously, determined to get to Sato's office on the upper floors. She knew to be caught meant potential death, but an indescribable force propelled her forward. Her daughter and Biyu were the only reasons she still wished to live.

Arriving at Sato's office, she pressed her ear against the wood, straining to catch any sound. She knocked softly. No response came from within, prompting her to retrieve the key hidden in her skirt pocket. Palms slick from nerves, she unlocked the door with a quick motion, glancing in both directions along the corridor before slipping into the empty room.

She was greeted by the pungent scent of stale cigarette smoke, threatening to choke her senses. She approached Sato's desk and began to look through the stacks of papers, examining each document, but they were merely contracts from local businesses, mixed in with old newspapers. Finally, her gaze fell upon the stack of documents Hiroshi had delivered. She skimmed through the list of names, lightly but methodically tracing her finger down the page. By the time she reached the end without spotting Qiang or Biyu's names, relief and anxiety warred within her chest. She felt a catch in her throat. They had not been apprehended, but she was no closer to knowing their whereabouts.

"No," Mingzhu whispered to herself, swallowing. "Qiang is safe. They are all safe. They have to be."

She returned the papers to their original order and scanned the desk again, unsure what she was hoping to discover. Sato had said himself that he and the young lieutenant had been careful. Still, she continued to search, moving files one by one, cautious not to disrupt their sequence.

Just as she was about to abandon her search, her eyes caught sight of a small notepad concealed beneath Sato's ashtray. With delicate precision, she extracted it, finding it blank. Upon closer inspection, she detected faint grooves on the paper's surface.

Footsteps passed outside, and she instinctively crouched behind the desk. *Keep walking. Keep walking,* she prayed. Sweat formed on her brow as the footsteps receded into the distance. Only then did she rise, her hand steadying herself against the desk's edge.

Returning her focus to the notepad, she held the top sheet against the window, allowing the moonlight to shine through it.

First Light at Feathers. Eighty-five.

The meaning eluded her. Hastily, she pocketed one of Sato's permission slips, folded it, and embarked on her silent retreat from the office.

Back in her room, she skillfully forged a permission slip in Sato's handwriting. Then, safely concealing it beneath her mattress, she spent the remainder of the night awake, consumed by the fear of being discovered for what she had just done.

The following morning in the hotel kitchen, Mingzhu was surrounded by other secretaries at the large wooden table, which served as their gathering point. The other women chatted among themselves in Japanese, ignoring her. Mingzhu had maintained a deliberate distance, avoiding unnecessary conversations since she had arrived. She trusted no one and was sure no one trusted her.

The head chef, Fung, was busy chopping away and managing eight other cooks. Together, they spent their days catering to the needs of the Japanese soldiers, captains, and colonels stationed in the headquarters. Fung, known for his reticence, had developed a fondness for Mingzhu, likely due to their mutual preference for silence. He consistently served her more food than the other secretaries, a gesture she sincerely appreciated.

As she ate a bowl of *zhōu* seasoned with scallions and white pepper, a young woman entered the kitchen, her face scrunched up in angst. Several secretaries began mumbling.

"That's the one I was telling you about," one of them whispered.

"She looks frail. She won't last a day under the general," another replied.

Mingzhu had overheard during the past few days about how General Tanaka had taken on a new secretary after firing his previous one for being too brown-skinned. Tanaka had a track record of firing his secretaries within two weeks, whether for racism or incompetence or some other made-up excuse. Mingzhu heard he had fired one simply because she was taller than him. The young woman approached the dining table and sat next to Mingzhu.

"I'll have what she's having, please," she said quietly to Fung.

"No more!" Fung shouted. He reached his hand into a bamboo

steamer, plucked out a *mántou,* and ungraciously chucked it onto a small plate for her. "You eat this."

Mingzhu watched as the young woman began taking small bites of the soft dough, the steam pouring from her mouth as she chewed. The other secretaries were right. This woman looked frail. Mingzhu's heart sank, thinking of Qiang. She pushed her bowl toward the woman. "I'm not hungry. You can finish it," she said.

The girl looked at her with gratitude before pulling the *zhōu* toward her and inhaling it in one full gulp, not even using the spoon Mingzhu had offered along with it. When she finished, she turned to Mingzhu with a smile and a shy laugh. "I'm sorry, what terrible manners. I haven't eaten much the past few days."

Fung gave Mingzhu a disapproving look before making his way to another stove, and the other secretaries leaned in closer to listen to their conversation.

"My name is Hana," the woman said.

"I'm Mingzhu."

"Who do you belong to?" Hana asked.

Mingzhu cringed at the question. She wasn't a dog. She didn't *belong* to anyone. "I work for Captain Sato. I'm his secretary."

"Ah." Hana nodded slowly. "I've been assigned to work for General Tanaka. I arrived in Hong Kong a few days ago, but I haven't met him yet."

The other secretaries lifted their hands to cover their laughter. Mingzhu was reminded of the women she used to meet for high tea and how they would do the same to her and Francine. She leaned closer to Hana and whispered, "I hear General Tanaka is fond of the scent of lemons. There are may chang shrubs planted right outside the hotel lobby. If you crush the leaves to release their natural oil and apply it to your wrists each morning, type quickly, and consistently lower your head in Tanaka's presence, you might just make it through."

"That is very kind of you, Mingzhu," Hana said. "I will not forget such kindness."

"How did you come to find yourself in Hong Kong?" Mingzhu asked.

Hana perked up at the question, her eyes wide. "I'm here to serve my country, to free Asia from all Western control."

"Ah, I see." Mingzhu sucked on her teeth and gave a short nod. "And you believe this was the best way to do it?"

The kitchen fell silent, and the other secretaries cast her a critical look before urging one another to leave.

"Japan will free Hong Kong," Hana said proudly. "You and I, we are the same. Just look at us. Our black hair, our dark eyes. Our skin. We can't let the Western powers take away what is rightfully ours."

Mingzhu shuffled in her seat. They were not the same. Not by a long shot.

"It's for the greater good, right?" Hana added.

Fung slammed a pot onto the counter causing Hana to jump. "You finish eating, you get out of my kitchen," he said.

Mingzhu took the opportunity to leave as quickly as possible. As she made her way to Sato's office, she realized just how naïve Hana was, and how brainwashed many Japanese were that came to work in Hong Kong. They wholeheartedly believed in their cause and were oblivious to everything else. Despite this, Hana reminded her of Qiang. Mingzhu could only hope that someone else would offer their bowl of food and a helping hand wherever her daughter was.

When Mingzhu entered Sato's office, he had not yet arrived. She took advantage of the moment, ensuring everything was in order. Had the notepad beneath the ashtray protruded as much yesterday? Mingzhu leaned forward to readjust it, but Sato entered the room just as she did so. Reacting quickly, she swept her hand across the desk.

"Cigarette ash everywhere," she said, dusting off her hands. "It's clean now."

Sato's left brow jerked as he approached her, his gaze shifting from the ashtray to Mingzhu. A lump formed in her throat, but she resisted the urge to swallow, choosing to cough and fold her hands behind her back instead.

"What are my duties today?" she asked.

"I have a meeting to attend off base this morning," he replied, walking toward the window and peering at the streets below.

"When will we leave?"

"You're not coming."

"What meeting is it?" Mingzhu asked, emboldened by the possibility that he had something to hide.

Sato eyed her suspiciously, his hand resting on the hilt of his sword. Mingzhu lowered her head, her confidence shrinking further every second Sato kept his eyes on her. "Many in your position have chosen execution over serving the Imperial Army. Are you here because you fear death?" Sato asked, catching her off guard. But Mingzhu did not hesitate to answer.

"Death doesn't scare me," she answered. "Never seeing my loved ones again does."

"You believe you will see them again?"

"I refuse to die until then."

His grip on his sword loosened. "I'll be back," he declared before leaving the room.

Mingzhu knew it was now or never. She seized a random stack of documents from Sato's desk and followed him, keeping her distance. The headquarters bustled with soldiers and workers, covering her as she weaved through the crowd, but she lost sight of him. Finally, she reached the main lobby and saw Sato exiting the building. She rushed toward the doors, but two guards intercepted her. Promptly presenting her permission slip, she fabricated a story about Sato forgetting some crucial documents, and to her relief the guards allowed her to pass. Outside, she spotted him in the back of a vehicle, pulling away from the curb. She hopped into one of the other black sedans.

"Where to?" the driver asked.

Mingzhu paused. Could this be her chance to escape? She could tell the driver to take her anywhere. She could make a run for it. Her chest constricted at the thought of getting caught, of the many checkpoints she would have to pass through, and the driver who might turn her in. How long would it be before someone noticed her absence? If she did not make it out of the city, she would be sentenced to death. She exhaled as she came to her senses. Sato was her only means of survival. And she had to survive.

"Follow that car," Mingzhu finally said, pointing to Sato's vehicle ahead.

Her eyes flitted between the retreating car and the streets. What had become of Hong Kong? Gripping the door handle, she witnessed

Chinese civilians reduced to servitude, digging trenches and clearing bodies. The acrid stench in the air stung her nostrils and made her eyes water, blurring her vision. Japanese tanks stood like an impenetrable barrier across the streets, their armored surfaces reflecting sunlight onto beggars kneeling in despair. Driving by what used to be a park, she witnessed soldiers marching across the grass, throwing people to the ground if they refused to bow.

When the car finally stopped, Mingzhu stepped out and found herself on a familiar street, full of bird shops. She and Qiang had purchased a cage for a canary here once.

She scanned her surroundings, but Sato was nowhere in sight. Most shops were boarded shut, and empty birdcages littered the street, piled haphazardly upon one another. She hoped the absence of canaries was because shop owners had released them before the occupation. The thought of the birds soaring freely, beyond the reach of war, offered her comfort. She imagined Qiang with Biyu, safe together, and her resolve strengthened.

Then, it struck her—the note she had discovered in Sato's office. *First Light at Feathers.* Could it refer to one of the bird shops? Determined, Mingzhu folded the documents she had hastily grabbed from Sato's office, shoved them into her pocket, and continued walking. Beggars scurried away as she passed by. With a jolt, she remembered her uniform, and a familiar self-loathing filled her heart.

She scanned the alleyways for any sign of him. Though she treaded lightly, the rain-soaked pavement and the stillness of the morning amplified the sound of her footsteps. Approaching the end of the street, she finally spotted Sato standing outside one of the bird shops, and she instinctively retreated behind a nearby pillar. Peeking cautiously out, she watched him slip a note into a doorframe. When he started walking back up the street, she pressed herself further into the shadows of the pillar. She observed him turning left into a small alley, followed by the sounds of a scuffle.

She edged closer to the wall and peered into the alley. A Japanese officer faced Sato, whose lip was bleeding.

Sato spat blood onto the gravel, anger emanating from him. "How dare you strike a captain?"

The soldier screamed, accusing him of being a spy, and leaped onto him. Their fists blurred through the air, the sickening thuds of blow after blow reverberating in the narrow confines of the alley. Mingzhu's pulse pounded as Sato was overpowered and cornered against the alley wall.

"I'll report you!" the soldier shouted, striking Sato hard in his ribs. He collapsed to the ground with a groan. "Admit it!"

"Who sent you?" Sato gritted out.

The soldier aimed his pistol at Sato and shot him in the leg. Sato cried out in pain, and Mingzhu slapped her hands over her mouth to keep herself from screaming.

"Answer me!"

"What nonsense are you spewing? Just wait until I get you back to headquarters!"

"You think you can fool us all, Captain? We've been watching you. Those secret meetings, the coded messages, they've caught our attention. We know you're a traitor."

Sato's eyes narrowed, and his voice was steady with a tinge of defiance. "I am a loyal servant to the emperor. I've dedicated my life to our cause."

Mingzhu kept her hands over her mouth, blood roaring in her ears.

"Admit who you are, or I will kill you," the soldier threatened.

Mingzhu spotted a broken piece of wood among the remnants of a birdcage. Silently, she crept toward it, her movements purposeful and controlled. Gripping the makeshift weapon, she turned the corner just in time to witness the soldier raise his gun, his finger tightening around the trigger. Without hesitation, she lunged, driving the sharp piece of wood into the soldier's neck with all her might. Warmth gushed over her hands, and the deafening sound of a gunshot filled the air, causing her to stumble back and instinctively squeeze her eyes shut and cover her ears. A split second later, another shot echoed through the alley, followed by a resounding thud.

"Open your eyes," Sato groaned.

Mingzhu slowly did as he asked. The lifeless body of the young soldier lay beside her, blood pooling beneath him from the wooden stake protruding from his neck and the hole in his chest. Sato had the soldier's gun. Mingzhu stared at her bloodied hands, her body trembling and her head spinning. Pain sliced through her chest.

"I killed him," she murmured, shock numbing her.

Sato struggled to rise, using the wall for support. He latched on to Mingzhu's arm for balance. "Pull yourself together. We need to leave," he said.

Mingzhu shook her head. "No," she asserted. "I killed him. I must bury him!"

Sato regarded her with a confounded expression.

Mingzhu could not stop shaking. "I killed him . . ."

"We are at war!" he shouted into her ear. "If you bury him, will you bury the other dead bodies lying out here, too?"

"I—"

"You told me today that you wished to survive, that you chose life over death."

"I did . . . I do . . ."

"Then we need to move," Sato said, rummaging through the soldier's pockets. "First, we must make this look like an accident—a robbery of sorts. Come, help me drag the body."

She gave him a stern look but remained cautious with her words. "When we get out of here, you must tell me what is going on—why that soldier accused you of being a spy."

Sato groaned, leaning to wrap the dead soldier's jacket around his wounded leg. "If we survive, I'll tell you everything."

As they emerged onto the street, a soft drizzle began to fall, washing away the traces of their encounter. Mingzhu couldn't stop shaking at the thought of having stabbed someone in the neck. She began to cry, her tears disguised by the rain streaming down her face. As she walked beside Sato, she knew, deep down, some essential part of herself had been shattered.

CHAPTER 17

Biyu's days at the factory had fallen into an unending cycle of fatigue, tension, and fear. The ceaseless clanging of machines and the hushed conversations among the workers formed the dissonant backdrop to her life now. The calluses on her hands, built up over the years, were tougher than ever.

She glanced around the factory, observing the faces of her fellow prisoners, each marked by a weariness that mirrored her own. As she sewed, her thoughts drifted back to her childhood, when life had seemed simpler and full of better possibilities. She remembered the sun-drenched streets, the laughter shared with Mingzhu, and the alleyways and markets of Shanghai.

Movement from one side of the factory knocked Biyu back to the present. Qiang, who sat beside her, motionless, was also deep in thought. Was she thinking of Shanghai, too?

A soldier closed in on them, and Biyu let out a short cough. Qiang quickly resumed her work. When the soldier walked past without paying any attention to them, Qiang lifted her foot from the machine's pedal and sighed. "I can't do this anymore."

Biyu kept sewing, her eyes darting between the needle and Qiang. "I know this is hard, Young Miss. The war will end soon."

"Can you be certain?" Qiang hissed.

Biyu pressed her lips together and looked back at her work.

"I'm sorry," Qiang said.

"It's all right," Biyu said. "I understand."

The soldier began making his way back around, and Qiang pushed her foot back onto the pedal. Just then, the large metal factory doors opened, and a troop of Japanese soldiers marched in. The thumping sound of needles piercing fabric came to a standstill as all eyes turned to the leader. Two officers from the factory ran to him in a salute.

"Lieutenant Nakamura, welcome," they greeted unanimously.

The lieutenant gave a curt nod before stepping into the vast space, his presence commanding attention.

"Sorry for the stench in here," one of the officers said, gesturing to the workers. "They smell like pigs."

"*You're* the pigs," Qiang mumbled.

Biyu tugged on Qiang's sleeve, a signal to keep her mouth shut.

"Show me the facility," the lieutenant said.

"Hai!" The officer turned to the workers. "Everybody up! Bow!"

As the lieutenant walked along the lines of workers, Biyu noticed Qiang lifting her chin, refusing to lower her head. Biyu felt uneasy at the way Qiang stared at the lieutenant, defiance radiating from her gaze.

When the lieutenant reached them, he stopped and looked Qiang in the eyes. Biyu felt nauseous. "Young Miss . . ." she began, prodding at her charge's arm.

The officer leading the lieutenant stepped closer to Qiang. "How dare you! Bow now!"

Biyu glanced between the lieutenant and Qiang. Was she going mad, or had a brief flicker of recognition passed between them?

"Do I need to repeat myself?" the officer shouted again, his spit hitting Qiang's cheek.

She wiped the saliva off with the back of her hand and said nothing. Her eyes remained on the lieutenant, her head slightly cocked.

"Why you . . ." The officer struck Qiang hard across the face. Biyu bit down on the inside of her mouth to keep from screaming and tasted blood. When Qiang didn't budge and continued to stare at the lieutenant, the officer hit her again. This time, Qiang stumbled backward, her hands cupping her cheek.

Biyu's own hands shook. What had gotten into her young charge? Biyu had always known Qiang had a rebellious spirit that far exceeded Mingzhu's, but she was taking it too far this time. Biyu tugged on Qiang's tunic with force.

"Young Miss," she barked, pressing her lips into a thin line.

"I won't bow," Qiang said. Her eyes blazed with rage.

The lieutenant tilted his head, his eyes fixed on Qiang. He didn't say a word. The officer took the opportunity to strike Qiang again.

"Young Miss!" Biyu caught Qiang by the arms before she fell to the floor. "Please, just bow. Please."

Qiang pushed Biyu away. "I won't bow," she said again.

The officer staggered back and waved his arms around. "You dare defy us? You must have a death wish." He stepped forward, ready to attack Qiang again.

Biyu would not let that happen. She leaped in without a second thought. "Enough! Stay away from her!" she shouted, colliding with the soldier. She pushed him back a few steps.

Stumbling, he regained his balance. "You little—" He reached for his pistol and pointed it at Biyu.

Biyu stood immobilized, staring into the barrel of the gun. Though terrified at the thought of dying, she found solace in knowing she had tried to protect Mingzhu's daughter. She closed her eyes and drew in a shaky breath. If this was to be her fate, then she would accept it without hesitation. "Enough," the lieutenant said. He looked away from Qiang. "Show me to my office."

The officer's eyes widened. "Lieutenant, she should be shot!"

"I prefer my workers alive," the lieutenant replied. "Now, show me to my office."

As the soldiers moved on, the two women grasped each other, knees weak. The workers returned to their stations, and the rest of the shift passed in a nightmarish haze as Biyu waited for the lieutenant to change his mind and shoot them both. When her shift ended, the realization sank in that she had to leave without Qiang, who had been tasked with an additional four hours of work, while Biyu had only two. Unwillingly, Biyu retraced her steps back to Francine's place from Middle Hill, braving the relentless downpour. Each stride back to the village sent shudders down her spine. How could she have pushed the officer like that? What a stupid thing to do.

Biyu warned herself not to think of the incident. Such terrible thoughts would only lead to bad luck. Picking up her pace, she raised her hands to shield her face from the rain. A crack of thunder blistered through the sky, and she didn't hear the sound of heavy boots nearing her from behind until it was too late.

The strike was quick. There was no time to retaliate.

Biyu crumpled to the ground. Before her, the muddied black boots of a Japanese officer pressed into the earth.

"Chinese bitch! This is what you get for disobeying us!" the Japanese officer shouted. His boots kicked mud into Biyu's nose.

She wanted to tell him to stop, but she wouldn't beg. She guarded her face with her hands as he continued to kick her in the stomach, the excruciating pain narrowing her vision until she was about to lose consciousness.

"Get off her!"

Francine pulled Biyu away and up against a wall. She wiped Biyu's face with the sleeve of her shirt and began crying. "Wicked, wicked men, you disgust me!"

Biyu could hardly open her eyes. Through slits, she watched as the soldier snatched Francine by the hair and pulled her to her feet. "You're getting in my way. Pathetic woman."

"Get off me, you animal!" Francine shrieked.

Biyu raised her arm, hoping to get Francine's attention, but her rib was cracked, and she fell onto her side in pain. Several other villagers had made their way out to the path to watch in fear. The soldier groped Francine and she dug her nails into the side of his face and tore at his skin. He pushed her off, whipped his pistol out, and shot her in the chest. She fell to the ground, then lay unmoving.

"Francine!" Biyu croaked.

The onlookers quickly returned to their homes, and Biyu began crawling toward her.

The soldier turned his pistol on Biyu.

"Stop!" a voice snapped. Two Japanese sergeants marched toward them.

"What are you doing?" one of them asked.

The soldier saluted, showing his lower rank. "This filth almost tore half my face off!"

Biyu hardly noticed them glance at her. Francine's eyes were open and unseeing. Gripping her body, Biyu began sobbing.

"Mind your tone, soldier. Where is your post?"

"Middle Hill Factory, sir."

"You're out of bounds, then, soldier," the sergeant said. "Get back to your post immediately."

"But these women—"

"These women are irrelevant. Those East River dogs have been in and out of these villages in swarms. We don't have the men to fight back today. Now, get back to your station."

The soldier took another look at Biyu, swore under his breath, and stormed off.

"Get the body off the path, woman," the sergeant ordered Biyu.

After they had left, Biyu cupped Francine's face in her hands and continued to shake her. "No, no, no . . . Please, wake up. You're not . . . you're not dead . . ."

A gentle hand landed on Biyu's shoulder, and she turned to see the neighbor, Wong Taitai, behind her, soaked from the rain. "Let's move her into the courtyard," she said tearfully. "It'll be dark soon."

CHAPTER 18

The rain had ceased, leaving behind a thick layer of humidity across the island, and the sun continued to hide behind stubborn clouds. Supporting Sato with one arm, Mingzhu used the other to push open the creaky door of an abandoned brothel. A musty odor wafted into her nose as she peered down a long corridor lined with fading red wallpaper that peeled at the edges.

"This room will do." Sato pointed to the closest door.

Mingzhu helped him inside and guided him to the bed. As she looked around, it was clear the Japanese had raided the place at the start of the war. She caught her reflection in a gold-framed mirror situated atop a vanity. Strands of wet hair stuck to her cheeks, and her hands were stained with small patches of the dead soldier's blood.

Sato groaned in pain and grabbed her arm. "Look around. There must be something we can use to stanch the bleeding."

"Stay here," Mingzhu said. "I'll be back in a moment."

She reentered the corridor and went further into the building until she reached a small kitchen. Hardly anything remained in the cupboards. Broken plates and glass littered the linoleum floors, and a rat lay dead in a corner, rotting away. From the window, the voices of soldiers neared. Mingzhu quickly ducked low as they walked past, careful not to make a sound. Once they disappeared, she finally found a small bucket and filled it from the tap. Thank goodness, the water was still running in this building.

On her way back to Sato, she investigated each room, trying to find something to stitch his wound. One room was filled with racks of *qípáo*'s and Western-style dresses. Setting the bucket down, she brushed her hand along the rack of dresses, feeling the satin against her skin, and wondered if she would ever wear something like that again. When Sato's distant groan caught up to her, she ripped down several dresses. Then, she came across a small box of needles and thread. "Perfect," she whispered.

Sato sat on the edge of the bed, his face pallid and his stare unfocused.

His trousers were soaked with blood. She met his eyes, searching for any sign of vulnerability. Sato had always been a man of veiled emotions, but in this moment, Mingzhu recognized his undeniable fragility. She couldn't help but think of Henry.

Mingzhu tore at his trousers with a pair of scissors until his leg was exposed and he let out a pained groan. "Let me tend to your wound," she said sharply.

"Do you know what you're doing?"

"I have some idea," she replied, snipping away at a rayon dress to fashion a piece of cloth. "My daughter used to get into all sorts of accidents. Whenever she hurt herself, I'd be there."

"You didn't have servants for that?"

Mingzhu frowned. "I know how to help my own child," she said.

"If you insist." Sato's shoulders relaxed. "Remember, this stays between us."

Mingzhu nodded, her movements careful as she began to clean the wound. Being so close to Sato in such a different setting was strange. Whoever this man was, Mingzhu didn't wish him harm. At least, not at that moment.

"Are you going to tell me why that soldier was after you? Why did he call you a spy?" she asked, unable to wait any longer. She needed to know if her suspicions were correct.

Sato's silence lingered as if he were deciding how much to reveal. "Can I trust you?"

"That's your decision. You can make that choice freely."

Sato chuckled. "Your husband must dislike your sharp wit."

She paused, distracted. "Do you know where he is?"

"Stanley, I believe."

"Is he alive?"

"Do you want him to be?"

Mingzhu pressed the cloth harder against Sato's leg until he let out another groan. "Tell me who you are," she said.

"I'm a fighter," Sato replied.

"That much is evident," Mingzhu said. "But for which side?"

"Can't you guess?"

"I want facts, not guesses." Mingzhu threw the cloth back into the bucket and picked up a needle and thread. "The bullet went straight through. You're fortunate."

As Mingzhu pointed a small needle at his leg, he asked, "Are you certain you know what you're doing?"

"Are you worried I'll butcher you with this tiny thing?"

Sato laughed. "You find me repulsive, don't you? Because of who I am."

Ignoring him, she pressed on his wound and pierced the skin. Of course, he was right. Why would she have any regard for someone who had kept her captive? Forced her to watch as dozens of people were taken into the woods and shot? Of course she despised him. But, at the same time, she knew there was more to him. And she knew she couldn't let him die.

"I am part of the resistance," he said calmly, as if the stitches were nothing more than a passing inconvenience.

Mingzhu paused, steadying her hand before pushing the needle through his skin again.

"I'm listening," she prompted, continuing to suture his wound.

"Have you heard of the East River Column?"

Mingzhu nodded.

"I work with them," Sato said.

"For how long?" she asked, jerking her head back.

"Since they were first established. Back in thirty-eight. Back then, they were two separate groups. They've been operating in Hong Kong since the occupation began eight months ago."

Had the occupation really endured for that long? Time had slipped away unnoticed. Despondency swept over Mingzhu. Had she become so entrenched in her role as Sato's secretary that she could no longer keep track of the passing days and months? Or had she simply refused to acknowledge the passing of time, not wanting to recognize that each day was one more that she had gone without her daughter and Biyu?

"They've set up several bases around the city. Out in the villages, too," Sato said. "There are three main camps. Tai Po, Sha Tin, and Sai Kung."

"The resistance is against the occupation," Mingzhu said. "You're Japanese."

"Well, aren't you a sharp one," he mocked.

"That makes you a traitor to your own people."

Sato leaned forward and grabbed Mingzhu's hand so she was forced to stop stitching. He looked at her intensely. "If your people raped, killed, and mutilated another race, would you stand back and do nothing?"

Mingzhu freed herself from his grip. "Of course I wouldn't!" she hissed.

Sato gestured to his leg for her to continue. "I was only a lieutenant when we fought Shanghai back in thirty-seven. I joined the army thinking I'd make my parents proud. I wanted my country to flourish and expand. I never thought we'd be killing civilians, too."

Mingzhu's hand stilled for a moment. "You were naïve," she said.

"I was," Sato admitted. "My captain made me do things I can't ever forget. Things I can't unsee."

"He made you?" Mingzhu asked incredulously.

"I didn't want to die," Sato said. "I'm not like you. I fear death."

"We cannot control death, Captain. I just hope that when the time comes, I am surrounded by my loved ones. That's all I can wish for."

Sato pressed his lips together. Mingzhu pushed the needle through his skin once more, noting his silence.

"So, what then?" she asked. "Are you trying to atone for your sins?"

Sato rubbed his chin and sighed. "My sins cannot be forgiven."

Mingzhu wanted to interrogate him further, but his expression made it clear that he had shared all he would for the moment. Men and war never ceased to baffle her.

"What about the lieutenant you spoke with the other day?" Mingzhu diverted the conversation. "Is he a part of this too?"

"You heard us?"

"You weren't exactly quiet," she replied, not wanting to admit she had intentionally eavesdropped.

Sato gave a rueful smile. "Yes, Hiroshi is one of us. But right now, Tanaka has flagged him. It serves us well that Hiroshi follows his commands for the time being and plays a loyal servant to the emperor."

"And what is it *you* do for the East River Column?" Mingzhu asked. She finished closing the wound, tied off the end of the thread, and chucked the needle into the bucket of water.

"I work with the Tai Po base. Brother Knife, their leader, manages weapons shipments that come in from Japan. Their mission is to infiltrate the shipments before they reach Japanese hands."

"What about the other bases?" Mingzhu asked.

"You do ask a lot of questions, don't you?"

Mingzhu gave Sato a demanding stare.

He sighed. "The Sha Tin base has been set up as a medical station. They're in charge of obtaining medical supplies and transporting them. They work most closely with the Red Cross."

"And Sai Kung?"

"I don't know much about Sai Kung. It's run by two brothers. They primarily infiltrate comfort stations around the three main islands and focus on civilian rescues."

"It sounds like a whole system has been put into place," Mingzhu remarked, dismissing the fleeting notion that Qiang or Biyu might have been ensnared in one of the comfort stations. She refused to entertain such thoughts; they were an omen of misfortune. Instead, she focused on contemplating the potential a resistance might hold. Mingzhu experienced a faint spark of hope for the first time in a while.

"The resistance is growing," Sato continued. "They're strong, but without intelligence, they'd be crushed by now."

"So, that's where you come in," Mingzhu said.

"Exactly."

Mingzhu helped Sato lift his injured leg onto the bed. "Here, rest against the pillow. I'll find somewhere to throw these," she said, picking up the bloodied towels and remnants of his trousers.

Sato grabbed Mingzhu's arm. "Thank you," he said.

Mingzhu sat on the edge of the bed, ignoring the fact that a man was already sitting on it. "When I heard you speaking with Hiroshi, he mentioned I could help. What is it you want from me?"

"What do you think I want from you?"

"I don't know," she said. "You had a chance to kill me, but you didn't. You have kept me by your side since the occupation began. For what?"

"I gather people who I think I can use. The day we met, you impressed me. The way you stood up to me, never lowering your head once. I knew you had been confronted before. Shanghai, right?"

"Yes."

"I knew I'd need someone strong in my corner. A woman. Someone people underestimate. I believe you can help."

Mingzhu clung to the bloodied rags in her grip. "How?"

"Hiroshi has been transferred to Middle Hill, so I need another informant."

"What do you need me to do?"

"Tanaka is suspicious. He made that obvious when he reassigned Hiroshi and severed our relationship. I need you to take on more responsibility."

"Do you think Tanaka sent that man after you today?"

"There's no doubt about it. The Americans have been increasing their movements across Hong Kong. Tanaka is getting impatient. So, are you with me?" Sato asked.

Mingzhu met his gaze, noting a flinty resolve that matched her own. If Sato truly was working alongside the resistance, this would be her opportunity to finally do something for her people. She would be a fool to decline such a partnership.

"I'm with you," she said. "From here on out, I'm with you."

Later, at headquarters, Mingzhu met Sato in his office as requested. The sun had finally appeared, and its early-evening glow broke through the window behind Sato's desk, drenching the room with soft amber light.

"How are you feeling?" she asked.

"I'll manage," Sato replied, motioning for her to sit across from him. He slid a small handkerchief toward her, with something inside. "Here, this is yours."

Accepting the bundle, Mingzhu uncovered her mala beads and jade bangle tucked within. Her heart skipped a beat. "You have held on to these all this time?"

Sato nodded. "It was never my intention for you to part with them. It was protocol. No prisoners were allowed to keep anything of value."

The tip of Mingzhu's nose tingled as she took the jade bracelet in her hands, its weighty coolness transporting her back decades earlier, when she stood before her parents outside the *sìhéyuàn.* Tears fell from the corners of her eyes as she slipped the bangle back on. The strength she felt emanating from the stone was immediate—as though she were whole again, even if she wasn't.

"Thank you," she said, looking at Sato.

"This war . . ." Sato began. "Please believe me when I tell you it's not what I want."

"I believe you," Mingzhu said, sniffing back her tears.

She stood to leave, and Sato picked up the string of mala beads. "You forgot these," he said.

"You can keep them, Captain." Mingzhu smiled softly. "May they offer you some semblance of peace, however small."

With that, Mingzhu let herself out. She didn't need the mala beads anymore. They were an object from a past life—a life that had shackled her to the traditions and duties of a wife she had never wanted to be. The mala beads tied her to no attachment. Not now, not ever.

Closing Sato's office door, Mingzhu's lips curved into a smile as she glimpsed the jade bangle gracing her wrist. Its return meant more than mere possession; it embodied her determination to press onward—to endure and survive—with the hope that one day she would give it to Qiang.

"Stay safe, my daughter," Mingzhu murmured softly, her heart hurting. "Wherever you are."

CHAPTER 19

In the stillness that enveloped the factory, Qiang sat alone. Her cheek still throbbed from being hit by the soldier earlier. A soft lantern above her station cast a blurry glow, and the machines around her that had roared with life earlier in the day now lay dormant.

For fifteen hours, her hands had been guided by the relentless rhythm of the factory. The vibrations had numbed her fingers to the point of agony. Fatigued, she lifted her foot from the pedal, and the mechanical hum stopped. Her palms were marked with red indentations and swollen from the heat. Shifting in her seat, she stared at the lines on her palms, carved like a road map of her destiny. Her mother's voice buzzed in her ears as she clenched her hands into fists. "Why do you always hurt yourself?" her mother had asked, rubbing Qiang's arm with antiseptic cream. The fresh scent of chrysanthemums had wafted in through the open window on a gentle breeze, blending with the herbal aroma of the ointment.

"I wanted to see outside, Mama," Qiang said. At six years old, she had hardly left the compound. The sounds of street vendors in the distance poured over the walls and into the house.

"And climbing the ginkgo tree is better than opening the door?" Mingzhu tutted.

"Baba doesn't let me go out," Qiang said.

"Your baba isn't here. If you want to go somewhere, then ask me. I will take you anywhere you want." Her mother's voice was as soothing as the melody of spotted doves in the garden.

"But Baba says girls should stay at home."

Her mother paused, her gaze drifting to the lanterns hanging from the courtyard walls before meeting Qiang's eyes again. "Maybe that's true for me, but not for you. *You* are different."

"How?"

"You're my daughter, and I say you can go wherever and do whatever you want."

Qiang's eyes glistened. "Really, Mama?"

"I would never lie to you. So, where do you want to go?"

"The cinema!" Qiang exclaimed. "I want to see the funny man with curly hair and a thick mustache!"

"Charlie Chaplin?"

"Yes, yes! Charlie Chaplin, Mama!"

Mingzhu laughed. "Then, we shall go to the cinema. We'll take Biyu with us."

"What if Baba finds out?"

"That's for me to worry about, not you." Mingzhu blew on Qiang's arm. "All better, see?"

Qiang winced. "Will I be okay, Mama?"

"Of course, my strong little one. You have a long life ahead of you."

"I do?"

Her mother took Qiang's hand in her much larger one, her fingers tracing the lines on her palms. "See this? This is your lifeline. Look how long it is!"

Qiang giggled. "It's really long!"

"Exactly, my dear," her mother said. "And it's a sign that you'll have a long, happy life. Just like this tree you climbed."

Now, in the factory, her fists still clenched, she prayed that her mother was right and that she would live a long life, but the possibility seemed absurd now.

The factory doors opened with a loud creak and Qiang jerked her head up to see a figure approaching. Hiroshi. She stood, knocking her seat to the ground, missing his boot by an inch.

"You may leave now," he said, picking up the chair.

Qiang studied him. He looked no different from the night in the courtyard beneath the banyan tree, though his hands were free of gold paint. "Do you remember me?"

"No," he said, his eyes falling to her bruising cheek.

Qiang wanted to believe him, but the slight twitch in the corner of his mouth gave away the lie.

"Where do you live?" he asked.

"Excuse me?"

"It's past curfew," he said. "How will you get home?"

Qiang had worked past curfew many times before. Though it was a good thirty-minute walk, she knew exactly how to return to Francine's. All she had to do was stay clear of the river.

"I can drive you," Hiroshi said.

"No." Qiang took a step back, startled.

"I'll walk with you, then."

"Absolutely not."

"What are you afraid of?"

"Is that a serious question?"

"You get home safe; I don't lose a worker."

"You *do* remember me, don't you?" Qiang narrowed her eyes.

"I've never seen you before," Hiroshi said again. He was lying, Qiang was sure of it.

"I don't need your help. I've walked home many times at this time of night."

"Patrols are everywhere after curfew. How do you avoid them?"

"What?"

At that moment, a soldier came running into the factory and began speaking to Hiroshi in Japanese. Some workers had been found stealing leather straps and trading them for food.

"I will deal with that tomorrow," Hiroshi told the soldier. "You may leave."

The soldier looked between Hiroshi and Qiang. A perverted smile spread across his face. "Yes, Lieutenant."

"You may leave, too," Hiroshi said, turning back to Qiang once the soldier had gone.

Like the first time they had met, Qiang couldn't quite hold her tongue. "What are you going to do to those people? The ones who stole the leather?" she asked.

Hiroshi cocked his head. "You understand Japanese?"

"A little," she replied. If Hiroshi could lie about not remembering her, she could lie about how much Japanese she spoke.

"The rules are clear," Hiroshi said. "Those caught stealing are sent to prison."

"You and I both know that's not what happens."

"I'm not sure I know what you mean."

Qiang was enraged by Hiroshi's mocking tone. His calm demeanor made her want to scream, but she refrained. Instead, she said, "Let's just say they get thrown out. You know, the same way one might throw out a chair, or even a vase."

Hiroshi's eyes remained fixed on Qiang's as she hoped he would finally reveal that he had met her before. But he merely asked calmly, "Do you often speak in riddles?"

Qiang bit down on her tongue. "Forget it. You have relieved me of my duties tonight. I will leave now."

Hiroshi lifted his arm to stop her. "Your talents are wasted in this factory. You should have become a translator. They are given better living conditions and food."

"What do you know of these translators?" Qiang asked, thinking of her mother. "Do you know any of them?"

Hiroshi's brow arched. "I know a handful. Mostly women."

Qiang's heart raced at the thought that her mother could be among them. She desperately wanted to ask Hiroshi for more information, but she didn't trust him.

"Why do you want to know?" Hiroshi asked.

Qiang ignored his question. Instead, she brazenly pushed his arm out of her way to leave. But then, she turned back to him. "You know, Lieutenant, I met a man once who told me of the art form *kintsugi*. Do you know it?"

"I do, yes. What's it got to do with me?"

Qiang shrugged. "I often wonder if the man I met still believes in such an art form, if he still wants to fix broken things. What do you think?"

Hiroshi pressed his lips together before answering, "I think I have asked you to leave, and you're wasting my time."

Without another word, she left him standing there in the near dark, the back of her neck hot. Pushing the door open, she glanced back to meet his piercing gaze. Her breath caught in her throat as she walked out into the night.

As she returned to Tseng Lan Shu, the constant high-pitched whirs of cicadas and the hushed rustling of leaves accompanied her every step. The acacia trees seemed like silent guardians, their branches forming shapes that looked like they were reaching out above her. With each careful step, she thought of Ah-Long. Where was he now? Was he with the resistance? Was he even alive? Mr. Gok's words still played on her mind.

You're just a girl. What do you know about fighting?

She moved with caution, fearful of running into soldiers, and when she finally crossed the bridge to Tseng Lan Shu, she sighed with relief. But as she neared the house, the sound of a woman crying immediately made her breath hitch in alarm.

She ran into the courtyard and let out a scream. Biyu was kneeling beside a lifeless Francine, her hands resting on her chest where blood had already begun to congeal. Biyu's face was purple like a plum, and her left eye bulged from its socket. Mr. Gok stood frozen in the doorway with Wong Taitai.

"Francine!" Qiang cried, falling to her knees next to Biyu.

"Young Miss, I'm so sorry," she sobbed.

"No," Qiang whimpered. "No . . . Please, no."

"Young Miss . . ."

Qiang turned to Biyu and cupped her swollen face in her hands. "Biyu, who did this? Tell me who!"

Mr. Gok screamed at Qiang's question, a cry that silenced theirs. He stared at them both for a long moment, the two women kneeling beside his only daughter. He stormed back into the house, where his footsteps rebounded across the wooden floors until his bedroom door slammed shut.

Wong Taitai approached the women and pleaded, "Qiang, you must convince Biyu to bring Francine into the house. She's been kneeling here for hours, and her clothes and hair are still soaked. If she stays like this, she'll wind up sick. Please, Qiang . . . Francine is gone. There's no bringing her back."

It was a small funeral, but nonetheless, it was done.

Qiang didn't care that the Imperial Army had banned people from performing such rites. She welcomed the prospect of soldiers turning up to cause a riot. She would cause a revolt ten times worse. The contempt that had once simmered away in her gut had now reached her throat. She wanted to vomit, to drown them in her hatred, to flood this entire land and watch every soldier be swallowed whole.

Qiang cleaned the blood off Francine's face and body while Wong Taitai helped dress her in a blue *qípáo* embroidered with yellow flowers. Francine hadn't brought much to her father's home, but a few beautifully woven silk dresses were among her belongings.

Biyu, whose movements were restricted by a broken rib, lit a small fire in the courtyard. They had no joss paper to burn, so Biyu used old newspapers that Mr. Gok had stored beneath his bed. She cut them up into square sheets and diligently folded them, tossing them into the fire. The smell of charred ink made the women sob harder.

Francine's body was carried out into the courtyard and wrapped in the bedsheets she had slept in. Qiang, Wong Taitai, and Biyu spent the next four hours digging a sizable hole in the mud near the lychee tree. All the while, Mr. Gok remained in his room. He lay in bed, his back to the door. Every time one of the women went to check on him, to ask him to bid his farewells, he ignored them. Eventually, as the midnight wind picked up, rustling along the village paths, Francine was fully buried.

Qiang, Biyu, and Wong Taitai knelt on the ground and bowed three times.

"May you find peace, Francine," Wong Taitai said. "May your spirit find its way through the afterlife to the next with no hardships. Do not come looking for us. Leave peacefully."

Wong Taitai's words had reason. The Chinese believed a murdered soul would come back in the form of a vengeful ghost. Qiang didn't believe in ghosts. She only believed in things she could see, could smell, and could touch. The spiritual realm was nothing but a figment of one's imagination—something hopeless people grabbed onto.

As Wong Taitai continued, Biyu whispered to Qiang, "She died because of me. I am the cause of this."

Qiang put an arm around Biyu, steadying her sobbing frame. She had no words of comfort to offer, no wisdom to share. Biyu had no reason to feel such guilt. If anything, Qiang was the reason the soldier had followed Biyu in the first place. How could she have been so foolish? She patted Biyu on the back and continued kneeling before Francine's grave. Eventually, exhaustion took over, and Biyu fell asleep in her arms.

Once Wong Taitai left, Qiang, who had become strong from the factory labor, carried Biyu into the house and put her to bed. She wiped Biyu's hair from her face and traced a finger along the cuts and bruises on her cheeks. She could find no way to resolve her anger. It kept growing and growing. Francine's murder, Biyu's beating, Hiroshi's lies—Qiang felt that she was boiling from the inside out. No, she should not have aggravated the soldiers, but they should not be here in the first place. None of this should be happening.

She tiptoed into the kitchen, pulled out a paring knife, and exited the house.

Thirty minutes later, Qiang was back at the factory, sneaking around the compound toward the makeshift cabins where the soldiers slept. Footsteps and drunken slurs filled the air. Qiang ducked, quickly hiding behind a bush. She gripped the knife tighter, sweat dripping down her back as two officers walked by. One of them, Francine's murderer.

"You sick dog!" one of the officers said, slapping his comrade on the back. "Did she beg for mercy?"

"They always do." He smiled ghoulishly.

Qiang could hardly breathe. She wanted to drive the knife into his chest until he was ripped open. She wanted to see what the insides of a heartless man looked like. She pushed herself up and stepped forward, but a twig cracked behind her. Before she could respond, a heavy cloth was pressed firmly against her nose and mouth.

Instinctively, she writhed in response, releasing the knife as her body numbed. Her consciousness fluctuated, and she caught glimpses of the blurred figure carrying her to the back seat of a car. Her head began to spin as she struggled to keep her eyes open. Just before she succumbed to darkness, the distorted voice of a man reached her ears.

You'll be safe there. I promise.

CHAPTER 20

Biyu woke to a voice mumbling from the courtyard. With difficulty, she pushed herself up and out of bed, one arm wrapped around her chest to ease the pain of her broken rib. She glanced at Qiang's bed, which looked like it hadn't been slept in. Making her way across the living room, she reached the front door and saw Mr. Gok standing before Francine's grave.

"Silly, silly, child," Mr. Gok babbled. "So, so silly."

Biyu placed a hand on the door for support, and the creaking sound caught Mr. Gok's attention. He turned to her, his eyes red and filled with grief.

"Mr. Gok," Biyu said, tears splashing down her neck. "I'm so sorry . . ."

Mr. Gok grunted, shuffling back into the house. As he walked past Biyu, he stopped so they were shoulder to shoulder.

"She was a silly, silly child," he said. "To die for what? For *you*?"

Biyu sobbed harder.

"No." Mr. Gok put a hand up to silence her. "I will not hear it. We all make our own choices in the end. Good or bad. My daughter, that silly, silly child. She died saving you. Fine. That was her choice. But you? No. You do not get to cry."

Biyu blinked and pressed her lips together, tasting the saltiness of her tears.

"For Francine, you must live on," he continued. "Do not waste my daughter's life by drowning in useless tears. Now, get out of my way."

When Biyu reentered the living room, Mr. Gok's bedroom door

stood closed. Despite the growling of her stomach, she refused to eat. After everything that had happened, how could she?

The clock on the wall struck six o'clock. There was still another hour before Biyu was due at the factory. She quickly checked the kitchen and bathroom.

"Qiang?" she called out.

There was no answer. She slipped her feet into worn-out sandals, threw a cardigan over her shoulders, and headed outside. Where had Qiang gone?

The village was slowly waking. The soft light of dawn cast the surroundings in muted tones, which seemed to mirror the occupation. Hushed murmurs and distant, muffled noises sounded as Biyu closed the gate to the house. Several other gates creaked open as a few villagers ventured out cautiously, exchanging furtive glances with her.

She knocked on Wong Taitai's door.

"Biyu." Wong Taitai rushed to her. "You should be lying down, resting."

Biyu shook her head. "Qiang isn't home. I don't know where she's gone, and I'm worried."

Wong Taitai patted Biyu on the arm. "Perhaps she needed some space after what happened. Maybe she went to the factory early or even went for a walk?"

"Maybe . . ."

"She'll come back. Don't worry. You should get back inside and rest some more. I can help look after Mr. Gok today if you need."

"Thank you, Wong Taitai," Biyu said before turning away.

For the next hour, Biyu pressed on, moving from one house to the next. She didn't want to rest. She needed to find Qiang and make sure she was safe. Each door that cracked open revealed faces stamped with fear and hunger, their eyes telling of the shared uncertainties of the time. When every door she knocked on resulted in nothing but headshakes, she returned to the house.

Please come back, she thought endlessly, déjà vu clawing its way into the back of her mind.

"Please, come back!" Biyu had called out, chasing Mingzhu down a path between a row of terrace houses and tea parlors.

The Qing dynasty had collapsed several years earlier, and in its place, the Republic of China was established. Biyu had just turned eighteen and was almost at her wits' end caring for her ten-year-old charge.

"Come on, Biyu!" Mingzhu had shouted back. "I have a surprise for you!"

"Young Miss, you can't just run out of the house without telling your parents! We'll get into so much trouble."

Mingzhu finally stopped running, causing Biyu to almost crash into her.

"You worry too much! All the time, you worry, worry, worry," Mingzhu said, crossing her arms. "*Fùqīn* has already left for the day, and *Mǔqīn* is praying in the ancestral hall. No one will catch us."

"But it's dangerous out here, Young Miss," Biyu said, her tone almost scolding. "Your *mǔqīn* will have me kneel in the heat again if she finds out."

Mingzhu pouted, then grabbed Biyu by the hand. "Trust me, Biyu. Once you see what I have for you, you won't care if you must kneel."

There was no arguing with her charge. The Fire Horse energy in her was too strong. Stubborn, yes, but strong. Biyu relented and followed the little girl toward the open markets near the Bund.

The scent of spices and herbs filled her lungs as they walked the narrow streets, which were an assortment of colors, bright silk banners fluttering in the breeze and lanterns swaying overhead.

They reached a market stall filled with finds from across Asia. Biyu watched as Mingzhu's eyes widened with excitement as she pointed to the array of goods on display. Silks in every hue imaginable hung like cascading waterfalls, while jade carvings of mythological creatures glimmered beside strings of freshwater pearls and bone-carved amulets, all artfully arranged to entice passersby.

Mingzhu placed her hands on her hips and looked up at the stall's owner. "Do you remember me, old man?" she asked.

Biyu pinched Mingzhu's shoulder.

"Ow!" Mingzhu cried. "Why did you pinch me?"

"Young Miss, you can't call him old man. It's rude."

"But he *is* an old man!" Mingzhu turned to the stall owner again. "Are you not?" she questioned bluntly.

Biyu's cheeks flushed in embarrassment, but the stall owner let out a sharp laugh. "Yes, little miss, this *lǎorénjiā* remembers you well! Are you here with money today?"

Mingzhu pulled an embroidered purse from her dress pocket and handed the entire bag to the man. "It's all there. I counted it myself," she said proudly.

"Very well," the man replied, taking the purse from her. After counting it, he crouched behind the wooden table and pulled out a small box. "Here you go."

"Thank you, old man!" Mingzhu grinned. She took the box from his grasp and turned to Biyu. "Here. Happy birthday, Biyu."

Biyu was shocked. "You got this for me?"

Mingzhu giggled. "Open it!"

Biyu did as she was instructed. A stunning silver butterfly pendant was inside. Crafted from polished silver, the butterfly's wings had a subtle beauty, with fine lines and patterns that mimicked the complex veins running through its real-life counterparts. Biyu felt her eyes sting.

"Do you like it?" Mingzhu asked, peering up at her.

"It is beautiful, Young Miss," Biyu said tearfully. "But it's too much. I can't accept this."

"You must," Mingzhu insisted. "When you look at the butterfly, you will always remember me. Especially . . ."

"What's wrong, Young Miss?" Biyu said, noting Mingzhu's sudden change of expression. "Why do you look so sad?"

Mingzhu kicked at the ground and huffed. "I know you're leaving, Biyu."

"What? Who told you that?"

"The nanny was talking to *Mǔqīn* about it. *Mǔqīn* said that once you turned eighteen, you would be free."

Biyu didn't know what to tell the little girl standing before her. She was right. Her contract with the Yue family had ended. For all intents and purposes, Biyu was now free. Free to find work elsewhere, leave the Yue house, and start a new life.

As she looked at Mingzhu, who had begun to cry, it hit her all over again. This little girl wasn't just her employer's daughter. She really was like a sister to her—more than she had ever expected.

"If I asked you to stay with me, would you?" Mingzhu asked, taking hold of Biyu's hand.

Biyu didn't have an immediate answer. A part of her had been waiting impatiently for her contract to end for years. She used to dream about what sort of life she would have without being someone's servant. But Mingzhu's birth had given her not only purpose, but also an education, a family—a new life.

Mingzhu tugged on her hand harder. "I can't live without you, Biyu. I don't want you to leave. Please, please, can you stay with me a little longer?"

Now, Biyu gripped her butterfly pendant, the memory receding along with the hope that Qiang was still in the village. She continued walking around Tseng Lan Shu, but Qiang was nowhere to be found, and she was filled with despair.

Before, when the Japanese had penetrated Hong Kong and the Tang residence, Biyu had briefly entertained the idea of fleeing alone. She had despised herself for even considering it. After all, what was her existence without both mother and daughter? Who was she without these women? She didn't know, and despite the faintest undercurrent of curiosity about her own identity, she couldn't bring herself to leave. Mingzhu needed her, and she needed Mingzhu. Biyu's duty was to safeguard Qiang, but as she traveled through the village searching for her, she felt a profound sense of failure. Even if she yearned for the freedom to discover her individuality in this world, she couldn't pursue it until Qiang was safe and reunited with her mother.

CHAPTER 21

Qiang blinked awake, squinting into the daylight penetrating a small gap in a canvas tent. The scent of mosquito incense and herbs made her cough. She tried to sit up, only to be met with a wave of dizziness that sent her sinking back onto a thin mattress, her head throbbing.

"Hey, you're awake!"

Turning slightly, Qiang saw a young girl sitting by her side. Her eyes were wide and expressive, shimmering with curiosity and innocence. Her dark hair was tied back in a loose braid over her shoulder.

"Who . . . where am I?" Qiang's voice came out as a hoarse whisper, her throat like sandpaper.

The girl offered a comforting smile and helped Qiang sit up. "You're safe now," she said. She handed Qiang a tin cup and helped her take a sip.

"Where am I?" Qiang asked again.

The girl twitched her nose. "We found you near the river. You were not awake."

Qiang massaged her temple, and memories began trickling back, fragments at a time. Flashes of Francine's lifeless body haunted her. "Francine . . ."

"Francine? Who is Francine?"

Qiang shut her eyes in pain and fell back onto the mattress. She recalled returning to the factory and seeing the man who had killed her mother's friend. Then, she remembered being guided into a car and a man's voice telling her she would be safe. She couldn't remember anything after that.

"I am Hao," the girl introduced herself, her voice a gentle reminder of the present moment. She couldn't have been older than eleven.

"Hao?" Qiang looked at her.

The girl gave a broad smile. "Yes. Hao. Brother Wu calls me Hao and so everyone calls me Hao. He says I'm a very good child. What about you? What's your name?"

"Qiang," she managed to say. "My name is Qiang."

"Like strong!"

Qiang gave a weak smile. At that moment, she didn't feel strong at all.

"I found you. I helped you. My ma and my ba always told me to help people."

Qiang offered a smile. "Your parents must be proud of you."

"I don't know. They aren't here."

"Where are they?"

"They're dead." Hao looked down at her palms. "They didn't give rice to the Japanese man that came to our village. The Japanese man said that they must give rice. But my ma and my ba said no, we will not give rice to you. So the Japanese man killed them."

Qiang felt deeply sad for the young girl's loss—and to have to witness such a horror, too.

Hao took the cup from Qiang's grasp. "Come with me. Brother Wu will see you now."

"Brother Wu?"

"He is the boss here. He can help you."

"Boss . . . ?" Qiang breathed out. Where had she ended up? She reached into her pockets, but they were empty. The knife she had carried to the factory was nowhere to be seen.

Hao sprung to her feet and made her way to a small chest. She pulled out a gray tunic and black trousers. "Here. You can wear these. You're so dirty."

Sure enough, Qiang's current attire was covered in mud. She reached out and took the clean clothes from Hao. "Thank you," she said.

Hao turned around to give her some privacy. As Qiang changed, she marveled at the simple act of kindness from someone so young.

"You can turn back around now," Qiang said as she buttoned up the tunic.

"You look good. Brother Wu will be happy."

"Will you take me to see him?" she asked, curious.

"Yes. I'll take you now. Brother Wu is a good man. He fights the Japanese."

Qiang followed Hao out of the tent. "Hao?"

"Yes?"

"Where are we?"

"We are in Sai Kung, Qiang."

All around, makeshift shelters and tents sprawled everywhere. Bamboo and thatch structures stood shoulder to shoulder, connected by a web of narrow passages, and Qiang struggled to keep up with Hao, who threaded through them expertly. These humble dwellings, woven from nature's raw materials, spoke of survival amidst adversity. Could this be the resistance she had heard Mr. Gok and Ah-Long speaking of?

Qiang blinked through the sunlight that filtered across the canopy of trees above her. Washing lines stretched like spider silk between the trunks, bearing shirts and dresses, uniforms, and traditional garments that harbored the stains of struggle and the marks of resilience.

"Why are there so many tents?" Qiang asked.

"Brother Wu says it's safer. We tried living in that big building over there before but it was bombed. Now, we hide closer to the trees so the Japanese won't spot us so easily."

As Qiang continued to follow Hao, people stopped what they were doing and watched her. Some women who were nursing babies quickly rushed back into their tents, while others stood and whispered to one another. The entire camp was filled with women and children, and Qiang heard Cantonese, the Hakka dialect, and English. There was hardly a man in sight. In the center of the camp was a gathering space, where a firepit crackled and danced vigorously, encouraging camaraderie. Older women circled the flames, sweat dripping from their temples as they threw chopped cabbage and potatoes into a pot. Whatever Qiang had imagined the resistance would look like, this was far from it.

Hao nudged her. "Brother Wu is here. You can go inside."

"Will you come with me?" Qiang asked. As the question came out of her mouth, she realized how immature she was to seek a child's comfort and safety.

Hao shook her head. "I have to go and cut vegetables. We will have a big dinner tonight."

"I see." Qiang squared her shoulders.

"Here." Hao took a piece of string from her pocket and handed it to Qiang. "You can use this to tie up your hair. You look dirty."

"Still?" Qiang gave a short laugh, taking the string from Hao. "Thank you."

Hao smiled and ran off toward the women near the fire. Qiang promptly tied her hair into a ponytail before entering the tent. Two men sat in quiet discussion, surrounded by large wooden tables filled with maps, documents, and weapons. They fell silent, turning to her with stern expressions.

The bigger man crossed his arms and leaned back in his chair while the slenderer one stood, making his way to Qiang with a smile. "You're awake," he said.

"I'm looking for Brother Wu," Qiang said.

"That would be me. Come, take a seat." The man gestured to an empty chair. He wore a light cotton shirt with the sleeves rolled up to his elbows, his forearms toughened by physical labor.

Qiang took a seat by the table. Brother Wu's hair was a salt-and-pepper mix that fell just above his shoulders, slightly tousled as if he hadn't bothered much with grooming.

Brother Wu smacked the other man's shoulder. "This is Brother Song. He doesn't take well to strangers. But he'll warm to you eventually."

"She could be a spy," Brother Song said, rubbing his rounded chin. "I say we kill her right here."

Alarmed, Qiang immediately responded, "I'm not a spy."

"Ignore him," Brother Wu said, taking his seat. "Tell me, who are you?"

"You're the East River Column, aren't you?" Qiang asked, ignoring Brother Wu's question.

"Why do you think that?"

"You must be," she said. "I've heard stories of you back in Tseng Lan Shu. With the camp, the weapons, what else could you be?"

"Well, we could be everyday civilians simply trying to get by, hoping for the occupation to end."

"Not with the number of weapons you have in this tent alone. You're the resistance. You must be. Not to mention, most people across the camp are speaking Hakka. The resistance is mainly made up of the Hakka population, is it not?"

Brother Wu gave a hearty laugh, and Qiang hoped he was impressed by her.

"And what if we are?" Brother Song asked, eyes narrowed.

"If you *are* . . ." Qiang sat up straighter. "Then, I want to join."

"Do you even know how to fight?" Brother Song snapped.

"I can learn."

"You can learn to fight?"

"Yes," she said, determined. "If you need me to fight, I will fight."

"What if we need you to kill?" Brother Wu interjected.

Qiang turned back to him and lowered her head.

Brother Song snorted. "She's obviously weak-minded. We don't need another useless mouth to feed. I say we get rid of her now before the others return."

Brother Wu raised a hand to silence Brother Song. He looked at Qiang intensely. "I'll ask you again. If we need you to kill, will you?"

Qiang's lips trembled as she thought of Francine and Biyu, the paring knife she had held in her hand. She looked at both men and replied firmly, "Yes."

"Well then, it's settled. Welcome to the East River Column."

After Qiang's introduction to the brothers, she found herself shadowing Hao through the camp. It pulsed with collective energy, a united determination to protect their homeland. Hao led her through various paths, introducing her to the faces of this community of fighters and survivors. She was searching for the familiar face she longed to see. But Ah-Long was nowhere. She didn't dare ask for him. She couldn't bear the thought of losing him twice. Not today.

Qiang couldn't help but be struck by the array of individuals she encountered. Each face held a story—had seen both tragedy and hope, weathered storms—and all of them conveyed the firm spirit of Hong Kong. As Hao made the introductions, Qiang acknowledged each person with a nod, absorbing their names and roles within the resistance.

At one end of the camp was a communal area where more pots simmered above small fires. Children darted around, chasing one another and laughing. Qiang couldn't remember the last time she had seen children so free.

"What's over there?" she asked, pointing to an ample space beyond the tents.

"That's our training ground. You can practice your fighting skills." Hao dropped into a squat and put her arms into a defense position. "Like this!"

Qiang giggled at Hao's demonstration, but then they passed some large chests filled with weapons, and her smile vanished. When would she be able to fight?

Hao took her by the hand and led her toward another tent. "Here you will find Ah-Yee. She's nice. Ah-Yee fixes many things, like clothes and shoes. If you break something, Ah-Yee will fix it."

Qiang peeked inside the tent where an older woman with silver hair tied in a topknot sat cross-legged, patching a pair of trousers. The woman greeted her with a smile. "*Nei5 ho2,*" she said in Cantonese.

Qiang's Cantonese wasn't as developed as the other languages she spoke, but she understood the basic greetings. "*Nei5 ho2,* Ah-Yee," she replied. "*Ngo5 giu3,* Qiang."

Ah-Yee nodded and went back to her sewing.

Hao pulled on Qiang and directed her to a lookout post. "Here we can see if any Japanese come through the mountains. And we can also see our own people come. Follow me."

Hao began climbing the wooden stairs that led up to a square bamboo landing. Qiang followed, unsure if it would hold their combined weight. But, of course, bamboo was more robust than most wood. Together, they looked out into the dense hills of the New Territories, the afternoon sun sitting bright in the sky. Qiang wondered how far she was from Biyu and if she was safe.

As the day wore on, Qiang began helping others with menial tasks like washing clothes, mending shoes, and chopping vegetables. Even though her hands were sore from the work, it was a respite from the factory labor. She kept as busy as possible. The more she focused on cutting snake beans, the less she thought of Francine and Biyu. When it began to rain, everyone scattered back into their tents, and Qiang quickly covered the pots with lids.

Hao ran toward her, rain running down her cheeks. "Come." She waved. "You will stay with me."

Hao shared a tent with a young boy named Dai Dai. "That's not his real name," Hao said as she squeezed rainwater from her cotton shirt. "He doesn't know his real name. So, we call him Dai Dai."

"Like little brother?" Qiang asked, sitting on a small wooden chair beside two cots.

"Yes," Hao replied. "He doesn't talk much, but he is a good boy. Here, take this."

Qiang reached her hand out to receive a steel bowl, a toothbrush, and a towel. "Thank you." She smiled.

"Brother Wu told me to give these to you. You're lucky. Not everybody here gets a toothbrush."

"Do you want it?" she offered it back.

"No, no. I have one. Dai Dai has one, too."

"Is the bowl for our meals?"

Hao giggled, smacking her palms over her mouth. She stood closer to Qiang and whispered, "You need to poo? You do it in the bowl."

"Oh!" Qiang blushed. "We cannot go somewhere more . . . private?"

"Brother Wu says it's too dangerous. It's safer to stay inside the camp. Only fighters go outside."

"I see . . ." Qiang wrinkled her nose, exhausted by her thoughts.

Over and over, Brother Wu's words sounded in her ears. *If we need you to kill, will you?*

Qiang's senses roused as she gradually woke from a deep sleep, hearing the rhythmic patter of raindrops hitting the tent. As she opened her eyes, the rain began to calm, giving way to the sounds of food sizzling over a fire outside. Hao was nowhere to be seen.

Something warm pressed against her back. Turning her head, she saw Dai Dai fast asleep, his tiny body pushed against hers. The corners of his eyes were crusted with sleep, and his little brows knitted in a furrow. She sat up slowly and pulled the thin blanket over him, stroking his head. Eventually, his expression of angst turned into one of peacefulness as he began to snore.

She wondered what the boy's story was—where he came from, where his family was, and if they were still alive. Unease raked her stomach. How many other children were out there, homeless and without their loved ones?

A whistle sliced through the air, soon joined by another. Qiang's ears pricked up. Climbing gingerly out of the cot, she slipped into the laced boots thoughtfully provided by Hao earlier. The whistle persisted, compelling her out of the tent. Around her, people stirred into motion, making their way to the bamboo landing. Standing on it, high above them, was Hao, a beacon of enthusiasm, leaping and waving.

Crossing her arms to ward off the breeze, Qiang followed. The sound of vehicles approaching grew louder, and the children who had been running around the day before were now eagerly looking out onto a small dirt road. When Qiang reached the others, she spotted two vehicles nearing, a small white truck with a large red cross painted onto the side followed by one that looked like a Japanese vehicle, and her heart started to hammer.

"Don't worry," Brother Wu said, appearing beside her. "It's one of ours."

Qiang exhaled, the tension in her shoulders fading as she turned to the convoy's advance. The truck's doors swung open, and two men hopped off. A small boy ran to one of them, his arms outstretched.

"Baba!" he squealed in delight.

The man crouched, picked up the boy, and cradled him tightly in his arms.

More resistance members disembarked. First, at least five people emerged, a mix of men and women clad in Japanese uniforms. Their faces were covered in grime and blood. Following them, around eight women of different ages stepped off the truck. One woman, the oldest, fell to the ground as soon as her foot met the soil. Her legs were shaking, and she had clearly been injured. Qiang saw dark purple and black lines running across her shins. Without hesitation, she ran toward the woman and grabbed her by the waist.

At that moment, another set of hands had also reached around the woman. Qiang looked up to see a familiar face. Her entire body eased. "Ah-Long?"

Ah-Long looked at her, and a smile lit his face.

"You're awake, Young Miss," he said. "Come, help me. I'll carry her."

She helped to lift the woman onto his back and walked back into the camp with them. When Ah-Long had settled the woman down for others to tend to, Qiang grabbed him by the shoulders and hugged him tightly, shaking from relief.

"I'm so glad it's you," she sobbed. "I'm so glad."

Ah-Long hugged her back. "Young Miss . . ."

Qiang dug her face into his shoulder and shook her head. "No. Not Young Miss. Please, don't call me that anymore."

"Shh, shh." Ah-Long patted her on the head. "I'm sorry. I will call you Qiang from now on. How about that?"

She looked up into his dark eyes. She hadn't seen him in months. She had been so angry when he left, and she realized now that she had not allowed herself to think of him for all this time. But, seeing him now in the flesh, his face flushed with color and his body in better shape than before, her heart was comforted. "Heavens, I've missed you so much," she half cried, half laughed.

Ah-Long wiped her tears with his thumbs. "I have missed you, too."

They stood, holding each other for a while, not realizing this was the first time they had had such close contact.

"Ah-Long, I need to tell you some—"

"And I have something to tell you, Qiang—"

"Who's this?" A voice appeared next to them. Ah-Long let go of Qiang and turned to a woman dressed in a Japanese uniform.

"Sook Ping." Ah-Long gestured at the woman. "This is Qiang. She is the daughter of my old master."

Sook Ping possessed a commanding presence. She appeared to be in her early twenties, with a lean frame that exuded confidence. Her black hair, neatly arranged in a bun beneath the Japanese uniform cap, framed her sturdy features. Her eyes were as dark and liquid as calligraphy ink and held a sharp intelligence and a hint of contempt.

Sook Ping spat on the ground near Qiang's boots. "Ah yes, I almost forgot you used to be a servant."

Qiang narrowed her eyes. Who did this woman think she was to speak of Ah-Long in such a way?

"So what?" Sook Ping studied Qiang. "You're a high-society girl with a good education and rich parents?"

"Sook Ping. Stop it." Ah-Long grabbed her by the shoulder, but she continued to survey Qiang.

"Listen, I was the daughter of a rich man, too. But here"—she waved her arm across the camp—"you're just another one of us. You're expected to pull your weight. Do you even know how to cook or sew?"

Qiang's upper lip curled. "I'm not here to just cook or sew. I'm here to fight."

Sook Ping smacked her hand to her stomach and laughed. She pulled a knife from her back pocket and pointed it at Qiang.

"Hey!" Ah-Long put an arm out between the two women, but Qiang lowered his arm and faced Sook Ping, confronting her with an equally powerful stare.

"Wah." Sook Ping sucked her teeth. "You didn't even flinch."

"I'm not afraid of you," Qiang said.

Sook Ping stepped back and put her knife away. "I'm not the one you should be afraid of," she said.

"Don't listen to her." Ah-Long ushered Qiang to the communal area, where they sat opposite each other on wooden stools. "Tell me everything. Why are you here? How?"

For the rest of the evening, Qiang didn't leave Ah-Long's side. She told him everything that had happened since he left Tseng Lan Shu—what had happened to Francine, to Biyu, and how she had been ready to kill, when someone smothered her with a cloth to the face. The next thing she knew, she was at the camp.

"Where did Hao find you?" Ah-Long asked, deep in thought.

"By the river's edge, she said—just down the dirt path."

Ah-Long scratched his chin.

"Why? What are you thinking?" Qiang asked.

"I think the person who put you there wants you to live."

"Do many people know about the camp here?"

Ah-Long nodded. "Many people know. Even the Japanese know we are here. But they're too scared to come close. We have a good defense. Before, we had a building closer to the water, but they bombed it. So, we set up camp here. There are more places to hide."

"Yes, Hao mentioned that to me earlier. So, you think whoever left me here, they are on our side?"

"I don't know." Ah-Long sighed. "You didn't see the person clearly?"

Qiang shook her head.

"You're here now. Let's not worry too much. I'm happy to see you."

"I'm so happy to see you again, Ah-Long."

"Are you sure you want to join us? It's dangerous. You're good with languages. Maybe I can ask Brother Wu to send you to the International Liaison Unit? You can help with translations."

Ah-Long's offer made Qiang pause. She thought of her mother. If she took the liaison role, there was a chance—however slim—that she might find her. It was a small hope, she knew, yet it tugged at her. But the reality of what she had seen at the camp was hard to ignore. Translation work was important but it was still one step removed. Qiang didn't want to stand back and be an observer.

"No, don't do that," she said firmly. "I want to stay with you and the resistance. I want to be part of something bigger."

Perhaps, when the war was over, Qiang could find her mother again. But right now, she had chosen her place—in the fight. Ah-Long smiled, lifting a small cup of water. "Then you shall join me on the training ground in the morning. I will show you how to use the weapons. Here, let us fight together!"

Qiang raised her drink to his. "We fight together!"

Bringing the cup to her lips and smiling at her friend, Qiang could almost forget the flash of Sook Ping's knife pointed at her throat.

CHAPTER 22

Biyu walked around Tseng Lan Shu and its neighboring villages for days, knocking on every door she encountered. Most of the houses she visited were empty, already vacated by their occupants. Wherever she walked, the reek of death followed. The Japanese weren't slowing down by any means.

Biyu clutched her stomach as another cramp took hold. She was hungry, but there was hardly any food. Now that Ah-Long, Francine, and Qiang were all gone, she was down to only her ration card and Mr. Gok's. And Mr. Gok kept getting points deducted for working too slowly.

Biyu believed she was responsible for Francine's death. She reminded herself every couple of hours how she was to blame, repeating in her head: *It's you. She's dead because of you.* No matter how hard she tried to turn off that voice, she couldn't. She would always feel responsible for Mr. Gok losing his daughter and for Samuel and his father losing a mother and wife. Even the idea of one day giving that news to them brought pain to her chest.

By the time she arrived back at Mr. Gok's, her feet had swollen to twice their original size, her stomach continued to roar louder than the persistent strikes of a gong, and her head wouldn't stop spinning from dehydration. When she reached the door to the house, a young boy, no older than ten, ran up to her.

"Biyu?" he questioned.

She glanced around. The boy was on his own, carrying a small satchel.

"Who are you?" she asked. She wouldn't readily give out her name, even to a child.

"I have no name," the boy said. "I bring news from Qiang."

Two Japanese soldiers turned the corner and onto the path. Biyu grabbed the boy by the shoulder and quickly dragged him into the courtyard, shutting the gate behind her and covering his mouth. Together, they crouched behind the gate until the soldiers passed.

"You don't have to cover my mouth." The boy pulled away from her grip. "I know to be quiet."

"I'm sorry, I had to be sure," Biyu said. She stood and brushed the dirt from her knees. "You said you bring word from Qiang? Where is she?"

The boy opened the satchel and pulled out a box of hawthorn cakes. "They're freshly made. Qiang says you should eat the smallest one first."

Before she could respond, the boy thrust the cakes into Biyu's hands and ran away.

"Wait!" she called, but he had already disappeared.

Biyu burst into the house and looked around to find that Mr. Gok was not yet home. She tore open the box to discover five freshly baked hawthorn cakes, just as the boy had said. They each formed a circular shape, but one was evidently smaller than the rest. Biyu grabbed it and ripped it open, revealing a rolled-up piece of paper. She wiped the sticky dough of the cake from the paper and unrolled it.

> Biyu,
>
> Please accept my heartfelt apology. I am so sorry for how I left. Anger consumed me after Francine's passing, and my mind was muddled. I went to seek vengeance on her behalf. A thoughtless error, on reflection. But it did lead me back to Ah-Long. And to the ERC! It's real, Biyu. The resistance is real. It's not just whispers, or stories villagers tell their children at night.
>
> Ah-Long and I are both well. I have decided to join the cause, Biyu. I cannot endure another day working at the factory, and working under the thumb of the Japanese. I want

you and Mr. Gok to join me here. So, I have sent a messenger to deliver you this note.

Should all go well, the same messenger will wait for you near the village river two days from now at dawn. He will bring you to me, and we can be together again.

Until we meet again, stay safe.

Qiang

Biyu shredded the note into fragments, shoved it into the hawthorn cake, and swallowed it. Her mouth and throat were so dry it was like eating a handful of stones. But she didn't care. She inhaled another two cakes, relishing their slightly tart flavor while sobbing at the revelation that Qiang was safe.

By the time Mr. Gok returned, Biyu had already prepared a small plate of the remaining two hawthorn cakes, a bowl of boiled carrots, and one egg and placed them on the small dining table. She sat opposite Mr. Gok and watched him eat.

"Mr. Gok," Biyu began. "I have a way for us to leave here in two days. Qiang has joined the resistance. She wants us to join her."

"Qiang?" Mr. Gok stopped chewing on a piece of carrot. "Qiang?" he repeated.

"Yes, you know Qiang? She was here with us? She disappeared a short while ago. She has brought word of her safety. She has invited us to be with her."

Mr. Gok swallowed the carrot and looked Biyu in the eyes. "Francine, ah, who is Qiang?" he asked.

Biyu's mouth fell open. "Mr. Gok, I'm—"

"Why do you keep calling me Mr. Gok?" he asked, confused.

He stood, grabbed his bowl and chopsticks, and entered the kitchen. Biyu quickly followed him, trying to tell him again that she wasn't Francine, but he wouldn't hear a word of it. He placed his bowl and chopsticks into the sink before looking out of the kitchen window and into the courtyard. His eyes fell to Francine's grave.

"Francine," he said, turning to Biyu. "Who is buried out there?"

Biyu didn't know what to do. Mr. Gok's health had been deteriorating, but she had no idea how bad it had gotten in these past few days.

Had the death of his daughter hastened his decline? Was he somehow still in shock, perhaps? So many questions presented themselves to Biyu, but she had no answers. There was only one thing she could do.

"Father," Biyu said, gently. "We should get away from here. It's not safe here anymore. In two days, I'll take you somewhere better."

Mr. Gok dismissed her with a firm wave of his arm. "This is our home, Francine! We live here. Why would I go anywhere else?"

"Because it's not safe, Father," Biyu said. "The Japanese are unrelenting. They're killing more frequently; soon, it'll be our turn."

"Let them try!" Mr. Gok yelled. "I will not leave my home because of a couple of Japanese dogs! This is exactly what they want. They want us to run away scared. Well, I'm no coward!"

Mr. Gok had raised his voice so much that Biyu quickly shut the window and tried to pull him back into the living room. "Come, let me help you to your room and rest. You have had a tiring day. We can talk about this again tomorrow."

Biyu had never ventured into Mr. Gok's bedroom before, and it turned out to be much tidier than she had expected. She assisted him in getting to the bed, where he leaned against the headboard. Just as she was about to leave, Mr. Gok called her back.

"Francine," he said, beckoning. "Fetch me that box."

Biyu followed where he pointed and retrieved a small mahogany box from the vanity.

"Now, open it."

Sitting on the bed's edge, Biyu obeyed. Inside the box was a collection of small newspaper clippings, all in black and white. Mr. Gok pointed at one of them.

"This one, I've never shown you before," he said. "Take a look."

Biyu unfolded the selected clipping, revealing a young Mr. Gok standing in a field with an arm outstretched into a wave. Beside him was a young woman holding a little girl, and all three were smiling.

"Is this . . . ?"

"That's us, Francine. It's you, your mother, and me."

Tears welled up in Biyu's eyes as she looked at the image of a young Francine.

"No need to cry. It's just a picture," Mr. Gok reassured her. "Look at our field, Francine. See how happy we were? This land is our home. We can't let the Japanese force us out. I'm telling you now, I'm never leaving. Even when I pass on, my spirit will remain here."

Biyu folded the clipping and placed it back in the box. She turned to Mr. Gok, taking his hand in hers, feeling the roughness of his calloused skin against her own.

"If you want to stay, then we'll stay," she said firmly.

It was the least she could do. She owed it to Francine to ensure Mr. Gok lived the rest of his life comfortably, even if it meant putting her own future on hold. Even then, what future was to be had? She did not know.

She would meet the messenger by the river in two days with a letter explaining everything. Biyu knew that Qiang would understand.

PART III

JAPANESE-OCCUPIED HONG KONG, 香港占領地, 1943

CHAPTER 23

By the time winter came around again, rumors that Tanaka had his eye on the position of governor-general had spread to every island that made up Hong Kong. Many soldiers in the Imperial Army supported him. To them, he was the epitome of what a leader should be like. He had graduated from the twenty-second class of the Imperial Japanese Army Academy in 1910 and had steadily risen in rank. Mingzhu recalled seeing his name in the newspapers her husband used to read, how Tanaka was known for his ruthless nature and lack of empathy for civilian life. That much was evident from his stint during the Battle of South Shanxi two years earlier, where over one hundred thousand Chinese soldiers had been slaughtered by the Japanese. Wherever Tanaka went, bodies mounted in staggering numbers. Mingzhu had met him several times at headquarters when she had accompanied Sato to his weekly meetings. During those gatherings, she often focused on Sato's voice to avoid fantasizing about killing Tanaka. Lately, though, Tanaka had not called on Sato.

"That son of a bitch," Sato hissed that afternoon in his office. "How dare he withdraw my name from the meeting tomorrow."

Mingzhu stood by his desk, squinting as daylight pierced the window behind him. "He's been keeping tabs on you since you returned that day. How are we going to get word to the resistance now?"

Sato leaned back into his seat. "I know nothing about the incoming weapons shipments or even any planned attacks on resistance cells. I have to get into that meeting."

"Perhaps you don't," Mingzhu said. She lowered her voice to a whisper. "His secretary is sick today. I heard her coughing and vomiting all morning."

Sato looked at Mingzhu, almost annoyed. "What has that got to do with anything?"

"You men have little room for patience, don't you?" Mingzhu mocked.

Since discovering Sato's allegiance several months before, she felt more comfortable around him. There were even times they joked and laughed together—a welcome respite from the current affairs they found themselves involved in.

Sato sighed. "Go on, I'm listening."

Mingzhu sat opposite Sato and began to lay out her plan confidently.

"You think this will work?" Sato asked after hearing her out.

"Just give me until lunch." Mingzhu straightened. "That's all I'm asking."

Mingzhu rapped on the door. "Who is it?" a frail voice croaked.

"It's me, Mingzhu."

A pause. Then, shuffling feet scurried to the door. Tanaka's secretary, Hana, appeared, her face gaunt and paler than a rice cake.

"Heavens, Hana, you look terrible," Mingzhu remarked, pushing her way inside.

Hana's quarters mirrored Mingzhu's—small and sparse, with only a bed, small bedside table, desk, and chair. The overwhelming stench of vomit emanated from a bucket by the window. Mingzhu fought the urge to pinch her nose, not wanting to distress the already ailing Hana. "What can I help you with, Mingzhu?" Hana asked, coughing.

"You're too kind, Hana," she said, placing a hand on Hana's back and helping her back into bed. "I'm here to help you."

Hana struggled to keep her eyes open as her head met her pillow. "Oh, that's good of you. But I have taken some herbal tonic. There's nothing else that can be done."

Mingzhu feigned tidying Hana's desk, noting the paperwork and typewriter in the center of the table. "Are you certain?" she asked.

Hana groaned in pain and turned onto her side. Mingzhu went to pick up a towel soaking in a basin on a small bedside table and sat next to Hana. She wrung the towel free of water and began smoothing it along Hana's face. "Someone should keep an eye on you. An uncared-for fever could easily lead to madness. You know that's true."

"I suppose . . ." Hana sighed.

"I'll just stay until your fever subsides. It's the least I can do. You have always been kind to me," Mingzhu said. And that was the truth. Since Hana had begun working as Tanaka's secretary, she had always sought Mingzhu's company for breakfast, and the two women found themselves comforted by each other's presence. But Mingzhu wasn't here for Hana. She had to focus.

A few minutes later, as Hana drifted into slumber, Mingzhu returned to the desk, pulled out a chair, and sat down. She sifted through a thick stack of documents near the typewriter but found nothing of interest. She examined another pile of papers, but they were merely correspondence about American bombings that had already occurred.

Then, she quickly scanned the contents of an opened file. It contained detailed notes about Tanaka's meeting with the other captains scheduled for the next day. Most of it related to inventory and staffing, but one point stood out as a priority item of discussion.

Tai Po. Ten Days.

Mingzhu read the words three times before slipping out of Hana's room and rushing back to meet Sato.

They had time. They could warn them. Mingzhu felt a rush of energy as she bolted down the stairs, a sensation entirely foreign to her since the occupation had started. She harbored the potential to assist them. She might save their lives.

CHAPTER 24

Qiang crouched lower, hiding among the density of large oak trees near Yau Ma Ti station yard. Her breaths came in shallow gasps as she watched the Japanese soldiers patrol the area, their bayonets glinting ominously in the dim moonlight. Beside her, Ah-Long and Sook Ping waited, their eyes reflecting the same mix of fear and courage. Several feet behind them was another team of resistance members, waiting for their signal to assist.

She had been with the ERC for almost two months now, and she still couldn't shake the disappointment of Biyu not being there with her. She understood her reasons, but this did not alleviate her own worries. She wanted Biyu to be with her so she could be safe. But she could not think of this now.

Brother Wu had planned their operation a few hours earlier and requested that Qiang join Ah-Long and Sook Ping to prove herself. This was to be her first mission. There was no room for failure. The plan was for Qiang to follow Ah-Long and Sook Ping and sneak into the comfort station, bringing out the women from within.

"It's getting dark. The soldiers will be heading to the kitchens soon," Ah-Long said.

Qiang watched multiple soldiers exit a large warehouse a few feet from the train tracks. As the doors opened, distressed cries of women spilled out into the night, sending chills down Qiang's spine. She had heard of the atrocities, and she had witnessed them before, but she had never thought of the Japanese creating actual stations for such crimes.

Her grip tightened around the cold metal of the pistol Ah-Long had given her moments earlier. It was an unfamiliar weight in her hand, and despite Ah-Long's hasty instruction, she doubted her ability to hit her target accurately.

"I think that's the last of them," Sook Ping said. "It's now or never."

"Come on," Ah-Long urged.

Furtively, the trio moved along the fringes of the forest, drawing closer to the warehouse, avoiding any stray beams of light from the occasional streetlamp. When they reached the train tracks, Ah-Long turned back and signaled for them to cross on his count.

One.

Two.

Three.

With a quickened pace, Qiang sprinted across the tracks, the rocky ground beneath her shoes jabbing into her heels. At one point, she almost tripped but steadied herself in time, but she dropped the pistol. Once safely on the other side, she pressed her back against the warehouse wall.

"You lost your pistol," Sook Ping spat.

"It is not her fault," Ah-Long said defensively.

Qiang pushed herself off the wall and took a step forward. Sook Ping yanked her back. "Leave it," she said. Turning to Ah-Long, she added, "Bringing her was a mistake."

Qiang wanted to argue but knew it was a fair assessment. Sook Ping brought her fingers between her lips and mimicked the chirping of crickets with a sharp whistle, signaling their comrades across the tracks to begin their approach. Together, they slipped into the warehouse.

The sight that greeted Qiang was beyond her worst nightmares. Her entire body tensed as she followed Ah-Long and Sook Ping further inside. The warehouse was vast, its windows sealed with wooden planks. The only light came from scattered oil lamps on the ground. Qiang felt like she had entered a realm of lost souls, where despair clung to the air.

Rows of small beds were tightly aligned against the walls, separated only by flimsy screens. Ah-Long drew the screens aside, unveiling women who seemed more like apparitions than living beings, their frail bodies reduced to mere skin and bone. With each curtain that Ah-Long pulled back, Sook Ping approached the bed, tenderly placing two fingers beneath the woman's nostrils, and either solemnly shook her head for those who had passed or signaled for one of the other members to carry those who still lived out to safety.

"There are too many," Sook Ping said.

Ah-Long agreed and turned to the others. "Split into two groups. One group follow Sook Ping. One group follow me. Qiang, come with me."

Sook Ping shot Ah-Long a piercing look, but he didn't acknowledge it.

Qiang shook her head involuntarily. This was all too much. Their broken bodies, bruises, and scars were all too reminiscent of Cai, Francine, and countless others that had been lost since the occupation began.

The warehouse doors burst open with a deafening crash. Ah-Long grabbed Qiang's shoulders, pulling her into a makeshift room where a young girl cowered, tears streaming down her face.

Gunfire erupted, bullets zipping in every direction.

"Retreat!" Sook Ping's voice cut through the chaos. "Save who you can! Retreat!"

Ah-Long attempted to pull Qiang away, but she resisted and crawled back to the terrified girl, yanking down a curtain and wrapping it around her shivering form. She scooped the girl into her arms, shielding her fragile head with her hand. "We can't leave her. Come on."

Together, they fought their way to the rear of the warehouse, smashing through a window and leaping out across the tracks. With the girl in her arms, Qiang sprinted for her life, bullets whizzing past her. One round struck a tree trunk just inches away, disorienting her, but she pressed on. She had to.

•

Safely back at base, members gathered the women into the medical tent and tended to their wounds. The potent smell of herbal tonics and alcohol simmered across the camp, momentarily soothing Qiang's nerves.

She began making her way to check in on Hao when Sook Ping walked up to her, their noses almost touching.

"You're not fit to be part of this team," Sook Ping said.

Ah-Long moved to step in, undoubtedly prepared to defend Qiang once more, but this time, Qiang gestured for him to stand back. She locked eyes with Sook Ping and responded calmly, "Today was my first mission. I was not prepared for what I saw."

Sook Ping emitted a maddening laugh. "Pathetic. I'm not having you endanger us again. Brother Wu was wrong about you. You might have a good head on your shoulders, but what use is it when your legs are weaker than a newborn!"

"Are you finished?" Qiang asked, her voice steady.

"Oh, I could go on," Sook Ping sneered.

"You don't know me," Qiang said. "I've only been here a couple of months, and during that time, I have trained every day with Ah-Long. You're not giving me a chance."

Ah-Yee and Hao stepped out from their tents, drawn by the conflict. They stood by Ah-Long, observing the tense exchange.

"A chance? There are no chances here, *Young Miss,*" she said mockingly. "One wrong step, and you're dead. We all are. The Japanese don't give chances."

"You're right," Qiang conceded.

"What did you say?"

"I said you're right. So, will you teach me, then?"

"What?" Sook Ping was clearly caught off guard.

"Will you teach me to fight?" Qiang asked again. "Ah-Long has been an invaluable teacher, but he doesn't train half as much as you do. I want to be as strong as you. I am capable. You'll believe it once you give me a chance."

Sook Ping groaned. "What have I told you about chances?"

"You said the Japanese don't give second chances," Qiang said. "You're not like them, though. You're better than that. Teach me."

Sook Ping took a few steps back, disbelief etched on her face. But as Qiang remained resolute, her gaze unwavering, it became evident to everyone present that Sook Ping could only say yes.

"We begin tomorrow," Sook Ping finally said.

As the group returned to the tents, a large truck sped down the dirt road and into the camp, almost knocking into the fence.

"Brother Wu's truck." Ah-Long rushed toward the camp's entrance. "Hao," he called out. "Find Brother Song. Something isn't right."

As Brother Song made his way through the camp, Brother Wu had already disembarked from the truck, accompanied by a handful of other members. Blood trickled down his forehead, staining his face. Ah-Long provided support, guiding him into a seat Sook Ping had fetched while Qiang hurriedly approached with a damp towel to stanch the bleeding.

"Brother!" Brother Song rushed over. "What happened?"

"It's the Tai Po faction." Brother Wu grimaced as Qiang continued to clean his wound. "They've been bombed."

CHAPTER 25

Mingzhu had been called to Sato's office. Walking in, she waved away the pungent odor of whiskey and cigars.

"You're drinking too much these days," she said.

"Take a seat," Sato said, raising a glass. "Let us honor the lives lost today."

"What do you mean? They succeeded?"

Sato nodded almost imperceptibly.

"You said you would get the message out immediately! You said the Tai Po faction would be safe."

Sato took a swig of whiskey and wiped his mouth with his hand. Then, he threw the glass across the room. It hit the wall and smashed onto the floor.

"What happened?"

"We got the timeframe wrong." Sato exhaled.

"No, I know what I read," Mingzhu said. "The document in Hana's room clearly stated the attack would come in ten days."

"I trust you," Sato said.

"Then, what happened?"

"Tanaka's men apprehended a young boy, the son of a resistance member. Under torture, the boy drew a map of the entire base. Tanaka took immediate action. Our warning, at least, got most of the children out."

Mingzhu stumbled back, taking a seat. Her shaking hand gripped the chair's arm. "What will happen now?" she asked. "You were tied to them. Were any other members of the Tai Po faction taken in for questioning? Will this lead back to you? To us?"

Sato smacked his hand on the desk. "How am I supposed to know? It happened only several hours ago. You always ask so many questions. Why this, why that! I don't have the answers, damn it!"

Mingzhu's lips pursed. She had a million more questions she could've asked, but there was no point.

"All I got was this," Sato said, picking up a small note from his desk and handing it to Mingzhu.

> We have been attacked. Brother Knife has been killed.
> Survivors will head east. Await our next message.

"They are without a leader," Mingzhu said.

"Hence the reason they're heading east. I believe they will join forces with the Sai Kung faction."

"The one led by the two brothers?"

"Yes. I'm reassigning you," he said.

Mingzhu offered a curt nod.

"I'm dispatching you to the *Hong Kong News* headquarters in Kai Ham, our closest post to Sai Kung."

Kai Ham, Mingzhu thought. Wasn't that close to Middle Hill?

"I thought their headquarters were in Kowloon?" she asked.

"The Americans bombed it weeks ago. The remaining staff have relocated; they're now using an empty school as their office. As you know, the Imperial Army struggles to fill certain positions here. Many Japanese still refuse to migrate to Hong Kong. So, I've put you forward as a translator. You start tomorrow."

Mingzhu straightened her back and nodded, agreeing to the new assignment.

"I need you to open a new communication line with the Sai Kung brothers. I cannot just sit here and wait for them to reach out to me," Sato continued. "Who knows if the Tai Po survivors will even make it to Sai Kung. We must be proactive."

"How will I connect you with them, though?" Mingzhu asked.

"Find the little ghosts, and you'll find your answer."

"Little ghosts?"

"Young volunteers. They're small enough to slip through the cracks, mostly unnoticed. Messengers for the resistance."

"Children, you mean?"

"They may look like children, Mingzhu." Sato shifted in his seat. "But the war has forced them to mature beyond their years."

"How exactly am I supposed to find them?"

"You're smart," Sato said. "You'll figure it out. Besides . . ."

"Besides what?"

"I have a feeling you will find yourself in good company." Sato grabbed another glass from the table and began to fill it with whiskey. "Now, get out of here. Report to me in the morning before you leave."

The car hummed along the road, the thump of the wheels against the pavement matching the rocky beat of Mingzhu's heart. Driving her was a young officer named Rensuke Aoki. Rensuke had been assigned as Mingzhu's driver and guard by Tanaka. How Sato persuaded Tanaka to sign off on her new role eluded her. Before she left, Sato had clarified that Rensuke was loyal to the Imperial Army and Tanaka and advised Mingzhu to be cautious and alert throughout her missions.

"Rensuke-san," Mingzhu began slowly, her breath fogging the cold window. "Have you been stationed in Hong Kong for a long time?"

Rensuke looked dumbfounded, as if he hadn't expected her to address him so directly and warmly. "Not . . . not very long, no," he replied.

Mingzhu offered a small smile, glancing at him through the rearview mirror. Rensuke was a young officer whose features were both sharp and composed. He couldn't be more than twenty years old. His complexion bore the warm hue of sun-kissed skin, an indication of his time spent outdoors, no doubt, and his neatly cropped black hair framed a face that carried an air of arrogance, accentuated by the faintest hint of stubble along his jawline.

"It must be quite an adjustment, being in a foreign place," she said.

Rensuke shrugged, his fingers tapping on the steering wheel. "It's different."

"Mm . . ." Mingzhu hummed.

"Things will settle eventually," Rensuke added quickly. "The emperor is mighty. Hong Kong is bound to thrive under our rule."

Mingzhu gave him a skeptical look. It wasn't as though Hong Kong was in complete shambles before the occupation.

"I see," she replied shortly.

Sato's plan might have sounded deceptively simple, but Mingzhu understood the complexities beneath its surface. As the car continued its journey and the landscape outside shifted from tall buildings to large fields, Mingzhu thought of Qiang. The road signs began to signal their approach through Middle Hill, and her heart clenched. She was so close to Francine's village in Tseng Lan Shu. She wanted so badly to ask Rensuke to stop the car so that she could look around the village and see that Qiang and the others were safe and well—but she knew she couldn't. The last thing she wanted was for Rensuke to find out she had family. So, as the car drove on, she prayed to her ancestors and called upon them for protection. *Please let them be there. Let them be safe.*

Light streamed through the car window, warming Mingzhu's face. Her reflection beckoned from the glass. She could hardly recognize herself.

Once, her hair had flowed like a river of silk, its deep black hue dark as a moonless night. Now, it appeared lackluster, strands coarser and dimmed by the harshness of her situation. The unrelenting stress had woven wrinkles at the corners of her eyes, and the healthy glow once adorning her cheeks had surrendered to a muted pallor as if the storm of war had drained her of life.

She tore her attention from the window and refocused on the road ahead. Whoever she used to be, that woman no longer existed. Mourning her would be useless.

The school appeared smaller than Mingzhu had anticipated. Its weathered structure stood before her like a forgotten relic of brighter days. From the telltale signs of smashed windows and holes in the roof, Mingzhu understood that disaster had struck here at the onset of the occupation. The roof, a patchwork of faded tiles, jutted and curved, and the wooden shutters that framed the windows were infected with mold.

As Mingzhu approached, she noticed a steady stream of people entering and exiting the school, carrying notebooks and newspapers. Soldiers patrolled the area, their faces stern.

Rensuke gestured toward the gate.

"Thank you," Mingzhu said, her steps carrying her along the muddy path.

She passed by occupied classrooms. News workers huddled together near a small heater, their typewriters clacking and pens scribbling furiously on notepads. The urgency of their work was evident in their furrowed brows and rapid movements. Each classroom mirrored the next, a sizable Japanese flag hanging from the walls within each, casting a shadow over Mingzhu. The crimson emblem commanded attention and stood as an embodiment of the control imposed by the occupation.

Mingzhu noted the similarity between the flag and the red veil that had covered her head on her wedding day—both the color of blood, both the symbol of oppression.

Rensuke cleared his throat. "You're to meet the lead journalist. Come."

Mingzhu peeled her stare from the flag and walked to the end of the hallway where the last classroom stood. At the door, she gave a quick knock before entering.

By the window, a figure caught her attention, and for the briefest moment, her heart stilled. The sight of him transported her back to that very first encounter at the house, a memory that felt both vivid and distant. His commanding stature, dark hair, and green eyes were as captivating as ever, and she almost forgot to breathe.

Henry.

Much like at their initial meeting, Henry stood there with a book in hand, a scene that seemed almost scripted by fate. His face lit up with an infectious enthusiasm as he closed the book, and it was as if the passage of time had not dulled his spirit. The memory of that bright spark during their first meeting resonated deeply as Mingzhu looked at him, a reminder of the connection they had shared from the beginning. Excitement tugged at the seams of her composure. There was a visceral urge to call out his name—to bridge the distance between them. But the weight of reality, in the form of Rensuke Aoki, held her back.

In that fleeting moment, as Henry stood by the window, Mingzhu's heart spoke volumes that her lips dared not utter. It was a reunion of unspoken words, a silent acknowledgment of the journey they had embarked upon separately, yet together. They stood looking at each other, and a bittersweet understanding hung between them.

"You must be the newly appointed translator." Henry propped the book onto the table and strode toward her. He reached out his hand with a broad smile.

Not missing a beat, Mingzhu slid her hand into his. She didn't shake his hand the first day they met. She wasn't going to make the same mistake twice. She offered a candid smile. "I'm Mingzhu," she said.

Henry's lips quivered. "I'm Henry Beaumont. I believe we will be working quite closely together here."

"I believe so," Mingzhu said, her face lighting up. "What were you reading?"

"That?" Henry tilted his head back toward the table. "*The Tale of Genji.*"

"By Murasaki Shikibu," Mingzhu said.

"Yes."

"How do you find it?"

"It's an eye-opening read. There's much to discover as it examines the intricacies of human emotions, the complexities of relationships, and the cultural and societal dynamics of the time."

"It sounds similar to another classic I know," Mingzhu said, a beam of delight gracing her lips. She wanted to name the book aloud but knew mentioning *Dream of the Red Chamber* or any Chinese novel would be foolish.

"I know the one you speak of," Henry replied, a note of mischief coating his voice. "In fact, I much prefer that one to this."

"Me too," Mingzhu said.

Rensuke put his arms behind his back and squared his shoulders. "Mr. Beaumont. I am Rensuke Aoki. I have been assigned to accompany this woman. I will bring her in every morning at eight and return her to headquarters by seven each night."

"Rensuke." Henry offered a curt nod.

Mingzhu couldn't hold back a scowl. Rensuke spoke of her like she was but an object. Something to be taken, moved around, and returned when the time came. She bit her tongue. This was not the time to air her grievances.

"You will show this woman around, Mr. Beaumont. I will follow," Rensuke said.

"Right, yes, of course. Follow me."

As they walked out of the classroom and back into the hallway, Henry suggested Rensuke make his way to the kitchens where other officers were having breakfast.

Rensuke shook his head firmly. "I have eaten. I will stay with this woman as directed by my commander."

"This *woman* has a name," Mingzhu muttered, and Rensuke ignored her.

"Very well," Henry sighed. "This way, then."

He guided Mingzhu with an air of earnestness, and she could not hide her joy. Even in these dark times, Henry's enthusiasm prevailed. His words painted a picture of the daily life unfolding within these walls under the shadow of the Japanese occupation. Of course, he was careful with his words, aware that Rensuke was only two steps behind him.

"How many staff work here?" Mingzhu asked.

"When we first started, we had almost fifty employees."

"And now?"

"Now we have about twenty or so."

From the corner of her eye, Mingzhu caught a glimpse of a small girl peeking through a window of one of the classrooms. When she turned to face the child, the girl vanished from view. Rensuke leaned in, attempting to glimpse what had piqued Mingzhu's interest. Not wanting to draw more attention to the situation, Mingzhu promptly redirected her focus to her conversation with Henry.

"I heard the Americans bombed the original offices in Kowloon," she said, continuing to walk.

"That's right. Many were killed by the blast."

"I'm sorry to hear of any deaths," Mingzhu said. "But I am grateful you were not injured."

Henry halted, turning to her, his expression tightly controlled. She could sense that he had much to say but was restraining himself. How she wished that Rensuke wasn't present.

They soon reached the doorway of another classroom and stood there, watching workers bustling about. In the corner of the room, a group of printers operated in unison, producing sheets of black-inked paper.

"What are they printing?" Mingzhu asked.

The corners of Henry's mouth turned down. He glanced at Rensuke before saying, "As you know, *Hong Kong News* is the only English-language newspaper available in Hong Kong now. We generate stories for English speakers to read. We also ship these papers out West."

Henry was withholding more than he let on, his demeanor revealing a hidden layer of concern. She had a clear understanding of the situation within the news office. The *Hong Kong News* was a mouthpiece for the occupiers that eroded any semblance of truth or objectivity, serving as a tool for the Japanese to manipulate public perception and obscure their own atrocities. Mingzhu harbored a certain resentment toward Henry for working at such a place. Still, she recognized her lack of moral high ground.

"So, tell me, Henry," Mingzhu said. "What is it you need me to do here?"

A few days later, Mingzhu had settled into her new routine of working at the news office, assisting in translating Japanese orders and official communications into English for the staff writers to then type out and distribute. Despite her reservations about the newspaper's affiliation with the occupiers, she found solace in being so close to Henry.

While Mingzhu was engrossed in translating a media release detailing how Japanese investments brought fortune to Hong Kong, Henry approached her desk. "Where's your shadow?"

"Even shadows need to relieve themselves sometimes." Mingzhu smiled.

"I'm back," Rensuke said bluntly before taking his usual seat behind Mingzhu, and Henry's face dropped.

Another man walked into the room. "The children are here, Mr. Beaumont."

"Ah." Henry looked at his watch. "Good. Let's get the papers onto the bicycles, then."

Mingzhu looked up at the mention of children. "Could I help?" she asked.

For days, she had been trying to find a way to get close enough to Henry to confide in him. She trusted him, and she knew her best chance of finding out which children to approach was through him. The only problem was Rensuke.

"I was hoping you'd ask," Henry said with a cheery smile. "Come, let's head outside."

Mingzhu followed Henry out of the building, and several other workers followed closely with stacks of freshly printed papers in their arms. Rensuke struggled to keep his usual two steps behind Mingzhu, and the other workers stumbled around as they walked.

"Why are you really here?" Henry managed to whisper.

Mingzhu glanced back at Rensuke, then turned to Henry. "I must speak with you."

"Women's lavatory. Midday," he said.

Rensuke finally caught up, sending Mingzhu and Henry into silence.

Mingzhu helped Henry and the workers hand newspapers to small children by the school's entrance. One girl stood out when she snatched a handful of papers from a boy her age and said, "You're weak. Look at me. Look at how much I carry."

Mingzhu couldn't hold back a laugh as she thought of her daughter. Qiang was just like this girl at her age—headstrong and brave. If this little girl was alive and surviving the occupation, then surely so was Qiang.

"You really are strong, aren't you?" she asked with a smile.

The girl looked at her and then looked at the Japanese uniform she was wearing. Mingzhu watched as the little girl's expression faded into fear.

She wanted to tell the little girl not to be scared of her. She tried to say that she was only wearing the uniform to survive, but a loud voice called over before she could say or do anything.

"Hao! Hurry up!"

The little girl turned to a slightly older boy and called back, "Coming!"

At midday, Mingzhu excused herself from Rensuke's presence and entered the women's lavatory. It was a small space with only two cubicles. It had begun to rain, and water had started trickling in from a small gap in the window above the sink. One of the cubicle doors was closed. She gave a gentle knock.

"It's me," she said.

The door clicked open, and Henry pulled her into the cubicle. Tightly squeezed in the space together, she thought back to when they had stood outside the *caa4 caan1 teng1*, when his arms wrapped around her waist. Her heart quickened as she caught a faint whiff of soap from his clothes. His body was a whisper from hers. She wanted to press herself against him and hold on to him tightly. The past and present seemed to blur, and she wanted to cling to the moment, a flash of intimacy amidst the chaos of the world outside.

Henry looked at her as though he had a million thoughts, his eyes searching hers. "Have I told you how good it is to see you again? After all this time?" he finally said. "I've been longing to tell you how sorry I am. For everything that happened at the house . . ."

The door opened, and Mingzhu brought a hand to Henry's lips, gently covering his mouth.

"Hurry up," Rensuke called out.

"This is the women's lavatory," Mingzhu said in anger. "Please!"

Grumbling, Rensuke left, slamming the door shut.

Mingzhu exhaled, her back muscles relaxing. As she pulled her hand from Henry's lips, he took hold of it and held onto her tightly, and she let him.

"I am so sorry, Mingzhu," he said again.

"I don't need apologies," she said, reluctantly pulling herself from his grasp. "What's done is done. We don't have time. I need your help, Henry."

"Anything," he said. "What do you need?"

"Sato sent me here. He is working with the ERC. The base in Tai Po was destroyed. I need to make contact with a little ghost. There are so many children here. Do you know who I should seek out?"

"Yes, I do," he said. "There's one—"

The door opened again. Henry quickly hopped onto the toilet so that his feet were out of sight should Rensuke look. "What's taking you so long?" Rensuke shouted.

Mingzhu wanted to open the door and slap Rensuke across the face for such insolence. She flushed the toilet and shouted back, "I'm done. Please leave so I may fix my uniform in front of a mirror."

"Fine," Rensuke said bitterly.

When he left, Henry stepped off the toilet and put his hands on her shoulders. "There is a girl, her name is Hao," Henry said. "She is with the Sai Kung base. Find her, and she will pass on any message you need."

Mingzhu felt an overwhelming urge to be close to him and instinctively wrapped her arms around his waist.

Henry held her tightly enough that she could feel the strength of his heartbeat. "I've thought about this day for so long," he said softly.

"What, us embracing in a lavatory cubicle?" She chuckled softly, then gently untangled herself from him. She saw the green eyes that had appeared in her dreams for countless nights. Leaning in, she pressed a gentle kiss to his lips. "I'm finding it hard to leave you."

Henry's touch was tender as he stroked her cheek. "I'm not going anywhere. And now that you're back in my life, I'm never letting you go again."

CHAPTER 26

Hunched low behind the weathered, corrugated walls of the factory warehouse, Biyu remained hidden from the view of the soldiers, perspiration beading on her neck. She clutched the packet of seeds tightly and awaited the arrival of the individual with whom she was scheduled to exchange the seeds for a radio.

Since Francine died, Mr. Gok had become increasingly prone to moments of forgetfulness, muttering to himself about people and events long gone. She wanted the radio to provide some semblance of stability—a return to normalcy in his life.

Footsteps approached, and Biyu tensed. A fellow worker, Geling, emerged from the shadows, clutching a battered radio in her hands.

"Here," Geling said, passing the radio to her. "Take it, quickly."

Biyu handed over the tiny bag of vegetable seeds Wong Taitai had kindly gifted her days before.

A soldier rounded the corner, his eyes narrowing at the sight of the trade.

"Stop right there!"

Geling shoved Biyu toward the officer before fleeing. Biyu's heart seized as the officer gripped her hair and pulled her close to his face. "You're about to pay a very fine price for what you have done," he spat.

The officer hauled her through the factory by her hair, the excruciating pain searing her scalp. The clamor of machinery halted as the other workers froze in horrified silence.

When they arrived at Lieutenant Nakamura's office, the officer kicked Biyu's legs and snickered as her knees came crashing to the cold, tiled floor. Nakamura stood there, reading a document.

"What is she doing here?"

The officer presented Nakamura with the diminutive radio as though offering a new toy to a parent to admire. "I caught her with this in hand. She was with another, but I didn't see her face properly. These vermin all look the same."

Biyu cursed silently at the word. How dare this officer refer to her as such? She hated the fact that she couldn't defend herself. She could do nothing but bite down on her tongue.

Nakamura motioned the officer away. "Leave us," he commanded.

"Hai!" The officer bowed.

"Wait," Nakamura said. "Find me some gold paint."

The officer looked perplexed. "Gold paint, Lieutenant?"

"That's what I said."

"Hai!" The officer bowed one more time before leaving.

"Stand up," Nakamura said, looking at Biyu.

She stood, rubbing her knees as she rose.

"What is the radio for?"

She delayed answering. What could she say to get herself out of such a predicament? The truth? A lie? Which one would save her?

"You may sit," he said, as if aware of her doubts.

"I'm fine to stand," she replied. Then, for good measure, she added a quick "Thank you."

He sucked on his teeth before taking a seat and playing around with the radio.

"You'll need a battery," he said.

Biyu hardly heard him. She was too busy trying to think of what to say. Perhaps she could tell the truth, and he would understand. She almost laughed at the thought of a Japanese man showing signs of compassion. If she lied, what would she say? The officer had already informed Nakamura that it was an evident trade he had witnessed.

He put the radio down and leaned back. "Tell me, what is the radio for?" he asked again.

"It's for my father," Biyu said. It was easier to call Mr. Gok her father. "He's listened to the radio every night for as long as I can remember. I want to give it to him so he doesn't feel isolated. I want him to hear voices from somewhere beyond . . . here."

"The stations are controlled and censored. Your father would hear nothing but Japanese news," he said.

Biyu considered his words. She knew the stations were under strict control. But what if there was one station that defied the status quo?

Nakamura picked up the radio again, opened his desk drawer, and placed it neatly inside. "This conversation is over. You may leave now."

Biyu eyed his drawer. "But—"

"Close the door on your way out," he said unapologetically.

Biyu sat across from Mr. Gok that night, a modest plate of boiled snake beans the only barrier between them. She couldn't banish the thoughts of the trade. Why did the lieutenant not reprimand her for having secured a radio? She was let off too easy.

"You're not eating," Mr. Gok said.

"Neither are you."

"No appetite."

Mr. Gok had lost a lot of weight since Francine's death. Biyu lifted two strands of beans between her chopsticks and moved them toward his mouth.

"Ahh," she said, managing a laugh.

He swatted her hand away. "I'm not a child, you silly girl!"

Undeterred, Biyu persisted, bringing her hand closer to his face again. "Come on, Father. Remember when I was little? You used to feed me like this all the time," she said, hoping that her words were fact and that Mr. Gok would surely remember such a thing.

He chuckled briefly, and then, with a grin that stretched across his gaunt face, he bit down on the beans, chewing with audible gusto.

"You were such a good child, Francine," he said.

"Of course I was," Biyu said.

"Don't be so overbearing. It's unladylike."

"We're in the middle of a war. There are no ladies here." Biyu snorted. "You see one?"

He laughed. A big belly laugh that she hadn't heard since arriving at the village. Together, they sat talking until the last strand of snake bean had been consumed.

After Mr. Gok had drifted into a deep sleep, a faint, almost imperceptible knock emanated from the courtyard. Wrapping a scarf around her neck, Biyu tiptoed outside, carefully unlatching the gate. Nestled between a rock and the swaying grass lay the radio she had attempted to acquire earlier. She picked it up and gingerly opened the back to reveal a battery inside.

She craned her neck toward the darkened path, but there was no sign of anyone. Quietly shutting the gate behind her, she pivoted toward the house. The flowers that Ah-Long planted had burst into full bloom once again. What a shame he wasn't there to admire their beauty, Biyu thought.

CHAPTER 27

Crouched behind a thicket of bushes, Qiang and Sook Ping blended into the night, dressed in black from head to toe, caps pulled low to conceal their faces. Having been pushed beyond her limits for several weeks by Sook Ping's trainings, Qiang finally received permission from Brother Wu to accompany her on a mission to scout a newly discovered comfort station. With shallow breaths, the two women peered through binoculars at an imposing structure a hundred meters away. Nam Koo Terrace loomed before them—its red brick exterior, its columns and symmetrical design, concealing the atrocities within.

Qiang adjusted the focus of her binoculars, scanning the building for any signs of movement. "There are at least six guards by the main entrance," she murmured.

"We're here to assess the parameters, nothing else," Sook Ping said.

"I know," Qiang said, refraining from bickering. What did Sook Ping think, that Qiang would simply barge in there? Continuing to survey the area, she pointed toward a side gate adjacent to the Ship Street steps. "There, that's a way in."

"Good spotting," Sook Ping said.

A flash of movement on the roof caught Qiang's gaze. "Did you see that?"

"What?"

Qiang pointed urgently. "Up there, look!"

"It's a woman," Sook Ping mumbled, aiming her binoculars at the top of the building. "What is she doing?"

Qiang peered through the binoculars again. On the rooftop stood a figure dressed in a long white tunic that fluttered in the night breeze. Strands of disheveled hair flapped around her face as she stood, her hands cradling the swell of her stomach.

"She's with child." Sook Ping's voice wavered with concern.

"No," Qiang murmured, panic in her voice. "She's going to jump. We must do something."

"What?" Sook Ping hissed. "Absolutely not. We're outnumbered."

With a swift motion, Qiang broke cover, dashing toward the building, her resolve unyielding despite Sook Ping's attempts to pull her back into hiding. She managed to get to the side steps of the building and hid low behind a wall.

Soldiers arrived in the courtyard, most of them drunk and unaware of the woman on the rooftop.

"Monsters," Qiang growled, her grip tightening around the handle of her pistol. With a quick, practiced motion, she checked the weapon's readiness.

But before she could take aim, Sook Ping grabbed her shoulder, causing her to stagger.

"Let me go!" Qiang hissed, her fingers itching to pull the trigger.

Sook Ping grabbed hold of her arm, grip firm. "This is not the way," she snapped. "We cannot allow ourselves to become one of those women there!"

Qiang hesitated, torn. She looked up at the woman again, catching her tilt her head skyward before throwing herself off the ledge.

Returning to camp, Qiang and Sook Ping trekked along the muddy paths in silence, their black boots caked with dirt. The dense vegetation of the woods masked them, and the stench of damp soil and decaying leaves, mixed with hints of distant smoke carried by the winds, signaled winter nearing again.

Besides their footsteps, the only other sound came from the occasional hoot of a brown wood owl perched high in the trees. Qiang closed her eyes briefly. She was back at the house on the Peak, sitting next to her mother in the garden. Her heart ached at such a thought, and she quickly shook the image from her mind.

A twig snapped underfoot, breaking the silence as Sook Ping lunged at Qiang and pushed her up against a tree.

"What do you think you're doing?" Qiang demanded.

"You almost blew our cover!" Sook Ping hissed.

Qiang hit her on the shoulder, breaking free from her grasp as Sook Ping had taught her. "Don't you ever push me like that again!" she shouted. "I could have taken them on! She was pregnant. She was alone! She would have been scared to death."

Covering her ears with her hands, Qiang collapsed onto the ground. She sobbed, her cries loud, her mouth gaping open as she struggled to catch her breath amidst the onslaught of emotion. "She was pregnant . . ." she repeated. The image of Cai, curled up in pain on the boat as they fled Shanghai, then dead on the floor with Jun, was vivid in her memory.

"I'm sorry," Sook Ping said quietly and crouched beside her. "Did you . . . did you know the woman?"

Qiang shook her head. "No," she said between sobs. "She reminded me of someone, that's all."

"A loved one?"

"Not at all," Qiang sniffed. "In all honesty, I quite hated her. But seeing the woman tonight, I don't know . . ."

"There, there. It's all right." Sook Ping gently patted her on the back, taking Qiang by surprise. It was the first hint of softness she had seen from Sook Ping in the months she had known her.

"I'm just *so* tired," Qiang said, taking a shuddering breath. "I'm so, so tired. How is any of this normal?"

Sook Ping lowered her gaze, seemingly unable to find the right words. "I'm tired, too."

"I just want this to end," Qiang continued. "I want this all to end. I miss my mama. I miss who I was before they came and took her away from me."

Sook Ping wiped the tears from Qiang's face with her thumbs. "I miss my family, too," she said softly. "Do you know where your mother is now?"

Qiang shook her head. "What about you? Where's your family?"

Sook Ping's lips trembled. "I wasn't home the day they invaded. I was with my father at our factory in Yuen Long. My mother and younger sister were gone by the time we returned to the house."

"Heavens." Qiang took hold of Sook Ping's hand. "What if my mama . . . what if your sister . . . what if they ended up like that woman?"

"Don't say that, Qiang. Don't even think it. You're right. None of this is normal. But don't give up. You'll find your family again one day. Just like I'll find mine."

"How can you be so certain?" The wind began to pick up speed around them, lifting leaves from the ground.

"Please." Sook Ping gave her a gentle shake. "Stop thinking like that. I need you to stay strong. I need you to be the woman I met when you first arrived at the ERC. Strong. Determined. Smart. Where is that version of you?"

"You think I'm smart?"

"Wholeheartedly."

Qiang gave a short laugh. "You know everyone back at the camp looks up to you more than they look up to me."

"That's not true. You know you have done a lot since you arrived. The people have taken a liking to you, Qiang. The children, especially, trust you a great deal."

"I suppose . . ." Qiang sniffled.

"I'm glad to be able to fight alongside you," Sook Ping said, putting an arm under Qiang to lift her back to her feet. "I may have been the one to teach you how to fight—how to survive—but you have taught me that we don't have to feel so alone. That we are just two women, in a sea of men, fighting for something that might change the course of this war. You taught me that what we do here *matters*. That was all you."

"I wish we could save everyone," Qiang whispered, noting this was the first time she was having such a heartfelt conversation with Sook Ping. Could it be that she was finally warming to her after all these weeks of training together?

"Believe me, there's nothing I wish more than that, too." Sook Ping tugged on her arm. "Come on, get up. Wipe the tears away. Don't ever let the men see you cry. You cry once in front of them, they'll never respect you again. And that's if they even respected you to begin with."

"You're absolutely right," Qiang said.

Sook Ping laughed. "I'm always right. Come on, let's get moving. Men may have started this war, but let's ensure that women help to end it."

That night, as she lay awake in her tent, Qiang wondered what life would have been like if Japan had never invaded. If, alongside her mother and Biyu, she was still living at the house on the Peak. She wondered what university she would have eventually enrolled at, what she would have studied, and who she would have become.

Taking a steady breath, she sought to calm her nerves. The gentle snoring of Hao next to her brought her comfort. Her life wasn't over yet. There remained a glimmer of hope, a chance to manifest those dormant dreams—all she needed was to stay strong. And so, with her mother in mind, she closed her eyes and fell into a deep sleep for the first time since arriving at the ERC.

CHAPTER 28

Cold winds slapped against the Japanese flags adorning the newspaper office's main entry. Mingzhu tightened her gloves, her legs trembling in the chill. She had arrived early, eager to intercept the children who came to pick up newspapers. Hao, who Henry had identified as the little ghost she needed, turned out to be the girl Mingzhu had thought a bore a resemblance to Qiang.

She stood beside a hefty brick column, using it as a barrier against the wind, and waited patiently. But then, Rensuke turned up.

"I thought you were having breakfast with the other soldiers," Mingzhu said, concealing her irritation.

"I'm a quick eater," Rensuke replied. "Why are you out here?"

"Headache," she fibbed. "Needed some fresh air."

Rensuke clasped his hands behind him and took a position close to her, his gaze locked on her movements. A small group of vendors began their setups along the roadside. Since the occupation began, Hong Kong's streets had grown largely desolate, except for a few retail stores and teahouses.

A rickshaw halted at the entrance, and Henry alighted. "Good morning," he greeted, brushing past Mingzhu to enter the building. His hand grazed hers as he passed, sending a flutter through her stomach. She diverted her gaze to the main street, hoping Rensuke hadn't caught the exchange. He didn't appear to.

The main door creaked open. A few workers emerged, their arms loaded with stacks of freshly printed newspapers. In the harsh morning light, the headlines caught Mingzhu's eye while the sharp scent of fresh ink invaded her senses. It was a smell she disliked, as it brought back memories of her husband at the dining hall of the Tang residence, perpetually buried behind the *South China Morning Post,* distant and preoccupied.

Soon, the children began turning up on their bicycles in a line. The workers started distributing the newspapers, efficiently packing them into the children's satchels and baskets. Their routine was well practiced, a daily ritual that spoke of their contribution to keeping the city's pulse alive, even as its heart was constrained by the occupation.

Mingzhu spotted Hao amidst the activity and knew she had to approach her. Briskly rubbing her hands together, she closed the distance between them, with Rensuke trailing close behind, focused. Mingzhu pretended to survey the nearby vendors. Finally reaching Hao, Mingzhu addressed her in Chinese, "Look at all these papers . . . how do you manage to carry them all?"

Hao, who had previously been fearful of Mingzhu, visibly relaxed as she responded in their shared language. Pausing in her task of loading papers onto the front basket of her bicycle, Hao remarked, "Your Chinese is really good."

Grinning, Mingzhu replied, "That's because I am Chinese."

Hao glanced at Mingzhu's uniform and asked, "But you work for them?"

Mingzhu nodded, but before she could say more, Rensuke intervened, placing a hand between them. "Return inside immediately and get to your work," he commanded.

Mingzhu's urgency grew. She needed to speak to Hao to convey a message to the ERC. Just then, a window on the second floor opened, and Henry's voice rang out. "Rensuke! You have a telephone call!"

"Me?" Rensuke looked puzzled.

"Yes!" Henry bellowed. "Does the name Tanaka ring any bells?"

Without hesitation, Rensuke left abruptly, heading back into the office and leaving Mingzhu alone with the children. She exchanged a grateful glance with Henry and mouthed *Thank you.* Seizing the opportunity, she crouched down to Hao's level. "Listen to me. Do not be afraid. Your name is Hao, right?"

Hao nodded, unsure.

"I need you to get today's paper to someone at the ERC. I know you have connections there."

Hao hesitated, shuffling nervously.

"You're a little ghost, aren't you?" Mingzhu whispered, trying to reassure her.

Hao shook her head aggressively. "Me? No," she said, scratching her head.

Mingzhu reached out, placing a gentle hand on the girl's elbow. "Even though I'm dressed like this, I'm Chinese. I'm not one of *them*. I can help you."

"I don't know," Hao mumbled, returning to loading papers onto her bicycle.

"Please," Mingzhu begged. "Just make sure this paper gets to your boss. Read the poem inside."

Two officers appeared before she could say more, urging the children to disperse. Mingzhu watched anxiously as Hao rode off, praying that her message would reach the ERC.

When Mingzhu returned to her desk in the office, there was no sign of Rensuke. She glanced around for Henry, only to learn he was entrenched in afternoon meetings. As the sun began its descent and the printers fell silent, Henry finally approached her desk.

"Have you seen Rensuke?" she asked.

"Come with me," Henry urged, motioning for her to follow, as he walked through the office, bidding farewell to workers with a nod and a smile as they left for the day.

Soon, they arrived at the kitchens. Poking her head inside, Mingzhu spotted several soldiers indulging in drinks and card games. Rensuke, sprawled in a chair with legs propped on the table, emitted snores accompanied by drool trickling from the corner of his mouth.

"What happened to him?" she whispered.

Henry leaned in, his voice hushed as he murmured into her ear, "Perhaps he indulged a bit too much?"

Suppressing a laugh, she turned to him. "What did you do?"

"I suspect there must have been some form of sedative in his water. Who knows?" Henry replied nonchalantly.

Another chuckle escaped her. "We could get in trouble for this," she cautioned.

"Look," he gestured toward the table, where empty bottles of imported beer lay scattered around Rensuke's feet.

"I admit, you have set the stage well."

"Forget Rensuke. I have something to show you."

In Henry's office, Mingzhu leaned casually against a cluttered mahogany desk, where papers and a sleek typewriter competed for space. The scent of leather wafted from the nearby chair, offering her a sense of warmth.

"What is it you wish to show me?" she inquired. Reaching into a cupboard, Henry retrieved a small gramophone, and she gasped with delight. "Where did you find this?"

"I stumbled upon it several streets away," he replied, placing the gramophone gently on his desk. "Shall we listen to it together?"

Mingzhu nodded.

"Hmm, it doesn't seem to be working," Henry said, giving the gramophone a light tap.

"You don't have to look that disheartened," she said softly.

"I had hoped we could . . . we could . . ."

"Dance?"

"Yes," Henry confirmed, moving closer to Mingzhu. He brushed a strand of hair from her face and tucked it behind her ear. "I've wanted to dance with you since the first day we met."

"The first day?"

"Yes," he said. "Since you walked into the library back at the house. I remember everything about you from that first meeting, Mingzhu."

She blushed, not knowing where to look.

Henry continued, "I remember your green *qípáo,* jade bracelet, brocade shoes. I even remember how your hair was pinned."

She took a step closer to him. "What else do you remember?"

Henry smiled. "I remember how your eyes lit up when you spoke about literature. How you sat on the edge of your seat, telling me of all the books and poems you wanted to share with me. And then, I remember seeing you at the dance hall at the hotel. I remember seeing you dancing with your husband. I remember how jealous I was."

She laughed. "Weren't you busy dancing with someone else? I'm surprised you noticed me there at all."

"I notice you in every room, Mingzhu," Henry said, his voice serious. "I especially notice when you're not there."

Mingzhu's pulse skipped. "Come, let's dance. We don't need music."

With that, she ran her hands along his arms, savoring the sensation. She guided his hands to her waist and placed her own behind his neck, drawing them close together. Mingzhu hummed a soft tune, and they swayed, wrapped up in each other's hold. Her cheek grazed Henry's jaw, igniting a flood of emotions within her. Within those four walls, safely in his arms, she pushed the thought of war aside.

"I've been thinking," Henry began, his voice barely above a whisper.

Mingzhu continued humming, leaning into him.

"I want you to return to England with me," Henry confessed. "When the war is over. Will you come with me?"

Mingzhu pulled back slightly, meeting his gaze. "Are the trees in England as green as your eyes?" she teased.

"Even greener," Henry affirmed.

"I must see for myself."

"Is that a yes? Will you come with me?"

Mingzhu didn't look away from him, and a smile played on her lips. At that moment, she thought only of herself. Despite wanting to find Qiang and Biyu again, this moment was not about them. For once, she wanted to be a little selfish. She answered, "When the war ends, I'll go anywhere with you, Henry Beaumont."

Henry's smile widened as he leaned in, pressing his lips against hers. There, for the first time in her life, Mingzhu finally knew what it meant to be in love.

CHAPTER 29

After enduring another exhausting shift at the factory, Biyu traipsed back into Tseng Lan Shu. Her stomach churned, reminding her she hadn't eaten since she had left the house almost fifteen hours earlier. She wasn't hungry, though. She had reached a point where her starvation had turned into an emptiness devoid of feeling. Buried in her pocket was a small tube of antiseptic ointment she had procured from a fellow factory worker. Her thoughts lingered on Mr. Gok, who had fallen ill with a severe rash on his hands and arms, accompanied by a fever.

Above her, the stars glimmered, as if they had come together to tell a story through dance—a performance just for her. Absentmindedly, Biyu touched the butterfly pendant dangling from her neck. Since Qiang joined Ah-Long in Sai Kung, Biyu had received messages via little ghosts every few weeks. With the pendant in her grasp, she sent a prayer into the night for the well-being of Qiang, and especially Mingzhu.

As she passed Wong Taitai's house, she saw her peering through the gate.

"Biyu?"

Biyu greeted her with a gentle nod. "What brings you out so late?"

"I've been waiting for you."

"What's the matter? Is it Mr. Gok?" Biyu cast a quick look into Mr. Gok's courtyard.

"He's fine. But I wanted to tell you I know what made him sick."

Intrigued, Biyu stepped off the path into Wong Taitai's courtyard. "What?" she asked.

Wong Taitai gestured behind her. "Do you know the row of abandoned houses over there?"

"Yes, I'm familiar with them."

"They're completely overrun with *fēngxìnzǐ*. With the recent cold weather, they've blossomed abundantly," she said. "Such adaptable plants, they are!"

Biyu drew in an uneasy breath. She vaguely recalled seeing hyacinths dotted around the village. "Do you think they have something to do with Mr. Gok's rash?" she asked.

"Yes! While they're beautiful, their bulbs are quite poisonous. I spotted Mr. Gok wandering around there a few days ago. He must have touched them!"

"*Fēngxìnzǐ,*" Biyu murmured. Something abnormal took hold in the pit of her stomach. An intention. A bad one. "You say there are many of them?"

"That area is completely overrun with them," Wong Taitai affirmed. "You must keep him away from there."

"Of course." Biyu nodded determinedly. "I will. Thank you, Wong Taitai."

As Biyu gently applied ointment to Mr. Gok's hands, her gaze followed his to the vacant corner of the living room where his wife's tablet had once rested.

"My wife," he murmured. "I miss my wife."

"I know you do," Biyu whispered.

"Do you have someone you love, Francine?"

Biyu didn't correct him. She hadn't corrected him for a while now. "I love Qiang, and Mingzhu—"

He interrupted her with a dismissive swat. "No, no, no. I mean the love that touches the heart. Have you ever experienced that kind of love?"

Deciding to sidestep his probing question, she continued applying cream to his blisters.

Once, many years ago, back in Shanghai, she had harbored feelings for another. It was the year Mingzhu had married into the Tang family. Shortly thereafter, visitors arrived from Tianjin, a city in the northeast of China. Among the visitors was a young man named Chen Yongnian. He was the son of a wealthy merchant and a cousin to Wei. He immediately took a liking to Biyu, and the feeling was mutual. Throughout his stay, Biyu found herself meeting him often, silently observing water lilies drifting in the courtyard pond together. They exchanged few words, as they hailed from vastly different worlds—he from privilege, she from servitude. When Yongnian eventually departed, Biyu never saw him again. At the time, such a love hadn't been worth the transgression, and she had let him fade into the back of her mind.

After Mr. Gok had drifted off to sleep, Biyu quietly exited his room and perched on a small stool beside Francine's grave in the courtyard. She recalled the day Francine had bravely leaped in to rescue her. She couldn't shake the thought that had begun to brew in her stomach earlier when she was with Wong Taitai. All those years ago, Biyu had willingly suppressed her desires, choosing duty over personal longing. However, now, under the occupation, she felt something new stirring within her—a desire to defy, to rebel. Serving the Yue family, the Tang family, and Mingzhu had always been an honor, but being forced to serve the Japanese was a different matter entirely. For the first time since the war began, she questioned the path she had been following. If Qiang was brave enough to join the ERC, then surely she could do something, too.

Biyu knelt beside the overgrown patch of hyacinths with a trowel clutched tightly in her hand, the wet soil staining the cotton of her trousers. She hesitated momentarily, her mind racing with the risks of her actions. Carefully, she began to dig, her movements slow and deliberate as she pulled the plants from the damp earth. Each root tugged free sent a surge of adrenaline coursing through her veins. Once she had collected a sufficient amount, she retreated to the safety of Mr. Gok's house. She set to work with trembling hands, grinding the hyacinth bulbs with a mortar and pestle.

The following day, Biyu sat at her station in the factory, sweat sticking to her palms. She was scared, but she tried to push those feelings away. What she was about to do was risky, but the prospect of striking back against her oppressors in such a way fueled her. Even if her actions affected only a few, it would still be meaningful. And, for Biyu, that was reason enough to proceed.

When the usual soldiers who roamed the factory decided to take a break and stand near the exit, talking and smoking away, Biyu knew this was her chance. She carefully pulled a small sachet from her trouser pocket and covertly sprinkled the powdered hyacinth bulbs she had prepared the night before into the linings of the uniforms she was stitching together.

She continued to do this until there was no powder left. That night, she fell asleep with a smile on her face.

CHAPTER 30

While taking stock of a carbine box with Ah-Long, Qiang felt a pang of envy toward Sook Ping, who was out on yet another mission. Since Nam Koo Terrace, she hadn't been put forward. Had Sook Ping said something to Brother Wu? Did she tell him of her breaking down? Surely not. Qiang remembered clearly how Sook Ping had said she was glad to be able to fight alongside her.

"Is something wrong?" Ah-Long asked, waving a hand in front of her face.

"I'm fine," she said.

"Are you sure? If you're tired, I can finish up here."

A grunt escaped from Qiang's mouth. In truth, she wasn't in the mood to discuss her thoughts or emotions, especially not with Ah-Long, who had been incessantly checking in on her well-being throughout the day. He cared, and she was grateful. But at the same time, she felt suffocated by his constant presence. He was always hovering over her.

"Qiang!" Hao ran into the tent with a copy of *Hong Kong News*.

"Get that awful thing out of my sight," Qiang said.

Hao smiled at Ah-Long. "Oh, good. You're here. Ah-Yee is looking for you." When he excused himself and left, she turned back to Qiang. "Where's Brother Wu, Brother Song? They didn't come back last night," she said, scratching her head.

"Hao, do you have lice again?" Qiang asked. "Come closer. Let me have a look." She ran her fingers through Hao's greasy hair, inspecting her scalp closely. "No lice. Thank heavens."

"Where's Brother Wu? Brother Song?" Hao asked again.

"They'll be back soon," Qiang said, concealing the painful reality. She couldn't bring herself to reveal the truth to Hao—how, in the past few days, additional women saved from various comfort stations had succumbed to despair and killed themselves. Brother Wu made sure none of the children were informed of what had happened, and together with Brother Song had taken the deceased to a nearby hill to be buried.

Hao pushed the newspaper into Qiang's grasp. "You must read this. There's a message for us inside," she said urgently.

Qiang flicked through the pages. Every headline she came across sent a stream of rage through her veins.

STRICTER CURFEWS ENFORCED FOR HONG KONG CIVILIAN SAFETY.

HONG KONG CIVILIANS CONTINUE TO THANK JAPANESE LIBERATORS.

HOW JAPANESE INVESTMENTS TRANSFORM HONG KONG.

"Lies upon lies!" she spat.

Hao tugged on her sleeve. "Look at the last page."

"What is it I'm supposed to be looking for?"

"Here . . ." Hao pointed to the bottom left corner where a haiku had been typed out.

Silent shadows meet,
Willow whispers in the night,
Fragrant hearts seek open light.

"Who told you to bring this here?" Qiang asked.

"A woman at the news office. She came to me today. She asked if I was a little ghost. I said, 'No missy, I am not a little ghost,' but then she told me not to be scared. She said she wants to speak with the boss. She said she wants to help."

Qiang scrunched the paper under her arm and crouched to meet Hao's eyes. "You have to be careful, Hao. This could be a trap. Did you tell the woman anything else about us?"

Hao shook her head. "She has nice eyes like you, Qiang. She dresses like a Japanese man but when she saw the Japanese men walk past, she was scared, like us."

Qiang sighed. What woman didn't fear the sight of a Japanese man under such circumstances? Nevertheless, the message had been delivered. She would try to decipher the haiku's meaning before Brother Wu returned. She wanted to prove she was capable of more than managing the stock.

A few hours later, Brother Wu examined the haiku, reading it aloud a few times. Brother Song read it only once before dropping into his chair, putting his feet on the table, and groaning from exhaustion.

"I think I've worked out its meaning," Qiang said confidently. Brother Song raised a brow, and she bit the inside of her cheek. Was he mocking her? She couldn't tell.

"Come closer," Brother Wu said to Qiang. "Tell me what you think."

Qiang ran her finger along the lines of the haiku.

"*Silent shadows meet,*" she said. "I believe this refers to two people or groups forming a connection based on mutual circumstance. The people or group intends to remain unnoticed."

"I can see that," Brother Wu said.

"*Willow whispers in the night,*" Qiang continued. "I think that's a location. I think it's here."

"Here?" Brother Song asked. "Why here?"

"Look around," she gestured outside the tent. "We're completely surrounded by willow trees. No other place in Hong Kong looks like this."

"What about the last line, then?" Brother Wu asked, rubbing a bruise that had formed on his elbow.

"*Fragrant hearts* must refer to us, to the people of Hong Kong. After all, Hong Kong literally translates to *fragrant harbor*. I think this haiku was written by someone who means to open a line of communication with us here, to work together in saving Hong Kong from the Japanese."

"You got all that from a haiku?" Brother Song asked. This time, he was definitely mocking her.

Qiang had had enough of his bitterness. She crossed her arms and looked him in the eyes. "When I was growing up, my mama read me many poems. English, Chinese, haikus . . . She used to spend hours talking with me, trying to interpret the writer's intent. If any of us can critically analyze this message, I believe it is me."

"The writer," Brother Wu interjected. He took the paper and looked at it again. "There is no name beneath the poem. Merely a stain."

"Show me," Qiang said.

Brother Wu laid the paper flat on his desk again and pointed to a tiny smudge beneath the word *light*.

Qiang quickly pulled open one of Brother Wu's desk drawers and began poking around until she found a hand loupe. She unfolded the loupe and slipped her index finger into the opening opposite the glass. Bringing it close to her face, she pressed the knuckle of her thumb firmly against her cheek. With the glass directly over her eye, she squinted. There, four tiny letters appeared.

OWPK.

Qiang looked up. "What does *OWPK* mean?"

Brother Wu took the loupe from her and had a look for himself while Brother Song wrote down the letters on a piece of paper. "You're smart, Qiang, I'll give you that," he said. "But this further proves you're unsuitable for the resistance."

"What does that mean?" Qiang bit back.

Brother Wu lowered the loupe and sat down. "Stop it, Brother. You're too hard on her."

"And you're too lenient." Brother Song exhaled. He looked at Qiang until he finally gave in and showed her the letters he had written. "It's called a Caesar cipher. Ever heard of it?"

Qiang shook her head, angered that Brother Song knew something she did not.

"The Caesar cipher is how we communicate with our allies. If this was intended for us, as Hao and you believe it to be, then we should be able to get a name from decoding it."

"How do you decode it?"

"We have an agreed letter shift. For every letter provided from the English alphabet, we shift four spaces forward."

Qiang took the pen from Brother Song. She could see that he was impressed by her enthusiasm.

"What does it say?" Brother Wu asked.

"Sato," Qiang said. "The name is Sato. A Japanese name."

Brother Song scratched his chin. "Isn't that the name one of the Tai Po members had told us about?"

"It is, indeed," Brother Wu said. "Where did you say Hao got this?"

"A woman from the news office told her to bring it to us," she replied.

"We'll send Hao back with a response tomorrow. If it is the man the Tai Po members have spoken of, we will have gained another ally."

"If not?" she asked.

"We still have little agency in this war, Qiang." Brother Song said. "Risks are to be taken. Remember that."

The loud clatter of pots and pans drummed across the network of tents. The cooking area had expanded to cater to the camp's growth since Tai Po survivors had migrated to Sai Kung. Simple campfires had given way to constructed hearths, their flames blinking intensely.

On the training grounds, Qiang had slowly become a force to be reckoned with, much like the storm's fury that stretched across the sky. The anger that once fueled her had evolved into a fervent dedication to the cause. Her heart was ablaze with certainty, and her relentless training routine spoke volumes of her unwavering resolve.

Sook Ping stood before her, feet locked to the soil, her arms stretched out in a striking position. She sprung her knife toward Qiang. "Again," she said. "You're getting better but still lacking in defense."

"I'm trying my best!" Qiang called through the pouring rain. The smell of wet earth filled her lungs, making her chest feel heavy.

Qiang and Sook Ping danced between strikes and parries, their blades sparking against each other. Each raindrop mingled with the sweat that their intensive training had produced. Qiang blocked Sook Ping's attack, her focus intense.

"Better!" Sook Ping shouted. "Again!"

Qiang gracefully stepped back before launching into another strike. As they sparred, their every movement seemed like a choreographed sequence. A measured strike from Sook Ping was met with an equally agile parry from Qiang. Sook Ping's strikes bore the precision of a seasoned fighter. In contrast, Qiang's movements carried the grace of evolution, reflecting her journey from a place of anger to one of purpose.

Hao interrupted their match, shouting from Brother Wu's tent. "Qiang! Sook Ping! Brother Wu is calling you!"

With staggered breath, Qiang pushed the knife into the leather pouch wrapped around her waist. "Coming!" she called back.

Alongside Sook Ping, she made her way across the damp earth, her boots sinking into the mud with every step. Inside the tent, Brother Wu sat in his usual wooden chair. His eyes met hers—his expression a blend of urgency and gravity. Brother Song sat hunched over a map, tracing pathways and routes with his finger.

Qiang greeted the brothers with a firm nod.

Brother Song returned the gesture while Brother Wu chucked her and Sook Ping a towel each.

"Qiang," Brother Wu began. "Brother Song and I are heading south on a weapons mission. Sato has given us information on a new shipment due in the morning. We've decided—"

"*You* have decided," Brother Song corrected.

"All right, *I* have decided to have you oversee the camp's management while Brother Song and I are on this mission. As Sook Ping will be joining us, you're the next in line to take on such a responsibility."

"Will Ah-Long be joining us too?" Sook Ping asked.

"Absolutely," Brother Wu said. "We need as much muscle as possible. This will be our first weapons mission in a while."

Qiang felt slighted. She didn't want to stay at the camp. She wanted to go on the mission, too. "Why can't I come?"

Brother Wu pushed himself from his chair and walked over to

Qiang. He patted her on the shoulder. "From what happened at your mission with Sook Ping, I know you are not ready. You still have much to learn when it comes to maintaining composure."

Qiang shot Sook Ping a frustrated look. "You told him what happened?"

"They asked, and I'm not one to lie." Sook Ping shrugged.

"Quiet, the both of you," Brother Song said. "Bickering women. What an earache."

"Brother Wu," Qiang said. "Let me come. I can help. Trust me."

"I do trust you," he replied. "That's why I'm leaving the camp under your care. Sook Ping tells me the people here trust you. The children look up to you, the elderly enjoy your company, and even most men listen to you when you speak. I have witnessed this, too."

"You said all that?" Qiang eyed Sook Ping.

"I told you, I don't lie about these things." Sook Ping smiled.

Brother Wu continued, "Besides, this is the first weapons mission we're going on since the Tai Po faction was bombed. Even though Brother Song and I are leading the mission, we are still learning, too."

Qiang considered her position. That Brother Wu trusted her to such an extent was a sign of respect, and she didn't want to disappoint him. She would do as he asked.

"I have a question," she said.

"Go on." Brother Wu smiled.

"Now that we are taking on the Tai Po faction's agenda, what will happen to ours?"

"You mean civilian rescues?" Sook Ping interjected.

"And the comfort stations," Qiang said. "There are still so many more. What will happen to the women?"

Brother Wu dropped his gaze. "Our priorities have shifted," he said. "The civilians . . . the women . . ."

"They're not our problem right now," Sook Ping answered bluntly, as though she didn't care, but her glistening eyes betrayed her. "The more weapons we stop from reaching Japanese hands, the sooner we can bring this occupation to an end."

"Sook Ping is right," Brother Song said. "There is nothing we can do for the women now. I'm sorry, Qiang. I know how invested you were in those missions."

Qiang couldn't help but notice Brother Song's sudden shift in demeanor. It marked the first instance since her arrival that he spoke to her with genuine softness. Despite his sudden kindness, Qiang couldn't stop wondering about the lives of the women she had yet to save. Was there nothing she could do?

Qiang assumed the role of acting camp leader with dedication. During the absence of Brother Wu, Brother Song, Sook Ping, and Ah-Long, she diligently made her rounds to visit every tent, ensuring the well-being of all women and children. She assisted those in need, whether it involved laundry, cooking, or sewing. She also attended to anyone needing medical attention and escorted them to the clinic.

Qiang reviewed the inventory checklist at the clinic, marking off depleted supplies such as bandages, alcohol, or stitching kits. In the afternoons, she supervised the Red Cross trucks delivering essential items, and for anything they couldn't procure through official channels, she dispatched little ghosts to nearby markets.

That night, she maintained a watchful eye over the fighters stationed around the camp perimeter. She couldn't afford to sleep soundly, fully aware that the lives of everyone on base were now on her shoulders. Although the situation was vastly different, she couldn't help but think of her mother, who had always overseen the house back at Victoria Peak. How had Mingzhu managed to bear the responsibility for every person within those walls?

When the members eventually returned the following morning, Qiang wanted to weep with relief. The mission had been a success, and six large containers of weapons had returned to the base with the members, with much of the rest destroyed. Hao had been sent back to the news office to relay the message to Sato.

While helping Sook Ping and Ah-Long move the weapons into one of the smaller tents, Qiang sensed an uncomfortable silence that hung in the air. Her comrades weren't even looking at one another. Did they fight again? They frequently argued, but something about this felt different.

"We've got quite the collection here," Qiang remarked, trying to ease the tension.

"Mm," Sook Ping grunted. "It went well."

"A successful mission, then." Qiang retrieved a small knife and held it out as if preparing to attack.

Ah-Long reached out, gently correcting her grip. "Steadier. Like this."

Sook Ping scoffed, rolling her eyes.

Qiang pulled away. "I can do it. I don't need help."

"I see you don't need my protection anymore," Ah-Long said. His tone was calm, but something else flashed in his eyes. Almost like disappointment.

"That's not—" Qiang began, but Sook Ping's sharp interruption cut her off.

"Stop being so overbearing. You're like an annoying brother."

Ah-Long's jaw tightened and his ears flushed. "I'm not her brother."

Sook Ping's mouth puckered into a suppressed grin. "Mm-hmm."

"You always say such inappropriate things, Sook Ping."

"I do? When?"

"All the time!" Ah-Long retorted. "You're always finding opportunities to mock me."

"At least you notice me," Sook Ping mumbled, and surprise flared through Qiang.

"What did you say?" Ah-Long leaned forward, staring at her.

"Nothing," Sook Ping said loudly, glaring at him.

Qiang didn't know where to look. She thought back to a few weeks earlier, when they had all gathered to celebrate a minor victory. Sook Ping had made a rare attempt at cooking, a task she usually avoided. The dish turned out decent, but Qiang remembered Sook Ping serving Ah-Long personally and watching him closely as he tasted the food. At the time, Qiang had thought Sook Ping was merely seeking validation for her cooking. It was only now that she realized there was probably a deeper meaning behind the attention. Should she say something? Or was it better to stay quiet and let them navigate their own feelings? Sighing inwardly, she shifted her attention back to the weapons scattered around and avoided eye contact with them both, determined not to get caught in the crossfire of their friction.

"You really know how to get on my nerves, Sook Ping," Ah-Long finally said.

"You don't think you get on mine?" she argued.

Without answering, Ah-Long let out a scoff and exited the tent.

"Idiot," Sook Ping muttered under her breath, and Qiang bit back a smile. She wouldn't meet Qiang's eyes as she turned to her. "What are you doing? There's no need to take stock of the smaller pieces."

Qiang paused, pistol in hand. "Why not?"

"I'll be distributing them to the little ghosts stationed in Black Hill."

"Black Hill? Don't you have to pass through Middle Hill to reach there?"

"It's the safest route," Sook Ping confirmed.

"I'll accompany you," Qiang said. "There's someone I must see."

CHAPTER 31

Waiting in Sato's office for his return, Mingzhu counted out the contents of her purse. It was all military yen. She was back in the city, and Sato had welcomed her with a modest sum in case of an emergency. In her entire life, there had been only one other occasion when she had possessed money she could call her own.

The first occurred when she was ten years old. At that time, she had desperately wanted to purchase a gift for Biyu, but her mother adamantly refused, asserting that servants were not meant to be indulged. Instead, Mingzhu struck a deal with her father, offering to assist him in transcribing court documents from Chinese to English, and he would pay her one silver coin per document. It wasn't that her father couldn't do the task himself, but she knew he would never say no to her. Especially if it involved writing. Once Mingzhu had collected three silver coins, she used the money to purchase a butterfly pendant for her closest friend.

Since then, any money she possessed always belonged to someone else. Until now. Despite her circumstances, she couldn't help but contemplate the possibility of a future beyond the occupation. She realized that her skills were in high demand and that she was valuable because of her capabilities. For a moment, she allowed herself to imagine a life where she wouldn't be someone's wife. A life where she would secure a job, earn her own income, and attain her own property.

The door opened, and Sato charged in with an optimistic expression. Mingzhu quickly stuffed the purse back into her trouser pocket.

"You're smiling," Mingzhu said. "Why?"

Sato gave a belly laugh and crashed into his seat. He poured a glass of whiskey and downed it before answering. "Guess where I have come from just now?"

"Where?" she asked.

"*Bah,* you're no fun at all," Sato said. "Tanaka called me into the weekly meeting. He invited me back personally."

"He did?"

"Sit down. Do you not get tired from standing all the time?" He waved at a chair opposite him. "You should have seen his face. This morning, he said my insights would be most useful to the other captains."

Sitting, she placed her hands on her knees. "What came of this meeting?"

"Tanaka was a straight shooter today. All plans, no chitchat. He's plotting another attack on a resistance base. We can warn them, Mingzhu."

"Which one?"

Sato huffed. "Well, that's the only thing he didn't disclose. But we know there are only two main camps left. Sha Tin and Sai Kung. Knowing Tanaka, he'll want to gut out the strongest first."

"Sai Kung has the most members," Mingzhu said. "They recently infiltrated one of Tanaka's shipments."

Sato shook his head. "He was furious. The soldiers on duty that day have been sentenced to death. Poor men."

Mingzhu didn't quite share his sentiments. "Will there be another shipment coming in?" she asked.

Sato poured another glass of whiskey. "Three days from now. Here." He pulled a piece of paper from his pocket. "Get this typed into a haiku in tomorrow's paper. Along with a warning of a coming attack."

"Am I to tell them we know nothing more about the attack?"

"There's not much more we can do now, Mingzhu. Hopefully, we will know more soon."

Mingzhu reached across the desk and retrieved the note. She scanned it quickly.

200 pieces
Route: Tokyo › South China Sea › Sham Shui Po
Transport: Kamikaze Maru
Expected Arrival: November 15.

A loud thud rattled the door, and Mingzhu stood to attention. When the door opened, Tanaka entered, followed by Rensuke. Mingzhu scrunched the note into her hand and bowed.

Tanaka gave a slight laugh. "This secretary of yours, Captain. Impeccable manners. So well trained." He had always been brash, but he had become even more unbearable since the talk of his impending governorship.

Sato laughed back awkwardly as he stood and offered a bow, too.

Tanaka looked around, his hands clasped behind his back. "We ought to get you a bigger office, Captain. You can move up two floors, be closer to me," he said.

"I would be honored." Sato gestured to the bottle. "Drink?"

Tanaka rejected the offer. He took a seat and squinted at Mingzhu's hand. "You look anxious," he said.

Mingzhu gave a stiff shake of her head.

"General," Sato said, drawing Tanaka's attention back to him. "What brings you here?"

"I'm taking some precautions over the next couple of weeks. Rensuke will continue to protect your secretary."

Mingzhu's jaw locked.

"That is . . . welcome news . . . I suppose," Sato said.

"As for you," Tanaka continued, leaning forward. "As you're important to me, I have assigned two of my finest officers to act as your security detail from now on."

Mingzhu composed herself so Tanaka would not see her distress.

"Two officers," Sato repeated. "That's hardly necessary. I mean, I don't really travel. My place is here."

"Well," Tanaka said wickedly. "You can't travel now anyway. Did you not hear?"

Mingzhu's ears perked.

"Hear what?" Sato asked.

"I issued a lockdown an hour ago. No one is to leave headquarters without my permission. It's merely a safety protocol. Nothing to be concerned about," he said, looking over at Mingzhu's clasped hands again. When their eyes met, he gave her a nasty smile.

"For how long will the lockdown last, General?" Mingzhu asked. Her head began to hurt but she refrained from reaching to her temples and rubbing them. "I'm due to return to the news office."

"That's not happening today," Tanaka said.

"General," Sato said, trying his luck. "When will the lockdown be lifted?"

Tanaka shrugged. "Could be tomorrow, could be the next day. Don't worry. Your place is here. Isn't that right?"

Sato stumbled over his words. "Well, yes. Right. But two officers. Is that necessary?"

"This isn't a discussion. It is an order," Tanaka said. He gradually stood and made his way toward the door, and Rensuke ran to open it. He turned to Mingzhu and Sato, a smile spread across his face. "Enjoy your evening," he said.

Immediately after he left, two officers swarmed in, greeted Sato with a bow, and proceeded to station themselves on either side of his desk. Sato cast Mingzhu with a look of desperation. There was nothing she could do to help him. At that moment, she didn't even know how to help herself.

"The document I need translated," Sato began, clearly referring to their interrupted discussion. "Will you be able to complete the task here at headquarters?"

"I will try my best, Captain."

With that, she left his office, Rensuke following closely behind. She had to figure out how to get the information to the ERC. But how? More important, she had to do something about the note in her hand. When Rensuke bent down to tighten his laces, she scrunched the piece of paper into her mouth and swallowed it.

Rensuke followed Mingzhu everywhere. For hours, she almost lost all hope in trying to get the message out to the resistance. Ever since the sedation incident at the news office, Rensuke had been on full alert. But when he finally excused himself to go to the lavatory, she knew this was her chance. She ran from her room, down the hall, and into the nurse's office. It was empty. She went straight to the telephone and began dialing the number to Lieutenant Nakamura's office at the factory in Middle Hill.

The line cracked, and Hiroshi's voice came through. Mingzhu sighed, relieved. But she had no time to waste. She knew the telephone lines were likely to be tapped. She would have to be mindful of her words.

"Listen to me," she said. "I have two messages for the children of the land."

"I'm listening," Hiroshi replied.

Mingzhu closed her eyes, imagining the note Sato had given her back at his office. She could see the weapons shipment information forming in her memory. "Two hundred unseen. Kamikaze's gift, night's dream. Fifteen western winds."

"I got it," Hiroshi said. "What's the other message?"

"There will be—" She stopped at the sound of footsteps approaching outside the room. There was no time to think of a coded message. "Base attack coming," she whispered and slammed the receiver back into place.

Glancing around rapidly, her eyes landed on a pair of scissors. She seized them and cut her palm open. As blood splattered onto her uniform and the floor, she hurriedly wrapped her hand with a handkerchief and hid the scissors in a drawer. Just as she finished, the door opened to reveal Rensuke, wearing a severe expression.

"What are you doing here?" he hissed.

"I hurt myself," Mingzhu replied, gesturing with her injured hand for emphasis.

"How?"

"I was trying to open the window back in my room," Mingzhu began, her voice faltering. She could feel her legs wobbling slightly. "It was stuck. I scraped my hand on the metal frame."

Rensuke's eye twitched. He ordered Mingzhu to return to her room and remain there for the rest of the night. Thankfully, Rensuke was just as ignorant as she had predicted. She spent the rest of the night awake, hoping with every part of herself that Hiroshi had heard her message.

CHAPTER 32

In the kitchen, frost began to form on the windows. Winter was drawing to a close, yet the temperatures remained low. Biyu and Mr. Gok sat on small stools, huddled around the brick stove where a modest fire crackled. She handed him a roasted yam. "Eat," she insisted. "It's hot, be careful."

"*Faan1 syu4, faan1 syu4, faan1 syu4,*" he stuttered. Yam, yam, yam.

"I've added salt today." Biyu smiled. "It should taste better than yesterday. Give it a try."

"I want to eat something green," Mr. Gok mumbled.

Biyu cast a rueful look outside toward the small vegetable patch. With factory work and the extra care and attention required for Mr. Gok, the snake beans that Ah-Long had planted remained neglected for months. "Eat the yam," she said again.

He took a hesitant bite of the vegetable, and the steam billowed from his mouth, mingling with the chill air. His health was rapidly deteriorating, and the Imperial Army had mandated his departure from the farm, leaving him dependent on Biyu's ration card, which could hardly sustain them. Throughout the day, Mr. Gok slept, only getting up in the evening to sit beside Francine's grave in the courtyard, wondering who lay there.

Some days, he forgot about the ongoing occupation entirely, but when reality resurfaced, he would descend into fits of rage, hurling objects around the house. For a while, Biyu worked extra shifts at the factory to earn additional points for rice and vegetables. But when Mr. Gok's health declined further, she remained by his side most of the day to prevent him from acting impulsively. Biyu still carried the sting of guilt from Francine's murder. She had made a solemn vow to herself to stay by Mr. Gok's side and look after him—a promise she couldn't easily break. And she didn't want to. Her affection for him had grown deep, akin to a father-daughter bond, a feeling she hadn't experienced since her days in Shanghai with Mingzhu's father, Master Yue, who had once briefly acknowledged her with a pat on the head and a rare word of praise.

"Finished," Mr. Gok said, wiping his mouth with the back of his hand.

Biyu assisted him from the stool and led him back to his room, where she helped him get into bed.

"Radio," Mr. Gok said.

"How about we don't listen to the radio tonight?" she suggested.

"Radio," he said again.

She sighed and reached for the small radio on his bedside table. "Only music tonight. Nothing else."

"Fine."

Biyu adjusted the dial until a woman's voice emanated from the speaker. Before she left for the resistance, Qiang had said that the radio exclusively broadcast patriotic Japanese songs. Still, Biyu believed it was acceptable for Mr. Gok to listen, considering he couldn't understand the lyrics. He could simply enjoy the melody and drift off to sleep.

As the song played, Biyu removed his slippers and helped him to put on a new pair of socks. She saw the calloused skin of a man who had toiled relentlessly for many years. The lumps and veins around his ankles proved he never knew the meaning of rest.

When he finally closed his eyes and fell into a deep sleep, Biyu went out to the abandoned houses, braving the cold, and began pulling out another batch of hyacinths. The chill of the earth numbed her hands, but the faint warmth emanating from the oil lamp provided some comfort. Since she had succeeded in her experiment, rumors began circulating around the factory about how guards stationed in a nearby village had succumbed to severe rashes and fallen ill. Apart from Biyu, no one knew the cause. Now that she understood the pain it inflicted on the soldiers, she was determined not to give up. Even if the hyacinths stopped growing, she would find another way to make her enemies suffer. With a fresh bunch of flowers and the trowel in hand, she made her way back into Mr. Gok's courtyard. Suddenly, a slight movement on the other side of the gate caught her attention. Alert, she clutched the small trowel. A shadow cast itself on the gate, and she raised her arm, preparing herself for what lay beyond.

"Who's there?"

"Biyu?" a voice called.

Biyu dropped the trowel, letting it clatter to the ground. Was she dreaming?

"Biyu?" the voice came through again.

Following the sounds of rustling over the courtyard wall, Biyu glimpsed the figure of a person climbing over and leaping into the courtyard. It was Qiang.

"Biyu!" Qiang ran to her and embraced her tightly.

Biyu wrapped her arms around Qiang and patted the back of her head. "Young Miss," she sobbed. She ushered Qiang into the house, noting how mud slathered her face to blend in with the landscape, and how her once slender, almost silk-like hands were now calloused and rough. She looked wild, more like a warrior of the forest than an aristocrat's daughter.

"Your hands," Biyu said, worried. How would she explain this to Mingzhu?

"Don't worry about that. I can't stay for long," Qiang said quickly. "I'm just passing through."

"Do you need water? Are you hungry?" Biyu started walking toward the kitchen but was pulled back by Qiang. "We have yams," she added.

Qiang shook her head, smiling. She pulled a small package from her pocket and handed it to Biyu. "They're extra ration point cards. You can use them at the market to get more food."

Biyu took them and tried not to sob.

"Biyu, listen to me," Qiang said. "This is very important."

"Tell me, Young Miss. I'm listening."

"I can't send any more little ghosts to you over the next few weeks. The Japanese have been kidnapping them and torturing them for information. We don't want to risk their lives for our cause any more than we need to. These ration cards should get you and Mr. Gok through in the meantime. Where is Mr. Gok?"

Biyu gestured to his bedroom door, where the sound of a Japanese singer's voice continued to flow from within. "I'm caring for him the best I can."

"Are you certain you can't return to the base with me, Biyu?"

Biyu held Qiang's hands. "Young Miss," she began. "I cannot even explain how proud of you I am. Look at the strong woman you have become! But no, I cannot come with you. Mr. Gok's health is getting worse. I don't want to burden the resistance members with our presence. Besides, Mr. Gok has clarified that he won't leave his home. Who am I to sway his thoughts otherwise?"

Qiang told her she understood the hardships and guilt Biyu faced. "Then stay safe, Biyu. I don't know how long this occupation will last, but I promise to do my part and fight for freedom."

"I don't doubt you will, Young Miss." Biyu smiled.

"I should go, then."

"Wait." Biyu took a small bundle from the dining table and handed it to Qiang. "Your mama's book. It's only right that you have it."

Qiang took the bundle, her lips quivering. "Thank you, Biyu. Mama will be glad to know we have kept this safe."

"Your mama is the strongest woman I know. She's alive. I can feel it."

"I feel it too," Qiang said, pulling Biyu into one last hug.

From the gate, Biyu watched as Qiang snuck off the path and into the forest. All the while, she held on to her butterfly pendant, whispering to the evening winds. *Where are you, First Madame? Where are you?*

CHAPTER 33

A few nights later, when the rain had stopped and the air had settled, Qiang wrapped a woolen shawl over her shoulders and sat outside her tent next to a small fire. She held her mother's copy of *Dream of the Red Chamber* in her hands, pretending for a moment that the book was her mother's hand instead. Pieces of paper poked out from the pages, and she opened the book to find a small stack of letters. She recognized the handwriting immediately.

Madame Tang, Qiang takes after your intelligence and wit. It is clear to me you have raised and loved her well. Sincerely, H.

Madame Tang, you're right. Li Qingzhao's poem "To the Tune of Lamentation" is breathtaking. In the last sentence, she writes: Trying to bring back the lost time. What do you make of such an ending? Will you share your thoughts with me? Sincerely, H.

Mingzhu, I hope you were not startled by the minor accident and that the burn on your hand has recovered. Sincerely, H.

Mingzhu, I eagerly await our next meeting. Sincerely, H.

Mingzhu, meet me at dawn in the library tomorrow. I have a poem I wish to share with you. Sincerely, H.

Overwhelmed by the revelation of the letters' contents, Qiang quickly tucked them back into the book. Despite her burning curiosity, she reminded herself that it wasn't her place to read anyone's private letters. But that didn't stop the questions from flooding her mind. Since when had Henry addressed her mother by her first name? When had their letter exchange commenced? And, lingering like an unspoken truth, was there a deeper connection hinted at within those pages, or was it merely her imagination?

"Qiang," Hao shouted. "Brother Wu is calling for you!"

"Coming!" Qiang stored the book back inside the tent, under her pillow, and made her way to the camp's entrance, where Brother Wu stood guard with several others.

"You called for me?" Qiang asked, rubbing her hands together for warmth.

"We've lost another two little ghosts to the Japanese," he said. The dark circles around his eyes were almost black in the moonlight. "Hao only just managed to get herself back here safely."

"They're too young to fight this war," Qiang said, wrapping an arm around Hao's shoulders and pulling her to her side.

Hao's face was reddened by the unforgiving winter winds and her eyes were wide and alert. Qiang felt sorry for her, for all the children suffering under the frightening conditions of the occupation. They should be free, playing in the countryside, giggling without a care, and weaving dreams for their future. They shouldn't carry the burdens of war, hiding in the shadow of fear.

"It's lucky Hao got back to us. One of Sato's men delivered a message to her," Brother Wu said. "Hao has never seen this man before."

"What's the message?"

Brother Wu sighed. "Hao didn't get the whole message from him. Soldiers began raiding the *Hong Kong News* office. Hao managed to get out safely because Sato's man helped her. He told her to send someone to meet him near Middle Hill."

A low mumble vibrated as several ERC members began talking among themselves. Some quickly raised their hands to offer themselves for the mission. *I can do it,* they said one after the other.

"If I might interject." Qiang stepped forward. "I worked at a factory near Middle Hill. I've been back there since, and I know the surroundings well."

Brother Wu contemplated her interruption. Then he nodded, his decision clear. "Very well. The mission is yours," he said. "Come, let's talk in my tent."

Qiang and Hao followed him inside, where the subtle scent of cedarwood welcomed them. When the other ERC members outside made their way back to their respective tents and were out of earshot, Brother Wu began talking. "There's an abandoned clinic in Tai Nam U, just outside Middle Hill."

"I know the one. I have walked past it many times," Qiang said confidently. This was it. This was the moment she had been waiting for, to finally be trusted enough to take on a solo mission. "When do I leave?"

Brother Wu leaned forward slightly, a rare trace of concern in his stern demeanor. "This won't be easy, Qiang. The Imperial Army has bolstered its grip around several borders. You must get in and out of there as quickly as possible."

"I understand," she affirmed.

Brother Wu picked a yellow ribbon from his jacket pocket. "Wear this in your hair. This contact will know to look for it."

Qiang took the ribbon from him, and Hao stroked it with a finger.

"If the contact finds you suspicious, he will ask you for a confirmation word," Brother Wu lowered his voice. "The word is *bauhinia blakeana*."

"*Bauhinia blakeana,*" Qiang parroted.

"You leave at first light," Brother Wu said. "You'll dress as a Red Cross volunteer. Sook Ping will drive the truck and wait for you to complete the assignment."

At that moment, Brother Song appeared. "You're sending her?"

"She can do this—" "I can do this—" Brother Wu and Qiang said in unison.

Brother Song placed his hands on his hips. "Fine. While you're there, see if there's anything worth taking from the clinic. We're low on supplies again."

"Absolutely not," Brother Wu said. "The mission is simple. Retrieve information, that's it."

"I can do it," Qiang interjected.

"I said no. Stick to the mission. Is that understood?"

Qiang bit down on her tongue and cocked her head, neither agreeing nor disagreeing with Brother Wu's direct order.

Ah-Long intercepted Qiang before she could hop into the truck, where Sook Ping waited in the driver's seat with the window down. His hair was damp with humidity, and his expression was strained.

"Are you sure you're ready for this?" he asked.

Sook Ping snorted.

"Yes, I am," Qiang replied firmly. "I know Middle Hill better than anyone. Stop worrying."

"I can't help it." Ah-Long placed a hand on her shoulder. "Wait here. I will tell Brother Wu that I wish to come with you."

Qiang held him back by the elbow. "I told you, Ah-Long," she said, her voice slightly raised, "I can handle it. Besides, you have your own assignment to focus on."

Sook Ping slammed down on the car horn. Qiang gave Ah-Long a quick smack on the arm. "I'll be fine. I'll see you in a few hours."

Qiang wanted to ask Sook Ping about the tension she'd noticed between her and Ah-Long, but as the truck roared to life and the rain-drenched camp slowly receded from view, her nerves about the mission ahead drowned out everything else. Her fingers instinctively touched the yellow ribbon in her hair.

"You'll be fine," Sook Ping said, echoing Qiang's own words, her eyes on the road ahead. "Remember everything we've gone over. Get in, get out. That's the mission." She cast Qiang a glance. "You better come back to us safe and sound, you hear?"

Qiang nodded. Sook Ping had become more than just her trainer and fellow fighter—she had been a quiet source of strength and camaraderie for quite some time now. Calm washed over her, and the bond between them warmed her soul.

Wires and signs hung off the blown-up concrete inside the clinic on the second floor. Qiang intended to meet the contact on the third floor, but a medicine cabinet caught her attention. She couldn't resist checking it out for any supplies. She pictured Brother Song's surprised yet pleasant expression as she returned with such goods. Perhaps she would finally win him over. Carefully, she walked over debris until she crossed the large ward and opened the cabinet. She threw anything she could grab into the small bag neatly clasped across her shoulders. Two empty bottles fell, rattling to the ground, and she froze. Sweat dripped down her back as shadows crept along the halls just past the entryway. Didn't Brother Wu say that the hospital was abandoned? Perhaps some civilians had sought shelter here. Looters, even?

As the shadows enlarged and boots stomping through the hallways grew louder, Qiang dropped to the ground on her hands and knees and huddled between a concrete slab and a bed, listening intently as two Japanese soldiers shouted back and forth to each other. When they finally passed the ward, she moved toward a door in the far corner and exited into a narrow stairway. Bricks and debris obstructed access up and down the floors. A small window had been shattered, and glass littered the ground. Accessing the third floor from here was impossible. She would have to return the way she came or leap out of the window and find another route.

Not wanting to encounter the two soldiers from earlier, she pushed herself onto the ledge, her legs trembling as she mustered the courage to jump. She heard her mother's soft voice steadying her.

You have a long life ahead of you.

Exhaling slowly, she leaped onto a mound of rubble, and a large metal shard sliced into her knee. Her body twisted, and a suppressed scream of agony escaped her lips. Blood coursed down her leg, saturating her cotton trousers. She scrambled to rise as swiftly as her legs would allow, but when the cold edge of a sword landed on her neck, she froze.

"Turn around," a man's voice ordered.

Slowly, Qiang turned until her eyes met with two Japanese soldiers. The one holding the sword to her neck was thinner than she was, and the one beside him was an older man who looked weary, as if in great discomfort. When the thin soldier saw her face, he smiled.

"A pretty one," he said. "It must be my lucky day."

Qiang's throat constricted as blood continued to gush from her wound, the flesh around her knee pulsating. She could take one of the soldiers, but injured, she wasn't sure if she could battle both at once. A movement from the window she had jumped out of caught her attention. Was she seeing things, or was someone standing there?

"Let's take her inside," the thin soldier said to the other. "She's far too pretty to waste."

The older soldier shuddered in disgust, scratching his neck. "This uniform is itchy as hell," he muttered, shifting uncomfortably. "She's all yours. I don't deal with Chinese women."

It took everything for Qiang not to strike him in the face. Whatever she was going to do to defend herself, she was better off returning inside the hospital with one of them first. She could fight one and then come back for this monster afterward.

"Fine, wait here for me, then." The thin soldier grabbed Qiang by the wrists and yanked her back inside.

Behind closed doors, the soldier tried to push Qiang onto a bed, but she resisted, standing firm. "Lie down!" he barked.

Qiang winced, her knee throbbing with pain, causing her leg to shake slightly. Her head was starting to feel light. Just how much blood had she lost? She met the soldier's glower with defiance and spat, "You must be deluded."

The soldier stared at her in surprise. "What did you say?"

Qiang lunged at him while pulling out a concealed dagger and stabbed him in the stomach.

The soldier screeched in pain and struck her with a heavy blow to the face, and pain exploded in her jaw. Qiang stumbled back, her knee giving out, and she fell to the floor. Blood pooled in her mouth, and she spat it out. With a hand clasped to his stomach, the soldier grabbed at her neck and pulled her to her feet. Without hesitation, she stabbed him again, putting her entire weight behind the thrust. The knife entered the soldier's stomach through his hand, and he let out another scream of pain and rage.

"You bitch!" he roared. He tumbled back, knocking over a metal trolley, sending clashing echoes down the halls. He reached for his pistol but was too slow as Qiang disarmed him, just as Sook Ping had taught her many times before. She pointed the gun to his head.

"Don't move," she ordered.

The soldier laughed. "Go on. What are you waiting for?"

Brother Wu's words buzzed in her ears. *If we need you to kill, will you?*

Qiang didn't know what to do. Her finger was on the trigger. She was ready, yet somehow, she felt hesitation consume her. She had practiced over a hundred times with Sook Ping. But seeing a real living human before her instead of the usual makeshift straw figures back on the base was different.

"Do it!" the soldier yelled again. His hands covered his stomach, and his body trembled.

Qiang shuffled, putting most of her weight onto the leg that wasn't injured. Loud footsteps approached the door, and the soldier let out another laugh, knowing his comrade was moments away.

The door crashed open, and the soldier who had been waiting outside stood before her with a gun pointed at her face. Qiang swung her gun toward him, and just as she was about to pull the trigger, a sword plunged into the soldier from behind. She gasped as he fell to his knees, revealing a face she recognized behind him.

Hiroshi Nakamura.

"You," she said, her voice shaking.

Hiroshi stepped over the soldier and wielded his sword at her. "Kill him," he ordered.

Qiang's knee finally gave way again, and she fell onto the floor.

"Kill him, or he will surely kill you," Hiroshi said. "Don't waste my time."

In pain, Qiang raised the pistol to the soldier again. Sweat dripped from her temples. She pulled the trigger and watched as the bullet pierced the soldier's chest and he collapsed, eyes glassy and unseeing.

Hiroshi approached her cautiously, his eyes drawn to the crimson stains on her trousers. He reached out to lift the fabric, but Qiang instinctively slapped his hand away.

"Don't touch me," she said.

Hiroshi pressed a finger to his lips, the distant sounds of marching feet outside amplifying the urgency of their situation.

"Lower your voice," he murmured, guiding her to sit on the bed. "Show me your wound."

She smacked his hand away again. "I said I'm fine. Let me go."

"Let you go?" Hiroshi appeared bewildered. "You're free to leave anytime, Qiang. Just let me help you first."

At the sound of her name, her heart skipped a beat. "You do remember me," she said.

"I do," Hiroshi answered.

He knelt in front of her and rolled up her trousers, causing Qiang to wince as he exposed the gash on her knee. He searched the room until he found a suture kit, which was empty save for a needle. Without delay, he tore off three buttons from his jacket and unraveled the threads, forming a makeshift suture. He began stitching Qiang's wound.

"Ow!" Qiang's knee jerked.

"This is all I have. I'm sorry," he said, focusing on her injury.

She was confused by the surreal moment—an injured Chinese resistance fighter being tended to by a Japanese lieutenant. Why was he helping her?

"Why what?" Hiroshi asked.

Qiang blinked, startled that she had spoken out loud. "Why are you helping me? What do you want?"

"Just let me finish this, then I'll tell you," Hiroshi replied.

Qiang couldn't shake the fear that this might be a trap. Was he helping her only to take her back to the factory as a hostage?

Once she was stitched up and the last traces of blood had been wiped from her leg, Hiroshi looked up at her tenderly, a thread of burden in his eyes. He took hold of the yellow ribbon holding her hair in place and, with a fluid motion, pulled it free. Her hair spilled across her shoulders, and she narrowed her eyes as Hiroshi held the ribbon between them.

"You're the one I've been looking for," he said.

"I don't know what you're talking about," she replied.

"The confirmation. Do you know it? Tell me, and I'll give you what you came here for."

"How can I trust you?"

The sounds of footsteps outside grew louder again. "We don't have much time. The code consists of two words. I'll say the first one, and if you can tell me the second, I'll give you the information Brother Wu seeks."

Qiang relaxed her shoulders at the mention of Brother Wu's name. "I accept those terms," she said.

"Bauhinia . . ."

Qiang swallowed hard. "Blakeana," she replied.

Hiroshi released a breath. "I'm glad they sent you. I have often wondered how you have been since that night."

"What you do mean, since that night?"

He ignored her question and pulled a brown envelope from his jacket pocket. He handed it to Qiang and told her to hold on to it safely.

"I asked you something," she said.

Hiroshi avoided her inquiring stare. "Let's just say I'm glad you're with Brother Wu and the others. You'll be safe there."

The last four words hit her like a sudden monsoon downpour amidst a scorching summer, washing away the dust of uncertainty she had up until then.

You'll be safe there. I promise.

"It was you," Qiang said, dumbfounded. "You're the reason I ended up at the resistance base."

"I couldn't let you attempt to kill that officer at the factory, Qiang. You had no skills. You would've been killed."

"Are you even Japanese?" Qiang asked.

"You like to ask questions, don't you?"

"Is that a problem?"

Hiroshi let out a small laugh. She caught sight of his dimples deepening and was momentarily swept back to the night she had met him before the war, the gold paint on his hands.

"You can ask as many questions as you like."

"So, are you Japanese, then?"

"My father was Japanese," Hiroshi replied.

"And your mother?"

"Chinese. From Shanghai."

"My mother is from Shanghai too," Qiang shared.

"My father was sent back to Japan during the battle of Shanghai. My mother . . ." Hiroshi's voice trailed off.

"What happened to her?"

"She was taken by the Imperial Army alongside my sister. They were sent to become comfort women. They died from starvation."

Qiang's eyes stung.

"Please," Hiroshi said, catching her tear with her thumb.

Qiang started at his touch and pulled away, wiping her face with the back of her hand. "Tell me, what message do you bring?"

"The first message is that there will be an attack on a base. I don't know when or where. That's all the informant said before the line went dead."

Qiang frowned. She did not want to convey this message to Brother Wu.

"The second message is a haiku," Hiroshi said. "I've read it many times, and something doesn't feel right."

Qiang cocked her head. "What do you mean?" she asked. She opened the brown envelope and retrieved a small note Hiroshi had written.

Two hundred unseen.
Kamikaze's gift, night's dream.
Fifteen western winds.

"Two hundred unseen," Qiang read aloud. "This is the number of weapons that are due to arrive?"

"Yes, I understood that line to be the same."

"I presume *Kamikaze* is the ship? *Night's dream* means the shipment will be arriving at nightfall?"

"Midnight, I believe," he said. "That's when most of the world is in a deep sleep. When dreams come to us."

"Fifteen western winds," Qiang said. She brought her hand to her mouth. "Fifteen is the date of arrival? Western winds . . . What does that mean?"

Hiroshi sat beside her on the bed. "That's the location. It's Sham Shui Po Pier. It's west of Hong Kong."

"This all makes sense, then." Qiang turned to him. Her shoulder brushed his arm, and Hiroshi promptly got back to his feet, his face reddening.

"Something doesn't feel right," he said.

"What do you mean? What doesn't feel right?"

Hiroshi pointed at the last line. "Japan has never sent weapons shipments to Sham Shui Po. It takes longer, and it's also closer to the Allied forces' line of sight. Why have they decided to dock here this time?"

"I . . . I wouldn't know," Qiang said. "I'll make sure to tell Brother Wu of your concerns. But, if you think about it, would it be so strange for them to change locations? After we infiltrated their shipment at Tai Koo dock, they're probably being cautious, don't you think?"

Thunder erupted outside, rattling the clinic's walls. "You should leave. If the tracks get too wet, you'll have trouble returning to base in this cold weather."

Qiang got to her feet. She had forgotten about her knee and the pain while she spoke with Hiroshi. When she put her weight on her injured leg, she fell forward into his arms.

"I'm sorry," she said, pushing herself from him.

Hiroshi cleared his throat, but no words came out. Instead, he walked across the room and peered outside the door. He gestured for her to follow him.

"Stay alert," Hiroshi said, his hand brushing against Qiang's waist as they moved out.

Back in the truck beside Sook Ping, Qiang kept her eyes fixed on her knee. She clutched the brown envelope as though her life depended on it. Her hands trembled slightly, and she struggled to steady her breathing. The impact of what had just happened pressed down on her, the image of the soldier's lifeless eyes haunting her mind.

Sook Ping reached out and placed a comforting hand on Qiang's arm. "You did what you had to," she said softly. "It's never easy, but it's . . . necessary sometimes."

Qiang stared at her muddied shoes. Memories of the night she had first met Hiroshi came flooding back, like the bright colors of a painted scroll unrolling before her. She recalled the dimly lit courtyard of the police station, the crafted kite, the towering banyan tree, and the sad cry of a little girl who had linked their destinies.

In the past, Qiang had sat in a vehicle, staring at her muddied shoes, lost in thoughts of Hiroshi. Today, under vastly different circumstances, she found herself doing the same. If her shoes were stained with mud the next time, would she meet him again?

CHAPTER 34

In the softly lit confines of the small bathroom, a single lamp cast a gentle flame, warding off the lingering remnants of winter's chill that lurked outside. Inside, the steam from the hot water smothered the air, surrounding the space in warmth. Biyu perched on a small plastic stool beside the bathtub, her elbow casually resting on its edge. Mr. Gok reclined in the tub, the shallow water barely covering his legs.

"Louder," he demanded, pointing to the radio by the windowsill, dripping water onto Biyu's slippers.

"It's loud enough," she replied. "Any louder and we will get into trouble."

"Trouble?"

The radio sputtered and crackled, and the song that had been playing stopped. Mr. Gok's ears pushed back as a voice erupted from the speakers.

Newly appointed governor-general of Hong Kong, General Hisakazu Tanaka promises to continue the good work on the emperor's behalf, making Hong Kong a land of opportunity for all Asian citizens.

Biyu snorted loudly and shook her head. She reached over to turn the radio off but Mr. Gok stayed her arm, his eyes clouded with confusion.

"Tanaka?" Mr. Gok murmured, resting a hand on the side of the tub. "That is a Japanese name."

Biyu turned the radio off and took hold of his trembling hand.

"Father," she began, as she always did, "we are in occupied Hong Kong, remember? The Japanese have taken over."

Mr. Gok clamped his mouth shut, the wrinkles around it deepening.

"Come on," Biyu said. "Let's get you out and dry, shall we? I got snake beans for us from the market. You said you wanted to eat something green, remember?"

"Something green," he repeated.

Her concern deepened as she helped him into a pair of trousers and a fresh shirt. The implications of a new governor-general worried her. What rules would this man impose? Would he reduce the rations even further? Would he change the curfew? What about the random arrests of civilians on the street? What would he do in response to that? Every time a new leader had come into power, they had promised a brighter future. They swore they were here to assist, but all Biyu had witnessed were people committing acts of violence and torture against innocent people. Biyu thought of Mingzhu, recalling her role as the first wife in the Tang family. Mingzhu had always prioritized the wants and needs of everyone and ensured the safety of those under her care. Surely, women would make better leaders than men, Biyu thought. Whether or not that was something she'd witness in her lifetime was debatable.

When Biyu helped Mr. Gok into bed, he stroked her head with a smile. "Silly, silly girl," he said. "My silly, silly, Francine."

It was clear his memory was faltering rapidly. Lost for what to do, Biyu switched the radio back on, and a soft melody filtered through the speaker as she sat beside him until they both fell asleep.

The morning sun brushed the sky with strips of orange reminiscent of turmeric as Biyu stood in the kitchen, heating water to prepare breakfast for Mr. Gok. She waved a bamboo fan to puff the fire. Just as the water began to simmer, the quiet was abruptly shattered by several gunshots.

Startled, she knocked the saucepan over, and scalding water splashed onto her feet, which luckily were protected by thick boots.

She quickly grabbed the saucepan from the floor with a towel, placed it into the sink, and ran toward Mr. Gok's room.

When she entered, the room was empty. Panic surged through her veins as she darted out and checked the bathroom. But her worst fears were realized when she reached the courtyard.

Beyond the partially opened gate, a grim scene unfolded before her eyes. Japanese soldiers had formed a line of villagers and people Biyu had never seen before. Their rifles pointed at a few of them. Her throat constricted in fear as she spotted Mr. Gok standing barefoot behind a gnarled tree. The ice on the ground was making him shiver, but he stood there, resolute.

"Mr. Gok!" she gasped, gesturing urgently for him to return to her side. He didn't respond, so she called out again a little louder. "Father!"

"Biyu!" Wong Taitai's voice pierced through the wall between their houses.

Biyu turned to a small gap in the wall and gripped Wong Taitai's hand. "Mr. Gok's out there. What should I do?"

"Stay quiet," Wong Taitai urged. "You have seen what they do to women. Keep your head down."

The stench of anxious sweat from Biyu's pits made her nauseous as another round of shots were fired, and a scream was heard from a few houses down. Wong Taitai moved her hand onto Biyu's wrist and tightened her grip.

"Monsters!" Mr. Gok bellowed, emerging from behind the tree.

"No, no, no!" Biyu called out. She jerked toward him but was pulled back roughly by Wong Taitai.

"Biyu, look at me," Wong Taitai pleaded. "Don't look out there. Just look at me."

Biyu refused.

"You must all die today!" Mr. Gok yelled.

Biyu watched in horror as he stomped toward the soldiers who had their rifles aimed high.

"Look at me, Biyu!" Wong Taitai begged again.

Hot tears ran down her neck as she turned to face Wong Taitai, shutting her eyes tight, knowing she couldn't witness what came next.

When another round of shots was fired, followed by the thump of a body falling to the ground, Biyu slumped to her knees. Wong Taitai held fast to her wrist, not letting go. An eerie silence fell across the village path, the only sounds coming from Biyu as she sobbed uncontrollably. "Mr. Gok . . ." she wailed, gasping for air. "Mr. Gok . . ."

CHAPTER 35

The moon hung low, casting shadows across the paved streets of Sham Shui Po. Dressed in the tailored uniforms of the Imperial Army, Qiang, Ah-Long, and Brother Wu blended seamlessly into the obscurity that cloaked the nighttime city. Soft whispers escaped their lips as they exchanged hurried conversations, their coats rustling. Only half of the forty-six members assembled for their covert mission had successfully obtained the coveted Imperial Army uniforms.

Standing near a lamppost, its dim light only just touching their silhouettes, the trio awaited the crucial moment. Soon, they would have to signal to the others concealed within the narrow alleys.

"Tell me again, Qiang," Brother Wu said. "What is our mission?"

Qiang bent over to tighten the bandage around her knee. "Ambush. Attack. Attain the goods."

"Good," he replied.

Qiang thought of the intricacies of their plan over and over again in her head. Yesterday, alongside Brother Wu and Ah-Long, she had painstakingly dissected the pier's layout, familiarizing herself with every pathway and concealed nook. She had passed on Hiroshi's concerns to Brother Wu and Brother Song, but both men had said what Qiang also believed—that the Japanese had chosen to disembark weapons at a different location due to their earlier success at Tai Koo dock.

A ship's horn blared into the night. When the vessel finally docked, a troop of Japanese soldiers began unloading the rifles. Qiang pressed two fingers to her lips—a sharp whistle sounded into the air, and their comrades emerged from the shadows, armed with weapons they had procured from a previous mission. The night exploded into pandemonium as the resistance fighters descended upon the Japanese soldiers guarding the cargo.

Amid the chaos of battle, Qiang maintained her focus. She and Ah-Long set their sights on the supply crates, where the invaluable cache of weapons lay concealed. They worked silently as they moved toward their target, planting explosive charges and disabling enemy vehicles. Every so often, Qiang would fend off a soldier, firing her pistol without hesitation this time.

Nearby, Brother Wu was surrounded by three soldiers, who were closing in on him. Qiang shot one of them, and he seized the opportunity to disarm one of the other soldiers with a swift motion and, stolen sword in hand, moved with calculated steps, parrying the third soldier and cutting his throat with precision.

"Get to the crates!" Brother Wu yelled.

"Come on, Ah-Long!" Qiang reloaded her pistol and cleared the path toward the weapons, shooting with accuracy at every encounter.

"Something isn't right!" Ah-Long shouted. "There are too many Japanese!"

A soldier restrained Qiang from behind. She elbowed him in the stomach and punched him in the nose. When he tumbled backward, she shot him in the chest and continued making her way toward the crates, but Ah-Long was right. Japanese soldiers were pouring from all sides of the pier.

Arriving at the crates, she hastily removed the wooden planks, paying no heed to the painful splinters that embedded themselves in her hands. They were empty.

"It's a trap!" Qiang shouted. She grabbed Ah-Long's arm and pulled him behind a car. Bullets pelted the vehicle. "They're closing in on us. We need to get our people out of here."

Ah-Long took hold of her hand, and they sprinted back from the pier. Qiang fired her weapon at every Japanese soldier she spotted, but the murky confusion of battle made it impossible to distinguish between friend and enemy. Resistance fighters caught in the crossfire also fell—some collapsing to the ground while others plunged into the cold harbor waters. When she saw another female fighter get shot, she rushed to help, but Ah-Long pulled her back, shouting, "We must go!"

Qiang struggled against his grip, her legs trembling with despair. The wounded woman fell to her knees and slowly closed her eyes, her arm outstretched toward Qiang.

"Argh!" Ah-Long groaned, collapsing to the ground and taking Qiang down with him. He clutched his lower abdomen in agony. He had taken a bullet.

"No!" Qiang knelt beside him, her hands pressing firmly against his wound, desperately trying to stem the bleeding.

Another gunshot rang out, narrowly missing the back of Qiang's head. She spun around to see an enemy soldier approaching, rifle in hand. She fumbled to retrieve the pistol she had dropped, the blood on her hands making it slip from her grasp. As the soldier prepared to fire at her, Qiang squinted as moonlight splashed across the blade of a sword. In one motion, the soldier's head was cleanly sliced from his neck and rolled to the ground. The body crumpled, and Qiang saw Hiroshi standing before her, sword in hand.

There was a movement behind him, and Qiang finally regained her grip on her pistol and pulled the trigger. Hiroshi's eyes widened as he turned around. The soldier who had attempted to sneak up on him lay dead.

Hiroshi hurried over to her. "Help me get him up. We need to get out of here."

Qiang assisted in hoisting Ah-Long onto Hiroshi's back. As they prepared to make their escape, she stopped. "Brother Wu," she said.

Hiroshi put an arm out to stop her. "He's strong. He'll be fine. I'll get you back as close to your base as I can. Let's go."

Another uproar erupted between Brother Wu and Brother Song. Qiang stood outside the medical tent where Ah-Long, who was being tended to, thankfully was still alive. Sook Ping hadn't left his side. Hiroshi was long gone. He had brought them back to the outskirts of the base to maintain the secrecy of his identity and left before Qiang had a chance to speak with him.

"You're just as responsible for this as I am!" Brother Wu shouted.

"We should have known. And her, with her code-cracking mastery, she should have been the first to know it." Brother Song glared at Qiang.

Brother Wu shook his head wildly. "The message was clear!"

"I don't care!" Brother Song spat on the ground near Brother Wu's boots. "We lost over thirty of our people! Thirty!"

Qiang stumbled back at his words. How had they been so clueless? She should have listened to Hiroshi's concerns and taken them more seriously. As she stewed in guilt, the brothers continued to argue.

"And now you wish to appoint her"—Brother Song pointed at Qiang—"as a supervisor? Are you mad?"

"Why not?" Brother Wu countered, his tone resolute. "You said it yourself! We've lost too many of our people today. We need more leaders."

Brother Song huffed. "Absolutely not! Anyone but her!"

Qiang's confidence was shaken. Perhaps Brother Song was right. She had been so sure of the message's meaning. From the other side of camp, Hao came skipping over to her side, and Qiang wrapped her arm around her small shoulders and gave her a hug.

"If it's because she's a woman—" Brother Wu began.

"There's no place for women in this war!" Brother Song bellowed.

"Half our fighters are women! Have you forgotten the tales of Liang Hongyu from the Song dynasty?"

"Bah!"

"Or what about Fu Hao from the Shang dynasty? She rose in rank and became a military general," Brother Wu pressed on.

Hao couldn't contain herself and jumped around, waving her arms up high, exclaiming, "Hua Mulan, too!"

Brother Song shook his head aggressively. "Mulan is folklore, you silly girl!"

"But Qiang isn't," Brother Wu declared.

"I swear to the heavens, if you proceed with this course of action, you leave me with no alternative but to relinquish my position," Brother Song thundered.

"Oh, don't be so ridiculous," Brother Wu retorted with an exasperated sigh. "Having another leader is a positive development. You and

I have been stretched thin, and just consider the multitude of new evacuees we've accommodated here over the past few months. We require more effective management. You have seen it yourself; the people here have taken a liking to Qiang. The women, the children—they all listen to her."

Brother Song turned his back on Brother Wu and faced the crowd of members, who had gathered around in groups. "I absolutely refuse to lead alongside a woman! If I depart today, who will join me?"

"Stop acting like a child," Brother Wu urged. "Let's discuss this together."

"No!" Brother Song pushed Brother Wu's arm away. "I swear that I am leaving today! I will ask once more. Who will stand by my side?"

The members all looked at one another, confused about what to do. Several scratched the back of their heads, while others looked everywhere but Brother Song's direction.

Qiang disliked witnessing the discord between the two brothers. All she had to do was decline the offer, and peace would be restored. As she stepped forward, intending to intervene in their dispute, Hao tugged on her tunic. "I will follow you, Qiang," she said. "To me, you're just like Hua Mulan."

Qiang warmed at Hao's words. This was her opportunity to demonstrate her worthiness for leadership, to prove that women could assume command and thrive amidst conflicts. She cleared her throat. "I accept the offer, Brother Wu."

Brother Wu's face broke into a wide grin while Brother Song stormed back into the tent.

"Leave him to me," Brother Wu said. "That stubborn man has no other place to go. He'll come to terms with it in a few days."

Late that night, Qiang couldn't sleep. It would be morning soon, and there was little point in trying. Panicked thoughts ran through her head. Could she trust the information Hiroshi had provided? Was he somehow entangled in a deceitful plot? She dismissed that notion. After all, he had been the one to introduce her to the resistance, and he had saved her and Ah-Long during the ambush. Surely, a deeper layer of the situation remained concealed from her. Turning onto her side and peering through the narrow opening in her tent, she spotted Brother Wu crouched near a flickering campfire.

The argument between the brothers troubled her. Unable to rest, she got out of bed, pocketed her pistol, and left the camp, seeking solace in the dense forest. She needed to clear her mind, to purge the harrowing memories of what had transpired at the pier. Her fingers closed around a fallen branch, its rough bark a minor distraction, and she trailed it through the overgrown grass, every so often smacking it against a tree trunk. The air was thick and smelled like frozen earth. Pausing, she looked at the dark sky above.

Throughout history, women consistently demonstrated their worthiness to assume leadership roles. Qiang couldn't understand why, with the passage of each decade, a fresh wave of men emerged, attempting to suppress women's true potential. How many more decades must pass before women could lead as men had done for centuries?

A sudden rustle nearby caused Qiang to tense, her hand instinctively reaching for her gun. "Who's there?" she called out, her stance firm, prepared for any threat.

A shadow darted past a nearby tree and then lunged toward Qiang, a knife narrowly missing her face. Reacting swiftly, Qiang pivoted on her feet, seizing the assailant by the arm and pinning them against a tree, disarming them with practiced ease.

"You have improved," a familiar voice remarked.

"Sook Ping?" Qiang pulled the figure closer, relief washing over her. "I nearly killed you!"

"I said you have improved, not that you were better than me." Sook Ping laughed, brushing bark from her face and hands. "What are you doing out here?"

"I can't sleep. You?"

"Same." Sook Ping shook her head and leaned against the tree. "Ah-Long has finally fallen asleep after taking some medicine."

"How is he doing?" Qiang asked.

Sook Ping pursed her lips, clearly biting back tears. "He'll live. The bullet missed any vital organs." She took a deep breath.

"I'm surprised you even left his side to come out here. I thought you'd be glued there until he was back on his feet!" Qiang said, attempting to lighten the mood.

Sook Ping pinched Qiang's arm. "I had to breathe some fresh air at some point. I'll go back to check on him soon. Someone needs to keep him from doing something reckless again. So, why can't you sleep?"

"The brothers' fighting has worsened," Qiang sighed. "Do you think Brother Wu made the right choice, appointing me as supervisor?"

Sook Ping nodded. "I do. It's not like they're asking you to be the head leader. You'll do well. You're a fast learner."

"Thank you." Qiang smiled. "I guess only Brother Song takes such issue with me."

"Don't worry about him. Brother Song has his own scars he's dealing with. Not everything is always so black-and-white, Qiang."

"What does that mean?"

"It's not my place to say." Sook Ping shrugged.

"Tell me—"

A whizzing sound pierced the forest's stillness, cutting her off. Qiang looked skyward, where an American fighter plane tore past at breathtaking speed. In hot pursuit, a Japanese aircraft closed in, firing round after round. Within moments, the American fighter was struck, and it spiraled down to the base of a nearby hill with a deafening crash.

"I'll go warn the others," Sook Ping said. "Will you manage?"

Qiang gave her a nod before sprinting through the forest, vaulting over fallen trees and maneuvering around branches that jutted like knives. The roar of the flames grew louder with each step, and the acrid smoke stung her eyes and crammed her lungs.

Reaching the scene, Qiang saw that a wrecked aircraft lay smoldering amidst the billowing smoke, its metal frame twisted and charred. Inside the fiery wreckage, she spotted the injured American pilot, his uniform singed and torn, trapped within the blazing inferno.

"Breathe!" she shouted in English above the roar of the flames. Steeling herself, she braved the searing heat and choking smoke to approach the wreckage.

The pilot, dazed and disoriented, groaned in pain. "Help! Please, help me!"

There was no time to waste. Her mind racing, Qiang assessed the wreckage for the safest way to extract the pilot. She wrapped her jacket around her hand and reached for a shard of metal, using it as a makeshift lever to pry open the wreckage's mangled cockpit. The intense heat licked at her skin as she struggled to free the pilot, her jacket providing just enough protection. Her lower back stretched painfully, but she kept trying. Finally, putting all of her might into one last heave, she managed to pull him from the burning plane.

Coughing, the pilot lay on the ground, his face smudged with soot. "Thank you," he managed to whisper.

Qiang helped the pilot to his feet, supporting his weight as they stumbled away hurriedly. The flames roared behind them, hungry and relentless. As they reached the forest, the fuel tanks exploded, sending a blast into the sky. Qiang shielded the pilot with her body as debris rained down around them.

The American looked at Qiang with gratitude. He pulled on an aluminum disk-shaped tag hanging from his neck and showed it to her.

Qiang read it with haste.

> I am an American airman. How many li away are the nearest Chinese guerrillas.

"Heavens," Qiang said. "I don't know whether you're lucky or unlucky. Come with me. We need to get out of here before the Japanese come."

"You speak English," the pilot said. "You saved me. I owe you my life."

"You owe me nothing. Come on. The Japanese will be here soon."

CHAPTER 36

Tanaka had ascended to the position of governor-general of Hong Kong, and the Imperial Army was busy organizing a lavish celebration in his honor. Inside the bustling headquarters, people scurried about to prepare for the event, but Mingzhu was preoccupied with other concerns. Had Hiroshi successfully conveyed the message to the resistance? Had their mission to infiltrate the weapons shipment been executed without casualties? And had they avoided whatever attack was coming for them?

Adjusting the collar of her uniform, Mingzhu paid no notice to the beads of sweat on her forehead. She stood amidst the opulent dance hall within the Peninsula. The morning light splashed into the hall through the large windows, and at regular intervals, her gaze met Captain Sato's, a silent exchange of understanding passing between them. The lockdown Tanaka had put into place had ended only an hour earlier, and Mingzhu and Sato made sure to remain at the headquarters for the celebrations to avoid raising Tanaka's suspicions.

Rensuke was there, too. His attention wasn't on Mingzhu but instead on his conversation with Tanaka's daughter. Rensuke blushed, shifting his weight from one foot to the other as he listened intently to the woman's words.

Nearby, several other secretaries engaged in animated conversations, helping themselves to the delicacies on the towering table before them. One woman nudged Mingzhu, urging her to partake, but she politely declined. Her focus remained fixed on another officer running through the crowd toward Tanaka.

She watched as the officer whispered something into Tanaka's ear. He then looked across the room, first at Sato and then at her. When his eyes locked on hers, the hairs on her neck stood at attention. Something wasn't right.

Sato's eyes widened, his posture stiffening, noting the exchange. He quickly beckoned to Mingzhu with a subtle yet urgent wave of his hand and mouthed the words *Leave. Now.*

Immediately, she made her way out of the hall and toward the lobby. She had to get back to the news office. Headquarters was no longer safe.

Keeping her head low, she managed to slip out of the hotel, only to be confronted by two officers. They quickly restrained her, stuffing a handkerchief into her mouth and tying her hands behind her back. Her cap fell off as she struggled, and tiny black curls of her hair hung about her forehead. The officers dragged her down the hallway to a small cleaning closet and locked her inside. Mingzhu battered against the door, trying desperately to free herself, until her arms were bruised and she collapsed, breathless.

Hours seemed to go by until the closet door finally opened, and two officers yanked her off the floor and forcibly pulled her into the hallway. One of the men tore the handkerchief from her mouth. The sun had set, and she saw the night sky through every window they passed. How long had she been locked inside?

She kicked repeatedly, her heels pounding against the carpeted floor with each forceful strike. "Get off me," she shouted.

"Shut up!" the officers said in unison.

They continued to drag her until they reached a door that she recognized. Mingzhu swallowed hard as the officers pulled her up and knocked on the door.

"Enter."

The men shoved Mingzhu inside. Tanaka sat behind a large oak desk, where a golden lamp illuminated the room, making his black eyes look sinister and penetrating. But that was not what made Mingzhu uncomfortable. What struck her was that Sato was there, kneeling on the floor with his head hung low. Blood dripped from the corner of his mouth, and one of his eyes was swollen shut. His hands were bound together and rested on his thighs. Centered within his palms were the mala beads Mingzhu had given him. And to his right was Rensuke, seated as though he had ascended to a higher ranking than Sato.

"Strip her," Tanaka ordered the two officers.

"No!" Mingzhu put her hands out as they neared her, pulling and tearing at her uniform until she was wearing nothing but a white camisole and tap shorts.

Tanaka ordered the two officers who had brought her in to leave. Sato looked away while Rensuke's ears turned red. Mingzhu instinctively crossed her arms to preserve what little modesty remained, but it proved futile. Anger and shame pierced her skin. She kept as still as possible, ignoring that her legs had begun shaking. She tried to focus on Rensuke's boots, counting the scuff marks along the edge and two mud spots.

One.

Two.

Three.

Tanaka lazily made his way to Mingzhu and leaned in until his nose touched her neck. "I have some questions to ask," he said, inhaling. "Sato here didn't seem to want to answer them."

Mingzhu was too frightened to look at Sato. She remained quiet.

Tanaka propped himself up on the edge of his desk. "Do you have any clue as to why you find yourself here today?"

Mingzhu tightened her arms around her trembling body and shook her head.

"I didn't quite catch that," Tanaka said, a disconcerting smile on his lips.

"I do not know, General," Mingzhu replied, her voice quivering.

"There's no need to be so apprehensive," Tanaka said mildly. "I merely wish to talk, that's all. Isn't that right, Rensuke?"

Rensuke straightened in his seat and nodded like a child. "Yes, General."

Mingzhu felt sickened by his naked desire to please Tanaka.

"See?" Tanaka said. "Rensuke is my witness. I am only going to ask questions. Simple."

But nothing about Tanaka was simple. Mingzhu had heard the chilling stories about his deeds—the atrocities he and his men had committed. Only a man as ruthless as him would ascend to such a position, appointed by the emperor himself. Mingzhu realized that her fate hung in the balance, dependent on her following words or actions. Her head throbbed, and she knew there was no way out.

"She knows nothing," Sato spat.

"Silence!" Tanaka turned his attention back to Mingzhu. "How long have you served under Captain Sato?"

Mingzhu finally glanced at Sato, who had started shaking his head, signaling her not to speak. "Just over two years," she replied.

She pondered this as she recollected the early part of her captivity, when she had marked each passing day by scratching the wall with the heel of her shoe. At some point during the occupation, she had stopped counting. Perhaps some part of her had wanted to suspend the relentless march of time. The more she focused on the passing days, the slower they seemed to crawl.

Tanaka tilted his head. "Are you loyal to him?"

"I am loyal to the emperor," Mingzhu lied.

Tanaka chuckled. "You were right, Rensuke. She has a sharp tongue."

Rensuke mimicked his laughter like a child emulating a parent.

"Lower your arms," Tanaka commanded.

Mingzhu's brows twitched with reluctance, her arms still crossed protectively over her chest.

"That was a direct order. Lower your arms."

Trembling, Mingzhu lowered her arms to her sides.

Tanaka stood and approached her again. Overwhelmed by fear, Mingzhu almost lost consciousness. Sato raised his head and gave her a reassuring glance, which she clung to as a means of support.

Tanaka lifted his hand and traced a finger from her shoulder to her hand. "Chinese women don't take care of their skin the same way Japanese women do," he remarked. "Such a shame."

"If you have questions, just ask them," Mingzhu hissed.

Tanaka drew away from her. "It has come to my attention today that your commanding officer here," he said, pointing to Sato, "is working with the ERC."

"I don't know what you're talking about," she said.

"Is that so?" he asked. "You know nothing of a weapons shipment?"

Mingzhu shook her head. When Rensuke looked at her again, she drew her arms back across her chest.

"So, you have no idea that a group of resistance members were informed of the shipment sent to Sham Shui Po yesterday?"

"No idea."

"How interesting," Tanaka said. "Then you probably have no idea it was part of a scheme. There were no weapons. Only an attack."

Mingzhu's teeth chattered against the inside of her cheeks. What had she done? Had she sent members of the resistance to their untimely deaths? Was this all her fault?

Tanaka strode to a chest of drawers on the opposite side of his office. Perched above the chest, a gleaming katana rested on a polished wooden base, its presence commanding. He picked up the weapon, walked back to Mingzhu, and pressed the blade against her neck.

"I'm not the most patient of men," Tanaka said. "I will ask you one last question, and I best like your answer."

For a second, Mingzhu pictured the blade of the katana cutting into her flesh. But no. She refused to die—not like this. She still had to find Qiang.

"Did you know Sato was working with the resistance? Were you working alongside him?"

"I know nothing of the resistance," Mingzhu said firmly. "Sato is a private man. I don't even know what he likes to eat for breakfast."

Tanaka clicked his tongue and retracted the katana from her neck.

"Prove it," he challenged, thrusting the sword's handle into her palm. With a firm grip on her, he forcefully moved her to stand before Sato, who remained on his knees. "Kill him."

Mingzhu attempted to pull away, but Tanaka encircled his arms around her, his breath hot on her neck. Within their shared grasp, he positioned the blade against Sato's shoulder, gradually guiding it toward his neck.

Sato raised his head, and Mingzhu's lips quivered as she locked eyes with him. At that moment, he offered her a nod, a gentle reassurance. Permission to take his life to save her own.

Tears pooled in Mingzhu's eyes, obscuring her vision of Sato. "I am not a murderer," she said to Tanaka. "I know nothing of the resistance. Please, don't make me do this."

Tanaka hissed into her ear, "Either he dies, or you die. You decide."

Mingzhu's legs weakened, but she remained standing with Tanaka's support. He clenched her hands tighter.

"I won't do it," Mingzhu said. And she meant it. No matter how much she resented Sato for her position in the occupation, she still owed him her life. He could have killed her, but he didn't.

"Useless woman!" Tanaka shouted, pushing her onto the floor. "Rensuke. Take her to my room. Now."

"No!" Sato pushed forward.

Mingzhu began crawling toward Sato, but Rensuke grabbed her around her waist and pulled her away. The officers outside came in to help him. As they dragged her out of the office, Mingzhu watched Tanaka throw the katana onto his desk. He reached for a pistol from his waist belt and shot Sato between the eyes.

"No!" Mingzhu screamed. The last thing she saw as the door closed was Sato's body crumpling to the floor, fresh blood soaking into her mala beads.

In a past life, Mingzhu had been in Tanaka's suite. Before the occupation, she, alongside her sister-wife and husband, had occupied this lavish suite at the Peninsula Hotel. It was during a gala hosted by the British chief secretary of Hong Kong.

The suite was a blend of rich, dark woods and sumptuous fabrics. Ornate furniture with refined carvings graced the living area, and heavy curtains framed grand windows that revealed views of the harborfront. Still without her uniform and dressed only in a camisole and tap shorts, she felt out of place. Looking at the space around her, she felt as though she had slipped into a time capsule. Everything appeared just as it had been before, yet she knew everything had profoundly changed.

Still reeling from Sato's death, she walked shakily to the door and pressed her ear to it. She couldn't hear anything but knew at least one officer was standing guard outside. When would Tanaka show up? She had to think of a way to get out. She wouldn't let herself fall prey to his vicious acts. No matter how much she longed to survive, to be with her loved ones again, this would be one step too far. She would rather burn to death than ever let that man violate her. But how could she escape? Where was the way out?

The officer outside spoke. "What is all this?" It was Rensuke.

Mingzhu pressed her ear to the door harder.

"General Tanaka has requested sweets and wine to be delivered here, sir."

It was Fung, the army chef.

Mingzhu leaped from the door and paced in a frantic circle. Her mind raced with thoughts of how to enlist Fung's assistance. What could she possibly offer him in return? Should she resort to begging? What would Fung want?

Rensuke spoke again. "You say General Tanaka asked for this?"

"Why, yes, sir." Fung lowered his voice. "You know how women get after a glass or two. I'm sure it'll make things easier for the general."

Laughter bounced between them, and Mingzhu's unease gnawed at her stomach like a bitter knot. The door swung open, and Fung casually strolled in, pushing a trolley concealed under a cloth.

"Good evening," Fung greeted her civilly.

Rensuke turned back to face the hallway.

"Fung—" Mingzhu started.

Fung raised a finger to his lips, urging her to remain silent.

"General Tanaka has taken a liking to you. It is your fortune to be blessed by such a man," he said loudly. "Come, enjoy the sweet treats and wine."

With a subtle motion, Fung lifted a corner of the cloth from the trolley, revealing a boot knife with a wooden handle between two bottles of wine. Mingzhu's eyes widened in astonishment. At that moment, Fung placed a hand over his heart, signaling to Mingzhu that he was on her side.

"Act fast," he whispered.

Mingzhu held her breath, offering a slight tip of her head.

Before leaving, he added, "If you need more wine, you know where I am."

When the door closed, Mingzhu quickly grabbed the knife, rushed over to the bed, and hid it under the pillow. She knew what she had to do next. She opened a bottle of wine and began pouring it into a glass. She took a sip, relishing its flavor. She had not had such luxury since before the war, and the tart, sweet feeling in her mouth made her want to cry. If she could, she would have drunk the whole thing. Instead, she smashed the glass against the bedframe and let out a scream.

Rensuke burst into the room, alarmed. "What's going on in here?"

Mingzhu sprawled on the floor, her hand dripping with blood. "Rensuke," she panted, her voice trembling. "It was an accident. Please, help me."

Rensuke's eyes darted to the shattered glass. He pulled a rolled bandage from his uniform pocket and wrapped it around her wrist. "Get up. The general can't stand the sight of blood on a woman. You must clean yourself up."

As he went to leave, she pulled the knife from beneath the pillow and, without a second thought, struck Rensuke in the back with so much force and rage the knife hit bone.

When he pushed back, recoiling in agony, Mingzhu yanked the knife out, adrenaline pumping, and closed in on him and slashed the blade across his throat. The heat of his blood sprayed her face, leaving a gruesome mask of crimson in its wake. She shuddered as Rensuke fell to the floor.

Mingzhu dropped the knife in shock and stood over his body, her gaze locking onto Rensuke's fading eyes, searching for answers that would never come.

"You . . . you . . ." He gagged, hands on his throat.

Mingzhu clenched her teeth. "May your soul find no peace."

Wasting no time, she crossed the room to the trolley Fung had brought earlier and removed its cover. Amidst the array of sweets and wines, she found a neatly folded maid's uniform. Wiping her hands and face on the bedspread as best she could, she changed into the provided garments and made her way out of the room, through the halls, and into the kitchen.

When Fung saw her, he immediately stood and rushed to her. "There is a truck waiting for you outside. Take this package. Now leave and never come back."

"Why are you helping me?" she asked, accepting the package.

Fung jerked his head. "You don't know?"

"Know what?"

"I don't have time. But just know that I am with Sato. Was . . . was with Sato." Fung frowned. "He knew this could happen, and he had made preparations. Despite his overbearing nature, Sato was a good man. He especially cared for you."

Mingzhu found herself unable to speak.

"Hurry, you must go." Fung pushed her out through the back door and onto a dark street, where the headlights of a truck flashed at them. "Go!"

Mingzhu gave Fung one last look before running to the truck. The doors opened, and a resistance member helped her inside. As the vehicle sped off, she emptied the package of its contents. Inside was a small bundle of military yen, along with a note.

We owe each other nothing.
Remember, you belong to no man.
May we never meet again.

Sato

She clenched the note in her hand, crumpling it. The mental image of Sato being shot replayed again and again. She squeezed her eyes shut with a deep breath, trying to steady herself. Everything had unfolded too quickly. She didn't even get to say goodbye. She recalled how she had despised him the first time they had met. The irony of mourning him now struck her as slightly absurd, and she let out a soft laugh. She imagined Sato being amused by her thoughts, and that alone kept her from breaking down completely.

CHAPTER 37

The pilot, Lieutenant Donald Kerr, was immediately taken to the medical tent, where several members attended to his wounds. Aside from his burns and cuts, he was well enough to speak with the brothers.

"There's no need to stand," Brother Wu said, as he entered the medical tent, putting a hand on Kerr's shoulder, and pressing him to lie back down.

"Tell us," Brother Song started, not wasting time. "Were you followed?"

Qiang stepped into the conversation. "I got him out just in time. The aircraft blew up, so the Japanese should assume he died in the blast."

"What were you doing out of the camp alone at this time of night?" Brother Song demanded.

"I—"

"Stop it." Brother Wu looked at Kerr. "Tell us, what is your mission? Who sent you?"

Kerr recounted his mission. He was a fighter pilot in the U.S. Army's air force and had participated in numerous air raids, flying a P-40 fighter plane. After several successes, he was assigned a scouting mission in Hong Kong alongside two other pilots.

"I can only hope they weren't shot down, too," Kerr said.

"What were you scouting?" Brother Wu asked.

"The Japanese have tightened border control over the past few months," Kerr said. "I was sent to scout the positioning of various checkpoints along the harbor."

"What do you plan to do with that information?" Qiang asked.

"What do you think?" Brother Song grunted. He turned his back to Qiang and faced Kerr. "Why are the Americans planning such an attack? What is the gain?"

"To cut the supply lines once and for all," Qiang said.

Kerr smiled. "Exactly."

"What can we do to help?" Brother Wu asked.

"I need access to a secure communication line with my commanding officer. Are your radios safe to use?"

"Of course," Brother Wu said. "We'll bring one to you now."

Qiang stepped closer to Kerr until her back faced Brother Song. "We know the city better than anyone else," she said. "If you're seeking information regarding troop movements and the arrangement of harbor defenses, we can help."

"Qiang is right," Brother Wu said. "From now on, consider us part of your mission. Once you recover, we will find a way to get you out of Hong Kong."

The pungent aroma of wild ginseng and various medicinal herbs flooded the campgrounds. Qiang's stomach emitted a low growl, and she couldn't remember the last time she had eaten. She spotted Ah-Yee and a group of older women gathered around a small fire, fanning the sizzling pots suspended above the flames.

As she approached, she caught sight of Brother Song at his post up in the guard tower. She didn't know what got into her, but instead of sitting comfortably beside Ah-Yee, she made her way over and climbed up to join him.

Brother Song hastily wiped tears from his face with his sleeves.

"Are you crying?" Qiang asked bluntly.

"Of course not! Damn allergies." Brother Song turned to leave when Qiang reached out to stop him. "What is the meaning of this?"

"Are you really going to quit if I am to lead alongside you?"

Brother Song swatted her arm away. "I've said it before: there's no place for women in war."

"There's no place for anybody in a war!" Qiang cried. "I know what I am capable of. I know I can make a good leader."

Brother Song gritted his teeth. "You know nothing." Without another word, he climbed down the ladder, leaving her alone with nothing but the view of distant fires and smoke sprinkled across the hills.

Not long after, Brother Wu appeared beside her with a small *mántou.* "You haven't eaten all day," he said.

Qiang dug in gratefully. "Why is he so hostile toward me?" she asked, her gaze following Brother Song as he walked back to his tent. "He treats me like I murdered him in a past life."

Brother Wu gave a short laugh. "That's not what it's about."

Leaning against the wooden beam of the tower, Qiang asked, "Then, what's his problem with me?"

Brother Wu sighed, his eyes looking for a focus other than her face.

"What is it? Tell me."

"You look like his daughter," he said.

"Brother Song has a daughter?"

"Had." Brother Wu lowered his voice. "She was killed."

"What happened to her?"

"She was strong, just like you," he said. "She was part of the resistance and fought alongside her father. But while they were out on a mission, the Japanese kidnapped her. They knew she was Brother Song's daughter, so they made an example out of her."

"No . . ." Qiang breathed.

"After they killed her, they hung her body from a light post at one of the main checkpoints in the city. Many civilians saw her hanging there. It was a reminder to never join the resistance or to defy the Imperial Army."

Qiang was speechless. There were no words to express her devastation and sadness for Brother Song.

"He doesn't hate you," Brother Wu said. "When he sees you, he sees his daughter. Too much pain."

"Brother Wu! Qiang!" Hao shouted.

Qiang peered down from the tower to see Hao pointing to the dusty road ahead. One of their Red Cross trucks was approaching fast.

"That's Sook Ping," Brother Wu said. "She was sent on a rescue mission. Let's go help her."

Qiang silently nodded and let her sense of duty guide her steps. All the while, she made a mental note to be kinder to Brother Song. She descended the tower alongside Brother Wu, positioning herself near the entrance as the truck stopped. Sook Ping jumped out and swung open the back door. Qiang moved forward, intending to assist, but when a woman emerged from the truck, she froze.

The whole world shifted beneath her feet as she locked eyes with her mother.

CHAPTER 38

As Mingzhu descended the Red Cross truck, the crumpled note from Sato pirouetted to the ground. The person she had yearned to see for the past two and a half years stood before her. She could hardly believe it.

"Mama!" Qiang surged forward like a rocket, wrapping her arms around her mother's waist.

Mingzhu could barely maintain her balance as her arms encircled her daughter, her hand resting on the back of Qiang's head. "Qiang! Is this real? Is it really you?"

"Mama!" Qiang cried. "It's me, Mama."

Mingzhu gasped, overcome with joy, falling to her knees with Qiang. "My daughter . . . my daughter . . ."

"Mama . . ." Her daughter's tears soaked her shoulder.

Mingzhu peeled herself from Qiang, tenderly holding her daughter's face. As their gazes met, her heart ached. Qiang had lost so much weight, yet the undeniable radiance in her eyes endured. A surge of feelings welled within Mingzhu, and she couldn't help but laugh and cry, her elation at their long-awaited reunion overflowing.

"First Madame . . ."

Mingzhu looked up to see Ah-Long emerge out of the medical tent, being supported by another resistance member. He went to bow but let out a groan from the pain, and she saw his middle was wrapped with bandages. Mingzhu went to him and placed a hand on his arm, a smile spreading across her face.

"Ah-Long," she said with warmth. "I'm so happy to see you." She started to cry once again, taking his hand in her own. "I cannot thank you enough for your silent words that day. I cannot. What happened?"

Ah-Long squeezed her hand. "A bullet. Nothing serious," he said bravely.

"Come, let's get you settled in," Qiang said.

Mingzhu tightly held onto Qiang as they entered the camp. Throughout the night, she couldn't take her eyes off her daughter, savoring every minute as Qiang led her through the base, introduced her to fellow resistance members, and shared a meal. To Mingzhu, it felt like she had transcended mortality and entered the celestial realm.

Inside a small tent, as they lay next to each other, Mingzhu continued to grip her daughter's hand, unwilling to release it. A small candle next to the bed flickered as the evening breeze picked up and filtered through the space.

"I've let you down," Mingzhu said, her throat tightening.

Qiang looked at her sidelong, a woeful expression in her eyes. "You have never let me down, Mama."

"I'm so sorry, Qiang," Mingzhu continued. She wanted to pour her heart out. She wanted to tell her daughter that not a day had gone by when she hadn't thought of her, when she hadn't cried herself to sleep wondering if she was alive, wondering if she would ever see her again. She wanted to tell her that if she could turn back time, she would never have left the house with Henry that day and would've fought as hard as she could to find her and be with her. She wanted to say so many things, but her lips trembled too much. Wordlessly, she let tears slip down her face.

Qiang turned to face her. "Mama," she said softly. "You don't have to say anything. I know what is in your heart, the same way you know what is in mine. We're together again. That's all that matters."

Mingzhu smiled. How did she have such a wonderful daughter? How did she get so lucky in life? "Tell me, Qiang," she said. "Tell me everything that has happened."

And so, throughout the night, until the sun began to rise, Mingzhu listened as Qiang recounted the tragic death of Cai, her escape with Ah-Long, and the trials she had faced with Biyu. She learned about Qiang's refuge at Francine's in Tseng Lan Shu, her work at the factory in Middle Hill, and the painful news of Francine's murder. Qiang's words painted an intense picture of her journey, and with each sentence, Mingzhu pitied yet admired her daughter.

"And Biyu?" Mingzhu asked. "Is she still unwilling to come here?"

Qiang nodded sadly. "We received news that Mr. Gok was killed a few days ago. Biyu has refused to join me here because she wanted to stay and look after him, but now that he's gone, maybe she will come after all."

"Can we send her a letter? Is there a way?"

"Of course, Mama," Qiang assured her. "We'll find a way to bring her to us."

"No," Mingzhu said.

Qiang looked confused. "What do you mean no, Mama?"

"I don't want to force her to do anything. You don't know this, Qiang, but many years ago, when I was much younger, I begged Biyu to stay with me, to follow me and forgo her freedom. And she did."

"Because you're her family, Mama. Of course she would stay with you."

"I don't want to ask her to stay with me again. She has a right to choose her own path. Let her decide what she wants, and we'll support her choice."

"I understand," Qiang said. "Hao is going out with Sook Ping tomorrow. If it's safe to do so, I'll ask her to stop by the village."

A while later, Mingzhu and Qiang sat outside the tent, where they watched the sun roll up behind the mountains, forming yellow streaks across the campgrounds. Throughout it all, Mingzhu never stopped smiling. Yet, beneath her smile, her thoughts drifted to Henry. Was he safe? Was he thinking of her, too? She wondered how she could get in touch with him. As the questions lingered, she squeezed her daughter's hand a little tighter, her mind shifting between the warmth of the present moment and the uncertainty of whether she'd ever see Henry again.

CHAPTER 39

Biyu hunched in the corner of the bathroom, her bottom bruised from sitting on the hard floor. She played with the radio, spinning the dial around and around, around and around. Her eyes were heavy, and she could taste the blood from her cracked lips.

Since Mr. Gok had been killed, she had become locked in a routine of self-despair. She didn't drink. She didn't eat. She didn't sleep. She was so dehydrated she couldn't even cry anymore. But instead of soaking her clothes with tears, her grief drowned her from within.

Wong Taitai, a persistent visitor, had been knocking on the bathroom door daily, pleading for Biyu to emerge, but Biyu had no desire to venture beyond the confines of the bathroom. Not when she knew that Mr. Gok's body lay just past the courtyard, discarded in a pit among a sea of other forsaken souls.

She had tried once. On the night he was killed, she had summoned the courage to go and retrieve his body from that ditch. But when she arrived, the overwhelming sight of countless lifeless faces staring up at her, twisted in desperation and fear, had frozen her in place. She couldn't find Mr. Gok amidst that horrifying tableau, and fear had clutched her heart like a vise. And so, she sat in the bathroom like a coward.

A while later, there was a gentle tap on the bathroom window. With some effort, Biyu pushed herself upright, using the wall for support, and cautiously approached the glass. There, she discerned the faint silhouette of a child.

"Who are you?" she croaked, opening the window.

"Hi! I'm Hao," the girl said with a large smile. She pulled the window open further and jumped into the bathroom, and Biyu wondered if she was hallucinating. "I have a letter. From Mingzhu."

"I *am* hallucinating," she said, falling onto the edge of the bathtub.

Hao closed the window and told Biyu to keep her voice down. "Is there anything I can eat here? I'm hungry. Or even just a cup of water?"

At the sound of the girl's stomach, Biyu stood up. "I can boil you some yams. Do you like those?"

Hao's eyes lit up. "Oh, I love yams!"

"Right . . . well, come with me, then."

In the living room, Biyu handed Hao a small portion of boiled yams and watched her chomp hurriedly. When Hao extended the plate toward her, she declined, unable to muster the appetite. She continued to face away from the courtyard, determined not to think of what lurked beyond. Even when the wind picked up, and the sound of crickets got louder, she remained facing Hao.

"You said your name was Hao?"

"Yes. Like 'good.'"

"What a lovely name."

"Thank you."

"And you have a letter for me? From Mingzhu?" Still, she did not truly believe it.

Hao chucked her chopsticks onto the table and wiped her mouth with the back of her hand, letting out a small burp. "Here."

Biyu instantly recognized Mingzhu's handwriting, and the loneliness that had gripped her soul for so long began to ease.

Dearest Biyu,

When I heard from Qiang that you're safe and well, my heart swelled in delight. I have reunited with Qiang here in Sai Kung. I never thought this day would come, but heaven has been kind. I remember you always telling me as a child that while fate is decided in the heavens, affection depends on humans.

Biyu, I have never been without you for as long as I can remember. I have never considered you a maid, but rather, a sister. You helped raise me, watched me grow, walked every long path with me, stood by me as I married into the Tang family, and helped me to raise my daughter. You gave up your freedom and happiness alongside mine. You held my hand through every misfortune, every sad day I had. Qiang is alive because of you, I am sure of it. There is nothing I can ever do to repay you for your love and dedication. But I promise I will make it up to you in our next lives. I promise to be your guide, your help, and your strength. I promise to be everything you have been to me.

Many years ago, you gave up your freedom for me. I can't have you doing it again. Enclosed with this letter is something I hope you will take as a token of my love for you. Let this token free you of all burdens here and remove any obligations you have to me.

May we meet again under different circumstances.

Your sister,
Mingzhu

As Biyu's tears spilled across the letter, the ink began to run, blending the words together. Knowing that Mingzhu was safe alongside Qiang gave Biyu a profound sense of peace.

"Here." Hao rummaged in her trouser pockets and pulled out another envelope.

Biyu opened it with shaking hands to reveal a small bundle of cash, a passport, and a ticket to board the SS *Macao*. She ran her fingers across the blurred image in the passport. She could hardly make out the woman's features. Beside the photo was the name Yan Mi.

"You're not Biyu anymore," Hao said. She picked up a cup of water and downed it. "The ship leaves tomorrow at noon. Someone will collect you and take you there safely."

"Is this a real person?" Biyu asked.

Hao nodded. "She was from a rich family. Her father paid us to get her out of Hong Kong."

"Where is she now?"

"She didn't make it," Hao said bluntly. "We have a whole bag of passports like hers. Mingzhu said this was the best one."

Biyu read Mingzhu's letter again. Despite the opportunity to reunite with Mingzhu and Qiang after all this time, a stirring within her signaled a long-overdue longing for freedom. At that moment, it felt as though her entire life flashed before her eyes. She recalled the image of herself as an eight-year-old girl walking the streets of Shanghai, being welcomed into the Yue residence as a maid. Memories flooded in—Mingzhu's birth, her marriage to Wei, Qiang's birth, and the Japanese invasion of Shanghai and Hong Kong. Through years of devoted service, Biyu had willingly surrendered herself to others. If she truly wanted to live for herself, it was now or never. With that, Biyu told Hao to sit patiently while she wrote a response back to Mingzhu.

> Dearest ~~First Madame~~ Mingzhu,
>
> I was happy to remain by your side all these years. I have no regrets. I accept your token of freedom and love. As Yan Mi, I will build a new life—a life that will make you proud. One day, when I become the person I am meant to be, I will find you again.
>
> Your sister

Biyu exited the house the following day and locked the door behind her. Passing Wong Taitai's house, she slipped an envelope under her gate. Inside was the key to Francine's house with a note.

> *I promise to return one day and give Mr. Gok the burial he deserves.*
> *Until then, stay safe.*

Furtively, she scurried through the trees and onto the bridge, skillfully evading the morning patrol passing by. She resisted the urge to turn to look back at the ditch where Mr. Gok lay. With her eyes fixed firmly ahead, she pressed forward.

At Kowloon Bay, several dozen people were already boarding the SS *Macao.*

Biyu offered the resistance member some cash for bringing her all this way. They refused, simply stating it was their duty, before hurrying away.

Taking a deep breath, Biyu stowed the money back in her bag. She pulled out the forged papers Hao had given her. Her fingers trembled as she began to walk across the boarding ramp where a Japanese soldier stood guard.

"Identification papers," he said, holding his hand out expectantly.

Biyu handed over the documents. Despite her insides writhing, she betrayed no indication of nervousness. The soldier studied the papers, scrutinizing the details closely. Biyu had memorized every line on the journey to the bay, ready to deliver to the soldier should he ask. Her name was Yan Mi. She was born on a hot August day and she never married. *Yan Mi, Yan Mi, Yan Mi.* Sweat formed above Biyu's lips, but she maintained her composure. She knew that her escape depended on this moment, and she couldn't afford any slip-ups.

The moment felt endless, yet the soldier returned the papers in a matter of seconds. "You may board," he said.

Biyu nodded but said nothing, her heartbeat accelerating. She walked past him, keeping her head low.

As she stepped onto the lower deck, she realized the boat was devoid of soldiers. The only servicemen were the crew. Biyu watched the soldiers down on the dock turn away a family of three, refusing to let them on.

"Please!" the father pleaded. "At least let my son through. His papers are legitimate!"

"Back away!" the soldier yelled.

The mother fell to her knees, clasping her hands together. "My son was born in Macao! He is not from here. Let him board, I beg you!"

The soldier lifted his rifle and shot into the air. Biyu turned away as anguished screams resounded. She forced herself to walk around to the other side of the boat where her back turned to the city. Rubbing the butterfly pendant, she looked at the vast expanse of open water stretched out before her. The waves glistened, offering a glimmer of hope—of a new life away from the horrors of war.

I'll come back one day, she promised. *I'll come back.*

PART IV

JAPANESE-OCCUPIED HONG KONG, 香港占領地, 1944

CHAPTER 40

Spring had finally arrived, but the sun refused to show its face in Hong Kong. Qiang didn't need the sun, though. Her mother's unexpected arrival at the camp a month earlier was all the warmth she required.

For several days, Qiang joined forces with the American pilot, Kerr, to maintain a secure radio connection with the Allied forces. The latest critical information indicated that a forthcoming attack was imminent, and Kerr urgently sought the assistance of the resistance in orchestrating the evacuation of civilians from Japanese checkpoints scattered along the harbor. While she busied herself with these matters, her mother spent most of her days reading to the children and helping Ah-Yee mend clothes.

Brother Wu formally appointed Qiang as ERC supervisor alongside Ah-Long and Sook Ping. Together, they embarked on the meticulous planning of complicated rescue missions designed to save as many innocent lives as possible.

In the wake of Sato's death, Brother Wu found himself deprived of any source of intelligence concerning weapon shipments. Consequently, the members of the Sai Kung resistance shifted their focus and channeled their energies back to the liberation of civilian hostages and the covert infiltration of comfort stations. Qiang wholeheartedly accepted these new missions.

Brother Song remained by Brother Wu's side despite his vocal disapproval of Qiang's promotion. Contrary to his earlier threats of departure from the base, he had decided to stay. Qiang was grateful for this and took it as a sign of his acceptance.

"We've cleared three checkpoints in the past week," Qiang said, pointing to a large harbor map on Brother Wu's desk. "There are too many civilian residences around the last few. We need to be careful how we approach this to not alert the enemy. We only just managed to escape unscathed the last time."

Ah-Long agreed. "Time is running out. The Allied forces' planned attack is just five days away. We need ideas."

Sook Ping, who had stood quietly beside Ah-Long the entire time, remained silent. Qiang could tell by the way she thinned her lips and tensed her posture that something was bothering her.

"Any suggestions?" Ah-Long asked.

After a moment, Qiang said, "What if we coordinate with local fishermen who know the waters well? They can help us discreetly transport civilians away from the danger zones. We could also create diversionary tactics, like small-scale disturbances or fires, to draw the enemy's attention away from our rescue efforts."

"That's it," Ah-Long said. "That's perfect. We can finalize the details together and begin preparations with the members."

Sook Ping finally spoke. "Are you sure you're fully recovered?"

"I'm as fit as a lion," Ah-Long said, patting his lower abdomen. "Here, hit me."

Sook Ping scoffed. "You couldn't handle me."

Just then, Hao burst into the tent, breathless. "There's a Japanese soldier outside the camp. Brother Wu wants to kill him, but the soldier keeps calling your name!"

"Me?" Ah-Long asked quizzically.

Hao shook her head and pointed to Qiang. "He keeps calling for you."

Qiang knew exactly who it was. She ran out of the tent and toward the camp entrance, where she saw Hiroshi kneeling in the mud, his arms in the air. Brother Wu stood before him, a gun pointed at Hiroshi's head.

"Stop!" Qiang shouted. "Don't shoot!"

"You know him?" Brother Wu asked.

"I do," Qiang said. "He's the one I met at the clinic."

Brother Song approached, wielding a knife. "He's the one who set us up!" he shouted, lunging toward Hiroshi.

"No!" Qiang shouted. She threw herself before Brother Song, putting her arms out to defend Hiroshi. "He warned me. He told me something wasn't right with the information given to us. If we had listened to him, we wouldn't have lost so many people that day."

Ah-Long had approached with Hao by his side.

"He's on our side," said Mingzhu, who was walking toward the unfolding scene. "He works . . . worked . . . for Sato."

Brother Wu lowered his gun.

Hiroshi finally spoke. "Tanaka has marked your base as the next in line for destruction. There's going to be an attack here six days from now."

Her mother pulled Qiang up, dusting dirt from her trousers. "How did you get this information?" she asked.

"Exactly! Sato is dead," Brother Song chimed in. "How do we know this isn't another trap?"

When her mother let her go, Qiang stepped forward, readying herself to defend Hiroshi again.

"I was given the information from Fung," Hiroshi said. "I have been in hiding since the day I met with your people at the pier."

"You were there?" Brother Wu asked.

"He saved us," Ah-Long said. "He got me and Qiang out of there."

"Fung and his wife took me in. I have been staying with them. Fung retrieved the intel when he was clearing plates from Tanaka's office. Tanaka has set his sights on this very base. Six days from now, he will be sending an entire unit here. We need to make preparations."

"We?" Brother Song scoffed.

"I wish to join your cause. I wish to fight with you."

"You're a traitor to your own people," Brother Song spat.

"His mother was Chinese," Qiang said, coming to Hiroshi's aid again.

"How do you know that?" her mother asked, shooting her a look only a mother could give.

Qiang shut her mouth and looked at the ground. From the corner of her eye, she noticed Ah-Long staring at her.

"Get up," Brother Wu said to Hiroshi. "Follow me. We will talk."

Qiang watched Hiroshi walk through the camp. Several people he passed gave him scornful looks, and some even spat on the ground where he walked, cursing him.

"Is there something you wish to tell me, Qiang?" her mother asked, placing a hand on her elbow.

"No, Mama. Nothing."

Qiang stood outside Brother Wu's tent, waiting for Hiroshi and leaning forward to catch their conversation, but she couldn't hear anything. She glanced over to see Ah-Long approaching her.

"Qiang, can we talk?"

"Can it wait?" she asked.

"Not really, no," Ah-Long said. She reluctantly followed him down a small path beside Brother Wu's tent. "I need to tell you something, Qiang."

"I'm listening," she replied, her gaze still fixed on the tent.

"I love you."

Her gaze flew to his. "I—what?"

He grabbed her by the shoulders and gave her a gentle shake. "I said, I love you."

"Ah-Long, I . . ."

His grip tightened, and his eyes, normally warm and kind, filled with pain.

"Ah-Long, let go. I . . . I don't feel the same way."

After a long moment, he released her and took a step back. "Is it because I am a servant?"

"What? No!" Qiang looked at him. "You have never been a servant in my eyes, Ah-Long. You're a fighter."

"Then, why could you not love me back?"

"Ah-Long," she murmured, not quite knowing where to look, "perhaps what you're feeling is just a relic of the past. In all honesty, I felt something for you once, too, but that was before the war, before everything changed, and we had to grow up so quickly."

"So, you liked me too?"

"Maybe. But that was before." Qiang kicked at the ground. "I don't have those feelings now. You're like a brother to me—someone I would never intentionally hurt or betray. You're my family, Ah-Long."

Someone coughed nearby, startling them. Hiroshi stood there, hands in his pockets, brows slightly raised. A lock of thick hair fell onto his forehead.

"You." Qiang felt a blush creep up her neck.

"I apologize for interrupting."

"You're not interrupting," Qiang said.

Ah-Long shot her a hurt look.

"Brother Wu and Brother Song want all of us together," Hiroshi said, tilting his head to the tent.

Gathered around, Qiang, the resistance leaders, and Hiroshi spent the next two hours creating a defense plan for Tanaka's attack in six days. The priority was to get all the elderly and children to safety. Sook Ping would lead two small groups to assist with moving them from the base to a secure location across the river. In the meantime, Qiang, Ah-Long, and Hiroshi would continue to focus on the Allied forces' mission, heading out to clear the remaining checkpoints of civilians. Then, once that mission was complete, every able-bodied man and woman capable of fighting would stand guard at the camp and await Tanaka's men. The plan was put into place, and the countdown began.

Later that night in their tent, Qiang held a small plastic-framed mirror in her hand and watched her mother brush her hair, which brought a tender smile to Mingzhu's face.

"I remember when I used to do this every morning," her mother said, her eyes misty. "But then, when you turned eight, you said, *I can do it myself, Mama!* You always made me laugh. You were always so independent."

Qiang patted the mattress, inviting her mother to sit beside her. Mingzhu sat, continuing to comb Qiang's hair. "I am so glad to be with you again. I never gave up hope that we would reunite."

"Me neither, Mama."

"Brother Wu told me about the mission you will be undertaking in a few days. It sounds dangerous."

"It's hardly a mission," Qiang downplayed. "And I'm very capable."

Her mother rested the comb on her lap. "I don't doubt your capabilities. You have survived this far throughout these awful occupations. You're more than capable."

Qiang relaxed. "You must promise me you'll leave the base with Sook Ping. You will go with Ah-Yee and Hao to the other side of the river and wait for me there."

"I'll help the best I can," Mingzhu said.

Qiang took the comb from her mother's hand and placed it on a small table by the bed. She opened the top drawer and pulled out *Dream of the Red Chamber*.

"Heavens," Mingzhu said, taking the book from her daughter and holding it close to her chest. "You have had this, all this time?"

"Biyu gave it to me when I went to see her. Mama, may I ask you something?"

"Anything," Mingzhu replied with a loving smile.

Qiang gestured to the book. "I . . . read the letters in there. I'm sorry."

Mingzhu hesitated, her gaze dropping. "Oh, Qiang. I'm the one who should apologize."

"There is nothing to be sorry for. Were you and Henry . . . were you both . . ."

Her mother pressed her lips together tightly and, after a moment, nodded. "Yes, there was a connection, and we wrote letters to each other for a while. We met occasionally, away from the house. We would go to this wonderful tea restaurant and eat the most delicious beef brisket noodles I've ever had."

Qiang's heart warmed, realizing that her mother had experienced such simple joys. "Do you still have feelings for him, Mama?"

Mingzhu's eyes reflected the complexity of her emotions—sadness, joy, longing. Besides Biyu, Qiang was the only other person who understood her mother's expressions and what they truly meant. She sensed there was more left unsaid. Yet, Qiang didn't need to know everything about her mother. Every woman was entitled to her own secrets—her own feelings.

"Let me ask you another question," Qiang continued. "If you

weren't the first wife of the Tang family, if you weren't with Baba anymore, would you be with Henry?" When her mother didn't respond, Qiang said, "You don't have to worry about my feelings, Mama. The only thing I want is for you to be happy. What happiness can be had being one of two wives to a man like Baba? I could never accept such conditions for a marriage."

Her mother put the book aside and took Qiang's hands into hers. "Listen to me, Qiang. You won't have to. You will have choices I didn't have."

She rubbed her mother's hands. "Life has been hard for you, Mama."

"It was a different time," Mingzhu said, lowering her voice. "I believe women will have more choices and more power in the future. I believe in that because I see you. I see what you can do, what you fight for, and I believe."

"You believe in me that much?"

"Oh, my sweetest daughter. I have so much faith in you."

Moved by her mother's words, Qiang teared up. "Mama, there's something I need to tell you."

"What is it?"

"It's Baba," Qiang said, taking a deep breath. "He has passed."

Her mother stilled, her gaze unfocused, and she let out a long, heavy sigh, her lip trembling as she closed her eyes.

"Mama?"

"What makes you think such a thing?" Mingzhu whispered.

"It happened in January when Stanley Camp was bombed."

"I had heard there had been a U.S. Navy attack where Stanley Camp was accidentally bombed by one of their aircraft. Dozens of people died there, they said. But how do you know your father was one of them?"

"Brother Wu managed to get a list of the deceased. Baba's name was there."

Her mother began to cry, and Qiang wrapped her arms around her, rocking her back and forth, just as Qiang herself had been comforted when she was a child. She couldn't tell whether her mother's tears were shed out of misery or relief. Her father's death signified her mother's freedom, something she knew her mother had always yearned for but had never openly expressed. It was as though whatever her mother could not attain or achieve in life, she somehow aspired for Qiang to accomplish.

As for Qiang, she knew of her conflicting feelings. When she first heard about his death, there wasn't much time to process the news. Even now, sitting with her mother, she was unsure what to feel. Her whole life, she knew her father was disappointed she wasn't a boy. The love that came so naturally with her mother just wasn't there with him. So, whether he lived or died, it meant very little to her now. Besides, how can you love someone who was never really there in the first place?

Holding her mother close, Qiang made an unspoken promise to herself. She would survive her upcoming mission. She would rescue as many civilians as possible and return safely. She was determined to keep her mother's newfound freedom from being marred by more loss and grief.

CHAPTER 41

While her daughter prepared for the upcoming mission, Mingzhu took on her new role beside Sook Ping. Together, they relocated refugees from the camp to the other side of the river. The plan was to start with the elderly and help set them up before bringing the children over. The newly chosen campsite, nestled within a dense forest on the opposite shore, remained hidden from prying enemy eyes. Towering banyan trees, camphor trees, and the occasional jacaranda swayed gracefully in the morning breeze. It was now the middle of spring, but a cold chill made Mingzhu shudder as she moved along the side of the hill with Sook Ping.

Offering gentle smiles and words of reassurance, they handed out blankets and clothing, ensuring everyone was comfortable. Although the refugees were frail and weary, their spirits remained resilient. They eagerly pitched in, assisting in constructing small tents and rudimentary cooking areas. Mingzhu patiently taught them how to peel the white, spongy bark from select trees for kindling. She also showed them how to bind bamboo together so that the tents would hold up should the weather change—survival techniques she had learned from Qiang and Hao over the past several days.

She helped men and women set up their beds and followed Sook Ping across the river and back into the main camp. Hao was squatting by the entrance, holding her face up with her hands, seemingly dozing in and out of sleep. When Mingzhu reached her, she crouched in front of her and picked her up onto her back. Hao wrapped her hands around Mingzhu's neck and yawned.

"What are you doing out here?" Mingzhu asked, carrying her back to the tent.

Hao rubbed her eyes and patted the pocket of her shirt. "Mr. Henry . . . letter . . . for you," she said sleepily.

Mingzhu tucked Hao into bed and took the letter from her pocket. She and Henry had been writing to each other since she settled with the resistance, and Brother Wu had agreed to help him join them soon.

Mingzhu,

Do you recall when we used to exchange letters and secretively tuck them away within the pages of "Dream of the Red Chamber"? Those moments were truly some of the most cherished memories of my life.

I'm writing this letter to convey a message that Brother Wu recently delivered to me from Hao. They informed me they would come to retrieve me two days from now. In anticipation of their arrival, I've already packed my belongings, which in all honesty, consists of more books than clothes.

It shouldn't prove too difficult. Most of the officers have been called away the past few days and the rest have grown weary.

I fervently hope that my journey to your side will be a brief one.

Until we meet again.

Sincerely,
Henry

The prospect of Henry's impending arrival at the base to be by her side, seeing him for the first time as a free woman, left her palms damp with eagerness. She knew that when Henry set foot on resistance soil, she would do nothing to stop herself from running into his arms.

. . .

The camp was quieter than usual now that most refugees had been relocated. Mingzhu threw a shawl across her shoulders and headed outside. The light pouring in from Brother Wu's tent painted a streak of yellow on the dirt, and she could see Qiang inside, deep in conversation, Hiroshi standing close to her.

Ah-Long approached Mingzhu with a hot cup of tea and handed it to her.

"Thank you, Ah-Long," she said, bringing the cup to her lips. "Jasmine?" she asked in English.

"Ah-Yee picked the leaves herself. They've been drying for weeks now."

Mingzhu took another sip. Ah-Long's English had advanced over the years thanks to Qiang's teaching. She noted Ah-Long's gaze toward the tent where her daughter was. She held back a smile. "When did you first realize?" she asked.

"Sorry, First Madame?"

"Please." Mingzhu gave a wave of her hand. "Call me Mingzhu. I haven't been the first madame in a long time."

"Sorry," Ah-Long said, scratching his ear.

"So, tell me," she said. "When did you first realize you loved my daughter?"

Ah-Long's face reddened. "I don't . . . I mean . . . I . . ."

"Have you confessed to her?" she asked, blowing on the tea before taking another sip.

"I have."

"Of course you have. You have always been brave."

"She doesn't feel the same way."

Mingzhu had long been aware of this fact. She remembered many years ago when innocence still lingered in their lives—when her daughter had once held a fondness for Ah-Long. It had always been so obvious. Those memories were imprinted in her mind—her daughter, seated beneath the garden pavilion, teaching him English, her cheeks flushed with youthful emotions.

But now that she had reunited with Qiang, Mingzhu recognized the transformation that had taken place. Qiang was no longer the young miss of a well-to-do family. Her daughter had grown into a woman, filled with courage and grit. It wasn't that Ah-Long was inadequate, but rather, it was that Qiang had outgrown her feelings. Mingzhu couldn't help but sympathize with Ah-Long, who had clung to those emotions for far too long. Love, she reflected, was not always kind.

Mingzhu heaved a sigh before putting the teacup on the ground. She patted Ah-Long's back like she would pat Qiang's when she was little. "You know, Ah-Long, *gèhuā rù gèyǎn.*"

"I haven't heard that phrase before. What does it mean?" he asked.

Mingzhu peered into Brother Wu's tent again. Qiang's gaze locked on Hiroshi as he spoke. She knew her daughter had developed feelings for Hiroshi, and even though Mingzhu had always warned her against forming relationships with the Japanese, the occupation had taught her that bad and good people came in many forms. Race was just a weapon evil forces used to split societies apart.

She gave Ah-Long another pat. "It means different flowers match different eyes. You may think my daughter to be the most beautiful flower you have ever seen, but if she does not see you as the sun, it doesn't matter how much time you spend showering her with affection. She will never bloom for you."

Ah-Long dropped his head and sighed.

Her words were harsh but loving. They were meant to be. Life was too short and unpredictable to yearn for someone who would never love you back. Even if the war ended today and life went back to how it had been before, and everyone who had died came back to life, she would still choose not to return to her position of the first madame. She would never settle again. She hoped that Ah-Long would move on, too.

Carrying a plate of food, Sook Ping emerged from the makeshift kitchen tent and deposited it into Ah-Long's lap. "Eat," she demanded. "You haven't eaten since this morning."

"I'm not hungry," Ah-Long replied, his gaze still set on Qiang.

Sook Ping followed his line of sight. "You're such an idiot, you know," she snapped before storming off.

Ah-Long turned to Mingzhu, wide-eyed. "She's always so mean to me. What's her problem?"

Mingzhu couldn't suppress her amusement. She laughed so loud and so hard that her eyes began to water and tears streamed down her face.

"What's so funny?" he grumbled.

"Oh, Ah-Long," Mingzhu said, trying to compose herself. "Stop wasting your time on my daughter or you'll overlook what's been right in front of you all this time."

"What . . ." Ah-Long looked down at the plate of food on his lap. Each piece of meat had been chopped into perfect bite-size portions, the vegetables neatly laid over the rice so that the soy sauce would soak into the grains. "Oh," he finally uttered, scanning the area for Sook Ping, who had already disappeared into another tent.

Mingzhu patted him on the back again. "You'll be fine, Ah-Long. Everything will fall into place eventually."

Later that night, before sleeping, Mingzhu sat by a small campfire and wrote Henry a response. She would have it delivered in the morning.

> Henry,
>
> You asked me once if I were like Lady Sun from the *Three Kingdoms* or a woman who lacked agency. Here is my answer.
>
> I am neither.
>
> As a daughter, I was Yue Mingzhu. As a wife, I was Tang Mingzhu. In both lives, I followed the path paved for me by men. Lady Sun was powerful, but even she fought for a man's dream. From this day forth, every step I take will be a choice I make for myself. I can only hope you will accept me for who I am. If you're still willing to take me with you to England, I will gladly join you.
>
> Until we meet again,
> Mingzhu

CHAPTER 42

The night was darker than any Qiang had ever seen, as if the heavens had cloaked the harbor in a thick blanket to conceal their intentions. She stood near the shoreline alongside Ah-Long, Hiroshi, and other resistance members, their breaths mingling with the salty sea breeze. The mission briefing stuck in her mind, and the demands of their task pressed heavily on her shoulders.

"Remember the plan," she said, and Ah-Long and Hiroshi nodded. Each had a specific role, and their success depended on seamless coordination.

Ah-Long would create a diversion to lure the Japanese away from the pier. Meanwhile, Qiang and Hiroshi would discreetly signal to the civilians concealed in the alleys and other resistance members, prompting them to cross the boardwalk and board the small awaiting boats that had been prepared for their escape. The attack on Sai Kung would come tomorrow, and they needed to be there to defend it. This was their last chance to save what civilians they could.

Qiang fixed the leather belt around her waist and pulled a pistol from within. She watched Ah-Long slip into the shadows. Seconds later, the distant sound of glass shattering and shouts filled the streets. The diversion had begun.

The Japanese soldiers stationed at one of the checkpoints rushed toward the commotion, their flashlights casting flickering shadows that danced along the boardwalk like *jiāngshī* spirits, their movements wild and unpredictable.

Qiang glanced at Hiroshi, her eyes locking with his determined gaze. They both knew the importance of their roles in this operation. With a silent nod, they set off along the narrow alleyways that crisscrossed the waterfront district. She pressed her fingers between her lips and whistled to the other resistance members. Shadows moved in the alleys, and families ran across the boardwalk and jumped into the boats. The mission was going smoothly. Two junks had already made their way far across the waters.

The sharp crack of gunfire resounded, and the shouts of Japanese soldiers drew near. The soldiers closed in, pointing their flashlights at Qiang. She raised her pistol and fired, taking down the first soldier with a precise shot to the chest.

"*Kuài diǎn! Faai3 di1!*" she shouted at the civilians. "Get in the boats!"

Hurried footsteps and cries of civilians rang out. Qiang continued to fight. She crouched behind several wooden barrels, bile rising in her throat at the stench of moldy fish.

"Stay down!" Hiroshi called to her. He had begun firing at the incoming soldiers.

Qiang had run out of bullets. She crouched lower and began to reload her gun, but one of the barrels split open as a soldier fired at it. Fish water splashed both on her and the deck. She quickly moved to another set of barrels. All the while, bullets continued to fly at her. She tried to reload her gun again, but her hands were soaked and she couldn't get a firm grip on the pistol. She scowled in rage. "Bastards," she spat.

"Watch out!" Hiroshi shouted.

Qiang ducked just as a soldier lunged at her with a knife. Hiroshi shot the soldier, causing him to fall to the ground. The soldier rolled in agony, pressing the side of his stomach. Qiang grabbed his fallen weapon and drove it into his neck.

"Get back!" Ah-Long's voice pierced through the chaos.

Qiang peered over the barrels. Ah-Long and other resistance members were making their way toward the pier. They threw a round of fire bottles that quickly dispersed the Japanese soldiers from the formation they had created.

As flames lit up the sky, Hiroshi leaped over the barrels, wrapping his arms around her and shielding her from glass shards. She felt his chest rising and falling deeply. He pulled her to her feet.

"Thank you," she said.

"Here, take this." Hiroshi handed her his gun and removed his sword from its sheath around his hips.

Qiang positioned herself next to him, then opened fire on the approaching soldiers. Meanwhile, several resistance members smashed the windows on the upper levels of nearby buildings and began releasing arrows.

"The civilians!" Qiang shouted to Hiroshi.

Together, they ran back toward the pier's edge and helped as many civilians into boats as possible.

The fight lasted another hour until the only thing left was the stench of death, rotting fish, and salt water. Qiang's eyes stung from the smoke surging from the fires that were still burning. Ah-Long approached her and Hiroshi.

"The checkpoints are clear. We succeeded."

"We should go before more troops come," Hiroshi said.

"Let's round up the members," Qiang commanded. "We'll take those we have lost back, too. They deserve a proper burial."

As the remaining members readied themselves to board the waiting trucks, a vehicle hurtled toward them at high speed, then screeched to an abrupt stop. Qiang covered her eyes to protect them from the wave of dust and dirt that lifted from the ground. Sook Ping jumped from the vehicle, her complexion pale and drained of all color.

"Ah-Long!" she screamed. "Qiang!"

Ah-Long grabbed her by the shoulder as she stumbled toward them. "What's happened? Why are you here?"

Sook Ping began hyperventilating. "It's Tanaka's men. They . . ."

"They what?" Qiang yanked on Sook Ping's elbow. "Tell us!"

"They're headed to our base. Now!"

Qiang ran to the truck, jumped in, and blared the horn. "Get in! *Hurry!*"

. . .

"This makes no sense." While Ah-Long drove, Qiang sat in the back of the truck with Hiroshi, Sook Ping, and several other members. "Tanaka was due to attack the base tomorrow."

Sook Ping glared at Hiroshi. "It's you! You gave us the wrong information. You want us to die!"

Hiroshi knitted his brows, the hurt evident in his expression.

"Stop it!" Qiang screamed. There was only one thing on her mind: her mother. Sweat dripped down her face and back. "Drive faster, please!"

Ah-Long pushed his foot down harder onto the pedal.

Qiang didn't realise it, but she had taken hold of Hiroshi's hand and held it tight while praying for her mother's safety.

Please, please stay safe, Mama.

CHAPTER 43

Mingzhu hadn't painted her lips such a bright red since the day she married Wei. Today, though, was special. She wanted nothing more than to present the most radiant version of herself possible.

She dressed herself in a red satin *qípáo* crafted by Ah-Yee from material donated by the Red Cross a few weeks earlier. Although the shade was not as remarkable as the red one she had worn on her wedding day, it still held the significance of a joyous occasion. She was confident that Henry would recognize the deeper meaning behind her choice of color. She brushed out the knots from her hair and rolled it into a bun, pinning it in place with a wooden hairpin. Almost as good as Biyu, she thought to herself and smiled.

Standing before the modest tent's mirror, she examined herself closely, tilting her head from side to side to ensure the even application of her finely milled powder. With a deft hand, she traced the lines of her eyes with a precise stroke of black ink, her jade bracelet sliding on her wrist. For the first time in what felt like an eternity, gazing at her reflection, Mingzhu didn't just appear beautiful, but she also felt a profound sense of beauty from within.

A subtle shift in the atmosphere beckoned her attention. Outside, the faint murmur of scuffling and hushed whispers intruded upon the tranquility. Mingzhu approached the tent's opening, peering out. Several camp leaders had begun pulling everyone out of their tents and were now shouting, gesturing toward the main gates. She ran to her bed and pulled out one of Qiang's knives from where it was hidden underneath. Outside, Brother Wu was rallying the members to his side. Near the front gate, trucks roared forward, kicking up clouds of dirt and dust as they screeched to a sudden stop. The Japanese flags cracked against the wind as the truck doors opened and soldiers barreled out, spraying bullets into the base.

Ah-Yee screamed alongside several other women for the children to enter her tent. "*Faai3 di1, faai3 di1!*" she shouted. Mingzhu noticed Ah-Yee's hands trembling, though her actions remained determined. The children who stayed behind had refused to abandon their parents, who had chosen to fight. The visible fear on their faces as they were ushered into the tent deeply pained Mingzhu.

The conflict between the Japanese forces and the resistance was a frenzied display of action and combat. Swords clashed with katanas, gunfire popped through the air, and explosions sent plumes of smoke and debris into the sky.

Brother Song hurled himself at two soldiers, punches flying in the air. He managed to knock down both soldiers with little effort but was immediately stabbed in the back by another. He crumpled to the ground, desperately scanning the base. When his eyes met Brother Wu's, his expression softened. He raised a fist, and before succumbing to his death, he shouted, "To the resistance!"

Brother Wu stumbled at the sight of his injured brother. He smacked a fist to his chest and roared, "To the resistance!"

A chorus of voices resounded through the campground.

"To the resistance!"

"Protect our people! Protect our home!"

"Free Hong Kong!"

Mingzhu ran toward Brother Wu and the others, her dagger a deadly extension of her will. Several bullets missed her but she eventually took one to the shoulder, causing her to drop the knife and let out a pained scream.

Brother Wu grabbed her hand. Together, they ran across the camp. "You must get out of here!" he ordered.

"No!" Mingzhu shouted, ignoring the pain screaming in her shoulder. "We must fight!"

"Like mother like daughter!" Brother Wu cried, throwing a table to its side and hiding behind it with Mingzhu. "If anything happens to you, Qiang will never forgive me."

Mingzhu flinched as a bullet slammed into the table. Her shoulder burned in agony. "You underestimate my daughter, Brother Wu. She is a very forgiving person."

Brother Wu's face was grim. He lifted his gun and fired at a Japanese soldier who was closing in on them. "Here, at least take this," he said, pulling a second pistol from his belt.

Mingzhu took it and winced. Brother Wu looked at her open wound and quickly pulled a bandage from his pocket and began wrapping it around her. "This should hold the bleeding for a while."

Soldiers began to close in on them again and Mingzhu raised the pistol and fired at them. Her aim was off, and she only managed to hit one soldier in the leg.

"Help!" Hao's voice pierced the air. "Help me!"

A Japanese soldier had grabbed Hao and was making his way into a nearby tent.

"Put me down!" Hao cried.

Mingzhu froze, remembering the women she had seen being dragged into the church back at the start of the occupation. Back then, she was unable to do anything. But now, everything was different. She was a woman standing alongside men and other women, fighting for a cause.

She smacked Brother Wu on the back. "Cover me!"

Brother Wu gave a firm nod as she made a desperate run toward the tent, the sounds of gunfire cracking around her.

Inside the tent, the Japanese soldier had begun ripping at Hao's clothes.

"Stop!" Mingzhu screamed.

She pulled the trigger, managing to shoot him in the thigh, and immediately ran to Hao, pulling her into a tight hold. Hao was crying and shaking; her little hands gripped Mingzhu's waist as though her life depended on it.

"I've got you," Mingzhu said, hugging Hao. "You're safe. I'm with you."

With Hao in her arms, she went to move forward, her heart

pounding. But a firm hand snatched the nape of her neck and forcefully pulled her in. With a startled cry, she tumbled to the ground.

"Run!" she screamed, releasing Hao from her arms.

Still shaking, Hao stumbled to the tent's entrance before turning back with a desperate look. "Mingzhu!"

The soldier pulled Mingzhu to her feet by her hair. She tried to pry herself free from his grip but the pain in her shoulder proved too much.

"Mingzhu!" Hao sobbed harder. She ran back and started kicking the soldier in the leg but was quickly pushed away.

"Go!" Mingzhu cried. "Get to Brother Wu!"

Hao ran out of the tent as fast as she could. The soldier pushed Mingzhu down, trapping her beneath his weight on the ground. His lips descended upon her neck hungrily, like a rabid dog, and it was clear the bullet he had taken to the thigh had done little damage. She thrashed with all her might, but he was too heavy. Desperation overcame her and leaning forward, she sank her teeth into his ear, and in revolt, tore the flesh from his head. The soldier squealed as he clutched the bloody void where his ear had been, leaving him vulnerable. Taking the opportunity, Mingzhu removed the hairpin from her hair and thrust it through the soldier's throat. He toppled to the side, blood spouting in all directions. Scrambling, Mingzhu inched her way toward the gun near the bed. With trembling hands, she fired numerous shots at the fallen soldier until he lay motionless before her.

She pushed herself up, her entire body shaking. She hurried to leave the tent, but as she ran to the entrance, a bundle of straw, lit with flames, was thrown inside. She stumbled back, instinctively covering her mouth with her hand.

The fire erupted around her, blocking the tent's entrance, and panic set in. She ran to the soldier, retrieved a knife from his belt, and began slashing at the thick fabric of the tent near the back, desperately trying to create an escape route.

Outside, the battle raged on. The fire had engulfed the dry grass of the camp and was consuming everything in its path. The heat was unbearable. Mingzhu's vision blurred from the smoke and the tent's frame began to collapse, sending her back to the bed.

She had to do something. Frantically scanning the space for something that would help, she eventually pulled the sheet off the bed, soaked it in a bucket of water nearby, and covered her mouth and nose. Gasping for air, she threw herself under a large table.

As the battle outside intensified, a barrage of bullets popped around her. Mingzhu whimpered, her heart heavy with grief. Tears streamed down her face, powerless against the flames that now danced perilously close.

Dizziness overcame her as the world spun in orange and yellow. She had lost too much blood. Coughing violently, she collapsed to the ground, her strength waning. Her eyes stung. Her shoulder had numbed. As she cried, the first flames began licking at her legs. A pained cry escaped her lips. She shut her eyes and thought of Qiang. Her grip on the sheet slackened, and soon, she knew nothing but darkness.

CHAPTER 44

Black smoke ballooned across the sky over the base. Qiang stumbled out of the vehicle and ran into the fray. The camp that had once been their safe haven was now a landscape of destruction as fires raged. The sour stench of burning wood and flesh hung in the air.

As Qiang pressed deeper into the camp, her footsteps seemed to echo in the desolation and the cries of the wounded swept through. She surveyed the scene, desperately searching for her mother. To one side of the camp, a small number of survivors had already begun gathering the bodies of their comrades.

At the sound of Hao's cries, her attention snapped to one of the few tents still standing. She hurried inside to discover Brother Wu and Hao tending to her mother.

"Mama!" Qiang's heart constricted at the sight of her mother's charred *qípáo* and blistered skin. She rushed to her side, sinking to her knees, and clasped her hands, showering them with desperate kisses.

Brother Wu's comforting grip on her shoulder did little to ease her anguish.

"What happened to her?" she hissed. "What have they done?"

Brother Wu's touch softened. "She was caught in a fire. We managed to get her out before the tent collapsed completely, but . . ."

Hao began wailing, snot dripping from her nose. Brother Wu took her by the hand and guided her outside. "It's all right, it's all right," he said softly. "Come, let's get you cleaned up."

Left alone with her mother, ash-covered and severely burnt, Qiang began to cry. "Mama . . ."

"Qiang." Mingzhu's voice was a rasp.

"Oh, Mama. Wait for me, I'll go and find a doctor."

Mingzhu's grip tightened. "Qiang," she pleaded. "Stay with me. Don't go."

Qiang swallowed her sobs. "I'm here, Mama. I won't go anywhere."

"My daughter . . ." Her voice faltered as she coughed. "Will you hold me?"

Without hesitation, Qiang climbed onto the bed, cradling her mother in her arms and tucking the cotton sheet around her. "You'll be all right, Mama. You'll be all right. I've got you. I've got you."

Mingzhu gave a light chuckle. "Do you remember when you ran away from home?"

Qiang nodded, tears blurring her vision. "Yes, Mama. I do."

"You had found your way to the local park," her mother continued, her voice growing weaker. "You were perched high in that tree . . ."

Qiang remembered that day like it was only yesterday. She remembered sitting up on a large branch, staring down onto the streets outstretched below. Rows of peddlers and food vendors had set up their shops, and were busy chatting away with potential customers. The sweet odor of *guihuā nuomǐ ǒu* streamed upward, making her stomach rumble. She had seen a little boy below clutching a whole lotus root skewered on a stick, its cavity filled with sticky rice and coated with osmanthus blossom syrup. But most of all, she remembered how her mother had kicked off her shoes and climbed the tree to sit beside her.

"Do you . . . do you remember why you ran away that day?"

"I do," Qiang whispered. "Baba was angry he had no son. He wanted—"

Her mother interrupted gently, locking eyes with Qiang. Her words were even more strained now. "And do you remember what I told you?"

Qiang's throat tightened. "You told me that I was your greatest gift."

"You're the best gift," her mother said, gasping for air. "The day you entered this world was the day I began to live, too."

"Oh, Mama." Qiang tightened her arms around her mother. "Stop talking like this, you're scaring me."

It was then that Qiang noticed the bullet wound in Mingzhu's shoulder, the blood that continued to seep weakly out, and terror gripped her heart.

Her mother coughed. "Listen to me. You're a strong woman. I didn't bestow the name Qiang on you for nothing. Your bravery has moved mountains, your strength has saved lives. I have seen it. I have seen *you*. Promise me, you will stay strong."

Qiang shook her head. "No, Mama. Stop talking like you won't be here. Stop it. Please." Her mother heaved, coughing up blood. Qiang wiped what she could from her mother's lips with the sleeve of her shirt. "Mama. Hold on, I'll go and get help."

"Nobody is coming, Qiang." She tugged on Qiang's arms, unwilling to let go.

"But—"

"Shh, shh." Her mother feebly slid the jade bangle from her own wrist to Qiang's. "I am always with you, Qiang. Always."

"Mama, no . . ." Qiang cried. "Stay with me. We can go to Macao. We can find Biyu. Please, I'll take you now. Please just stay with me."

Mingzhu extended her hand to touch Qiang's face. As she softly brushed her cheek, tears streamed down her face and neck. She managed a faint smile before gently closing her eyes.

"No, no, no!" Qiang wailed. "Mama . . ."

With a strained exhale, Mingzhu's hand slipped from Qiang's cheek and dropped onto the bed.

And then, Qiang was alone.

Time ceased to have meaning. At first, Qiang could hardly breathe, let alone move. She didn't know how long she clung to her mother, resisting any attempt to release her grip. She barely noticed how the rest of the group took turns to look in on her. Sook Ping and Ah-Long brought food, which she left untouched, while Hiroshi frequently approached with a cup of water, only to have Qiang turn her head away each time. She remained in the tent with her mother until well after the sun had dipped below the hills and the sound of grasshoppers entered the night.

Eventually, Hao tiptoed in with a book in her hands. She placed it gently on the edge of the bed. It was her mother's copy of *Dream of the Red Chamber*. A gust of wind flapped against the tent, and for an instant, she thought she heard her mother's voice.

I am always with you, Qiang. Always.

Just then, Ah-Yee entered, holding a fresh outfit, a small makeup kit, and hairpins. "It's time," she whispered.

Qiang knew she had no option but to heed Ah-Yee's direction. She couldn't hold on to her mother for the rest of her life, no matter how much she wanted to.

Setting aside the makeup and hairpins, Ah-Yee unfolded a stunning gold *qípáo*. "We'll bid your mama farewell in elegance," she declared. "She was a brilliant woman."

Hearing her mother referred to in the past tense made her feel sick. Qiang interjected, "Not that. Is there something simpler?"

"Simpler?" Ah-Yee looked puzzled.

"Perhaps a plain cotton tunic and trousers," Qiang suggested.

"But your mama was a woman of status, Qiang," Ah-Yee said. "She was the main wife of the Tang family. She—"

"My mama lived up to that role her entire life," Qiang interrupted, firm. "I will not let her die tethered to such a status or to the Tang name. Please, go and find something simpler for her to wear. My mama will leave this world in peace. She will leave a free woman."

The next morning, on a small hill, where the grass swayed gently under the warm caress of the morning sun, Qiang knelt before a humble mound of earth serving as a makeshift grave. Blades of grass, thick and lush, carpeted the ground around her, their tips glistening with dewdrops. All around, the sky was splashed in hues of red. With trembling fingers, she traced the letters of her mother's name scratched onto a simple wooden plank.

明
珠

"Mama," she whispered, the word catching in her throat. She leaned back slightly, pressing the backs of her hands against her forehead. With a heavy heart, she bowed three times, paying tribute to her mother.

Rising, she reached for her mother's copy of *Dream of the Red Chamber* nestled safely in a worn satchel by her side. Clutching the book to her chest, she sought solace in its familiar pages, imagining her mother's comforting presence beside her. Tucked within its folds were letters from Henry, tokens of a love her mother had dared not fully embrace. As she flipped through the pages, Qiang's eyes caught sight of thick pen lines underlining a certain passage.

> Upon oneself are mainly brought regrets in spring and autumn gloom
>
> A face, flowerlike may be and moonlike too, but beauty all for whom?

Her curiosity was piqued as she noted her mother's handwriting in the margins.

> *In this life, we miss each other.*
> *In the next, we meet again.*

Qiang's chest tightened. She had yearned, with every fiber of her being, for her mother to taste the sweetness of freedom. She had imagined an end to the war where her mother was liberated to embrace her feelings for Henry. She had wished for her mother to savor all life's joys, because if anyone deserved this happiness, it was her. But such dreams would forever remain unfulfilled.

With her mother's words close to her heart, Qiang stood and looked over the expanse of Hong Kong's green landscape. She lifted her chin, feeling the breeze against her skin. Despite the hardships she had endured, she knew this was not the end but a new beginning. With her mother's spirit as her guide, she vowed to live on.

. . .

Over the next few days, Qiang pushed herself to be the leader her mother had believed she could be. Each morning, she rose before dawn and sat by her mother's grave until the others began to stir. Then, alongside Sook Ping, she organized members into different teams to tend to the injured, ensuring that every wound was treated with care. The children, who had lost their innocent smiles and loved ones, were a priority to her. She made sure they were safe, fed, and clothed, often taking time to comfort them with gentle words and hugs. She directed the able-bodied survivors, working with them to rebuild the still-salvageable tents until her hands were blistered and sore.

Qiang sent a few members to search for Henry and several others who were supposed to have arrived at the camp the same day as the attack. But Henry was nowhere to be found, and word eventually came that the newspaper office had been bombed. She feared he had become another victim of war, just like her mother. A part of her wished this wasn't true, yet a small part found comfort in the thought that her mother and Henry might be together in the afterlife. Despite the uncertainty of this, she continued to lead the camp with fearlessness.

That night, as she sat down with Sook Ping by a fire, a faint radio sputtering in the distance crackled to life. A voice emerged from the static, and the camp quieted.

To our good and loyal subjects. We entered the war to secure Japan's survival and stabilize East Asia, not to infringe on others' sovereignty or expand our territory. However, after nearly four years of war, the situation has turned against us. Our enemy has begun to employ a new and devastating bomb, the power of which to do damage will see many innocent lives taken. Should we continue to fight, not only would it result in an ultimate collapse and obliteration of the Japanese nation, but also it would lead to the total extinction of human civilization.

Numerous resistance members gathered around the radio, their ears pricked with curiosity. Others paused their tasks, standing with anticipation while some murmured between themselves, their expressions hopeful. For several days, rumors of a possible surrender had circulated across the camp. The voice cracked through again.

Such being the case, how are we to save the millions of our subjects, or to atone ourselves before the hallowed spirits of our imperial ancestors? This is the reason why we have ordered the acceptance of the provisions of the joint declaration of the powers. We cannot but express the deepest sense of regret to our allied nations of East Asia, who have consistently cooperated with the Empire toward the emancipation of East Asia.

Shock raced up Qiang's spine, and Ah-Long scowled at the radio, his eyes red.

"It's over?" Sook Ping began to laugh. "It's over!"

Cheers and screams pierced the air. Brother Wu started sobbing into his hands while Ah-Long and Sook Ping began jumping up and down and joined the crowd in elated cries of joy. Qiang stayed where she was, her focus drawn to the hill where her mother was buried.

"It's over," Qiang muttered, rubbing the jade bangle on her wrist. "It's finally over."

Sook Ping must have noticed Qiang's distant gaze because she stopped celebrating. She walked over and gently pulled Qiang into a hug, holding her close. Not far off, Hao screamed in delight, her face glowing from the firelight. Ah-Long picked her up and spun her around, her giggles resounding through the camp, lifting the weight of occupation from everyone's shoulders. After a moment, Sook Ping released Qiang and joined Ah-Long, and they began jumping around with the other children.

As Qiang refocused on the fire, she saw Hiroshi standing a few paces away. Although he appeared calm, there was a dash of hesitation in his look. When she eventually locked eyes with him, a gentle smile spread across his face. He gestured toward the camp's entrance, and she nodded. She made her way to the gate and sat on a patch of grass beside it. The cool earth beneath her was a welcome relief from the heat of the fire. As Hiroshi crouched to sit next to her, the distant sounds of celebration continued to filter through.

"There's something I need to tell you," Hiroshi said. An indescribable sadness simmered in his gaze. "I want you to hear it from me."

"I already know," she said. "I overheard you and Brother Wu."

The day before, Qiang had eavesdropped on the conversation between the two men. Brother Wu had offered Hiroshi safe passage to China along with a new identity, but he had declined. He explained that accepting such an opportunity would be an act of cowardice in his eyes. And so, he expressed his desire to surrender to the British navy, be returned to Japan, and face trial for his actions.

"You heard everything?" he asked, his eyes never leaving hers.

She nodded. "Is this what you truly want?"

"It's not a matter of what I want, Qiang. It's about doing what I think to be right."

Pained, she let out a shaky sigh. "Japan will never forgive you for siding with the ERC—for siding with Hong Kong."

"And I wouldn't forgive myself if I hadn't." He gestured to the sky. "My mother wouldn't forgive me either."

The tip of her nose stinging, Qiang tried her best to blink back the tears but the thought of losing him was just too much. She let the tears roll down her cheeks while fighting hard to remain composed. "When do you leave?" she managed to utter.

"Tomorrow," he said. "Ah-Long will drive me into Kowloon. I will report to the British there."

Qiang started pulling on the grass, ripping it up in chunks. Her mind raced. Maybe she could ask him to stay? Persuade him to reconsider? But what could she really offer him? As she tore at the grass, she realized she didn't even know what her own future looked like. So, what right did she have to change his course?

"There's something else I need to tell you," he said, reaching for her hands and gently brushing off the grass that had stuck to her skin. "You and me? We'll meet again one day."

She gave a nervous laugh. "You believe that?"

"You don't?" he asked. "Think about it. From our very first meeting beneath the banyan tree, to the factory where you stood up to me, to this moment right now. Every step I've taken during this war, every path I've walked, has only ever led me to you."

Qiang's heart skipped a beat. His words were warmer than the touch of his hands.

"So, of course I believe," he said. "And I hope, so very much, that you do, too."

An abundance of words lingered on her lips, but she remained silent. The past three years and eight months had been filled with so much pain, suffering, and loss. The enormity of it all was overwhelming, and exhaustion settled over her as she sat beside him. The evening wind began to pick up, brushing strands of her hair across her face. She shifted closer to him and gently rested her head on his shoulder, Hiroshi's warmth offering her solace. Her hands were snuggled securely in his grasp, a small yet comforting connection. As she closed her eyes, she thought of the path she had traveled. She would never forget the aches of war and the terror that was so unfairly and unkindly passed onto her and so many others. But if she had to do it all over again, she would have picked the same path that led her to the resistance. Because once she knew her strength, and her will, there was nothing that could stop her. And it wasn't just her. It was every other woman that defied the occupation and fought for her home. The old saying held true and would remain so for the rest of time.

When sleeping women wake, mountains move.

EPILOGUE

SHANGHAI,
上海,
1950

Qiang opened the wooden shutters to reveal the courtyard outside. A spotted dove perched delicately on a branch of a camphor tree, ruffling its feathers against the breeze. The plum trees, their branches heavy with blossom, swayed gently, casting dappled shadows on the stone pathway below. Over the walls, distant shouts of vendors and merchants rushed through. She imagined her mother sitting in this very spot as a child, practicing calligraphy, staring out at the same camphor tree. The sun pierced through the morning haze, casting a warm light on a letter in her grasp.

Dear Qiang,

Since my last letter, Marco and I have settled into a comfortable rhythm with the new bakery. It's a little piece of paradise for us, and we now have eight different pastries on the menu! Can you believe it? From pastéis de nata to pork chop buns. Although we may not be blessed with children of our own, I find contentment in the small, everyday miracles of this life.

Most nights, I find myself reflecting on the journey our lives have taken since the occupation. It is a blessing that we can now share these moments of peace and joy despite the trials we faced. I will never forget receiving your letter after the

Japanese surrendered. How I wished I could be there for you. How I could have been there with your mama.

Your mama is always on my mind. As I write this, I am taken back to the very first day I met her. I remember stepping into the Yue household in Shanghai. I was so nervous! Those years of being with her were filled with lessons and warmth. Though the war brought its share of hardships, I never truly suffered because her kindness and wisdom were a constant source of strength. In my deepest heart, the love I have for your mama is unwavering. Everything she did to support me in this life is something I hope to repay in the next.

Qiang, she would be so proud of you and everything you have achieved in the last few years. I wish she were still alive to see how you have transformed her childhood home into such a wonderful school. I can imagine the smile on her face.

I must go now, but I will write again soon. Marco and I are eagerly looking forward to your visit this Christmas. Until then, take care.

With all my love,
Biyu

PS. Send my regards to Hao, too. I am so grateful you have each other.

Smiling, Qiang tucked the letter back into its envelope. Finding Biyu after the war hadn't been too difficult, since Qiang had noted the details of the fake name and passport they had given her to escape to Macao.

The previous Christmas she had stepped off the steam ferry and run into Biyu's arms, struck by how radiant she looked. Marriage suited her, and Marco looked at Biyu as if she were the center of the universe. The bakery had been brand-new at the time, small but cozy, painted a cheerful yellow with green trimmings, and the buttery aroma of freshly baked goods made her stomach growl even remembering it.

Inside the bakery, Biyu had taken a seat next to her. "Well? How's Hao? How's the school?"

"It's all going well. Enrollments are increasing. We've secured more funding, too."

"Oh, how wonderful. Your mama would be so proud." Biyu choked back tears, and Qiang felt her own rise, her heart aching, and Biyu squeezed her hand. "I'm sorry. Let's talk about something else."

"It's all right," Qiang said. It wasn't that she didn't want to talk of her mother. It was that, even after five years, it still hurt. She offered Biyu a brave smile. "I haven't seen you for almost a year. How is Marco?"

Biyu wiped a tear and laughed. "As incorrigible as ever! But I still can't believe we found each other. I can hardly believe my luck."

Qiang had squeezed Biyu's hands in hers. She was so proud. So happy. If her mother were still alive, she would be just as happy, too. When Qiang visited Biyu and her husband Marco for Christmas each year, she was always confronted by the idea that she might never find a love as potent as the one her mother and Henry shared, nor a love so sincere and kind as the one Biyu and Marco had.

To Qiang, love was, and remained, unreachable. Whenever she allowed herself to ponder love, often late at night while the rest of the world slept, her mind conjured the image of a man beneath a banyan tree, his hands speckled with gold paint.

For years, the question of his survival had haunted her, an incessant ache in her heart. She knew she might never uncover the truth. And so, she had to accept that sometimes in life, a connection made wasn't always something you could keep. But it could be something to remember, something to hold on to when all else seemed lost.

A soft knock interrupted her thoughts. "It's me," Hao said. "He's here! He's finally here!"

Qiang slipped the letter into the pocket of her trousers and hastily left the room. Following Hao, she noticed how they were nearly the same height. She thought back to the first time they had met at the camp. How small yet fearless Hao had been. Her hair, once braided loosely over her shoulder, was now cut into a bob that framed her round cheeks.

Following the bombings of Hiroshima and Nagasaki in 1945, the British had officially regained control of Hong Kong. Most resistance cells, including Brother Wu's, had relocated to China. He had wanted to take Hao with him, but she had asked to stay with Qiang. At that time, Qiang hadn't known where she would go or what she would do, but how could she reject a displaced child? Other resistance members who remained were just as lost. The British government failed to credit them, especially with all those whispers about ties to Communist factions in China. It stung—the same people who had fought tooth and nail for this city were left questioning the purpose of their fight.

Soon, Qiang had found herself adrift with few options. With some money from Brother Wu, she was able to rent a modest room in Hong Kong, where she started working as a bar hostess in Wan Chai. Her life fell into a dull routine during that first year, and at times, she found herself longing for the days of the resistance and missions with the ERC. Any extra money she earned was spent on Hao's schooling.

For a while, Sook Ping and Ah-Long lived nearby, too. Once Sook Ping confessed her feelings, the two were inseparable. Together, they found work in construction and would often visit Qiang. In the second year, Hong Kong had truly begun to recover. The city buzzed with increasing activity and the return of tourists and expats alike. By the third year, news arrived that her mother's cousin who had inherited the family home had died, leaving the *sìhéyuàn* to her, the only surviving member of the Yue descendants. Bidding farewell to Ah-Long and Sook Ping, Qiang and Hao moved to Shanghai.

"You're lost in thought again, aren't you?" Hao teased.

Qiang gave a light shake of her head and laughed. "I was thinking how tall you've grown since we first met!"

Upon reaching the large red door, Hao turned the handle and swung it open, revealing a man standing at the threshold. Qiang eagerly stepped forward, her arms outstretched. "Henry!" she cried. The years seemed to melt away as they hugged.

"Qiang." Henry's voice was thick with emotion. "It's so good to see you."

Pulling back, she took a moment to take in Henry's appearance.

The occupation had ended just five years ago, but the lines around his eyes told a different story, as if time had been less forgiving.

"You must be exhausted," Hao said, taking his suitcase. "I'll take this to your room."

"Thank you, Hao," he said before turning back to Qiang. "She's grown so much."

"She has." Qiang gestured into the house. "Come, let's have some tea."

Qiang led Henry through the *sìhéyuàn,* pointing out the intricate details of the transformed rooms as they walked. In one of the larger rooms, a slender woman sat surrounded by children, her infectious laughter mingling with the sound of pages turning as she read from a book.

"How many students live here now?" Henry asked.

"We have thirty-six boarders," Qiang replied. "But we also have another ten or so that come through during the day for lessons. Those children still have homes to go back to."

"War takes too much . . ." His gaze was suddenly drawn to the ancestral hall. From outside, Qiang could see the portrait scrolls of her ancestors swaying against the wind. "May I?" he asked.

Inside, the space was decorated with rich wooden beams, detailed carvings, and a low altar decked with incense holders and offerings. As the candles flickered, their gentle light spread throughout the room, creating warm shadows on the walls and bringing out the sophisticated details of the painted scrolls depicting the Yue ancestors.

Qiang watched as Henry's eyes fell upon one particular scroll, his breath catching in his throat. "Mingzhu . . ."

"I painted that last year," Qiang said. "I was worried that if I left it too long, I'd forget what she looked like."

"Beautiful," he replied softly, his eyes wet. "You've captured her perfectly."

Qiang gave him a gentle pat on the shoulder. Henry exhaled deeply, his struggle to hold back tears evident. She approached the altar with practiced grace, lighting the incense sticks with care. The tiny flames flickered like fireflies, while the smoke curled upward. "Here, let me show you," she said softly. She guided him through the ritual, explaining each step as they bowed together. Taking a few steps back, she watched as Henry stood before her mother's portrait, absorbing the moment.

Last year, she had received word from Brother Wu of Henry's whereabouts. She managed to track down an address in London and immediately wrote to him. When Henry replied, he described his injuries from a bomb explosion at the *Hong Kong News* office. Although he had planned to meet Mingzhu at the ERC base, his injuries had prevented him from doing so. He told her how local Chinese civilians rescued him and he had escaped to Singapore aboard a sampan. From there, with the help of the British navy, he returned to England. In his letter, he also mentioned that he had never given up hope of finding Mingzhu and had continued searching for her through his Hong Kong connections but to no avail.

And so, Qiang had been the one to tell him of her mother's fate. She thought she wouldn't hear back, but eventually he did respond, saying he had needed time to process the shock. For a while, Qiang exchanged letters with him frequently, their shared grief filling the pages. It was a comfort, though she wondered if true healing would ever be possible. When he had asked to come visit, she hadn't hesitated to say yes.

Henry finally turned from Mingzhu's portrait. "You mentioned tea?"

Later that evening, Qiang and Henry attended a private fundraising event at a grand mansion along the Bund. Standing next to Henry, clad in an evening gown of emerald green—her mother's favorite color—a discomfort settled into her stomach. The home belonged to a wealthy Englishman and his wife. The ballroom was a sight of opulence, with the smooth marble floors and the scent of expensive perfume lingering in the air. The room was buzzing with glasses clinking, people chatting, and jazz music softly playing in the background. But, having witnessed the brutal realities of war up close, Qiang struggled now to see this excessive lifestyle with the same enchantment as before.

"Do you really think they'll want to donate to our cause?" she muttered, playing with her earring.

Henry nodded, briefly shaking hands with a man walking past.

"You know these people are always in a rush to donate to charity. It's all part of their image."

Qiang paused to absorb his enthusiasm. "I guess we can't return empty-handed," she finally remarked. She understood that his efforts were not solely focused on the school; they were also a way for him to maintain a connection with Mingzhu, the last tangible piece of her he could still hold on to. So, it wasn't unexpected when, over tea earlier, he expressed his desire to stay in Shanghai and work as a tutor in the *sìhéyuàn*.

Qiang weaved through the sea of guests, offering her hand in greeting and engaging in casual conversations from time to time. With every interaction, her confidence grew in soliciting donations, leaving no doubt in anyone's mind about her capabilities. After an hour of introductions and polite exchanges, she was parched. She excused herself from Henry and a few others, her heels clicking on the floor as she made her way toward the bar.

"Gin rickey, please," Qiang said to the bartender, her eyes drifting to the dance floor, where couples swirled to the music. Her lips curved into a gentle smile as she recalled the night she had met Hiroshi. Thoughts of him came often—unexpectedly—like quotes in a book you'd underscore and come back to revisit later. Accepting her drink, she downed it in one swift motion, feeling the sting as it hit the back of her throat.

Several feet away, a group of men laughed, tears pooling in their drunken eyes. Their bellows were so loud, Qiang almost didn't catch the conversation between two women behind her.

"I saw the most exquisite *kintsugi* gallery the other day," said an older English woman. "Some temporary exhibition."

Qiang froze, her ears perked.

"Who was the artist?" her companion asked.

"Oh, how should I remember? Naka something."

Hearing that, Qiang whirled around and approached the woman, who startled. "Where is the gallery?" she asked, unintentionally grabbing the woman's wrist. "My apologies," she quickly recovered, letting go.

"It's just a few blocks from here, on Avenue Joffre, dear," the woman replied, taken aback by Qiang's intensity.

"What did the artist look like?" Qiang pressed. "Was his name Nakamura? Was it?"

The woman, now visibly uncomfortable, edged away. "I . . . I really don't recall, dear. Please, enjoy the rest of your evening."

She hurried off with her friend, leaving Qiang standing there, pressure building in her chest. Since the British had given up their extraterritorial rights after the war, Avenue Joffre was now Huaihai Road. It was a place she had visited many times before. How had she not noticed a new gallery? Her head swirled. Could it really be him? He had mentioned his mother had been from Shanghai. Was it possible he had returned here? She needed air.

She climbed the grand staircase and stepped onto the balcony, where she was surrounded by the hum of traffic and the blaring of ship horns from the docks and the faint smell of street food wafting up from the Bund. A familiar image formed in her mind: a man beneath a grand banyan tree, his hands decorated with flecks of dazzling gold paint, his dark eyes fixed on hers.

When he had asked her if she believed they would meet again back then, she had remained silent. Now, she looked out across the horizon, where the setting sun painted the sky the most brilliant shades of orange and red and gold, and she knew her answer.

"I believe," she whispered, her words carrying across the Huangpu River into the promise of tomorrow. "I believe."

HISTORICAL NOTE

The Japanese Occupation of Hong Kong lasted three years and eight months, and the wounds inflicted upon those who endured such horrors continued to course through the generations that ensued. Following the Japanese invasion and the subsequent Battle of Hong Kong in December 1941, various local guerrilla groups merged to form a unified resistance movement. It wasn't until December 1943 that these groups, including the Huiyang Bao'an People's Anti-Japanese Guerrillas and the Dongguan Model Able-bodied Young Men Guerrilla Team, were formally amalgamated and named the East River Column.

This movement, drawing heavily from the local Hakka ethnic community, played a pivotal role in the lives of Hong Kong's inhabitants. They set up their main operations in Sai Kung, working closely with local villagers while combating collaborators and bandits. Even children as young as six, often referred to as "little devils" (or "little ghosts" in *When Sleeping Women Wake*), took up critical roles within this resistance. Serving as couriers, smugglers, and guides, these young members were instrumental despite the looming threat of torture and execution if captured. The efforts of the East River Column were crucial in expediting the Japanese surrender in 1945.

Due to the resistance's association with the Chinese Communist Party, the British authorities refused to officially recognize its contributions post-war. Consequently, as a writer, I relied on the stories passed down to me by my family and the historical sources I was able to access.

There are several characters in this book that are inspired or based on real people. The character Hao, for example, was inspired by a video I watched during my research from the *South China Morning Post.* Titled *Hong Kong's Unsung Guerrilla Fighters of the Second World War* by Dayu Zhang, it featured a woman recounting her experience as a "little devil."

Another character in my novel, Lieutenant Donald Kerr, was a real person. Kerr served as a fighter pilot in the US Army's 14th Air Force. On February 11, 1944, he participated in an air raid over Hong Kong, piloting a P-40 fighter. While on the mission, his plane was shot down above Kowloon. Despite this, he successfully parachuted to safety and hid before Japanese soldiers could find him. He was later rescued by members of the East River Column, who guided him through the New Territories into southern China, eventually handing him over to the British Army Aid Group.

The character of General Tanaka was based on Hisakazu Tanaka. He was a lieutenant general in the Imperial Japanese Army and served as the Governor-General of Occupied Hong Kong during World War II. After Japan's surrender, Tanaka was arrested for war crimes, convicted by military tribunals for atrocities committed by his troops, and was executed in 1947.

While I have taken creative liberties in *When Sleeping Women Wake,* I have made a conscious effort to remain historically accurate in depicting key locations and settings. For example, the Peninsula Hotel in Hong Kong, an iconic building with a rich history, was commandeered by the Japanese military and repurposed as their headquarters during the occupation. Similarly, Stanley Camp was one of three major internment camps established by the Japanese, where civilians, including Allied nationals, were detained under harsh conditions. Another significant site, Nam Koo Terrace, a colonial-era mansion, was tragically converted into a comfort station, where women were forcibly held to serve as wartime "comfort women."

The following texts served as the bedrock of my research for this novel: *Battle for Hong Kong, December 1941* and *The Occupation of Hong Kong 1941–45* by Philip Cracknell; *Three Years Eight Months: The Forgotten Struggle of Hong Kong's WWII* by Jenny Chan and Derek Pua; *Tales of Old Hong Kong: Treasures from the Fragrant Harbour* by Derek Sandhaus; *East River Column: Hong Kong Guerrillas in the Second World War and After* by Chan Sui-jeung; and *The Fall of*

Hong Kong by Phillip Snow. Other valuable resources include www.gwulo.com, www.pacificatrocities.org, and the Hong Kong Museum of the War of Resistance and Coastal Defence.

In the novel, the spelling of location names is consistent with the "Hong Kong Historic Maps—Reference 1941." Sourced from the National Library of Australia, this map was crafted to complement Sir David J. Owen's February 1941 report on the future control and development of the Port of Hong Kong.

Lastly, for those who love books about books, *When Sleeping Women Wake* references several classics. One key text is the *Four Books for Women* (女四書), an educational collection for young Chinese women, widely studied by noble families during the late Ming and Qing dynasties. Originally separate works, they were consolidated by the Duowen Tang publishing house in 1624. The collection includes *Lessons for Women* by Ban Zhao, *Women's Analects* by Song Ruoshen and Song Ruozhao, *Domestic Lessons* by Empress Xu, and *Sketch of a Model for Women* by Madame Liu. Other notable works referenced are *Dream of the Red Chamber* by Cao Xueqin, *Romance of the Three Kingdoms* by Luo Guanzhong, *Midnight* by Mao Dun, *The Tale of Genji* by Murasaki Shikibu, and *The Elements of Style* by William Strunk Jr. and E. B. White.

ACKNOWLEDGMENTS

Writing this book has changed my life. It has allowed me to resurrect beloved childhood memories and breathe new life into historical moments that might have otherwise faded away. Through years of research and personal reflection, I unearthed narratives of bravery and defiance, honoring the spirit of those who came before me.

Consequently, there are many people to thank.

To my agent, Laurie Robertson, who's been such a bright light in my life. I still remember those early days of working together—constantly checking my email just to make sure it wasn't all a dream. I'll never forget how much I cried after signing with you—happy tears, of course. With you by my side, I can be the writer I've always wanted to be.

Endless thanks go to international rights agents Rebecca Wearmouth and Lucy Barry at Peters Fraser Dunlop. Because of you, *When Sleeping Women Wake* has found a home at Garzanti S.R.L. (Italy) and Éditions Leduc (France).

To my incredible editors and publishers, Natalie Hallak (Ballantine), Cassie Browne (Quercus), and Rebecca Saunders (Hachette): you have made my childhood dreams come true. The journey has been seamless, and I've learned so much from each of you. I am a better writer today because of you all. No number of words will ever be enough to express my gratitude. The support you have shown means the world and I'm still pinching myself at how lucky I am.

Elena Giavaldi, thank you for the stunning US cover—you captured the essence of the novel so beautifully and I can't wait for the world to see what you have created. To my UK and ANZ designer, Hazel Lam. From the moment we connected on Instagram, I knew you were the perfect fit. The fact our grandmothers are from Hong Kong only strengthens our bond.

The warmest gratitude and love to my dear friend, Manuela Ocampo. Thank you for reading my earlier drafts, for the wonderful morning walks where we discussed my characters, to screaming and jumping with joy throughout every milestone this book has reached. Anyone would be lucky to have you in their corner.

Emily Formentin, the sister of my soul. Oceans separate us, but my heart is always with you.

Alex Dicker, my oldest friend and honorary brother, you are my home away from home and it has been that way for as long as I can remember.

Pam Gan, thank you for reading my earlier draft and supporting me all the way from Singapore.

Priscilla Jia and Cousin Alan, thank you for checking my Chinese. Don't worry, it was checked again!

To my high school English teacher, Adrian Tilley, who, unlike the other adults at the time, saw how much I loved the written word and treated me like an equal.

Special thanks to Carlie Slattery, who provided such invaluable editorial feedback on my earlier draft. I am forever grateful.

I'd also like to acknowledge the incredible writers and creatives I've met along the way, with whom I've formed beautiful friendships: Ayesha Inoon, Genevieve Novak, Jess Ho, Di Lebowitz, Anita Patel, Lauren Chater, and the wonderful Juhea Kim.

To LinLi Wan at Pantera Press for reading the first few chapters and offering feedback. I hope Biyu's character is everything you hoped she would be.

A heartfelt thank you to Erin Wen Ai Chew (周文愛) of *Being Asian Australian* for giving me a platform to share my voice, allowing me to interview and connect with some remarkable Asian-Australian leaders.

To Kirsten Han at *Mekong Review,* Erin Cross at *HerCanberra,* Emily Riches at *Aniko Press,* Jess Lomas at *Books+Publishing,* and Tony Huang at *The Hong Kong Review*—thank you for publishing my articles, reviews, and short-form writing.

Incredible thanks to booksellers across the globe. I appreciate the work you do and hope to meet as many of you as I can over the coming years.

Kannika Afonso for your incredible talent behind the camera, which resulted in breathtaking author photos that I am beyond thrilled with.

Shari and David, for your kindness, care, and extraordinary annual Christmas puddings.

Aunt Alice, you have known about me wanting to write this book since the beginning and have always been there to listen when I needed someone to talk to. Your endless support and kind nature has offered me comfort over the years. You are the best aunt any niece could hope for.

Mum and Dad, thank you for bringing me into this world. Thank you for working hard to raise me, and for putting me through an International School in Hong Kong. It has not gone unnoticed how much you both have had to sacrifice. I am who I am today because of you.

To my beautiful baby girl, Lady. You are the most wonderful Dachshund in the world. Thank you for keeping my feet warm.

Mark, my love. I could write an entire book about how much I love you, but I'm a little spent after this one. So, I will simply leave you with one of my favorite quotes from the brilliant Eileen Chang. Whenever I read this, I think only of you: *You meet the one you meet among thousands and tens of thousands of people, amidst thousands and tens of thousands of years, in the boundless wilderness of time, not a step sooner, not a step later. You chance upon each other, not saying much, only asking softly, "Oh, you are here, also?"*

Lastly, and most importantly, to my grandparents. In this life, we were fated to meet yet destined to part. Whatever time we have left, I will strive to be there for you both. For anything I have missed out on over the years, I will make up for in the next life.

WHEN SLEEPING WOMEN WAKE

EMMA PEI YIN

A Book Club Guide

DISCUSSION QUESTIONS

1. Discuss the significance of the title, *When Sleeping Women Wake*. How does it reflect the themes of agency and resilience in the novel? In what ways do the characters demonstrate resilience and agency in the face of adversity?

2. How do the historical events of the Japanese occupation of Hong Kong shape the lives and decisions of Mingzhu, Qiang, and Biyu? How does the novel address the racial and cultural tensions during the Japanese occupation? What impact do these tensions have on the characters?

3. Analyze the relationship dynamics within the Tang family, particularly between Mingzhu and her daughter Qiang. How do these relationships evolve throughout the story?

4. Discuss the role of language and communication in Mingzhu's survival. How does her affinity for languages affect her choices and interactions?

5. How does the author portray the concept of resistance? What motivates the characters to support the East River Column fighters? How does the novel contribute to our understanding of World War II's impact on Hong Kong and its people?

6. Explore the themes of love and hope in the novel. How do these elements help the characters endure their struggles? What role does friendship play, particularly between Mingzhu and Biyu? How does their relationship influence the narrative?

7. Reflect on the emotional journey of the characters. How do the experiences of Qiang and Biyu differ from those of Mingzhu? What factors contribute to their divergent paths? How do their personal transformations mirror the broader historical changes occurring in Hong Kong?

8. Discuss the impact of war on the social hierarchy within the Tang household. How do power dynamics shift as the story progresses? In what ways do the characters challenge traditional gender roles?

9. How does the author use symbolism to convey themes of survival and resistance? Identify key symbols and their significance.

10. Consider the ending of the novel. How does it resolve the characters' journeys, and what message does it leave with the reader?

© KANNIKA AFONSO

Emma Pei Yin is an Australian-Chinese writer and editor. Her debut novel, *When Sleeping Women Wake*, has been published globally, translated into multiple languages, and was longlisted for both the ARA Historical Novel Prize (2025) and the Australian Indie Book Awards (2026).

She is the founder of yinfluence editorial, an agency supporting PoC, queer and neurodivergent writers by connecting them with editors and mentors who understand the stakes of telling stories from the margins. She also co-hosts *Served With Rice Poddy*, a trans-Tasman literary and cultural podcast and visual series recorded across Australia and Aotearoa New Zealand that centers conversations about books, publishing, identity and community through food-infused discussion.

Her work and commentary have appeared in *The Canberra Times, The Australian, Mekong Review, Being Asian Australian, The Hong Kong Review, Vogue, Harper's Bazaar,* and more.

@emmapeiyin on X and Instagram